The Company of the Wolf

ALSO BY DAVID WRAGG

Articles of Faith
The Black Hawks
The Righteous

Tales of the Plains
The Hunters

DAVID WRAGG

THE COMPANY OF THE WOLF

HARPER
Voyager

Harper*Voyager*
An imprint of
HarperCollins*Publishers* Ltd
1 London Bridge Street
London SE1 9GF

www.harpercollins.co.uk

HarperCollins*Publishers*
Macken House,
39/40 Mayor Street Upper,
Dublin 1
D01 C9W8
Ireland

First published by HarperCollins*Publishers* Ltd 2024
1

A catalogue record for this book is available from the British Library.

ISBN: 978-0-00-853377-9 (HB)

Typeset in Sabon by Palimpsest Book Production Ltd, Falkirk, Stirlingshire

Printed and bound in the UK using 100% Renewable Electricity
at CPI Group (UK) Ltd

This book contains FSC™ certified paper and other controlled sources
to ensure responsible forest management.

For more information visit: www.harpercollins.co.uk/green

For my friends in the east

ONE

They were definitely lost.

The mist was getting thicker, swallowing the forest around them, taking all sound with it, leaving only a smothering hush. The morning sun was an ivory smear somewhere overhead. Javani stared up at the nearest trees, pretty sure they were oaks, their neighbours dwindling dark stripes in the grey fog beyond. The broad leaves were undeniably orange. The entire forest had been gloriously autumnal for some time – vivid shades of yellow, amber, viridian and indigo – and the foliage was becoming sparser by the day, a slow rain of golden leaves accompanying every breeze. Beneath Javani's boots, a lush carpet the colour of blood stretched away into the mist, punctuated by fists of lichen-rimed rock and springing shrubs of vivid green. Fallen trunks, furry with moss, lay half-swallowed by the forest floor. Unseen birds chittered mutely overhead, the odd grey little finch swishing between branches, murky shapes in the fog. Everything smelled wet and fresh. If the sun ever made it through, Javani thought, it might be quite pretty here.

The hush was broken by some vicious swearing from down the slope, where her mother was attempting to coax the last of the ponies up to the ridge.

'Do you want a hand?' Javani called.

'No,' Ree snapped back. 'Stay with the others.' A grunt and another stream of invective followed. 'If either of those little bastards decides to follow you down, we'll never get them all up again.'

'Is your leg all right?'

'Fine. It's fine. Nine fucking *hells*!' Javani heard the swish of Ree's walking staff. 'Listen to me, you plum-brained plug, in the sight of all the gods I will beat you insensible if you do not move your stubby little arse up this fucking hill!'

'She knows you won't.' Javani didn't bother hiding her smile. 'They've travelled with us too long.' She stroked the nose of the pony beside her, who offered a polite snort in return.

A cry of triumph indicated the last pony's belated change of heart, and a moment later Ree crested the slope beside her, near-dragged by the stout animal, despite its load. Her limp looked no better.

'See?' she said, between pants, her thick white hair plastered around her face. 'I can be persuasive, kid.'

'Don't I know it.' Javani waited for her mother to catch her breath, allowing her a moment of rest before the inevitable: 'We're lost, aren't we?'

Ree didn't miss a beat. 'We are not.'

'Would you say you know where we are?'

'That's not important.'

Javani rubbed her arms. The forest was definitely chillier, as well as increasingly leafless. 'You don't think it's important?'

'We know where we're going: over the Ashadi. We just keep heading west, and we'll get there.' Ree started forward again, staff in hand, yanking the pony from the wiry shrub it had begun munching. 'Come on, we've wasted enough daylight for one morning.'

Javani reached out a hand to intercept her. 'Ree! Ma. Listen.' Keeping a tight grip on the lead rope of the other two ponies, both happily investigating the same bank of ferns, she shuffled in front of her mother. 'We have been crossing the Ashadi for weeks now. Months, even. And we're still not across. Look around us.' She swept a hand around the mist-choked forest. 'The leaves have turned, and now they're coming down in spades. There are more beneath our feet than above our heads. It's colder and colder in the mornings.'

'Nice to see a season turn, eh? Makes a change from the plains. You don't get colour changes like this with a load of sandy rocks.'

'Ma!' Javani scratched at her neck. Something had bitten her there, she knew it. 'Do you think we might have gone wrong somewhere? There are . . . There are more mountains than there should be.'

She already knew the answer – their westward progress across the mountains had been impeded by peaks of staggering height, and their efforts to find a way around had merely driven them further south along the range for weeks while getting them no closer to their goal – but the real question was whether her mother would admit it. That the landscape had changed was undeniable – they'd journeyed from arid slopes, through juniper forests, now into cloud and mist and autumn colours, ever-changing birdcalls and night-sounds, new trees and thorny carpets – yet somehow they were still no closer to their intended destination.

Ree took a long breath, still fighting the effects of the climb, and rested her staff against her shoulder as she slicked damp hair from her eyes. 'Come on, kid, we skirted the big ones; these are barely even mountains. Just, you know, self-important hills.'

'But we're not over them, are we? We're not in Arestan, the land of rice fields and vineyards and a sea as blue as sapphire, are we?'

'No. Not yet. But we know it's to the west, and we know which way that is.'

'Do we?' Javani gestured at the misty glare overhead. 'We can't see the sun through the trees and the mist for half the day, and the days are getting shorter and shorter. We've not seen our lucky hawk for ages, although I know he's still out there.' For once her mother did not attempt to disabuse her of the notion that the hawk she claimed to see from time to time was likely multiple birds and none was imbued with the spirit of a man who'd died to protect them. 'And Moosh's tip about the moss on the trunks . . . Well, it was horseshit, wasn't it?'

Ree gave her a sad smile. She knew Javani still cried, sometimes, for her friend; more than once she'd wrapped her arms around her in the night, when the sobbing was too much. 'It was. But I'm sure he believed it when he told you.'

Javani sniffed. 'Poor Moosh. He'd have laughed to see us now. Wandering the Ashadi, supplies dwindling, one pony lost, following what I'm *pretty sure* is an animal trail, not any kind of actual path.'

'It's a path.'

'Can we head back to that road? If we check the map again, maybe we can—'

Ree fixed her with an icy glare. 'You want to double back? To travel days backwards, and downwards, and upwards again, gods help us, just in case . . . What? In case we missed a turning?' She wiped a hand across her clammy brow. 'Kid, you need to understand something: it was not a very good map. You get that? The map was, what's the word, indicative at best. But we know where we're going, and if we keep putting one foot in front of the other, we will get there. You hear me? These mountains can't fight us off forever.'

Javani's head was shaking. 'I don't like it, I don't like it up here. It's so quiet! You can't see more than ten feet in front of you! It feels like the trees are trying to eat us!'

'Now you're just being silly. Have some water and let's get moving.' Ree held out her waterskin.

Javani reached for the skin with a scowl. 'Fine.'

Ree did not release her grip.

'Uh, Ree,' Javani said, tugging gently on the skin.

'Shh. Don't move a muscle,' Ree growled out of the corner of her mouth. She was holding herself rigid, staring over Javani's shoulder.

Javani fought the urge to turn and look, instead keeping herself still. 'What is it?' she mouthed.

Ree's voice was a low murmur. 'Fallow deer. Upwind of us, but watching. Move slowly. Get the bow.'

'What? Me?'

'You're closer, and the pony's between you and the deer. Come on, before it spooks.'

'But—'

'Kid, you want to moan about our supply situation or do you want to do something about it? Move like ice, get the bow.'

'But I don't want to—'

'Now is not the time for infant squeamishness, kid. I will watch but you must shoot. And gods know your archery needs practice.'

'Can't I use the little crossbow—'

'Not at this range, and not with any chance of killing it cleanly. Get to it!'

Muttering to herself, Javani reached a slow hand to the pony's laden side where their hunting bow was stashed. 'Bad in the wet, bad in the dry, not enough bolts, never goes where you aim it – might as well sling the wretched thing.'

'Hush your grumbling. You never know when a little surprise might come in handy. Now string the bow out of its eyeline.'

Javani did as she was told. Stringing the bow was hard enough at the best of times, let alone when attempted in absolute silence behind a pony's legs. It wasn't as if the hunting bow was any more accurate than the little hand crossbow, anyway . . . at least in her hands.

She slid one of the few remaining arrows from the quiver at the pony's withers and notched it in the bowstring, then stepped carefully back as she drew, lining up her shot on the still-oblivious deer. A gorgeous thing, now she saw it clearly as the mist rippled between them: tawny coloured, its upper coat dappled with fine white spots, small antlers branching up from its head like cupped hands. It was standing completely still.

'I want it recorded that I strenuously object to this action,' she muttered.

'Objection noted. Now remember what I taught you? Hold your breath, draw when you're ready to shoot—'

'Yes, yes! I've got it.'

'Then get a fucking move on!'

Javani sighted along the arrow over the pony's back, and drew back the bowstring. 'Sorry, deer,' she whispered. She loosed.

The arrow screwed off into the oaks, wide and high and wobbling as it flew, skimming off the underside of a branch and crashing to the leaf-thick floor. The deer started, dark eyes wide, then sprang away into the mist and out of sight.

Behind her came Ree's heavy sigh. 'Damned right you're sorry. You shut your eyes, didn't you? Nine hells, kid, we talked about this. Don't hesitate. Identify what you want and go for it, don't second-guess yourself.' She leaned back against her pony's side, shaking her head. 'Well, what are you waiting for? Go and get the arrow.'

Muttering and huffing, Javani trudged through the shin-deep dead-leaf carpet, kicking red and soggy foliage up before her. She hadn't shut her eyes, she was sure of it. Maybe it was just the will of the gods that she shouldn't be taking the life of an innocent animal. No matter how hungry she and Ree got. She bit her lip at the thought. Their travelling provisions had been generous, Ree planned like a pessimist, but most of the packs over the ponies were tending to empty. And when they ran out, she knew Ree was going to suggest eating one of the ponies. That was something she absolutely would not—

What in hells was that?

A sound, from down the ridge's far side, through a thick cluster of moss-furred trunks, the branches above increasingly skeletal. It had sounded like a, not a shout exactly, more like a cry. Someone in distress? Her pulse quickened, and she stopped herself, forcing a slow breath. Probably just an animal. They'd seen no other humans for too long, and now she was anthropomorphising the call of a, uh, quail, probably. Or maybe a partridge. She had no idea what either sounded like.

No. She heard it again, and this time she was sure – it was a person, and they were in trouble. She stood paralysed: run to help, or go back for Ree? What if it was someone cornered by a dangerous animal? She hadn't even found the arrow yet. But getting Ree meant doubling back, marshalling the ponies, Ree limping over with her staff . . . Nope, no time.

With only a mad, expressive wave back to her mother and the ponies, she set off for the clustered hornbeams at a run, marvelling as yet more forest loomed out of the mist as she crested the ridge. She half-slid down the slope, dodging thorny shrubs, leaving dark and muddy grooves in the leaf-covering, keeping her attention fixed on the origin of the sound. She could hear other things now, over the sound of her thumping feet and the rush of blood in her ears – the burbling splash of moving water, metallic jingling, possibly murmured speech?

She reached the trees, still half-sliding, and slung her way through the nest of trunks and out the other side, inwardly delighted at her nimble steps. She erupted from the grove down a slippery chunk of bank, and tumbled down onto a wide, empty patch of ground, devoid of trees and kicked mostly clear of leaves. A trail. No, a road!

A few feet away, a mule stood. It looked at her sidelong, then flicked an ear and returned its attention to cropping at the brush along the roadside.

Her excitement drained. Had she simply heard the mule? They could be noisy buggers, that was true, and a fellow who'd come through Kazeraz once had claimed he'd made a mule sing. The mule hadn't been around to corroborate, of course, but that was rather the nature of the teahouse stories. This one might be a chatty cousin.

'Shit,' muttered Javani. She'd gone through one knee of her trousers, was covered in mud, and a throbbing from one forearm suggested she hadn't navigated those trunks quite as deftly as she'd thought. She looked back at the mule, which was now pointedly ignoring her, as mules do. It was heavily laden with sacks and had a lead rope hanging loose on the soft mud of the road.

Brushing the worst of the mud from her knees, Javani stood, and froze. Beyond the mule was a stretch of open road, curving away down the slope, then another mule. Another three mules, in fact, all equally laden with heavy sacks. And between those mules and the first stood three men, their cloaked backs to her, looking down at something on the ground.

Javani edged sideways until she could see what it was they were standing around. Her gut sank as her suspicions were confirmed. It was a huddled figure. One of the men swung a kick at it as she watched.

'Shit,' muttered Javani.

'Had enough?' the kicker spat at the person on the ground. His accent was thick, from far to the south and east. 'Or still got that mouth on you?'

'Sounds like he's done talking,' chuckled another, with a similar accent. 'Come on, Fingers, let's get the goods and be off.'

The man called Fingers was narrow and stringy, looming like a birch-trunk over the prone figure, fists clenching and unclenching. All three men were very dirty, as was the man on the ground, but presumably for different reasons. 'What's that? You still got some fight in you?'

Javani was shocked to find herself edging closer, and vowed to discipline her heedless feet. Craning forward, she just caught the strained words of the beaten man.

'I only said . . . please let me take the mules back . . .'

Fingers kicked him again. 'No. You fucking dolt.' He swept one hand around in a narrow circle. 'Come on, boys, let's get back to the fire. And we know there's good eating on a mule.'

Javani swallowed. What we have here, then, is a robbery; these men are brigands, and they're robbing this man, who is, what, a merchant? A farmer? She peered at the sacks on the nearby mule. One seemed packed with wool, another grain. Was there a market somewhere nearby? Either way, it was a pretty solid assumption that the brigands were armed, and that in a moment one or more of them would come up the road towards her to get the last mule, at which point, she would . . .

She would . . .

'Shit,' muttered Javani.

TWO

This was one of those times, Javani thought, when you had to make a choice. She could turn, run and hide, and leave the poor merchant/farmer to be robbed and maybe even murdered, or she could intervene, and maybe save the man's life. Maybe.

'They're over here!' she called at the top of her lungs. 'Archers, form up!'

The men by the mules flinched in surprise, then as one turned to look up the road towards her. She ducked behind the lone mule, which was now regarding her with a wary stare. Best if they saw as little of her as possible. She was disheartened to see they were wearing mail beneath their grubby cloaks.

'The fuck was that?' one said, his gaze swinging wildly. 'Did someone say "archers"?'

'Who else is operating up here?' hissed another.

Lanky Fingers looked closest to being in charge. 'Grab the mules, let's get gone.' He stepped away from the man on the ground, who began, ever so quietly, crawling towards the trees at the roadside.

Javani felt her shoulders unclench. Her gambit had worked. They were running.

'I'll get that one,' Fingers growled, gesturing towards the lone mule, behind which Javani cowered. Tension returned to her shoulders like a whipcrack.

Fingers was coming up the slope towards her. When he saw her, saw he was dealing with a small, grubby girl who was very nearly thirteen but not quite, and a total absence of archers, things were going to go sideways very rapidly.

'Shit,' muttered Javani. It was possible she hadn't thought her gambit all the way through.

The mule gazed at her reproachfully, as if asking what she'd expected to happen. 'How was I to know they'd come for you?' she hissed at it.

The mule chewed slowly, mulling the question, but produced no response.

Javani looked from it to the muddy bank at the roadside, and the thicket of hornbeams she'd scampered through on her arrival. Not a chance of scampering back without Fingers seeing. She crouched lower. The mule gave the slightest shake of its head, registering its disappointment.

'Kid.'

Ree's voice was low, almost inaudible, but it went through her like a wave. Javani snapped her gaze up, and there was her mother, nestled in the thicket, her staff discarded and not a pony in sight.

'Catch.'

The hand-bow sailed from the trees and into Javani's grateful hands. She filed her astonishment at catching it cleanly away for some deserved basking later, assuming there was a later, slid a slim bolt from the grip and set about cranking the weapon. She was more than familiar with its workings; she'd been on the wrong end of plenty of examples already in her young life.

'Now what was— Boys! Get up here!' Fingers had seen the movement of the hand-bow, if not what it was and where it had gone.

The other two brigands came lumbering up the slope, trying to convince the three weighted mules to come too. The mules looked to be every bit as intractable as Javani's ponies, which at least reassured her that there was some truth in bromides. Fingers took a cautious step towards Javani's mule, trying to peer around it.

'That's far enough.' This time, Ree's voice carried clear across the morning, cleaving the wood's misty hush like a blade. 'Leave the mules and get out of here, before you and your comrades gain some punctures.'

Fingers froze. Ree was standing just proud of the thicket, the bow gripped in her hands, an arrow nocked and ready. Javani wondered if it was the one she'd lost, or one of the last few from the quiver. If they never found her arrow, she knew she wouldn't hear the end of it.

'Who the fuck are you?' Fingers barked. He seemed genuinely baffled. 'Do you not know who we are?'

'Hush,' Ree replied, her eyes steady on Fingers, arms extended, ready to draw back on the bow. 'There are sixteen archers in the trees around you right now. I give the signal, you and your boys drop where you stand. This is your last chance: leave the mules, and get out of here.'

Fingers licked his lips. He was youngish, Javani thought; it was hard to tell under the grime. He was pale and dark-haired and possibly from the lands of the distant south – she had heard accents like his before, but not for a while, not since they'd been travelling north to Kazeraz themselves.

'I don't believe you,' he growled, and lunged behind the mule, grasping for its rope.

'Kid, do it!' Ree snapped.

Teeth gritted, Javani raised the hand-bow and pulled the trigger.

There came a soft *plink*, then a howl of outraged agony.

Javani opened her eyes.

Fingers was on his back on the road, the hand-bow's slim bolt jutting from the meat of his thigh. He was staring at it in disbelief and bellowing.

'You were warned.' Somehow, Ree's voice cut over the sound of his honking, and the shouts of his two comrades as they broke into a run towards him. Javani had always been impressed at her mother's tone of command, which seemed to work on nearly everyone except Javani. 'Kid, reload,' Ree added in a low, decidedly non-commanding voice.

Javani began to reload, as Ree swung her bow on the two remaining brigands. 'Take him and get out of here. Now. Or none of you sees another sunset.'

The two men looked at each other, and one visibly swallowed. Whoever these lads were, Javani thought, they were clearly not very bright. Three of them, armed and armoured, against two smallish, barely armed women with one and half bows between us, they could rush us and beat us to a pulp before we got another shot off. But there was something about the way Ree spoke to them. Her confidence, her assurance, her unflinching *dominance* . . .

'I'm going to count to three,' Ree called. The men sprang forward, abandoning the mules and scooping up the convulsed Fingers, draping his arms across their shoulders.

'One.'

The brigands wheeled around like a five-legged cart and set off at what struck Javani as a fairly impressive clip back down the road.

'Two.'

Their pace increased, each jolting step sending another howl from Fingers into the morning air. They passed the mules, passed the patch of sodden mud where the merchant/farmer had lain, and disappeared around the curve of the hillside, swallowed by the lingering grey curtain of mist and the ruby vegetation.

'Three,' Ree sighed, and slid back against the trunk behind her. 'Breath of the gods, that was exciting, eh? You still whole, kid?'

Javani patted herself down. 'Think so. You?'

'Leg's hurting like a vicious sow, and I'm not sure how well I tied up the ponies, but it's not like you gave me much warning. Your signalling and crisis communication needs work, kid.'

'Yeah, I know.'

'And don't think I've forgotten about that arrow, either. It's not like we can replace it up here – you see many geese about?'

Javani shrugged. 'Maybe. I'm not that good on birds.'

Ree shook her head, eyes half-closed in amused resignation. 'Your education really hasn't been a triumph, has it?'

Javani had another go at brushing the mud from her clothes. 'I blame the parents.'

Someone cleared their throat on the far side of the mule. Javani hadn't even heard the approach.

'Ah,' said Ree with a bright smile. 'Kid, isn't it time you introduced me to your friend?'

The man said his name was Sweeper. It was an odd name, but no stranger than Fingers, and Javani was in no place to judge. Ree made no comment, which Javani thought was remarkably magnanimous of her. He was very dirty, most of it fresh from the look of him, and covered in welts and bruises. A nasty blow on his cheek was leaking dark blood down past his chin. Ree introduced herself and Javani, but volunteered no details of who they were, or what they were doing, which was probably for the best.

'You didn't have to help me,' he said, offering a look of downcast apology. He seemed young, and unsure, and very sore, but it was hard to tell under the dirt and injuries.

'You think so?' Ree replied, one eyebrow arched.

'They'd probably have stopped hitting me eventually,' he said, still not meeting her gaze.

'How charitable.' Ree inclined her head towards the mules, weighed down by their bursting sacks, now reunited by Javani. 'And you still have your goods, and your mules.' Her voice was slow and clear, as if she were speaking to a child, or someone hard of hearing. Or perhaps someone who'd recently suffered several blows to the head.

'Ah. Yes.' He didn't exactly look delighted. Maybe those head-hits really had addled him. 'Thank you.' He swallowed, looked around as if unsure, one hand on his bloodied cheek. 'Well.'

'Do you have somewhere you should be going?' Ree was peering into his eyes, perhaps looking for signs of concussion. 'Somewhere you were taking all this?'

'Oh, yeah, right. Right.' He nodded, swallowed again, his gaze still wandering. His accent was from somewhere around the plains, Javani thought, although she had no idea what would qualify as a local accent in the Ashadi. His eyes focused suddenly, and he turned to Ree and Javani. 'Would you come with me? It might make things . . . easier.'

'Would we get a hero's welcome?' Javani asked, not entirely sarcastically. She'd had a moment of true fear back there, a reminder of a time she'd hoped to put behind her forever, and was keen to identify some kind of silver lining.

'Oh, yeah, maybe. Why not.'

'Where are you going? A market? A farm?'

'Yeah, something like that.'

Ree nodded. 'We're amenable. Kid, get the ponies.'

'But I—'

'I'm not going back up that bank. Come on, hurry now.'

They made for an odd procession as they plodded up the road beneath the forest's ruddy canopy. The mist was finally lifting, at least a little, and glimmers of late autumn sun set the remaining leaves aflame. It really was a staggeringly beautiful place, Javani thought, mist and all, and such a wholesale change from the barren vistas of the plains and the desert where she'd spent her childhood. Not that they hadn't had their own stark beauty, but there's only so much love you can have for a landscape that wants to kill you.

Sweeper led the procession, his mules roped together, making steady, uncomplaining progress, and impressing Javani no end. She and Ree followed, leading their three ponies, who seemed small and squat beside the mules, and much less heavily loaded. Worryingly so. One of the ponies had lost a shoe somewhere in all the excitement, which had slowed progress and darkened Ree's mood.

'Something's really off about this,' she muttered as they walked, her staff in her hand and the bow (and hand-bow) stowed back on the pony.

'He's pretty shaken up, I guess he's not normally so . . . vague?'

'Look at the tracks, kid. Do you see it?'

Javani looked.

'Mule tracks,' she breathed. 'Going the other way. We're going back the way he came.'

Ree nodded. 'So where was he going before, and why is he going back now?'

'And where are we going now?'

Ree mimicked the man's boggle-eyed, drifting stare. 'Something like a farm, something like a market,' she muttered. 'Up here? When we've seen nothing and no one for weeks?'

'Where do you think those brigands came from? Do you think they'll be back?'

Ree cast a look over her shoulder, and her face grew solemn. 'Don't know, and don't know. I'm certainly keen to get back to wherever this fellow is from, assuming it's where all the stuff on his animals came from. Can't be just him there, not with all that.'

'Makes me wonder,' Javani said, one grubby finger on her grubby chin. 'Why wasn't he armed? If he was taking all this valuable produce somewhere – why's it just him, no guards, no nothing?'

Ree shrugged. 'Maybe he thought the hills were as empty as we did.'

'Maybe. Good thing we were there to come to his rescue.'

'I can't imagine that bandit agrees.'

'No.' Javani found herself frowning. 'I never shot anyone before. Do you think he'll be all right?'

'Probably. Those bolts are small, and you didn't hit an artery, or we'd have been slipping in his gush. Chin up, kid, it could have been far worse.'

'Yeah?'

'You could have hit him in the unmentionables. Gods know what kind of noise he'd have made then.'

Despite herself, Javani snorted. 'Have you ever hit anyone in the unmentionables?'

Ree pulled a half-smile. 'Maybe. But never deliberately. It's hardly sporting.'

'That doesn't surprise me.'

'Oh, really?'

'Really. You're a terrible shot with a bow.'

'Why you little—'

'Wait! Do you hear . . . *a lot* of water?'

THREE

It came out of the mist in stages, as at last the feeble sun fought its way through the low cloud and lit the mountainside. A waterfall, cascading over dark rock in thick sheets of white water, its spray sparkling in the thin shafts of sunlight. Before it a ravine, or at least a break in the rock, a sudden interruption in the hillside's winding climb, over which lay draped a narrow rope bridge. And beyond the bridge, rising in green terraces was . . .

'A village,' Ree breathed, wiping spray from her face. 'There's a whole village up here. This wasn't on the map.'

'I'm told it wasn't a very good map.' The kid was squinting through the drifting chunks of fog. 'You could almost call it a little town.' She paused. 'Gods, is it a trading post? Are the Guild—'

'Relax, kid. No Guild this far up, remember? Just look at the place. No pennants, no gates . . .'

The kid looked. 'Yeah, where are the walls?'

Ree's gaze followed the rim of the rock from the rope bridge, away from the waterfall and out of sight around the side of the far ridge. 'I guess the walls are the landscape.'

The settlement sat on a projecting escarpment, fringed by the waterfall and its ravine at the nearest edge, sweeping around the curve of the river that dropped into the valley below, and around the stark expanse of grey mountain that loomed above. The terrain of the escarpment had been worked into precise terraces, thick with buildings in neat rings, radiating from the uppermost.

Aside from the bridge ahead of them, Ree saw no other way to reach it.

Sweeper had reached the rope bridge, which swayed in the wind more than Ree felt entirely comfortable with. It wasn't that long, or that wide, and had thick oak planks strung between what looked at least sturdy knots. He turned, still rubbing at the cut on his cheek, and waved for them to approach.

'The mules can be a little reluctant, bridgewardly,' he said with a nervous grin. The bruises were really coming out on his face now, one side swollen and shining beneath the mud. 'I tend to take them the long way round. I can . . . I could do the same for your . . . your ponies, if you like?'

Ree's mouth was pursed. 'How long is the long way round? What would we be doing?'

'Relax, Ma,' the kid muttered. 'Look.' She gestured to the road's edge, where a narrow trail cut back down the slope beneath them, turning hairpins until it reached the valley floor beyond the waterfall's foot. Through mist and spray, Ree saw a much more substantial bridge over the river at the valley-foot, then a similar winding trail up the escarpment on the far side, steep and sparse, leading up towards the settlement's edge.

Sweeper offered an apologetic smile. One of his teeth was chipped, but Ree couldn't tell if it was fresh. 'Takes a time longer, thought you might want to cross here. Say . . . say hello.'

'I'm not sure about—' Ree began.

'What about our hero's welcome?' the kid cut in. 'Won't that be harder without you to introduce us?'

He shook his head vigorously. 'Oh, no. Much better, like this.' He extended a hand for the lead pony's rope, and the kid handed it straight over. 'See you there?'

'Kid! How do we know—'

'Come on, Ma, you're not going to slog your way down there and back up again just to keep an eye on the ponies, are you? Our hero's welcome awaits.' She swung back to Sweeper. 'You'll be all right with all the animals? Our girls can be, uh, difficult.'

'Yeah. Animals seem to find me reassuring.'

Ree took another look at the swaying bridge, its ropes slick with waterfall spray, its boards shining. She took a sharp breath. 'Well, then. See you there.'

A man stood at the bridge's far end, arms folded, waiting less than patiently for them to cross. Ree took her time, noting the man's thick woollen kaftan and peevish demeanour. Quality wool, too. She concentrated on putting one foot in front of the other, ignoring the grumbling sparks of pain from her right leg with each pace. A strong smell of animals wafted over the damp breeze.

'Who's this?' The kid was at her side, not escorting, not minding, just keeping close. Ree resented her conscientiousness as much as she appreciated it. *I'm not yet that old and decrepit*, she thought. *Still, the bridge is slippery.*

She eyed the wooden baton that hung from the man's belt. 'I'm guessing this is our first taste of the town's guardians.'

'Halt!' the man barked as they set grateful foot on the solid ground of the bridge's far side. A small hut stood to one side of him, possibly a guard post, and piled beyond on a patch of open ground were stacks of timber in impressive volumes, as well as coiled ropes and what could have been pulleys, laid flat. Clearly some building work was in its early stages.

'Can we not get a mite further from the edge of this chasm?' Ree enquired with a sweet smile.

The man sniffed. 'Stay where you are. There's no plague here, we won't have it. All new arrivals are to submit to inspection, by order of the Council.'

Ree's smile was undimmed. 'And who's that?'

His eyebrows lowered, although it wasn't clear if this was in anger or incomprehension. 'The village council, who make the laws and take the decisions that guide us and bind us, that council.' He blinked. He wasn't as old as Ree had expected, as old as his stature and manner had suggested. She'd have been surprised if he was even thirty, the skin fresh and unblemished on his jowly face.

'And who are you?'

'I ask the questions!' the man near-shrieked.

'Well, go on then,' the kid replied, leaning a hand on one of the bridge's anchoring posts. 'Ask away.'

The man was flushing, which amused Ree no end. He cleared his throat, one hand now gripping the baton at his belt. 'State your business here.'

'You know,' Ree said, leaning against the other anchor post, 'that's more of a command than a question.'

He looked from one to the other. 'Well?'

'Well, are you going to ask a question?'

His eyes went wide, and for a moment Ree thought he might try to strike her. Then a clear voice called out through the thinning mist. 'Gumis, do we have visitors?'

Ree looked beyond Gumis, their temporary obstacle, to see a woman descending the terraces, moving quickly down the banked-earth steps with obvious enthusiasm. She was old – Ree caught herself; the woman was probably the same age as her, her hair shot through with enough white to make great winding stripes in her braids. Her robes were loose and functional, and evidently of the same tough, undyed wool as the man blocking their path. He looked at her with obvious deference.

She reached them swiftly, as Gumis glowered, and offered them a bright, warm smile. 'Welcome, travellers. I am Camellia, a member of the Council here.'

Ree offered a bow of her head. 'We've been hearing all about you.'

'We don't have plague,' the kid added.

Camellia's brow furrowed, and she glanced at Gumis, who had remained in peevish silence. 'And you've met Gumis, our constable.'

Gumis grunted. Ree grinned. 'Indeed we have. I believe he was about to ask us our business here.'

'Which is?' he growled.

'Just passing through.'

'And do you have names?' Camellia asked with an open smile.

'I'm Javani, she's Ree,' the kid volunteered. 'We're on our way to Arestan, crossing the Ashadi.'

Ree put up a finger. 'One moment, please.' Gripping the kid's sleeve, she wheeled the girl into an involuntary huddle, facing back across the swaying bridge.

'Gods' haemorrhoids, child,' she hissed, 'have you lost your tiny mind? We are fugitives! What if there really are agents of the Miners' Guild in this place? We can't go broadcasting our identities and agenda!'

The kid only pursed her lips, eyebrows raised. 'Come on, Ma. No Guild this far up, you said so yourself. Our troubles are way behind us, that way. *That* way. No, that way. Maybe.' She turned back to Camellia without waiting for a response. 'Pleased to meet you.'

'Arestan, you say.' Camellia's smile had faded. 'Well, you are welcome here. Respect our laws and customs, and you may stay as long as you wish before you continue your journey.'

'Much appreciated,' Ree said slowly, and met the kid's glance. Adherence to law was an odd thing to lead with, wasn't it? What was their expectation otherwise? The kid's eyes said she agreed.

'Weapons!' barked Gumis.

'Excuse me?'

'Do you have on you any weapons of war, any tools of death or injury, or anything that can be used to kill or maim?'

Ree considered. 'Yes.'

'Surrender them immediately.' Gumis shot a look at Camellia. 'Please.'

Ree looked at the man sidelong. 'Why?'

Camellia cleared her throat. 'This would be the first of our laws. No weapons are permitted within the community. We live in peace here, and it is no place for tools of war.'

Ree gave them a deeply distrusting look, then ducked her head to the kid's level. 'What do you think, kid?' she murmured.

'I think maybe Sweeper wasn't addled from his injuries. Maybe they're all like this? But' – she gripped Ree's arm – 'we need supplies, we're down a shoe on one of the ponies, and we're still due our hero's welcome when Sweeper turns up with his mules and all his goods intact. We can always trade some of Aki's smaller stones if that doesn't do the job.'

'I hear you.' Ree stood straight again. 'We accept. I've got, let's see . . . three knives, one sword, and the kid here has, what? Two knives, is that it? Three, there you go. Then of course, there are the bows on the ponies.'

Camellia frowned. 'The ponies?'

The kid nodded. 'Your man Sweeper is bringing them up the long way. Along with his mules.'

Relief coloured her face. 'He brought home the mules? That's wonderful.'

The kid was nodding along with her, a broad grin spreading across her face. 'Not just the mules, but everything on them.'

Camellia's smile froze. 'What?'

'Yup, Ree and I arrived in the very nick of time, saved—'

'The mules are still laden?'

'As I said, we arrived, well, *I* arrived—'

'Dear gods above!' Her hands wrapped her head. 'Dear gods!' She turned and strode away from them, back towards the terrace steps, in the direction of the eventual exit of the long way round.

The kid met Ree's gaze. 'Now what do you suppose that's about?'

Ree's teeth pulled at her bottom lip. 'That may have been your hero's welcome going up in smoke, kid. Come on, let's go and see what's going on.'

She took a step, only to find the inflated form of Gumis once again blocking their path.

'Weapons!'

Ree followed Gumis's strutting form as he led them up through the terraces, trying to keep a lid on her simmering frustration despite the flares of pain from her leg at each brisk step. She'd not even been allowed her walking staff. Low timber buildings of elm and oak clustered on the rising ground, laid out in well-organised banks, broken by well-buttressed terrace walls with wide-cut steps. The mist was almost entirely gone, burned away by the sluggish late autumn sun, revealing the stark wall of grey rock rising behind the settlement, blocking further passage west.

'What about cutting food?' she demanded of Gumis's back. 'How am I supposed to do that?'

'We have communal implements,' he tossed back over his shoulder. 'Crafted from horn and bone, and only allowed in the hands of a select group.'

'Would that group include you, by any chance?'

His smirk gave her the answer.

'You know, Gumis,' she muttered, 'I could probably kill you with just my—'

The kid tugged at her elbow. 'Look at this place, Ree. These aren't shacks and lean-tos. They've got a market, that could be a teahouse, I'm guessing that's a temple, back there are grain stores, right? Past the barns?'

Ree scanned as she walked, and grunted reluctant agreement.

'Gumis,' the kid called, 'what was all that timber for at the bridge? Are you building something there?'

He was glossy with pride. 'The village is in the early stages of construction of a water mill, powered by the fall. It will be unlike anything for a thousand leagues in any direction. The fixings in the rock are already in place, and we'll be done in time for the first harvest.'

'You'll build it over winter?'

'Winter here isn't as sharp as in the high places.' He sniffed again. 'And we are hardy people.'

The kid leaned back in, her voice lowered. 'It's a pretty decent set-up, right? Looks almost like an army camp. It's got zones.'

Ree grunted again. Hens and geese pottered past them on avian business as they proceeded, and the smell of ruminants and their emissions was more powerful than ever. Bleats and squawks floated on the air.

'You have a lot of cattle here, Gumis?'

He shook his head. 'No cattle, but plenty of sheep and goats. And fowl.'

Ree eyed the grain stores, tall, conical buildings of loose stone and packed earth mortar. 'And you farm wheat?'

His pride was impossible to miss. 'And spring barley.'

Ree gave him a single beat. 'Then what the fuck do you cut it with? How do you shear and slaughter the animals? Stern looks? Sharp words?'

Gumis sniffed and came to a halt, his chin jutting. 'My apologies, travellers, but I think we have a miscommunication. I am escorting you not as your guide, but as your guard. You are strangers here, and have no right to demand anything of us.'

The kid stared back at him from beneath raised and sceptical brows. 'You're guarding us?' she asked, deadpan.

Gumis resumed his stalk, leading them wide of what must have been the main square, a wide expanse of open ground on the uppermost terrace, and towards the descending steps on its far side. 'The slaughterhouse and tannery are outside the community boundary,' he muttered. 'As are several other dwellings, for reasons that need not concern you.'

Ree ignored him, looking up at the stark rockface that hemmed in the settlement along its western side, all the way from the waterfall and its bridge, around the back of the terraces and then out of sight, around the mountain's shoulder. Now they were closer, she could see breaks in the rock, platforms and ledges, and what looked like stairs carved or hammered into the pale stone. A construction of ropes dangled from the uppermost ledge.

'What's up there?'

'None of your business!' Gumis snapped.

'Constable Gumis!' called a deep, rolling voice across the square. 'Who is this?'

They turned to see an enormous man ducking out from the doorway of what Ree now recognised as the grandest building yet. Timber-framed with a stone footing, it featured ornate carving on the pillars either side of its wide doorway, although at this range, she couldn't see of what. It struck her as the first purely decorative aspect she'd seen to anything since entering the settlement.

The man emerging from the doorway was vast, as tall as any Ree had ever seen, and substantial with it. He looked like a structural column. Like those of Camellia and Gumis, his robes were wool, but as he came closer Ree spotted its finespun softness, the dyed thread embroidered at cuff and collar. His clothes also appeared to fit him, which meant they could have been made for nobody else; you could have clothed the kid four times over with the same fabric.

'Look at the size of that bastard,' the kid whispered, her eyes wide in wonder.

'Master Keretan.' Gumis appeared to bow at the large man's approach. Gumis wasn't particularly tall to begin with, a little more than Ree's own modest height, and the man loomed over him like a siege tower. 'Travellers. Passing through.'

The new man looked the newcomers up and down. 'Has Camellia . . . ?'

Gumis nodded. 'She has.'

Keretan hmmed, then turned his lofty gaze on Ree. 'What brings you to us?' His voice was so deep it seemed to tremble through the earth.

'Just passing through,' Ree replied, trying not to crane her neck.

'We're crossing the Ashadi to Arestan,' the kid added, to her mother's annoyance.

The man hmmed again, a low rumble. Gumis was openly sneering. 'A limping old woman and a child? Get over the high places? With winter around the corner? Ha!'

Ree fixed him with a steely glare. 'Old?'

He somehow missed it. 'And don't think you're staying here, either, we're quite full. As soon as this mess with the handover is resolved, you're out again, make no mistake.'

Ree had taken a step forward already, one hand reaching for a sword that wasn't there. 'The only mistake around here is being made by your mouth, Constable Gumis. If you'd care to test my resilience, I'd be happy to duel you at your leisure. We can step outside your boundaries and use real weapons, or I can beat you insensible with that little stick of yours. How's now for you?'

The kid was pulling her back as the words left her mouth. 'Ma! No.'

Ree shook her off. 'What? I've won every duel I've fought. Nearly.'

'Please don't threaten one of the first people we've met in ages.'

Gumis appeared to be vibrating with outrage, but Keretan put one heavy hand on the man's shoulder. 'Peace, constable. Words can wound as sure as arrows, but what's said in anger can be mended more readily than spilled blood.' His heavy brows lowered. His head was very square, his scalp shaved and gleaming, his beard as thick and wide as his head, and very grey. Ree guessed he was older than her, but he could simply have been weathered by the atmospheric conditions. 'Now what was this you said about a mess with the handover?'

'Keretan!' Camellia was at the top of the far steps, robes flowing from the speed of her climb. Slinking behind her, bloodied and battered and looking thoroughly ashamed, was Sweeper.

'Keretan,' she repeated, her eyes wide. 'We have a problem.'

FOUR

The grand building was, apparently, the Council House. Inside, fires burned in twin fireplaces, either side of a wide patch of flooring, matted with woven reeds and laid with rugs. Ree had to admit the place was well constructed, the roof timbers stretching overhead between stone chimneys, allowing even Keretan plenty of headroom.

The big man folded himself on one of seven low wooden seats, hewn from old stumps and finely polished, set in a shallow curve beneath an odd display mounted on the chamber's far wall. Ree squinted in the low and flickering light.

'Nine bastard hells,' she whispered. 'Is that what I think it is?'

The kid gave her a level look. 'And what do you think it is?'

'A set of armour of one of Arowan's Golden Lancers. Although,' she squinted again, 'it looks pretty mangled. And from the size of it, it can only have belonged to one person here.'

Keretan caught her stare, and gave a slow, acknowledging nod. He didn't seem proud, or keen to discuss why a giant set of gleaming cavalry armour might be hanging from the wall of the Council House, but Ree got the impression that Keretan was a man who was happy to let his stature do the talking. No wonder he appeared to be the head of the Council.

The rest of the Council was gathering, such as it was. Keretan was the only one sitting so far: Gumis refused to let Ree and Javani out of his sight, Camellia paced on the matting before the seven seats, and two newcomers engaged in animated conversation by the door, apparently about something else entirely. They were older men, what hair remained turned silver, one stooped and leaning on a stick, the other taller, talking down his nose. They were, presumably, what passed for village elders. In the background, Ree saw Sweeper quietly pick up a broom and begin sweeping the matting by a fireplace. It seemed his name was entirely literal.

Camellia was out of patience. 'Mani, Volkan, please! We must discuss matters urgently.'

The two older men abandoned their dispute, apparently unresolved, and made shuffling progress to opposite ends of the Council seats. Gumis sat down beside Keretan, his beady eyes fixed on Ree and Javani, with a look as intimidating as his young face could muster. Ree shook her head in amused disdain.

'Very well, Camellia,' said the stooped man, the stick now resting between his knees. Ree eyed it with envy. 'What is the matter? Volkan and I were in the middle of a very tense game of stones, and if we don't get back to it soon he will claim infirmity and abscond.' He looked up, as if noticing the two extras in the chamber for the first time. His wrinkled features spread in delighted surprise. 'And who are our guests?'

Ree took a step forward and a breath to speak, but the enormous Keretan caught her eye, his hand raised to forestall her. Against her own expectations as much as anyone else's, she stepped back. The man exerted an astonishing level of natural authority, and it wasn't just from his size. He was measured and sober in manner, and had shown little in the way of emotion at any time since she'd first seen him. She waited to see what he'd do.

'Camellia?' Keretan said, with a slight motion of his open palm.

Camellia had yet to take her seat. 'Where is Lali? Has she arrived?'

Ree eyed the empty seats. Assuming Camellia ever sat, there would still be two left over. Maybe this Lali was another village big hitter?

A clatter from the doorway behind them announced a late arrival, a girl older than the kid, but possibly not much, carrying a bundle of what could have been parchment around a pen and ink set. Ree locked her features as the girl bustled past, determined not to show surprise. Somehow, they had to be trading with the plains, even as deep into the mountains as they were. There had to be a trade route she and the kid had missed, perhaps cutting south-east? Ree and Javani had come from the northern side, perhaps that excuse for a road they'd stumbled over had been the trade path's end.

The girl bowed to Camellia. 'I'm so sorry, Mother Camellia, I wasn't aware that—'

'It's no trouble, Lali,' Camellia replied with an indulgent smile. 'This was unscheduled, and you're here now.' The girl sank to the floor before the arc of seats, cross-legged, unfurling her parchment bundle and cracking open her pen and ink set. So, Ree mused, not much of a big hitter after all. Lali set down her inkpot on the matting, and artfully dipped one of her sharp wooden pens, making some vigorous test scratches at the parchment's edge until she was happy with the amount of ink on the nib.

Mani, the old fellow with the stick, leaned forward in his seat. 'Please, my dear,' he said in an avuncular tone, 'have a care with your marking. Is it not enough that the poor animal died for you, that you should make such a mess of its hide?'

Lali's cheeks darkened and her head bowed, and she put the pen to one side.

Camellia cleared her throat. 'If we are all ready . . . ?'

Ree's eyes darted once more to the two empty seats. Five out of seven wasn't bad, she supposed.

Without any further delay, Camellia launched into the meeting's preamble, noting the date (was it so late in the year already?) the names of those present, and the urgent nature of the assembly. She remained standing as she spoke, her pacing stilled but her nervous energy no less present, while Lali's pen scratched, gently, at the parchment from the floor.

'So, to the matter at hand,' Keretan rumbled, his dark eyes shifting slowly from Camellia to Ree and Javani, then to Sweeper, who was sweeping around a set of gleaming pots in the corner. 'Sweeper, please join us.'

The man shuffled over, broom still in hand. His wounds looked pretty dreadful in the flickering light of the fires and what Ree took to be tallow candles on clay stands, but he moved without gasps and winces, which was more than Ree imagined she'd do in his place.

'You returned to us with the mules,' Keretan continued, 'and their cargo still on them. Why did you not make the exchange?'

'Ah, Master Keretan, gracious councillors,' Sweeper said, his eyes on the woven reeds, 'there was the most dreadful confusion . . . I can't . . . I can't really explain it.'

Ree's mouth twitched. The exchange. She flicked a sidelong look at Javani. The kid was looking back, brows raised, lips pursed. Expectant. *Are you going to say anything?*

Not yet, Ree told herself. Let's see where this is leading, before we go blundering in again. For a start, she wanted to know what all that produce was being exchanged for.

Camellia was still standing, ducking her head to meet his gaze with earnest eyes, her braids swinging. 'Sweeper, please, you must tell us exactly what happened. We must make this right.'

'I'm so sorry,' was all the man would mumble.

Ree sighed to herself. Time to make herself even more popular. 'He was set upon by brigands,' she called from the back of the room. 'Can't you see he's been beaten near-senseless? No wonder he can't give you a straight answer.' Unless, she added to herself, that really is what he's normally like, in which case I can't help you.

'Then why does he still have the cargo?' said the second old man, Volkan, a pinched, narrow face on a vaguely cone-shaped head.

'Because we saved him!' the kid shot back. 'We arrived in the nick of time, and not only stopped him being beaten to a mushy pulp, but drove off the bandits before they could make off with your produce.'

Ree followed straight on. 'I'm sorry Master Sweeper couldn't get to his exchange as planned, but it was probably best he return for some care and attention, yes? You can try your exchange again later, perhaps a mite better guarded, if I may offer a suggestion?'

Camellia nodded. 'Yes, of course, we must rearrange it forthwith.' She paused, brows dark beneath silver braids. 'Brigands? You drove them off? How?'

'Shot one in the leg,' the kid retorted with what Ree was sure was more confidence than she felt.

'How many were there?' Camellia pressed, then the colour left her face. 'What did they look like?'

Keretan was leaning forward on one elbow, his eyes intent, licking dry lips. 'Kindly describe those you saw.'

Ree exchanged looks with the kid. 'Three of them,' the kid said. 'Shabby cloaks, shabby mail underneath. One was called . . . er, a nickname, Fungus?'

'Fingers,' Ree corrected.

'Oh, sweet mercy.' Camellia's hands were either side of her head, fingers burying themselves in her braids. 'Oh, mercy of the gods be upon us.'

'What?' said the kid, brows knitted. 'What's the issue?'

Ree was shaking her head. 'Are you telling me that Fingers and his crew were your exchange partners? That . . . that beating we witnessed was part of some arrangement?'

'No.' Keretan's voice cut over Camellia's anxious rambling. 'No beating was part of any arrangement.'

Ree could feel her eyebrows climbing. 'But apart from that, you were turning all that . . . *stuff* over to Fingers and his goons? In exchange for what?'

Gumis was up from his chair. 'None of your business!'

Keretan waved a peevish hand. 'Gumis, please. Sit down.'

Ree put her hands up. 'No, no, he's right. This is none of our concern. We're just passing through, right, kid?'

The kid grunted. She was frowning deeply, staring at Sweeper who remained staring at the floor, hands locked on his broom.

'And we're a little low on supplies, so if you wanted to thank us for saving your friend here—'

'You've saved no one,' came Camellia's voice in little more than a whisper. 'The exact reverse. Oh, mercy of the gods . . .'

'Camellia.' Keretan was getting to his feet, immediately huge even beneath the building's high beams. 'All will be well. As our traveller says, we can make the exchange again. If we send a message now, we might even have it done before sundown.'

'They *shot* one in the *leg*,' Camellia whispered, wide-eyed.

'And they were beating your man half to death,' Ree called back. 'Would have been the whole way there if we hadn't shown up when we did. Are you telling me you'd rather they'd taken all he had and left him bleeding out by the roadside, never to return?'

She waited.

'Well, that's horrifying.'

'You don't understand.' Deep lines dug beneath Camellia's eyes. 'It's not as simple as that.'

'Clearly.' Ree cricked her neck. Her leg was aching from standing. 'Well, we've used up too much of your time, so we'll be taking our leave – and our weapons.'

Gumis took a step down towards them. 'Happily,' he growled.

'Wait.' Keretan's hand was up again. 'It would be a shame if we gave the impression that we're ungrateful for your actions in bringing Sweeper home to us. He's a valued part of the community.' He took two giant steps forward and laid a gentle hand on the downcast man's shoulder. 'We would be happy to offer you supplies for your onward journey in return.'

Gumis went to speak, then, perhaps for the first time in his life, thought better of it. He continued to glower at Ree.

'Much appreciated,' Ree replied, ignoring Gumis. 'We'll be out of your hair before the day is over. Arestan is still that way, right?'

'Your leg.' Mani was hobbling up now, the meeting seemingly dissolving around them. Ree felt a pang of sympathy for Lali and her note-taking endeavours. 'Does it pain you much?'

Ree kept her voice cool. 'Only when I use it.'

'Would it be unkind to suggest you and the girl would benefit from some rest somewhere comfortable before you continued your journey?'

'Well, I'd have to ask *the girl*.'

The kid tugged at her elbow. 'Get him to define "comfortable".'

Mani had already turned to Keretan, looming overhead. 'Keretan, we can put them up for a day or two, wouldn't you say? Allow them a little respite before they move on. Arestan is no easy journey from here.'

'It's not?' The kid was still gripping Ree's arm. 'Then what in hells have we been travelling all this way for? We've been crossing the mountains for months, how are there still more bastard mountains?'

The Council House was quiet but for the dying echoes of her shriek. The kid cleared her throat. 'What I mean is . . .'

Mani offered a munificent smile. 'I can't make a proclamation on your route-finding, but Arestan remains to the west of us. Whether you can make it from here . . . I also can't judge. None of us on the Council ever tried the journey, and *some* of us,' he coughed, 'are now far too old to try.'

'Several have left us over the years,' Volkan added, although his attention seemed to be elsewhere, 'and not returned, but that proves little – perhaps they reached their destination, perhaps they did not, but none came back to tell us, and far more have stayed here, and made a home for themselves.'

Mani nodded, his white moustache bristling outwards as he smiled. 'It's nice here, after all.'

Keretan was looking at Camellia, who shook her head, resigned or defeated or simply preoccupied with whatever disaster was unfolding in her imagination. 'You and the child may stay for the night, if it please you. On your departure, we will ensure you are well-supplied for your onward journey.'

'Thanks,' Ree said, and meant it.

'Child?' the kid growled.

'Mani, will you show them out? Unless you have anything to add to our business?'

'Joyously nothing, Keretan.'

FIVE

The mist was gone, and the day shone golden, the wooded hills around them bright and burnished in the sunlight. Even the grey wall of rock behind them seemed to glow. The day still had some chill to it, but Ree could no longer see her breath when she huffed. The stink of animals and their emissions remained ever-present.

Mani excused himself for a moment while he conversed with a passing villager, a burly, youngish man, later named as Solheil, who pointedly paid the newcomers so little attention that his curiosity couldn't have been more obvious. Ree and Javani stood on the wide steps that led up to the Council House, watching chickens meander aimlessly across the square and basking in the meagre sun.

'Funny bunch, eh?' the kid said after a moment.

Ree scratched at her nose. She wanted a sit-down and a hot bath. 'They are indeed. Interesting mix of accents, too.'

Mani came wandering back, his stick leaving small divots in the soft ground. 'So sorry to keep you waiting, ladies. You could lodge in the stables, of course, but I think we can rustle up something a little more salubrious, if you're prepared to loiter a little?'

Ree chewed at her lip for a moment. 'Stables? Is that where our ponies are?'

He nodded towards the lower terrace. 'I understand so.'

The kid followed his nod. 'You have other horses?'

'No, these are winter stables, for the sheep and the goats. And the mules, of course. Your ponies will be in good company. Would you care to see them? Will they be worried about you?'

Ree hesitated a moment, scanning his expression to check he was joking. Not even a twinkle to his eye. The man was serious.

'Maybe. But they've had worse.' She paused. 'One of them needs a new shoe. Do you have a farrier here?'

'We do.' He beamed, moustache gleaming in the sun, then he paused in thought. 'Perhaps you'd care to meet her? She's a bit of a walk, but I think you might find it worthwhile.'

'Any chance of getting my staff back? My leg's pissing razors, as we say in the east.'

Mani looked pained. 'Ah. Confiscated by our constable?'

'The very same. But he's allowed his little truncheon, is he?'

Now there was a twinkle in the old man's eye. 'The baton of office could never be confused with a weapon, young lady.'

Ree fought down a smile at that; no one had called her 'young lady' in over a decade. 'Call me Ree. So, no weapons at all around here?'

A man strode into view from the other side of the terrace, walking briskly, his head high, his grizzled features impassive, almost hostile to their surroundings, looking neither left nor right but staring off to infinity. Unlike the other wool-clad villagers they'd seen, this man wore soft leather, and Ree's mouth fell open as she saw what he carried slung over his shoulder.

'That man—'

Mani turned, slowly, as the man crossed the square. 'Ah. Anri.'

'He's got a fucking bow!'

'And arrows!' the kid added.

The man took the stairs beside them two at a time, paying them no heed at all. 'Camellia!' he bellowed through the doorway.

Camellia appeared, looking flustered, perhaps still wrought over the ruined exchange, perhaps from her rude summoning.

'Anri,' she said. Her eyes went to his bow and back, but she said nothing. Ree wondered if the bow was the problem, or the arrows. What danger was a bow, after all, if you had nothing to shoot?

'Six rabbits,' Anri growled, 'and a hart.' His voice was deep and throaty, with the strong, mellifluous accent of the distant Hindmarch. 'If you're wanting them dressed, it's extra.'

'Anri, at the moment there are other priorities—'

He leaned back from her, dark eyes flashing. At least one of his front teeth was missing beneath his salt-and-pepper whiskers. 'Or I can take them back? Leave them to rot in the forest? There's less out there to hunt by the day.'

Camellia rubbed at her face with both hands. 'Of course not. I'll square everything with the Council.'

'Good.' He turned on his heel and began marching away, back towards the bridge.

Mani shook his head with a sigh. 'A sorry business.'

'That he's allowed weapons?' the kid prompted. 'Why is he allowed weapons and nobody else?'

Camellia was still in the doorway. 'Anri does not live in the settlement, but outside it. He,' she cleared her throat, 'pops in from time to time.'

Ree gave her a level look. 'And he's allowed to wander through with a bow and full quiver, but I'm not allowed a staff to take the burn from my leg?'

The councillor wasn't meeting her eye. 'He is a hunter; those are the tools of his trade. We know him, and know he will not harm anyone.' She left the rest unsaid: you, we don't know, and you could be some kind of stick-wielding mass killer.

'These laws of yours seem a little more flexible than you implied. What about knives? I need a knife for any number of reasons during a given day, none of them relating to blood-letting. At what point does a knife become a weapon?'

'When it is used to force an opinion.' Camellia's voice had lost its warmth. 'Good day.' She swept back inside.

'Ma,' the kid whispered. 'Please. For a little while, could you stop making enemies of everyone we meet?'

Ree flexed her jaw. 'That depends on them as much as me.'

'I'm not one to give advice,' Mani said in a voice that Ree very much took to mean he was someone who gave advice, probably on a frequent basis, 'but I have found that suspicion tends to breed suspicion.'

'And what's the alternative?'

He spread his palm. 'An open mind, and an open heart. Lead with love, and love will be returned to you.'

Again, Ree searched his face for signs of a joke, and found nothing. She flicked a glance at the kid. She seemed just as nonplussed.

'I'll bear that in mind.'

Sweeper came shuffling out of the Council House, his battered face unimproved by the sunlight. He blinked when he saw them still standing on the steps.

'Ah, Sweeper,' Mani called, 'how are you feeling? The ladies would like to meet the smiths – do you feel up to walking them over?'

He nodded, uncertain at first, then with greater conviction. Ree caught Mani's eye. 'Are you sure about this? He needs a rest more than we do.'

The old man replied with a beatific smile. 'He likes to help. Let him help you.' He extended a twig-thin arm. 'Come, I'll walk with you as far as I can. I imagine you may have more questions.'

Sweeper led the way, the kid following a pace behind, staring gormlessly at the surroundings as they made their way through the settlement, while Ree and Mani, arm-in-arm, brought up the rear. Ree wasn't entirely clear who was supporting whom.

'Does something amuse you, Mistress Ree?'

'Please, just Ree.' They took careful steps together around a pile of what she hoped was goatshit. 'I was trying to remember the last time I had a man on my arm.'

Mani's own smile widened in turn. 'I'd be surprised if it was long, but I'm honoured to be the current holder of the position.'

Ree cleared her throat. 'What is this place, Mani? How did you come to be here, so far from the rest of the world?'

His smile faded, his features softening in introspection. 'We call it Ar Ramas,' he said, his old voice squeaky, whistling through his moustache.

Ree dredged through her memories of Serican dialects. 'The stopping place?'

'The resting place,' he corrected. 'For those who had reached the end of the road, and could go no further.'

'Crossing into Arestan?'

He nodded, his breath coming a little heavier now. They'd left the initial banks of houses around the square and were travelling upslope along a trail, past a wide circle of stones that could have been a threshing floor, stone-walled food stores and neatly stowed farm machinery under projecting canopies. 'The first of us rested here, then more arrived, making the same journey, with all they could carry on their backs or drive before them. And more stayed.'

Refugees. 'You were fleeing the war?'

He cracked a sad smile. 'Which? The collapse of Arowan was just another notch on tragedy's belt, as Volkan puts it. Many had already fled Vistirlar, and found Serica no more welcoming. Droughts, famine, plagues – and then peace, and plenty. Here, at the edge of everything.'

'You never tried to push on? Cross the rest of the way?'

He was panting now, the climb taking its toll. Ree eased to a stop and reached down to rub at her calf, its grumbling no better. Ahead of them, the trail narrowed as it reached its apex, the stark face of grey rock to their left, the sheer drop of the escarpment towards the valley bottom to their right, then beyond the hillside stretched, revealing a rolling sweep of green pastureland hemmed by sharp shoulders of thickly wooded hills, vivid and shimmering in the morning sun.

Mani nodded at her leg, his breathing slowing. 'Does it pain you very much?'

'It's still healing. It'll settle.'

'And she never rests it properly!' came the kid's voice from ahead. She was standing on an exposed chunk of silvery boulder, looking out over the landscape, hands on her hips, silhouetted by the sun like a miniature explorer of new lands. Ree supposed that in a sense, she was.

'I like your daughter,' Mani said, with a nod. 'She's vivacious.'

'That's one word for it.' From their vantage Ree could look out over the sweep of the valley, the village and its surrounds, take in the clusters of wool-wrapped figures engaged in any number of meaningful tasks. 'What do the members of the Council do? When everyone else is . . . working.'

Mani wheezed a chuckle. 'Oh, we still work, where we can. Keretan leads the work crews, and is something of a stonemason himself. Camellia trains the spinners and the weavers, and sees to so much more besides. Gumis minds our borders, ever watchful.

And Volkan . . . ensures that any scheme or proposal is thoroughly tested.'

'And you, Mani? Are you out milking the ewes at dawn's crack?'

He laughed again, a sound like standing on a punctured bellows. 'Not any more, no – they wouldn't trust me! But they let me hang around nonetheless.' He took a long breath and raised his stick. 'You asked if we ever tried to push on.' He swept the stick around in a wide arc before them, taking in the florid hills, the grey and snowcapped peaks, the pasture, the neat, well-built homes, the waterfall and winding river. 'Why would we? We came in search of a better life, and we found it here. Peace, and plenty. Besides,' he extended his arm for Ree again, 'I hear the climate on the far side is very hot and humid. Quite unpleasant.'

'I've always heard it was paradise.'

'For rice, maybe, but too wearing for an old man like me.'

They resumed their walk, over the crest of the rise and into a gentle descent. The pasture spread before them, lush and verdant despite the lateness of the year, a waving sea of tall wildgrass speckled with vivid purple and yellow blooms. A thick ribbon of dark smoke from a wide-timbered building at the pasture's edge drew Ree's eye. It had the look of a forge.

'Everyone here was trying to cross into Arestan and gave up, then?'

He snorted, still a little wheezy. 'Not quite. Once the first of us settled, some volunteered to take word back to those we'd left behind, and return with as many as would come. Our path is well-trodden, and there are still occasional trips for trade. But we try not to have too much contact with the world beyond – not that we would turn away travellers, of course!'

'There's a quick way down to the plains from here?'

He chuckled again, a little creaky huff. 'There's a way, but you'd need to move a mountain or two out of the way to make it quick. It's still a long, hard path to take.'

'Huh.'

'It's a shame you won't be staying longer, Just Ree – we're so close to Sun's Night now, it will be a splendid occasion. I've been drying garlic in preparation myself.'

Ree thought of Keretan's gracious offer of a single night's accommodation, then pursed her lips. She was being unfair; she was the one who had insisted they were pushing on, and the settlers had offered them whatever they needed for their onward journey.

'Best we move on, but thank you.' Ree dodged what this time she was sure was a large pile of sheep-eggs. 'But . . . are you going to fill me in on exactly what this exchange was that the kid and I have disrupted? That involved your friend Sweeper nearly getting his guts kicked through his teeth?'

Mani's face fell and, as a cloud covered the sun, he suddenly looked sallow and frail. 'It is a sorry business,' he said, his voice scratchy. Without either suggesting it, they came to a stop looking down on the pasture, now patterned with a patchwork of cloud-shade. Sweeper was still loping ahead, his head bowed, sliding easily through the long grass, and the kid was following amiably.

'The men you encountered,' Mani said with obvious difficulty, 'are professional soldiers, part of a free company.'

'Excuse me? They're fucking mercenaries? What are they doing here?'

He took a heavy breath and went on. 'The exchange was a, hm, contractual payment.'

'For what?'

'For their services.'

Ree took a step away, fingers at her temples, the pain in her calf forgotten. 'Hold on, hold on – you said you're the only people up here, right? We're miles from anywhere, weeks from the plains . . . How, *how* is there a free company operating up here, and what services could you possibly need from them?'

He tried to reply, stumbling over his words. 'F-for our p-protection, you see? For p-peace.'

She could hear the kid's voice in her head – *Ma, why are you bellowing at an old man on a hill?* – and she took what she hoped would be a calming breath. But now she saw the shape of the board, and understood the placement of the pieces.

'Forgive me,' she said. 'Your business is your own.'

He nodded, but his smile was a delicate thing. 'They keep us safe,' he said, but it rang hollow, a response of rote.

Ree released some of her frustration in a heavy sigh. 'Ar Ramas is paying a mercenary company for protection. So what happens if you don't pay? You're left unprotected? Or,' she tilted her head, 'something else?'

'It won't come to that. Camellia will rearrange the exchange.' He rubbed a hand over his chin, momentarily pulling at his moustache, which sprang gloriously back. 'I do wish you hadn't shot one of them, though.'

'More than you wish they hadn't near-murdered your friend? What was he doing there on his own?'

Mani's tone was firm, corrective. 'He volunteered. I told you, he likes to help, and we let him. It makes him happy, which makes us happy.'

'I'm not sure getting his face repainted made him happy. But you can relax, it was a short bolt from a hand-bow, and it didn't hit anything important. If that merc can keep the wound clean, he'll be fine.'

'I do hope so.' Sadness entered his eyes. 'Nobody deserves such things.'

Ree pulled a face. 'I don't know, I think some people do, but I like to judge on a case-by-case basis.'

'Ma! Are you coming or what?'

Mani hefted his stick. 'I think this is as far as I go – I'll only have to go down the hill and back up, and it'll take me the rest of the day. I'll leave you in Sweeper's care, and I do look forward to seeing you later. It's poetry in the Council House tonight, but if you're still around tomorrow there's a puppet show if the little one is keen.' He inclined his head. 'You are very welcome here, Just Ree.'

'See you later, Mani. And, you know . . . sorry. For how I can be.'

He offered her one last bristly smile. 'We must love everyone as they are, not as we would have them.'

Ree puffed her hair from her eyes. 'Well, I guess I'll try.'

SIX

The forge was in fact two separate buildings, assembled from timber and stone, and an open-sided, covered area above a giant, half-submerged boulder. Something that could have been a half-finished ploughshare lay across it. A glowing fire lurked behind, enclosed by a shield of baked stone, sending dark smoke into the crisp morning air. The place looked deserted.

Sweeper stuck his head around the forge area, then walked to the first building, a snug-looking hut that shared a wall with the back of the forge, where the fire stood. He knocked at the doorway and shuffled back, one hand rubbing at his bruised ribs. 'Vida? Mariam?'

After a moment, a stout woman emerged from the dark of the doorway, wearing a thick and well-used leather smock, her wide arms bare. Her hair was short, running to grey on top but still dark behind her ears. 'Sweeper? What in the name of all the gods happened to you?' Ree recognised her accent immediately: Arowani, from the upper city. An accent she'd grown up around herself.

Sweeper ignored her question, his eyes somewhere in the churned earth by his feet. 'Visitors, Vida. Travellers, need help.'

Vida looked past his shoulder to take in Ree and the kid, lurking within the fire's warm glow. Her impassive expression didn't change. 'Is that so?' she said.

'Vida, who is it? Is it Sweeper?' called a woman's voice from inside the hut. This one was lighter, and with a similar dulcet Hindmarch accent to Anri's, the surly hunter. 'Ask him if Lali's finished with the Council yet.'

'Visitors, Mariam,' Vida called back over her shoulder, not taking her eyes off Ree and the kid. Ree was beginning to feel very inspected. The woman in the doorway was giving nothing away, her dark eyes steady, and she was making Ree uncharacteristically uncomfortable.

Another woman emerged from the doorway behind Vida, quite striking in her contrast. The newcomer was tall, willowy even, with an open, expressive face, and cascades of glossy dark hair, which she was in the process of retying.

'It's visitors, is it?' she said, anchoring the hair in place and resting an affectionate arm around Vida's shoulders. 'Well, there's a rare treat!' Ree couldn't tell if there was sarcasm in her words; she seemed plain-speaking enough.

'You're the smiths?' she said, attempting to gain some measure of conversational foothold.

'Vida by here is,' Mariam said, ruffling the shorter woman's hair. 'I'm more of a . . .'

'Dogsbody,' supplied Vida, with the slightest smile. Mariam squeaked with affected outrage. 'I'm Vida, she's Mariam.'

'Ree.' Ree jerked a thumb at her chest, then towards the kid, who waved. 'Javani.'

Sweeper bobbed his head and began to shuffle away. 'Be leaving you to it. Things to do, things to do.'

'Thanks, Sweeper,' Ree said, feeling vaguely uneasy at the retreat of his battered form. 'And do clean those scrapes, you don't want anything to fester.'

He nodded his head, too much, and continued his progress back towards the main settlement, silent steps through the grass. Mariam watched him go, her face furrowed with concern. 'Do you know what happened to him, then?' she asked, barely above a whisper. 'Is it something to do with the emergency Council meeting?'

Ree could hear Gumis's voice screeching in her ear. 'Not really our business, sorry.'

Vida was watching her closely from behind cool eyes. 'Fair enough,' she said. 'We're not ones for getting too close to Council business. Now what was it you needed? Apart from a bath.'

Ree let it slide – the woman had a point. 'One of our ponies has thrown a shoe. I'd really like to get her re-shod before we push on.'

Mariam's eyes lit up. 'Ponies? How many do you have? Where about are they now?'

The kid had crept forward, drawn in by Mariam's enthusiasm. 'Three – two girls, one boy. They're plains ponies, they've travelled all the way from Kazeraz with us.'

'I don't know where that is,' Vida grunted. 'Plains ponies, eh?'

Ree nodded. 'Plains ponies.'

Mariam's hand gripped Vida's wide arm. 'We could breed them, Vi, think what a difference they'd make!'

Vida was watching Ree from beneath thick silver brows. 'Would you consider trading them? We're short of draft animals up here and, as Mari says, they'd make a real difference.'

The kid took another step. 'You don't have *any?*'

Mariam gave a sad shake of her head. 'No horses, no oxen, just some increasingly crotchety mules, who were never much good at pulling anyway, even in their younger days. And fewer and fewer of them . . .'

'Couldn't you breed the mules?'

Ree didn't look at her. 'Mules are sterile, kid.'

'They always seemed pretty grubby to me.'

'Just . . . You can't breed them.'

'Oh.'

'And even if we had a donkey or two, they'd be bloody useless for threshing,' Mariam went on.

'They shit on the grain,' Vida clarified. She was still watching Ree. 'I'm guessing we're wasting our time, though. You're not much inclined to trade.'

'You'd be correct. We need those ponies, and we're only staying the night before we push on.'

Mariam's face fell. 'Oh, that's a double shame, that is. It's been so long since we had visitors, I was hoping to make a real fuss of you, and Sun's Night is right around the corner. We've got the masks ready and everything.'

'I made no joke about the bath,' Vida added. 'We can discuss the shoeing once you're refreshed. Mari, start heating some water, I'll get the tub.' With a nod, Mariam ducked back inside.

Ree's hands were already up. 'Really, we just need—'

The kid pulled her hands down. 'Ma. You said it yourself, you need a bath. I need a bath. We both need a bath. There'll be time to sort out the horseshoe later.'

Ree looked at the kid sidelong. 'When did you get so fucking sensible?'

'I'm sure I didn't pick it up from you,' she shot back with a grin.

Vida was staring at them, her gaze flicking from one to the other. 'You're mother and daughter, and you talk to each other like this?'

Ree shrugged. 'We're still new to it.'

The frown deepened. 'But she must be at least eleven.'

'I'm nearly thirteen!'

Ree shrugged again. The thought of a hot bath was beginning to supplant all others. 'What can I say? It's complicated.'

Javani, as junior visitor, had to wait her turn for the bath. Ree's contented sighs and splashes from behind the forge only made her all the more impatient. She left her mother to it, and wandered around the smithy, poking things, while Vida kept an eye on her from the corner. Mariam had gone to the other building, a long, wooden structure, from which came a hubbub of childish voices.

'You know,' Javani said.

'Yes?' Vida replied.

'For a blacksmith . . .'

'Yes?'

'You don't have a lot of metal in here.'

'Is that right?'

'All the other smithies I've seen were full of horseshoes, chains, hammers, tools, farming equipment, you know. Old bits of armour. Swords, probably. I suppose you don't have many of them here.'

'Indeed we don't.'

'But you don't have much of the other stuff, either.'

'We have enough to get by.'

Javani sniffed. 'If you say so.' She continued her wandering, towards the back of the forge where a giant mound of fur was piled beside the fire's stone enclosure. 'What's this for?'

'Careful—' came Vida's warning, but too slow. The fur pile raised its head, then pushed itself to its feet. Javani took a step back as a vast, muscular dog took shape before her, his thick coat the colour of sand but for a dark, stubby and grey-bristled muzzle and floppy ears, his shoulder almost at her chest. He shook himself, sending up a great cloud of dust.

'Hello, boy.' Javani reached out a tentative hand for him to sniff. He was by far the biggest dog she'd ever seen.

'Careful,' Vida repeated. She hadn't moved from her corner, which Javani took to mean the danger couldn't be that great. 'He doesn't take well to strangers, don't crowd him.'

The dog extended his giant, block-like head and sniffed her hand, then gave it a tentative lick with a great pink tongue. Javani wondered what might still be on her hand from their recent adventures. She risked giving him a scritch behind the ears with her other hand, and he leaned happily into it.

'Huh,' came Vida's voice from over her shoulder. 'Normally he's very standoffish with new people.'

Javani grinned. 'I guess I have some experience dealing with old dogs.' From the other side of the wall, she thought she heard the splashing stop. 'What's his name?'

'Tarfellian. Named after the defender of Arowan, in the great siege. A hero who kept the forces of darkness at bay, just like our old boy here.' She'd wandered over, and gave the dog's meaty flank a solid pat. He gave her a welcoming sniff, tongue lolling.

'What kind of dog is he?'

'Guardian. Minds the livestock. This old fellow came out with me and Mari, like you and your ponies. Watched over the animals, saw off predators of any sort. Made our life here possible.' Javani detected the faintest crack in her voice. 'Father of the pack, his grand-pups are still roaming the hills, watching our flocks, and now he can rest by the fire. He earned it.' She gazed at the dog with undisguised affection.

Javani gave the big dog another scritch, and he leaned himself against her with a contented huff, almost pushing her over. 'Well, he's a very good boy,' she said.

'He is,' came Vida's tight reply. 'You can give him a brush, if you like.'

'Kid!' Ree's voice came through the wall like a saw. 'Find out if there's tea.'

Vida met her questioning look. 'I'm afraid not.'

Ree appeared a moment later, emerging dressed with a finespun woollen towel around her shoulders, mopping a drip from her ear. 'You're up, kid. I hope I didn't leave it too filthy.' She turned to Vida. 'Is that a samovar I saw back there? Made from, what, an old armour casing? Did you make it? It's extraordinary.'

'No tea, Ma.'

Vida sighed. 'It's hard to get here. It should grow in this climate, but we've had no luck yet. We have to make trips for it, and no one has made a trip for . . . a while now.'

Ree looked unperturbed. 'But that's a working samovar otherwise, yes?'

'It is.'

'Then I have good news – the kid and I still have some tea in our saddlebags. Kid, run and get the tea, will you?'

Javani blinked. 'What? Run to the stables? Now? What about my bath?'

'If you're quick, maybe it'll still be warm when you get back.'

Vida put up a squarish hand. 'Don't burden yourself, young lady. I need to inspect your pony for the shoe, I'll make the trip – if you'll tell me where to look?'

'Ah, I'll come with you. I should check on the horses anyway,' Ree sighed. 'Kid, get in the bath, I can smell you from here.'

'I'm going!'

'How can we pay you for the shoe?' Ree asked as Vida pulled a thin cloak around her shoulders. 'What's your currency up here?'

'No currency,' the stocky woman replied. 'We're a co-operative.'

'So you barter with each other? Every day? That must be exhausting.'

'No landlords, no tenants, equal shares in all things. Makes things easier, not harder.'

Ree followed her to the edge of the forge. 'But how do you deal with freeloaders?'

'People find ways to be useful,' Vida said, setting out up the slope as Ree followed. 'Some more effectively than others.'

* * *

Mariam was waiting when Javani finished her bath, which had been both still warm and not too filthy after all, although a long way from clean. At least the worst of the grime was gone from her hands and knees, although it would probably make her far less interesting to Tarfellian the dog.

'Ah, Javani, is that better?' Mariam was beaming. 'This is Lali, one of our other young people.' The girl from the Council House was there, the one who had arrived late and taken notes. She gave Javani a flicker of a smile, and something that might have turned into a wave if it had kept going. 'She's going to show you around a little while I prepare some food. All right? Lovely, see you in a little bit now.'

A moment later, Javani and Lali were standing outside the forge, looking out over the hillside. 'Uh, hi. I'm Javani.'

'Lali.'

'Have you lived here long?'

'Yeah, nearly all my life, I think.'

Javani's mouth pulled to one side. 'You think?'

The girl shrugged. 'I'm an orphan. Lots of us are – lots of us young folk, I mean. Mariam is sort of our brood mother.' She gestured down the slope, where what had to be at least a dozen children of various ages and sizes (but all most likely younger than Javani) tumbled and shrieked. 'Nobody's really sure about my early days.'

'I get it, I was an orphan, too,' Javani blurted.

Lali looked at her sidelong. 'Isn't that woman your mother?'

Javani swallowed, feeling the heat in her cheeks. 'It's, uh, complicated.' Desperate to change the subject, she nodded at the girl's ink-stained fingers. 'Your writing's good? I mean, good enough that the Council . . . use you?' All the wrong words were coming out.

Lali's mouth creased as if she were tasting something unexpected and not wholly pleasant. 'Yes. Mariam teaches us. Can you write?'

Javani pulled at the neck of her still-grubby shirt. Ree had taught her letters, of course, but had made it clear that, as with so many other things, practising was on her, and she'd had, well . . . other priorities. 'I don't, uh, get to do it much.'

They stood in uncomfortable silence for a moment, Javani's cheeks still burning. 'You're going on to Arestan, then?' Lali said, to Javani's relief.

'Yeah. That's the plan.'

'Why?'

The question blindsided her. Why *wouldn't* you want to get to Arestan? Land of plenty, of possibilities, no mining, no Miners' Guild, no scrabbling in the dirt for a living with no hope on the horizon . . . A place where you can make a *home*. A life, not an existence. No more running, no more panic and desperate battles, no more arguing over every damned-by-gods triviality. Somewhere you could be happy. But somehow phrasing that to Lali, on the gentle slope of the pasture, wildflowers and tall grass swaying around them, the younger kids playing below them, seemed harder than it should have. 'We've, uh, got family there,' she muttered eventually, almost wishing it could be true.

'Huh. Exciting.'

'Yeah.' The silence was creeping back, and Javani moved to banish it. 'I hear no one from here has come back from crossing the high places. Do you, uh, do you think they made it?'

At once, Lali's face became animated. 'You know, it's not true, what they say.'

'Which bit? Who say?'

'That nobody ever came back across. Someone did.'

Sudden excitement flared, and Javani leaned in, at last finding some measure of common interest. 'Who? When?' And after a moment, 'Why?'

Lali's voice was a conspiratorial whisper. 'Someone you wouldn't expect.'

'Who?'

Her eyes were wide. 'Sweeper.' She stood back, waiting to see the impact of her words.

Javani mulled. 'Sweeper? The, you know, helping guy?' She mimed his shuffling walk.

Lali nodded firmly, brows cranked high. 'There's more to him than people think.'

'Well, I'd certainly hope so,' Javani muttered. 'When did he come back? Why?'

'See, that's it – he didn't come *back*. He came *from* there, when he arrived here. First person ever to arrive from the west.'

'And he's talked about it?'

Lali's arms were crossed. 'It's what everyone says.'

'Uh, right. Sure.'

Silence descended once more, and this time Javani didn't fight it. She'd clearly offended Lali by not being more impressed. Lali looked around, then back down at the raucous children on the slope below.

'Do you want to come and meet everyone, then?'

Javani grimaced. 'Lali, can I be honest? Tomorrow, Ree and I are going to be back on the road, and we're probably not going to come back, well, ever. I don't mean any offence to you or your friends, it's just I don't really, I'm not good at . . .' She swallowed. 'I don't make a lot of friends. Would it be all right if I just, you know, stayed by myself?'

The older girl stared at her for a moment, her expression hard to read, then said, 'Suits me.'

Without another word, she walked off down the slope, towards the boisterous, joyful children, leaving Javani in the shadow of the forge.

SEVEN

Javani sat on the hillside beneath the cloud-streaked sky, wrapped in her thoughts, completely oblivious to the man's approach. She'd made a mess of things with Lali, she knew, but in a way her cold departure had been an enormous relief. Javani had meant what she said: a life of constant travel had left her struggling to make meaningful connections with people, and on the rare occasions she'd managed it, well, they'd ended very badly indeed.

It wasn't as if she'd had much time to herself over the preceding weeks. She and Ree had been travelling almost in each other's pockets, barely a moment of peace or solitude in their trudging progress over the seemingly endless mountains, for safety as much as camaraderie. It wasn't like they talked that much of the time – Javani got tired during the long days, Ree got breathless on the steep climbs, and as the weather had turned, her leg seemed to pain her more. She supposed you could describe the remainder of their time as 'companionable silence', except it hadn't been all that friendly. After what had happened in Kazeraz, Ree now seemed possessed of the need to train Javani in all the skills she'd neglected for the first dozen years of her existence, not least archery, and the truth was that Ree was not a very good teacher – or at least not to her daughter. It had always been that way – Edigu, the foreman on their lost farm, had been the one to teach her to ride properly after years of Ree's errant instruction.

Javani wrapped her hands around her shins and rested her chin on her knees, earning a fresh reminder of the hole in her trousers. What had happened in Kazeraz? Ree's past had come knocking, and it had been looking for Javani, the daughter she'd never admitted she'd had. People had come to the town, hunters. They'd killed her best friend in front of her, then tried to kill her, too. She and Ree had been forced to flee, had left everyone and everything behind, everything they'd owned, everything they'd been building, and even then had lost another friend in the escape. Ree had been injured, and her refusal to recuperate had only made both her injury and moods worse. And through no fault of her own, Javani now had powerful enemies – the throne of Shenak, the all-consuming Serican Miners' Guild – who might yet hunt them still, might catch them should they slow their pace.

And what had she learned of Ree's past, after all that? Ree still refused to talk about it in more than generalities, but Javani's own memories of their early years together had taken a different tenor: Ree's quick temper when baulked, the unexpectedly violent accidents that had befallen many of their would-be obstructors. Suddenly it didn't seem so coincidental after all.

And now her mother was her mother. They'd never been especially close when they were niece and aunt, and the revelation of Javani's true parentage hadn't magically transformed their relationship into an intimate bond, but they were trying. Mostly. Javani wasn't convinced that Ree's promise of 'partners' was anywhere close to bearing fruit, and her mother still didn't seem to listen to her anywhere near as much as she should; instead, Ree was trying, in her own ham-fisted way, to catch up on more than a decade's worth of mothering by inexpertly instructing her daughter in skills both martial and survivalist. Or at least the outcome was inexpert; sum total so far: zero animals hunted, one bandit shot in the leg. The memory of the man she'd hit, Fingers, pained her. She hoped Ree was right and he would be fine. It would be nice, she thought, if she could make a life in which she never needed to shoot a bow again. Maybe the people of Ar Ramas were onto something after all . . .

'Not playing nicely with the other children, then, is it?'

She started. The sullen hunter, Anri, was standing right beside her, a hint of a smirk on his gummy, bearded face. He'd approached in silence, from upslope and downwind, never letting even his shadow enter her peripheral view. The bastard. Ree would have applauded.

With great care and deliberation, Javani leaned back against the wildgrass and the spreading silver-edged rosettes of a cluster of pinnate leaves, affecting total relaxation as her hammering heart-rate slowed. 'I hear I could say the same thing to you,' she retorted. 'Not wanted inside the village? Something you did, or is it,' she wafted a hand as if steering a bee from her face, 'the smell?'

He flashed something between a grimace and a smile, the black and silver bristles of his beard flexing over the dark of his mouth. 'Got my reasons. They've got their way of doing things, I've got mine.' He jerked a thumb at his chest. 'Need me more than I need them, isn't it.'

With that, he straightened the bow on his shoulder and set off towards the trees at the pasture's edge, his quiver bouncing with his steps, somehow weaving his way through the grass, leaving barely a trace of his passing. The bastard.

'See you later, Anri,' Javani called, lying back against the hillside. 'Or not, I guess.'

Ree's leg was really grumbling now, but the stables were in sight at the foot of the slope. She tried to keep the breathless edge from her words.

'Why do you and Mariam live so far from the others? Differences of opinion?'

Vida was keeping an easy pace, walking with swinging strides. 'No. The anvil stone is in the pasture. So that's where the forge is. So that's where I am. So that's where Mariam is.'

'But it's just you working in the forge?'

'No. I have apprentices.' She forestalled Ree's next question. 'Today is a rest day, at least according to Camellia. They're probably learning scripture somewhere. While spinning wool.'

Ree gritted her teeth from the effort of keeping up. Nearly there. She could feel a vein at her temple throbbing, just above the old scar. 'You're not entirely in tune with Camellia?'

Vida gave her a short, sidelong look. 'No.'

'No? You're not in tune?'

'No, you will get nothing further from me on that matter.'

Ree smiled, despite her aches. It had been worth a go. 'You say "no" a lot, you know that?'

'No.' Vida pulled up short, eyes searching ahead. 'Huh.'

Ree came to a stop beside her, grateful for the rest. Sweat was dripping down her back, and the day was not warm. She'd need to go straight back in the bath at this rate. 'What is it?' She tried to follow Vida's gaze, towards the stable building, no, beyond it, towards the far edge of the village, by the waterfall and the rope bridge where first they'd entered.

There: a cluster of figures stood on the bridge's far side. Hazy at this distance, but it looked like dark cloaks, and maybe even just a flickering glint of mail. 'Any chance those people at the bridge are another set of lost travellers?'

Vida's expression hadn't changed.

'No.'

Vida was moving as fast as Ree had seen her, making for the bridge at a swift lumber. 'You don't need to come,' she grunted.

'Not my business?'

'No.'

'I'm inclined to disagree on that score. If those folks are who I think they are, then their presence here may be a direct extension of my business.'

'Hm.'

Camellia intercepted them as they reached the lower terrace, coming from the direction of the Council House with Mani hobbling at speed some distance behind her. When she saw Ree, her eyes went wide, the cords of her neck standing out for a moment. A welcoming smile bloomed immediately, but it was an obvious veneer to the anxiety that rode beneath.

'Mistress Ree,' she said brightly, trying to move past them, 'you have no need to concern yourself with this – please, take some time to rest your leg.'

'Leg's fine, thanks, Camellia,' Ree lied. 'Thought I could repay your hospitality and make myself useful.'

She saw Camellia's throat bob as she swallowed, and the woman took a long breath through her nose, then the bonhomie fell away, revealing the nerves beneath. 'It might be better if they didn't see you, don't you think? After what you did?'

Ree pushed on past her, forcing Vida and Camellia to start walking again in her wake. 'And after what they did, I think there should be someone present to hold them to account, don't you? Keep this so-called mercenary company honest?' Camellia tried to speak again but Ree rode right over her. 'How many of you live in this place? Two hundred? More?'

'More,' Vida replied as Camellia spluttered.

'Two hundred and eighty-seven,' Camellia declared. 'Excluding Anri's household, at his insistence.'

'And how many able-bodied adults? What we used to call "fighting-age", once upon a time.'

Camellia visibly paled. 'You can't possibly—'

'Camellia, I saw the state of these so-called mercenaries this morning, when they were making off with your hard-earned produce and beating one of your people to insensibility in the process. They are threadbare and ill-equipped, probably deserters, and whatever lines they've fed you of their no-doubt magnificent heritage of professional soldiery, these men are simple bandits. Just stand up to them, present a demonstration of your numbers and your community's strength, and make it clear that there will be no more "exchanges" like that I witnessed today.' She put up a hand. 'It'll be obvious to them that they're hopelessly outnumbered, and not even these boys will be stupid enough to try to attack you. Drive them off now and be done with this farce.'

Camellia was shaking, but it took Ree a moment to realise it wasn't from fear. 'Thank you for your counsel,' she said in a hard, brittle voice. 'I regret, however, that you know nothing of us and our arrangements.'

Mani had finally caught them up, still smiling, but clearly drained by his forced march. 'Just Ree,' he cried happily, 'you'll be attending our little gathering with our mercenary friends?'

She extended her arm to him. 'Of course – that is, if nobody minds?'

Camellia was breathing hard through her nose. 'You are free to do as you wish, Mistress Ree. I would, though, implore you to keep your counsel until it is requested.'

Ree gave her a tight half-smile. 'I'll see how the mood takes me.'

EIGHT

Gumis was already at the bridge, puffed up with self-importance, one hand firmly gripping his baton of office. One of the cloaked figures, seeing Ree and the others arriving, took a step towards the bridge.

Gumis bawled at him. 'Not another step, sell-sword!' The baton was waved in a menacing fashion.

The man put up a hand and stepped away. 'No transgression was intended,' he drawled. 'But I'll mind you to attend how you wave that implement, lest there be a misunderstanding.'

Camellia came to a stop before the bridge's end, her robes loose and swinging, with Vida to one side. Ree noticed that although Vida was carrying nothing in the way of weapons, or even potential weapons, she still somehow gave the impression that she was fiercely armed, just from how she stood. Ree and Mani moved to one side, relaxing their mutual grip as they took a seat on one of the long timbers laid out beside the bridge. Ree found herself wondering how timber was handled with no axes, saws, or even planes. The more she thought about Ar Ramas's laws, the more impossible quirks she found.

'Let the man across, Gumis,' Camellia said, her voice weighed with foreboding.

'Just you! Leave your weapons,' screeched Gumis at the man at the other end of the bridge, who gave an acknowledging nod and began to make his way across. Beyond him, Ree saw three other figures, two in dark cloaks, one bare-armed. One of the two cloaks could have been one of the men from the roadside, he was suitably tatty, but the other one was too clean, too well-turned-out, as was the man making his way across the bridge. The bare-armed man deserved a second look, too, as the arms in question were roughly the width of one of Ree's thighs. The man's head was shaved but for two great stripes of hair along his skull, knotted and braided in rings and dyed flame red. Further rings decorated his exposed ears, with one more at his nose. He looked cold, but was the closest thing to a potential genuine mercenary Ree had seen so far.

The lead man had crossed the bridge, and placed his boots on solid ground with evident relief. He looked tall, or at least, he was lean enough to give the impression of height, with a slight slant to his swagger, as if he were walking into a strong wind, his thumbs hooked into his empty sword belt. Watchful eyes, little more than dark creases against the glare, peered from a square-jawed face dusted with silvering stubble, matched by the gleaming streaks at his temples. Ree had to admit he wasn't all that bad to look at.

'Who's this?' she whispered to Mani. 'Bandit leader?'

Mani's face crinkled with a mirth she didn't feel. 'An emissary from our free company friends.'

The man looked around the assembled villagers, taking in Camellia and Vida before him, Gumis glowering on one side, and Ree and Mani on the timber pile to the other. He swept a curt bow, his manner jerky but confident, then addressed himself to Camellia.

'My lady Camellia.' There was the drawl again. The man's accent was from far away across hills and plains, and presumably he was, too.

Camellia nodded in response. 'Chapter Captain Manatas.'

'There has been, I understand, an altercation.' He paused, but Camellia did not reply, and nor did anyone else. Once again his dark and serious gaze swept those present, and lingered for the briefest moment on Ree before passing on. She saw a tiny twitch to his features, a narrowing of the eyes, a tension around his mouth – curiosity, or intrigue? Perhaps a newcomer was unexpected, or perhaps his fellow bandits had passed on a description of their assailants, and he was trying to work out if she was the vanquisher of his gang. Either way, she did not care.

He cleared his throat, and this time addressed them all. 'Now, you know me here. I'm a fair man, only interested in doing what's fair. We have a contract,' he reached into his leathers and drew out a goatskin pouch, bound with thongs, which he set about untying, 'freely entered into and agreed on all sides, and we are fortunate that the drafters of this document,' from the pouch he pulled a folded parchment, which he hefted in one hand, 'had the foresight to cover us for any eventuality.'

Camellia took a half-step forward. 'We will, of course, make the exchange—'

'What we have here, Lady Camellia, is a breach.'

She fell quiet. 'Yes, of course,' she mumbled.

'You know me.' He patted the folded document against his mail-clad chest. 'You know I'd let this go, if it were up to me. But I have to answer to my commander, the captain-general of my company. And he,' Manatas broke off with something that was halfway between a grin and a wince, 'he is a man who is *inflexible* in his ways. He believes that a word given is a bond of iron, and a contract must be upheld, or else all is anarchy.' This time he did smile, a quick flash of decent teeth. 'Sounds pretty funny when he says it, too, what with the accent. Anyway, you know the terms. The boys and I are here to collect our delinquent payment, plus the penalty stipulated herein.' He patted the contract again. 'We'll wait while you prepare it.'

Camellia was staring at the ground. Vida remained silent, stoic, immovable as granite. Beside Ree, Mani sighed, then pushed himself to his feet. 'Well, fair's fair,' he said. 'Camellia, let's go to the stores. Vida, will you assist?'

Ree jumped up, ignoring the jolt from her calf. 'What in nine bastard hells are you doing?' she hissed.

Camellia strode over, her face held rigid. She kept her voice low. 'We are atoning.'

Ree matched her volume, although the supposed mercenary was taking pains to stay out of earshot by the bridge. 'For what? You haven't done anything wrong. How dare he demand ever more from you, and how dare you consider paying it! These men might call themselves mercenaries, but they are common thieves.'

Camellia's eyes were wide but she kept her voice controlled. 'Everything Captain Manatas said is true. We signed a contract with them. We agreed to their terms. We have breached those terms, and we are liable for a penalty. It is understood.' She took another long breath through her nose, her hands pressed together. 'Our equilibrium has been disturbed, and we place no blame.'

'No blame,' Mani added, helpfully.

Ree could feel the muscles of her jaw throbbing. She swivelled on her good foot and marched on the man by the bridge. 'Let me see that,' she snapped, snatching the document from his hand.

'By all means, do check it over,' he called to her retreating back as she limped away. 'We have copies.' He turned away, his attention back to his boots. 'Gods know we keep the clerks busy enough,' he muttered.

Ree was scanning the document, parsing the formal text with a part of her brain that had long been dormant and was quite happy to stay that way. As she turned over each page, her incredulity grew.

'This isn't an agreement, it's a one-sided nightmare,' she hissed. 'It's formalised extortion however you slice it. These clauses aren't penalties, they're punishments!' She shook her head, wiping at the waterfall spray that misted her forehead with the parchment. 'How long has this been in place?'

Camellia was stone-faced. 'Two years,' Mani said, the cheer lost from his voice. 'A little more, maybe.'

'Two. Years.' Ree rubbed at her eye, the contract still in her hand. 'You've been paying these terms for two years, and you haven't starved?'

'We are blessed here,' Camellia intoned, 'and we are grateful.'

Ree leaned in closer, until her head was barely a hand's span from Camellia's. 'And how many times in that period have they come to your aid, in these near-deserted mountains, relative to the number of times they've beaten and injured your people, the very people that this worthless document claims *they're here to protect*?' She realised she'd lost control of her voice, almost shouting point-blank at the councillor. The woman only tilted her head back, her expression unchanged.

'It is no shame to bear the scars of survival and endurance.'

Camellia raised a hand when Ree moved to speak again, and she knew further efforts would be wasted. Camellia was not going to be convinced.

'We shall atone,' she went on, 'and settle our obligations. They will settle in their winter quarters, we shall be safe with our stores. We have enough.' She closed her eyes for a moment, as if repeating a mantra. 'Even with the penalty, we have enough.'

'Fine.' Ree spread her hands, letting out a breath of her own. 'Like the man said,' she nodded at Gumis, who was watching her with undisguised animosity, 'it's not my business. Tomorrow the kid and I will be on our way, and you can keep whatever ludicrous arrangements you and your people can agree on.' For a moment she caught Vida's eye, and was convinced she saw disquiet there, but the smith's gaze shifted immediately, looking past and through her, and whatever connection she thought she'd found was lost.

Camellia, Mani and Vida turned and walked away from her, heading, she presumed, in the direction of the stores or stables, ready to drag the mules out again. She wondered if they'd get them back this time.

Ree turned away, and found Manatas staring right at her, his brow furrowed, his lips slightly parted, a man trying to work out a conundrum – or possibly trying to remember where he'd left his other glove. 'You're the aggressor,' he said.

'I'd have called it a spirited discussion, that's all.'

His head took the slightest tilt. 'From what those boys described, I was expecting, well . . .'

'Someone taller?'

'Something like that.' He rubbed a hand across his brow. 'They made it sound like an army came at them.'

'Maybe it did. They just didn't see all of it.'

His nod was slight, his eyes flicking past her over the village and the wooded hills beyond. 'Maybe. At least two, for starters.'

'Perhaps they should have thought twice about kicking the shit out of an innocent farmer, then.' Ree looked away, then locked gaze with him. 'How much do you want, bandit?'

'Excuse me?'

'You heard me. I know how this racket works. How much will

it take to get you and your other little bottom-feeders to pack up and leave, and not come back?'

He took half a step back, jaw dropped open, one hand clutched instinctively to his side. Had she genuinely offended him?

'My lady—'

'Ree.'

'Ree.' He placed a hand on his chest and offered the same short bow from earlier. 'Inaï Manatas, Captain, Ninth Chapter of the Company of the Wolf.'

'Inay?'

'Ina-i. My mother was Tabashti.' He cleared his throat again. 'My lady Ree, everything I said before was the gods' truth. My captain-general has a firmly held belief that things should be done a certain way. You, or a member of your secret army, have injured one of his men in the performance of his contractually agreed duties, and that, I am afraid, has consequences.'

Ree shook the parchment. 'I've looked over this so-called contract. In its simplest form, it's an abomination. You can't possibly believe it's just and equitable.'

He looked away. 'That is not at issue—'

'Horseshit! This entire fraud rests on the pretence that this is somehow a fair arrangement, that everyone benefits.' She shook her head, teeth bared. She should walk away, she knew she should. It was Not Her Business. It was Never Her Business. And yet. And yet. The parchment curled in her grip. 'I think it's time for a little renegotiation, don't you?'

'Now, what do you mean by that?'

'I'd like an itemised list of the services your so-called company has rendered over the contract term, by return.'

Colour darkened his cheeks. 'Would you kindly stop referring to everything about my professional existence as "so-called"?'

Ree met his fervid gaze. 'Naming a thing doesn't change what it is. Here.' She tossed the bundled parchment to him, and he snatched it before it could spread and flutter on the breeze. 'Whichever down-and-out notary you got to draft this absurdity for you, they stitched you up. There's a standard provision in the codicil, presumably copied from a *real* contract, for renegotiation after the initial term.

A term which I believe has passed. So take that back to your captain-general, Chapter Captain Manatas, and see what he has to say. You'll get no payment today, or until new terms are agreed.'

The man swallowed, still trying to stuff the loose pages back into their pouch. 'My lady, I think you misunderstand the situation here—'

'Just Ree. You've stated you're a fair man, and that your captain-general is a stickler for contractual accuracy. What am I misunderstanding, exactly?'

Camellia hove back into view from the direction of the stables, moving briskly, her face flushed. Her expression seemed primarily one of relief, which lasted exactly until she saw Ree and Manatas standing in obvious dispute. She increased her pace.

'We will have the mules loaded shortly, captain—' she began, breathless as she came to a halt beside them. Ree cut her off with a hand.

'Save your people's efforts, Camellia. There will be no payment today.'

Camellia stared at her, incredulous, then deeply suspicious. Her gaze snapped to Manatas. 'Captain?'

He managed at last to force the bundled pages into the pouch, and the pouch back inside his mail. 'The lady Ree has, for want of a better term, drawn my attention to certain clauses in our contract of service. She believes a renegotiation is due.' He looked distinctly uncomfortable, one hand straying to the mail collar at his neck, but, Ree noted, he was not explicitly disagreeing.

'She does not speak for us,' Camellia averred. 'Gumis, what have you been doing?'

'I had to watch the bridge in case more came across!' came his blustering reply.

Camellia turned her ire on Ree. 'What have you done? Please, in the name of peace, do not make things worse for us!'

'You're being exploited, Camellia, you're being ridden like a feast-day donkey by these criminals, but you can hang them on their own shabby paperwork. You're entitled to renegotiate, and I suggest you do so from a position of strength.'

The councillor only stared at her, not exactly dumbstruck but rendered speechless by what had to be a combination of shock, outrage and growing fear.

Manatas cleared his throat. 'I'm thinking perhaps our time here is at an end.'

Ree barely glanced at him. 'I'd say so, bandit. Go back to your so-called captain-general and tell him the fat days are over. If the people of Ar Ramas deign to sign another agreement with you, it will be a free choice, and the terms will be very different.'

The corners of his mouth flexed down as he sucked in his cheeks. 'I fear they will,' he murmured. 'I'll be bidding you good day for now.'

'Don't fall off the bridge and die on your way out.'

He shook his head as if dazed as he stepped back onto the bridge. 'I will endeavour so not to do.' He shot one look back over his shoulder. 'We *will* speak again.'

Ree watched with arms folded. 'I'll see if I'm busy.'

He made his steady way across without another look, then summoned his men with inaudible words. By the time Ree's heart had slowed, they were already descending the winding trail into the opposite woods, and were soon out of sight.

She turned to find Camellia's eyes boring into her.

'What,' hissed the woman, 'have you *done*?'

Still wiping crumbs from her clothes, Javani arrived at the Council House with Mariam in time to hear the end of the argument. Vida had sent word that something was happening, and it involved Javani's mother, but the crowd gathered by the building's open doorway would have been a pretty stark giveaway for anyone who was otherwise oblivious. It was the largest number of the settlement's population she'd seen in once place thus far, and she was grateful for some kind of crowd to blend into.

'Why did you insult him so? Why did you inflame things?' Camellia's raised voice carried easily over the square. 'We must restore equilibrium!'

'You are being extorted. All of you!' came Ree's hot reply. 'You're being screwed, for the sake of the gods. How can you be at peace with that, with this *abuse*?'

'We keep our people safe.' That was Keretan, the big man who sat beneath the mangled armour. 'We do what we must to keep things that way.'

'It won't stay that way. You must know that, you're not fools.

You're not fools, are you?' Javani could picture Ree pacing inside, staring down each in turn. 'If you don't stand up to them now, they will take, and take, until you have nothing left.'

'Stand up to them?' Keretan's voice growled with warning. 'You mean take up arms?'

'There will be no violence!' Camellia sounded terrified.

'It needn't come to that, if you—'

'Indeed it need not,' came Keretan's definitive reply. 'We would be grateful, Mistress Ree, if you would retire to your lodgings, and leave at daybreak tomorrow. What you do with your life then will be your own concern, and none other's; the same will also be true of us.'

Javani barely caught Volkan's parting words, as Ree came marching out of the Council House with a face like thunder. 'I can only pity your daughter.'

Ree went straight past her, limping in the direction of the smithy, the muscles of her jaw standing proud. Javani wasn't even sure if she'd seen her.

She turned to follow, and found herself face to face with Lali, the older girl whose company she'd spurned before lunch. Javani found herself immediately awkward and immobile, struggling to summon the words to repair any offence she might have caused, to reassure the girl that she wasn't unfriendly, just itinerant, and it truly was nothing personal.

'This is all your fault,' Lali said, dark eyes burning with scorn.

'Wh— How—?'

'You should never have attacked them. You attacked them unprovoked, and now you're just making everything worse.'

Javani felt blood rush to her cheeks, heard her pulse in her ears, but it wasn't shame, it was fury. 'Unprovoked?' she squeaked. 'They were beating the living shit out of Sweeper, and in the process of stealing your mules. All we did was tell them to stop.'

Lali didn't back down. 'Your ma shot one of them. That's worse than anything they did.'

Actually, that was me, Javani went to say, already picturing the look of shock in the girl's eyes, but then the wave of guilt caught her – actually, I'm not proud of that at all, and I wish I hadn't done it.

Lali must have read her flicker of doubt as defeat, and went to press her advantage. Javani was acutely conscious of the people around them, people she didn't know, normal, honest people who, whether they wanted it or not, were being hammered with the inescapable conclusion that she and her mother were armed insurrectionists. 'If you'd never got involved, this would all have blown over by now, and we'd have no cause to be afraid.'

She knew she should turn and walk away, but it would have looked so much like acknowledging it, like admitting Lali was right. 'So you're saying,' she growled, 'that your neighbours should be happy to submit to beatings from armed goons on a regular basis, in the interests of making your life easier, but there's no cause for anyone to be afraid?'

Lali's expression had stretched itself to an outright sneer. 'I wouldn't expect a bloodthirsty plains-dweller to understand.' A flash of doubt showed in her eyes. 'Maybe it's not your fault. Being raised among murderous, lawless degenerates, their only language violence, where the gift of life itself is cheaper than—'

Javani had heard enough. 'I'm going now.' She excused herself as she slid gently between the members of the as-yet-undissipated crowd, most of whom were polite enough to affect surprise at her existence, and set off after her mother.

NINE

Inaï Manatas, Captain, Ninth Chapter of the Company of the Wolf, would not sit down. He paced the flattened earth of the camp, mashing the thickening mulch of gold and flame-coloured leaves into the hillside with every circuit. His lieutenant watched him with concern in his eyes.

'Captain, will you come and sit down? You're making everyone nervous.'

Manatas shook his head firmly, continuing his fearsome circular march, hands clenched at his back.

'You're troubled, captain?'

'I am *vexed*, Arkadas.' Manatas continued to march, one finger now raised. 'And most sorely. What you see before you is not apprehension but the manifestation of bridled rage.' He came to a momentary halt. 'And a degree of apprehension as well, perhaps.'

'About this nonsense with the contract? You don't think we can straighten them out?'

Manatas resumed his pacing as his lieutenant gave a weary shake of his head. 'About what this nonsense with the contract *means*, Arkadas. It *means* they will drag their heels on the winter payment. It *means* it will require time and energy and perhaps even the threat of no small number of reprisals to see us made whole. It *means* there is now a large and swelling probability that we will not be shipshape when Ridderhof arrives.'

Arkadas sucked in his cheeks. 'You think he'll be unsympathetic? I figured an increase in our numbers might go some way to getting things back where they ought to be.'

Manatas halted again, turning to face the seated man. 'The issue at heart is not about whether the situation can be remedied, which of course is only a matter of time and the correct levers of persuasion. The source of my vexation is that when our illustrious captain-general arrives with his entourage and the rest of the travelling circus in tow, I will not be able to present the exemplary output of a well-run company chapter, up to date with its accounts and spinning like a well-made top. I will not be able to turn over the reins of this outfit, get the stamp on my tour and bid this no-doubt pretty but strikingly isolated part of the world goodbye as winter puts its jaws on the mountains and begins to squeeze.' He took a hard and angry breath through his nose. 'I will, instead, be presenting *this*.'

He swept his hand around the camp, taking in the sagging tents and the abandoned attempt at building a permanent food store, the half-built picket wall, the steaming, untended fires. His jaded gaze wandered across the loose piles of rusting equipment, the wooded corner where Ioseb of Cstethia, known as Fingers, lay in convalescence, the other members of his crew almost certainly harassing Tauras.

'All I wanted was to leave this place in a better state than we found on our arrival. Now I will never get out of here,' he sighed, then threw up his hands. 'And it was all so damned-by-gods unnecessary!'

'The white-haired woman?'

'The same, Arkadas, the very same.'

'She was one of those who ambushed the take?'

Manatas wheeled on the lieutenant, who shuffled back on the damp sack he sat on. 'Now just how certain are we of this ambush story? The way she told it, those Vistirlari galoots were the ones engaged in primary violence.' He shot another look towards where Ioseb's comrades, Zurab and Rostom, were definitely, definitely harassing Tauras. The big man was walking from one to the other, clearly looking for something, with each sending him to the man he'd just left. Manatas found himself clenching his teeth, his mouth tight. 'I cannot abide these Vistirlari,' he said quietly. 'Ill-trained, undisciplined, never served in a proper army . . . Just miscreants who spent a few months marching with a church rabble long ago, and never lost the habit of piracy. And Ioseb has made no secret of his feelings towards my command.'

'His thwarted ambitions are no concern of yours, captain,' Arkadas chided. 'He had no realistic claim to the captaincy, even before our . . . uh, posting.'

'I fear the person with the greatest need to hear that is Ioseb. Perhaps then the camp would not *fester* so.'

In truth, Manatas had struggled to blame Fingers/Ioseb for his hostility towards his captain; however unlikely it was that he would have been granted the chapter's command had it not been for Manatas and his staff's sudden arrival, the man and his cadre believed it nonetheless. It was the resulting indulgence of Ioseb's resentment that had precipitated the parlous state of the camp, Manatas's considerate leeway gleefully distorted to the point of outright sabotage. But now their time was up, and his indulgence was spent.

'You believe this woman?' Arkadas leaned forward, his head tilted, deep lines across his forehead. 'You're not inclined towards her, captain? She had a striking countenance I'll admit, even from range.'

'Arkadas, that you should even give voice to such a question only lessens my esteem for you, which pains me somehow deeper than my current troubles – all the more so for the unexpected nature of the assault.'

'You're right, captain, I apologise and withdraw.' Arkadas bowed his head. 'But you're still more inclined to take the word of an aggressive stranger over that of our own brothers-in-arms?'

Manatas looked once more towards the Vistirlari. They had sent Tauras in a wide circuit of the camp, clearly still searching for something, while they smirked at each other with private glee.

'It's possible that I am.' He looked beyond to where Ioseb convalesced. 'How is our invalid? Finding our accommodations to his liking?'

'He surely complains enough for three men,' Arkadas replied, twisting on his sack to follow Manatas's gaze. Rotten grain leaked from a small split at its base, pulsing with his movements as if slowly bleeding out. 'Only time he's quiet is when he's sleeping.'

'How long until he's back on his feet, creating fresh disasters?'

'Hard to say. The bolt came out without trouble, and the wound is far from grave, but his hygiene falls somewhat short of the company standard. Bau has done what she can, but I will be praying for him, despite my opinions of the soldier in question.'

Manatas let out a long breath. Their medic was high-strung enough at the best of times, forever threatening to resign her commission and return east to purportedly lucrative civilian work, and prolonged proximity to Ioseb might prove a final straw. He hoped his lieutenant's prayers would speed things along, and another pleading conversation as she packed could be avoided. 'You're a good man, Arkadas. The company is lucky to have you.'

'And I the company, captain.' Arkadas rummaged in one of the satchels slung from the strapping that crossed his torso. 'I have the bolt here. It's, well, it's very small, captain.' He held it up in one hand, and Manatas regarded it, head tilted.

'It is, indeed, lieutenant. It seems wrong to call it a bolt at all.' He sniffed. 'No wonder his wound is not grave.'

Arkadas replaced the bolt, then adjusted his seat on the grain-sack as if uncomfortable, sending out another dribble of rotten grain between his boots. 'Ioseb requested we notify his cousin of his injury.'

'His cousin?'

'He's serving in one of the chapters down-valley. Apparently they're close. I took the liberty of sending one of the runners.' He looked up, brows pinched, mouth downturned. 'Did I overstep, captain?'

Manatas waved a hand, his attention already shifting. 'Not at all, Arkadas. Prudent to notify next of kin. Just in case.'

Arkadas asked something else, his tone grave and manner awkward, but Manatas was no longer listening, his agreement distant and murmured. Tauras had completed his circuit. The Vistirlari now had him looking for whatever it was between the roots of a tree at the camp's edge, digging with his hands while they guffawed at his back. Manatas's knuckles went white.

'Motherless hoodlums,' he growled, surging forward. Arkadas leaped to his feet behind him, urging caution, but Manatas could not stop himself. He would not stop himself. A morning's worth of contained anger seethed within him, packed in with a further year's compressed rage, and a few decades of frustrations and sour turns beneath that, and the restraints were coming loose.

'What in the name of all the gods of sea and sky is going on here?' he roared.

The Vistirlari jumped to attention, one of them throwing up a salute in reflexive shock. Tauras pushed himself to his feet, his pale eyes wide in confusion, his earth-caked hands leaving muddy streaks on his clothes. 'Cap?' he said.

Manatas kept his eyes on Zurab and Rostom. They were both staring straight ahead, not meeting his gaze. 'What are you doing, Tauras?'

Tauras tried his best to dust off his palms, but succeeded only in smearing more wet mud over himself. He offered an apologetic smile. 'We were trying to recover some lost equipment, cap.'

'Is that so?' The Vistirlari were each attempting to outdo the other with their ten-thousand-yard stares. 'And what manner of equipment was this?'

'One of the special knives. The special knives, cap? Tell him, Zurab!'

'Yes, Zurab, tell me what kind of special knife was missing from my camp, on top of all the other horrors around here.'

The Vistirlari coughed. 'Just a knife, captain,' he said, his southern accent still thick enough to stretch his words.

'One of the left-handers,' Tauras added brightly.

Manatas nodded once, his lips sucked together, the fury draining back inside him to form a hardened crust of resentment once more. 'You were digging, Tauras, for a left-handed knife?'

The huge man bounced his head up and down with excitement. 'Exactly, cap. I've never even seen one before, and the lads were so desperate to find it, weren't you, lads?'

Rostom was doing a better job of keeping his composure. 'Sure were,' he mumbled through gritted teeth, eyes still on the distant horizon. The corners of Zurab's mouth were fighting their way inexorably upwards.

Manatas wrapped a palm over his fist and cracked the knuckles of his left hand, then his right. 'Tauras, the company thanks you for your diligent assistance in this matter but you are now relieved.

Clean yourself up in the stream and see if you can't bring some of our cook-fires back to life. After that, you are on watch. Dismissed.'

'Yes, cap. Thank you, cap.'

'Now, as for you two.' As Tauras thumped merrily away, Manatas swivelled on the Vistirlari, who still strove to avoid his eye. 'Soldiers, I am going to ask you not to do anything like that again. As Arkadas reminds us,' he nodded to his lieutenant, who stood a few paces behind, watching with sombre eyes, 'the company is a great extended family to us all, and we in this chapter are like a little household within the branches of that great tree. So you be kind to your siblings, and in turn you will be cared for. Do you understand?'

Rostom nodded, eyes front, but Zurab opened his mouth. 'You our daddy now?'

Manatas held his eye. 'Respect travels in two directions, Zurab. I can no more demand your respect than you can ask for mine. But you can respect the company that employs you, and the professional soldiers serving alongside you, and the customs and regulations that keep us alive and paid. Thousands have marched beneath our pennant, and our chapter is but a fraction of a greater whole.'

'When it comes to greater h—'

'At this point, Zurab, the custom is to be silent.' Feeling the kindling of his rage once more, Manatas tried a different tack. 'Now why aren't you caring for your compatriot? Surely it would help raise his spirits and speed the healing process?'

This time, Rostom answered. 'He complains too much. Tells us it's our fault he's injured.'

'Is it?'

They exchanged a quick glance. 'We were ambushed,' Rostom ventured. 'Didn't stand a chance.'

Zurab seemed to be hard of learning. He took a step forward. 'And what are you doing about it, Daddy? We hear tell that you backed out of the payment after some old woman—'

Manatas stepped directly in front of Zurab, so they were almost nose-to-nose. The Vistirlari's eyes crossed. 'Zurab, I have warned you once that your conduct must conform, but I have not been clear, and that is my sin to redress. Allow me to complete the second half of the picture: we are a military operation. We are professional agents of chartered violence. That means we are by nature capable of acts of sudden and intense savagery, when occasion and contract dictate. Thus the norms that bind our behaviour outside those occasions are agreed, adhered to, and enforced, by necessity, because we cannot, as men of professional violence, behave in an ungoverned manner. We are not barbarians, we are not marauders. We are paid to provide a service, and provide it we do, in exchange for a more generous fee than any of us would see if we turned our hands to the soil. Yes?'

Manatas moved back half a step, allowing Zurab to focus on him again. 'Because if we slip, if we traverse that line that demarcates the conduct of a professional outfit doing honest work for honest pay, then we become the bandits that that woman called us. So understand me, both of you: if you fail to conduct yourselves in a manner worthy of this company, you will be punished. And if that punishment does not correct your course, you will be expelled. And it will be a lonely life in these hills for a soldier without a company and without a contract, especially with winter's breath at our necks. You think the Guild would take you? You make it as far as the flatlands, their riders would cut you down when they caught your stink on the wind.' He glared at each in turn. 'Are my words comprehended?'

Rostom grunted, his gaze still focused somewhere on the wooded mountainside opposite, but to Manatas's astonishment Zurab opened his mouth to speak again. 'You can't expel us. You don't have the authority. You're only here because—'

Manatas leaned into the man's face again, getting a noseful of his days-old reek. 'Captain-General Ridderhof could be here within the week, and he surely does. All it would take is a word from me. Is that where you want us to wind up?'

At last, Zurab shook his head. Manatas stepped away, hands re-clasped behind his back, feeling some of the tension drain from his shoulders. 'Dismissed. But do me the favour of further consideration of what I have imparted.'

The Vistirlari relaxed in turn, shuffling away towards Ioseb's quarters. 'We'll certainly . . . *bear* it in mind,' Rostom chuckled as he turned.

Manatas stopped, his head tilted. His voice when he spoke was light, almost delicate, as if testing the air to see if it would take the weight of his words. 'What did you say?'

'Nothing, nothing,' Rostom muttered, but Zurab couldn't help himself.

'No need to get so . . . *grizzly*,' he sniggered.

One quick step brought Manatas's elbow against the man's chin, striking down and across. As he dropped, a knee followed into his chest, slamming him to the dank earth and pinning him, as a blade the length of his hand pressed against his exposed and bobbing throat. Rostom lunged to intercede and jerked to a halt, finding a second blade jutting from Manatas's extended arm, the gleaming tip gently pricking the leather of his thigh.

'Rostom,' gasped Zurab, 'help!'

'For the first time in your accursed existence,' Manatas hissed, 'I implore you to close up your mouth and open your ears, as it is plain to me that you have failed to comprehend what you were told.' He leaned forward, pushing the last of the air from Zurab's lungs. 'The first failing was mine, but this one lies heavy on you. I will say this once more but that will be the last time. We are men of violence. You will conform to our standards, or you will fall victim to them.'

Zurab made another plaintive noise, and Manatas pressed harder. He kept the second knife puckering the leather of Rostom's frozen leg, and nodded over his shoulder. 'I need you to understand something, for your benefit and that of the company at large. You see behind me, there stands Lieutenant Arkadas, who cares more about the company than any other who serves. Do you see him making any move to separate us? To rescue you? Do you hear any appeals to my better nature?'

Zurab gurgled. Spittle was frothing at his lips.

'That is because Lieutenant Arkadas knows better than most that discipline is what holds a unit together, is what holds a company together, and if I cannot demand your respect then I will command your fear, because command you I must. I have known captains who would carve the skin from your face at this time, cut the ears from your skull or sever your digits, and should I choose to mirror them, not a man in this camp would stop me.' He stared into Zurab's wide, wild eyes. 'Do you understand this? No one would do a thing, because they understand. We are men of violence, and must be curbed with the necessary means.'

He raised his knee an inch, and Zurab sucked in a gasping breath. 'I will not repeat myself. Be grateful I have no passion for disfigurement.' He rose slowly to his feet, ignoring the pop from his knee as he stood, and slipped the knives back into their sheaths at his belt. Zurab lay on the ground, taking great honking breaths. Rostom hadn't moved, and Manatas thought he saw a dark patch at the front of the man's trousers, not far from the nick he'd left in the leather.

'By the gods,' Manatas muttered, 'did you forget what sent me here? People think Tauras is simple, but I swear you two are the stupidest men I've ever had the misfortune to command. You will clean yourselves up and make yourselves useful in getting this camp straight. Now, get out of my sight.'

Manatas walked slowly to the camp's edge, Arkadas keeping pace a step behind, and looked out across the valley. The afternoon was waning, the coppery sun drifting towards the great grey peak, its shadow at the valley floor beginning to lengthen, the vivid crimson and gold of the slope beneath them losing its fire as the light faded. Already mist was rising in the valley again, the silver coils of the river at its foot obscured by a dim fuzz of cloud.

'Arkadas, I have let myself down.'

Arkadas said nothing.

Manatas stared at the rotting leaves between his boots. 'It is an ugly thing to draw a blade on a man in your command, let alone two at a swoop. Especially after . . .'

'They gave you ample reason, captain.' Arkadas paused, then ventured, 'It was an abject thing to raise the bear, and you did little more than bruise their pride.' He left the 'this time' unstated.

Sucking his lip against his teeth, Manatas shook his head. 'To allow such provocation to yield brutality is to let another pull your strings like a puppeteer. No man in possession of his faculties should answer words with violence.'

'Unless those words are a call to war, captain, or an incitement to harm those we are bound to protect.' It was clear that Arkadas did not want him to brood on the path that had led them to the cold mountainside.

'Well, yes, I guess there are circumstances.' Manatas ran a hand along his chin, feeling the rasp of his stubble against the cracked skin of his fingers. 'The world is messy, Arkadas, and people are complicated.'

'So I'm told, captain.'

'We are compressed, Arkadas, we are pressured like steam. The Miners' Guild and their "peacekeeping" have robbed this company of its trade in the flatlands, and we are driven to these high places, these fringes, and forced to ply our trade with dregs, with those unsuited to this life and its demands. This company is not what it was, Arkadas, and it may never be again.'

'So you have remarked, captain.' There was an edge of discomfort to the lieutenant's voice. Arkadas did not like to hear of the company's diminishment, no matter the truth of the words. Their numbers scattered across the range were likely only a few hundred now, and discipline decayed like a sun-warmed corpse. 'More than once.'

Manatas rubbed at his eyes. He needed a good night's sleep, a state unchanged in at least a decade. 'How I wish Keds were here. She always had a way of seeing the path through things.'

Arkadas shifted behind him. 'Think she'll be coming through with the captain-general?'

Manatas nodded, one thumbnail resting against the edge of his teeth. 'If we have the gods' favour. She'll have her chapter in a better state than this embarrassment, that's for damned sure.'

'Her promotion was our loss,' Arkadas murmured.

'But the company's gain,' Manatas finished, trying to make himself believe it. 'She'd never have tolerated the malfeasance of those Sink-rats this long.'

'Perhaps you should seek their expulsion after all? When the captain-general arrives.'

Manatas sighed. 'We both know a word to Ridderhof's adjutant from me won't achieve much. Botrys hates me almost as much as I disdain him.'

'I wouldn't take it personally, captain,' Arkadas replied with a soft smile. 'I hear tell Botrys takes issue with anyone he suspects is smarter than him.'

'Well that's got to be damned near everyone,' Manatas said with a weary laugh. Across the valley, a few lights already twinkled as the residents of Ar Ramas lit their candles and stoked their cook-fires. At least Tauras had got one of the fires in the camp going again, blessings upon him, but the rest of the place was going to need serious work before the captain-general and his court came rolling in. The Vistirlari and their antics had really dropped a dung-surprise in his oats, that was for certain. Ambushed, or sent packing from despicable acts? And by whom, armed with what?

He looked back across the valley, his eyes narrowed. 'Let me see that little bolt again, will you?'

Arkadas fished in his satchel and passed the slim quarrel across. Manatas held it up to catch the flickering light of the cook-fire along its length.

'Now what manner of weapon fires something like this?' he murmured. 'There is something afoot in these hills, Arkadas, and we are not seeing it all.'

TEN

Javani had nearly caught up with Ree when she pulled up short, a few paces shy of limping all the way back to the forge. 'Nine gut-shitting hells!' she hissed.

'What is it, Ma? Your leg?'

Ree stood with a hand on one of the forge's supporting posts. 'In all the excitement, I forgot to get the tea from the stables.' She rested her head against the post. 'I was really looking forward to a cup of tea.'

With cautious steps, Javani approached her mother's back. 'I could . . . I could go back and get it? I know which bag it's in. I think.' Although the thought of bumping into Lali again, the ferocity of her judgement, the finality of her scorn – and the thought that it had spread to others in the settlement, that they all blamed her and Ree for what had happened – sent hot little needles into her gut.

Ree waved a loose hand. 'No, kid. Not now.' Her head was still against the post.

Javani edged closer. She could see the back of her mother's collar was damp with sweat, despite the chill of the afternoon. 'Ma? Are you all right?'

Ree turned her head, twisting against the pole, and cracked a smile. 'Just tired, kid. Missing my stick.' She pushed herself back from the pole and nodded in the direction of the line of forest at the pasture's edge. 'I'd go and get myself a new one if I didn't expect Constable Gumis to snatch it off me like it's a demonic totem to be cast into a bottomless chasm.'

It was hard to match her mother's smile. 'Did you have to, um, antagonise them like that? They've been nothing but kind to us since we arrived, even if they are a bit, you know.' Javani waved her hands either side of her face. Lali's sneering expression was hard to shift from her mind's eye. 'They made it sound like you put everyone in danger. I thought it wasn't our business?'

Ree's smile faded. 'You're right, kid, a nice bunch they may be, but right now their collective stupidity and cowardice will see them eaten alive before winter's end.'

'You really think so?' The notion struck Javani somewhere in her chest, a cold, dizzy feeling that made her want to shiver. Despite Lali's hard words, she really didn't want harm to come to her or anyone else in Ar Ramas. She thought of the shrieking children playing peg-bat in the pasture, the adults she'd seen playing stones, the generally relaxed air to the place – at least until Ree had stirred things up again. It really is peaceful here, she thought. For once it doesn't feel like everyone is trying to get somewhere else, or is wishing they already were. Present company excepted, of course. 'Won't they just pay the bandits off after we leave, and go back to how things were?'

Ree hitched up her belt, flexing her bad leg. 'You're making the same mistake as they are there, kid. Assuming that what they had was some kind of balance, not a downward slide.' She held out her forearm, palm down, illustrating flat versus tilted before Javani's nose. 'It's a human failing. We think that because something's always been a certain way to us, that's how it always will be. We forget.'

'What?'

'That no matter how bad they seem at the time, things can *always* get worse.'

'Ah, there you are!' Mariam was crossing the pasture with long strides, Vida a few paces behind, carrying something bundled in her arms. 'Lost track of you in all the silly nonsense. Come on in to the hut, there's food waiting.' She swung her long tresses over her shoulder as she nodded to Javani. 'The young lady already had a helping, but she looks like she could use some feeding, doesn't she?'

Ree's smile returned. 'Finally, someone in this place is talking sense.'

* * *

Ree ate heartily, to an extent that would have shamed her had she not felt so famished. The abundance of the smiths' spread astonished her – warm flatbreads, slick with butter, mountains of hard, crumbly cheese, fresh yoghurt and green herbs, root vegetables she didn't recognise, alongside apples, quinces and wild cherries, and even a few nuts. Mariam watched her eat with a look of near-maternal pride, which Ree found a little odd as the woman had to be a decade her junior, but she wasn't inclined to make an issue of it.

'It's not always like this, mind,' Mariam cautioned as she offered another flatbread. 'Today's a rest day, and I was laying something on for the children, but you know what little buggers they are at sitting down tidy to eat a proper meal.'

All eyes turned to Javani, who was hovering by the doorway, looking out over the hillside, a half-eaten mound of cheese still on her platter. Ree gave a genial nod of agreement, her mouth too occupied with chewing to speak. Two things were becoming obvious to her: the first, that she'd been more worried about their supply situation than she'd let on to the kid, and had without active consideration begun restricting her own food intake for the last couple of weeks; the second, that if this meal was anything close to a fair representation of the pre-winter provisions of Ar Ramas, the settlement was staggeringly rich in produce. No wonder the bandits were hovering like flies.

'Drink?' Vida had been sitting quietly while her wife chattered and Ree shovelled food into her face. Now she offered something from a drooping skin, two carved wooden cups in her hand.

Ree eyed the skin. It was dark and mottled. 'What is it?'

'*Kipir*. Fermented goat milk,' Vida replied, her gaze steady. 'Not strong.'

'We let the children drink it every now and then,' Mariam added brightly.

'Shame,' Ree said, and extended a hand for a cup. She marvelled at the vessel's lightness, the intricacy of the carving and smooth finish. She remembered the extraordinary samovar she'd seen when bathing. 'This is a fine piece of work. Yours, Vida?'

Vida poured a generous slug into the cup. 'No. Metal is mine, wood is Mari's. Pots, too.' Mariam flushed and chattered, down-playing her evident skill.

'Lot of fine craft around here,' Ree murmured, thinking of the tightly constructed stone and timber buildings at the village's centre, the ornate pillars of the Council House. It made a stark contrast with the mudbrick efforts down on the plains, and her own attempts to build a permanent cabin on her since-abandoned farm. In Kazeraz, only the Guildhouse could have laid any claim to Architecture, and it had taken the purloined wealth of the entire region to accomplish that.

'Lots of fine crafters,' Vida replied, hefting her own cup.

Ree gave the contents of her cup a sniff, then took an exploratory sip. 'Not bad,' she said, taking another. 'Not bad at all.'

'If you finish that, there's fresh in the skin over by the doorway,' Mariam gestured to the dangling goatskin bag, not far from the kid's head. 'We give it a knock as we go in and out, we do, keep it mixing while it bubbles.'

The kid was looking over. 'Can I—?'

'Far too boozy for you, kid. Why don't you go out and play?'

The outraged, disgusted look the kid shot her provoked such a sudden snort of laughter that Ree was lucky not to send *kipir* through her nose. Clearly, that was not the reaction Javani had been aiming for, and she stormed out into the fading afternoon.

'Ah, she's a bright girl, she is,' Mariam beamed at the kid's absence. 'She'll be a bright young woman soon enough.'

'No rush on that score,' Ree muttered, chancing another swallow. 'The kid will be a kid a good while yet.'

'You'd best prepare.' Vida was leaning back against the wall of the hut, her arms folded. 'You'd hate to be ambushed by womanhood.'

'It can happen faster than you think, mind,' Mariam added, with wide, earnest eyes. 'Your girl may change very fast, very soon, and it would be best for both of you if you were at least predisposed—'

Ree raised her palms, brows rucked. 'I appreciate the concern, but really, I think we'll be just fine for now.' You don't need to tell me of the shock of sudden blooming, she thought grimly. By the time I was her age, I'd already been traded for political favour. Or was I a little older? Suddenly Ree wasn't sure. It had been a long time ago, after all. She blinked the thought away. The kid was different, that was what mattered. Things would be different for her.

She needed to change the subject, and it seemed an apt moment to confront the obvious head-on. 'You're not kicking us out, then. Thank you for that.'

'Of course we wouldn't!' Mariam protested, but Ree was watching Vida. The big smith had seen what had happened at the bridge, or at least the first part, and had been an eyewitness to her bollocking from the Council. Her face gave nothing away as she turned the fabulous cup in her hands, then she shrugged, a delicate lift of her heavy shoulders.

'Can't say some of the same thoughts haven't occurred.'

Ree rocked back on her stool, her eyes wide with vindication, but Vida raised a scarred hand. 'No. A thought is one thing, in the quiet of your own mind. But public words are action, and you acted strongly today.' She chewed at her cheek for a moment. 'Especially for someone so newly arrived to our situation.'

Mustn't overplay this, Ree thought. She kept her voice level, dampening some of the righteous excitement she felt. 'You agree, though? This contract, this *arrangement* – it's not just absurd, it's only a prelude.'

Mariam was watching her with serious eyes, her customary animation stilled. Vida was as measured as ever. 'A prelude,' she said, a question without inflection.

Ree met her gaze. 'Tell me how it came about. This place has been here for, what, at least ten years? More? But this plague of supposed mercenaries has been here only the last two. What happened?'

Mariam glanced at Vida, her expression broadcasting her thoughts as if she'd spoken them aloud: a desire to tell all, a fear of what might happen if she did, worry about what might happen if she didn't, concern for Vida, concern for the children in her care. Mariam was not a hard person to read.

'It was trading that did it.' Vida spoke slowly, her voice low. Although it was still daylight outside the hut, the room felt darker when she spoke, and Ree was suddenly grateful for the candles that Mariam had lit in the corner sconces when they'd sat down. Real wax, too, she noted.

'All of us who came to this place, almost without exception, found it by accident,' Vida went on. 'Like you, trying to cross the Ashadi. Trying to start a new life somewhere better.' Mariam put a long-fingered hand on her arm, and she clasped it. 'That's the foundation story, at least.' Vida pulled a tight half-smile. 'Truth is, we knew about this place before we set off. Friend of a friend, cousin of a cousin. It had almost mythical status by the time it reached us, but we believed.' She met Mariam's gaze. 'We needed to believe.'

Ree shifted on her stool. 'So you brought your tools and gear up into the mountains, just in case.'

Vida nodded. 'Packed everything we had onto a wagon, then onto the animals, following the trail, the ghosts of those who went before.'

'We weren't the only ones, though, were we,' Mariam added. 'Lots of folk were keen to come with us, but they all fell away. Illness, injury, or just . . . you know.'

'They gave up on the dream,' Ree replied. It was hard not to compare them with her and Javani, trekking for weeks through endless mountains, in search of a paradise that might not exist after all.

'But we found it,' Vida concluded. 'First new arrivals in a good while. And us turning up got people thinking, and then talking.'

'And then arguing,' Mariam said with a rueful smile.

Ree rubbed her chin. Her *kipir* was gone, and she was positively inclined towards another cup. 'Disagreements over whether the place needed new blood, and how to proceed?'

'Indeed.' Vida noticed her empty cup and moved to stand, but Mariam beat her to it, swishing around the table with impressive grace to retrieve the fresh skin from the doorway. 'But more than that.'

'Trade.' Ree gratefully extended her cup to Mariam for a strained top-up.

'Trade,' Vida repeated, doing the same. 'You may have noticed, this place is . . .' She waved a vague hand.

'Bounteous,' Mariam supplied, getting herself a cup.

'I was going to say "well-appointed". Ample grazing, excellent timber, fertile land, a climate for spring wheat and sweet barley that can't be matched on the plains.'

'Bar the rain, of course,' Mariam interjected. 'And we have bees!'

Ree glanced at the candles again. 'I gathered.' Not to mention, she added to herself, the setting was extremely defensible. Given the attitudes of the founders, could that have been simple coincidence?

'But we don't have everything.' Vida took a long drink from her cup. 'I'm a smith. I've got all the wood I could wish for to stoke my forge fire, but, to use a professional term, fuck-all metal – aside from what folks brought with them.'

Ree sucked at her teeth, nodding in appreciation. 'It's the opposite problem from the plains – all the ore you can mine, no bloody trees. Think you've got enough for a horseshoe?'

Vida chuckled. 'Never did get to checking your pony, did we? We'll sort it tomorrow.'

Ree crossed her legs before her, wincing at the stiffness in her calf. Thank the gods she was off it at last. 'The traders won out, then?'

'Anything we couldn't grow or farm up by here,' Mariam said, reaching forward to top up Ree's cup again, 'we had to get from somewhere else.'

Ree dipped her head in thanks. 'Which meant travel in and out of the mountains. Which meant the chance of people following you back.'

Vida nodded slowly, staring off into the hut's corner. Ree already knew there was nothing there. She was remembering, and doing so with guilt.

'We were glad of some new arrivals, mind,' Mariam said, her brightness now sharp-edged and brittle. 'It helped reassure us that Ar Ramas really had a future, that we'd be able to build, and grow, and the children would carry it on after we were gone.'

'At first it was a small thing,' Vida said. 'One of the trips down the mountains had a run-in with some vagrants – deserters, desperate refugees, who knows? They were lucky to escape with their lives, but nearly all the goods were lost.'

Mariam leaned her chin on one hand. 'You can imagine the arguments in the Council, can't you.'

'Let me guess – Camellia wanted to abandon all trade, someone proposed arming the next trip so they could defend themselves instead, and she went up like a powder-store?'

Mariam moved her hand fast to cover her smile, a small, nervous thing, but Vida gave a bleak chuckle. 'Close enough. But then someone had an idea.'

Ree had already seen it. 'Mercenaries. They guard the trips to and fro, take a share of the profits, and nobody in Ar Ramas need dirty their hands with a weapon. Win-win.'

Vida was staring into the corner again. 'And as it happened, representatives of something calling itself a mercenary company had recently arrived in the foothills. They weren't hard to find.' She trailed off.

'It was almost as if they were already looking for us,' Mariam finished, the light gone from her voice.

They sat quietly for a moment, sipping the dregs from their cups as the candles burned down. It was getting cold again.

'I can probably follow it from here,' Ree said at length. 'It started small, seemed reasonable, things seemed to be going well, but then after a couple of trips there seemed to be more mercenaries in the hills, and less and less of the produce was making it to be traded, until somehow it was all going straight to the mercs and you had no idea what you were paying for any more.'

Vida grunted. 'The long and short of it. They have a permanent camp across the valley, must be around twenty garrisoned there now, but they're part of a bigger group that come through on rotation every season. The payments have got more frequent, and more demanding.' Her knuckles whitened around the cup.

'We still have enough, mind,' Mariam was quick to add, 'even with what we give them, we're well-stocked for winter, even for the festival and all. Nobody will go hungry. And this is the last payment of the season.'

Ree kept her tone even. 'Is it, though?'

'A prelude,' Vida growled.

'A prelude.'

'You think they'll keep demanding more and more, until someone does go hungry. Or worse.'

Ree leaned forward and placed her cup down with both hands, then looked at them each in turn. 'Just ask yourself: why wouldn't they?'

ELEVEN

Javani seethed. Go out and play? As if she was an infant, not someone who that morning had (nearly) single-handedly seen off a bandit ambush, shot a man in the leg (reluctantly) and rescued poor Sweeper. Not to mention getting them this far after that mess in Kazeraz. She'd happily never enter a mine again as long as she lived.

She kicked around the empty forge, her feet scuffing the baked earth, then sat down beside Tarfellian the enormous hound, who was maintaining his tireless vigil of snoring as close to the glowing fire as prudence would allow. He raised his giant greying head as she clambered down beside him, giving her a meaningful sniff, then slowly licked at her hand. Definitely some cheese still on there somewhere, she thought. Satisfied he'd got what he could, he curled his head back into his great pile of body and produced a loud, exhausted sigh.

'You and me both, old man,' Javani said, rubbing his flank. She looked around the forge. It was neatly ordered, but she'd meant what she'd said to Vida earlier: there was a distinct lack of metalwork in it. Maybe it was all somewhere else, perhaps in a hidden store.

Go out and play, indeed. Go out and face Lali again, or any of the other children, who had no doubt by now been fully informed that she and her mother were murderous savages from the flatlands, come into the mountains to stir up trouble and create suffering. It's not our fault, though, she thought sourly, it's in our nature, we don't know any better – we folk of the plains are but simple creatures, prone to violent outbursts when confused or frightened. Well, isn't that just like everybody else? It hadn't taken much to inflame the passions of this supposedly peace-loving enclave, and despite a lot of words about love and serenity, everyone seemed to get stressed and nasty just the same as people did closer to sea-level.

She sighed. It would have been nice if Ree hadn't gone to such lengths to rile them all up, though. Not that she didn't have a point, of course – her mother *always* had a point, she was the pointiest person Javani had ever known – but, well, there were ways of expressing yourself, weren't there? And it really was nice here. Some part of her was desperately sorry they'd have to leave in the morning, but she knew it was for the best. It was definitely for the best. Wasn't it? Getting to Arestan was what mattered. Arestan was a paradise, everyone said it. In Arestan, they'd make a new life, a better life. A world away from scratching a living in the dust of the desert, from slogging ill-tempered through endless mountains. In Arestan, they could be who they were supposed to be. Whatever that was.

The sun was getting low, brushing the stark grey peaks that loomed over the settlement's western flank, casting them into jagged silhouette. The slanted light caught something bundled beneath a workbench, an odd cluster of points at one end. Giving Tarfellian a valedictory rub, she shuffled across the forge floor towards the workbench. There, tightly bound in sacking, their very tips exposed and gleaming in the reddening light, she found dozens of arrows.

'Well, well, well,' murmured Javani.

Two more bundles lay beside the package of arrows, far longer and thinner. She teased the sacking off the first, revealing the proud curved tip of an unstrung bow, made from two woods of different rich hues. Javani licked her lips. There were reels of string laid out on the bench above, and now she knew them for bowstrings; the loops were a clue, after all. So Vida and Mariam were making bows and arrows, in defiance of the Council's edicts? Or were they just looking after them for someone else?

And would they miss one if she borrowed it?

A short while later, having scuttled away from the forge to the nearby treeline with a long bundle pressed against her body and a fistful of arrows tucked in her shirt, the fletchings tickling her with every step, Javani successfully strung the bow. It was longer than Ree's, and far harder to bend, but she guessed that was rather the idea. She'd anointed a thick oak (probably an oak, most of the trees seemed to be oaks) with a large and obvious knot as her target, well out of sight of the forge and the pasture, and where a missed arrow (perish the thought) would come to rest harmlessly in the slick and festering leaves of the forest floor.

She knew her archery was far from good. She knew it mattered – their experience with the deer had been testament to that, and had they not immediately encountered Sweeper and his bandit friends, and from there found Ar Ramas, her missed shot could have meant eventual starvation for her and her mother. It was not a thought she cherished; she hated the idea of killing something, being responsible for inflicting pain and suffering on a blameless animal, especially one so pretty as a deer. Wasn't there a way she could just eat plants without starving? Mani had hinted at as much. It was possible that the elders of the settlement may have some positive notions after all.

But until she could confirm a life of guilt-free nutrition, she needed to improve her bow work. And while Ree remained a terrible teacher, Javani never got a chance to practise without her mother looming over her like an angry goddess, jabbering impossible commands and snapping at every perceived imperfection before she'd even got a shot off. She needed a chance to practise by herself, without anyone sneering or sniping, just taking her time, on her own.

She nocked her first arrow, lined up on the tree knot and drew back the string.

'You're going to miss.'

'Shitting piss!' she squeaked as the string leaped from her hand and the arrow flew off somewhere into the thinning golden canopy. She rounded on her critic with eyes of burning fury. 'You *made* me do that!'

Anri sucked in his gummy lips. 'No, I didn't. You were always going to miss that, you were.'

'I was not.'

He shrugged. 'You were, plain as day.'

She snatched another arrow from the bundle at her feet and waved it under his nose. 'Leaving aside for a moment you sneaking up on a young woman in the woods, how would you possibly know whether I'd miss or not? You've never even seen me shoot before.'

Her waves of indignation bounced straight off him, his eyes like twinkling creases in his grizzled face. 'Leaving aside for a moment the fact you've stolen my bow, and are in the process of losing my arrows one by one,' he retorted, 'any daft bugger can see you'll miss if you shoot like that. Just look at your feet.'

'What's wrong with my feet?' Javani glanced down. Her boots were worn and muddied, but she had a firm, comfortable stance. She felt confident as she hefted the bow.

'Kypeth's teeth,' he muttered. 'What lummox taught you to shoot, then?'

'My ma.' Javani felt suddenly self-conscious, staring at her feet again as if they'd suddenly give away their secrets. A floppy, ruddy leaf was stuck to the toe of her left boot, but unless that was some sort of code she was none the wiser.

'She as bollocks as you at this?'

Her cheeks were getting hot, her neck prickly. 'She's a dead-shot with a crossbow.'

'Great comfort, that must be,' he chuckled, his beardy face not quite pulling as far as a sneer. 'Learning you wrong on purpose, was she? As a joke, like?'

'Hey!' Javani would cheerfully mock her mother's teaching ability, skill with a bow, or indeed any other area she felt fell short of ideal, but hearing this bristly ruffian impugning Ree was a direct line to her core of rage. 'I could still jam this arrow—'

'No, you can't.' He'd already snatched it from her hand – she'd barely even seen him move. As she stammered, he plucked the bow from her grip. 'Lost enough arrows for one day, you have,' he growled. 'You're lucky I'm not making you go and fetch that one and all.' That was, she had to admit, a step up from Ree, and come to think of it that was rather how they'd ended up in this mess to begin with.

She kneaded her palm where he'd whipped the bow from her grip. 'You talk a big game, Anri,' she said sullenly, 'but I bet you can't even hit that knot.' She gestured not at the large knot she'd been aiming for, but a much smaller one above it, a thin pale circle in the fading light.

He shook his head as he bent to rebundle the arrows. 'No.'

'You can't hit it? Really?'

'Of course I can hit it, you infant, but you'll not goad me. Now bugger off.'

Javani didn't move. In fact, she stepped in front of him, blocking the last of the light. She knew she didn't react well to being dismissed by adults, but she couldn't fight her instincts. She'd recover some face here if it killed her, figuratively speaking. 'Won't let me take a proper shot, won't take a shot himself – what are you afraid of, Anri?'

'Told you, didn't I. These arrows are hard to come by.' He rose to his feet and propped up the bow, moving to unstring it.

She was as close to his face as she could manage; he was a fair bit taller than she was. 'Then don't miss, and I'll go and get it from the tree. Come on, what are you really scared of? Embarrassing yourself in front of an *infant*?'

For a moment she saw a flash of tooth in his black-and-silver whiskers. 'Right pain in the scrotum you are, aren't you?' His fingers had paused, the bow not yet unstrung.

Javani grinned, although she wasn't exactly sure what a scrotum was. It was probably near the liver. 'Tell you what, you hit that little knot, and—'

He leaned down and yanked a handful of arrows from the bundle, stabbing them into the soft turf, then nocked the first and drew. The arrow flashed from the bow, whipping past Javani who turned to follow its flight. It thumped into the little knot, a little north of perfectly in its centre. That actually disappointed her a little, but she'd made her point. She'd ground him down, and that was what mattered.

She put up a hand. 'All right, I'll admit—'

Before she'd turned more than an inch, a second arrow slammed into the knot, this time south of its centre.

'. . . uh . . .'

A third followed, slipping just to the right of the other two, its fletching brushing theirs as it quivered. Javani stared at it, her words half-formed, and waited for the final arrow. When it didn't come, she turned back to look at Anri.

The bastard had his eyes shut.

'You—'

He loosed the final arrow. Javani didn't bother turning to watch its flight – she heard its impact in the knot with absolute clarity in the quiet woods. She knew exactly where it had hit.

'Nine hells,' she breathed.

Anri opened his eyes, looked past her towards the tree, then merely grunted. He glanced at Javani when she stood immobile. 'Go on, then,' he said.

'Huh?'

'Go and get them, then.'

Shit.

She licked her lips. 'Can you teach—'

'No. Go and get them.'

'Please – I know we're only here until tomorrow, but can you tell me—'

'No. Get my fucking arrows.'

'At least tell me what's wrong with my feet!'

He let out a heavy breath through his nose, what remained of his teeth gritted, and set off towards the distant, now-perforated tree. 'No.'

She dogged his steps, kicking up decaying leaves as she hurried after him. 'Why not?'

'Not my problem, are you.'

'Well, no, but I don't have to be,' she babbled as he set about tugging the arrows clear of the trunk. 'Like I said, we're off tomorrow, but if you could just give me some pointers, I could practise on my own, I'm sure I could pick it up from there. Please? I'm Javani, by the way, I don't think we were ever properly introduced—'

'Don't care.' He turned and starting pacing back towards the arrow bundle.

'Come on, please? Just the feet thing, how long could that take? I'll—'

He stuffed the arrows back into the bundle with slightly more care than his rough manner would have suggested, then hefted it along with the still-strung bow. 'Dense as piles, aren't you?' he muttered, then tapped his chest with a forefinger, enunciating his words. 'Not. My. Problem.'

'Kid? Where are you?' Ree's voice carried through the trees. 'It's getting dark, get your arse back here, pronto.'

Anri gave her a sardonic, toothless grin. 'Mam's calling. Run along.'

Javani hunched her shoulders, feeling the heat of her breath in the chilling air. 'This isn't over,' she snapped to the man's retreating back.

'Doubt it,' came his breezy reply.

TWELVE

Ree's foot was tapping the forge floor. 'Where the fuck have you been? I was considering preparing to become worried about you.'

The kid looked flustered and upset, and her clothes seemed to be dirtier than ever. For a moment it looked like she would storm straight past, if only she had somewhere to storm to, but Ree put out an arm and hauled her into a sort-of hug, sort-of restraining hold.

'Hey. *Hey.*' She tilted her head, at last catching the kid's surly and downward gaze. 'What's up? What happened out there?' Her eyes narrowed. 'Do I need to put together some sort of improvised weapon from the scraps in this smithy and go out and stab someone?'

That got a reluctant grin. 'No, Ma, nothing like that.' Ree was aware that the girl was hardly hugging her back. They'd never been especially tactile, especially when their relationship had been a little more arm's length, so to speak, and while Ree was trying to bridge the gap as she went, she was never far from the thought that she'd left things a little too late.

'What was it, then?'

'Remember that hunter, Anri?'

'The one who swans around with a bow and a full quiver in this sacred weaponless district? Oh yes, he made an impression.'

'I ran into him in the woods.' The kid looked momentarily furtive, and Ree waited for the tenuous lie, but somehow an honest answer arrived instead. 'The smiths, they make arrows for him, and bows, too.' This was interesting. Very interesting. Ree remembered Vida's words as they'd eaten: *Metal is mine, wood is Mari's*. Another loophole in the Council's laws, or underground activity? 'I found some, thought I'd go out and, uh, do some training.'

'Ah. Far be it from me to criticise the spirit of endeavour, kid. And gods know, you need the practice.'

The kid went on, her eyes wet in the yellow light of the lantern Mariam had hung outside the hut. 'But Anri caught me. He was . . .'

'What, kid?'

'He was a *dick*.'

Ree snorted. 'I'm afraid, my dear, as you grow, you're going to find that for a depressing swathe of menfolk, that is the natural state. I wish I could promise you otherwise.' She squeezed her around the shoulders, and for a moment Javani rested her head against her. Little weed was taller than Ree remembered. Shit. Had the smiths been onto something when they spoke ominously of sudden blooming? Ree chased the thought from her head; there was plenty of time yet, and they had other priorities.

Mariam appeared in the doorway behind them with politely noisy footsteps. 'Still hungry, anyone? There's plenty of food left, and some won't be as good tomorrow.'

Ree took a step from her daughter. 'Kid? It must be at least half an hour since you last stuffed your face.'

The kid shrugged. 'I could eat again.'

Mariam beamed, waving Javani over. 'I wonder where she puts it!'

Shit. Definitely growing.

'You're more than welcome to bunk with us this evening if you're reluctant to take up the Council's offering,' Mariam said as she ushered the kid back inside the hut. 'Vida and I can sleep in the hall, or we'll make up beds in the forge.'

Ree cut her off with a firm gesture. 'No, thank you but no. We'll bed down in the stables, if it's all the same. We've been away from the ponies too long, they're going to be missing our company.'

Mariam's brow crinkled, unsure but too polite to disagree, as beyond her Ree heard the kid's outraged groan at the notion of sleeping in the stables.

'Well, if you're sure . . .' Mariam said. 'All the goats and sheep are in there, mind, for the winter.'

'I know. They'll keep the place warm, at least.'

'That they will. And pungent! Mind you,' Mariam went on with a slightly dreamy smile, 'it's not like we're too far off rooming with ruminants ourselves – we generally burn sheep dung through the winter, and it's a lot like sharing a hut with a small flock! We dry it for at least two years first, of course,' she added, as if to do otherwise would be unthinkable.

'Of course,' Ree echoed. 'Just sheep dung? What about goat? Seems like you have more of them.'

Mariam's mouth formed a horrified O. 'No. Never burn goat dung. Never.' She shuddered, and Ree was astute enough not to ask for more details. Besides, the kid's revelation had set her thinking, and she wanted to test the ground.

'Your constable, Gumis – he's the one who enforces the Council's edicts, is he?'

'Hmm?' Mariam seemed wrong-footed by the sudden change in subject.

'The laws on carrying weapons, and whatever else there is, I guess. How's it all enforced?'

'Enforced?' Mariam's cheeks were pinched, clearly pained at the line of questioning. 'I don't suppose there's any kind of active enforcement, see – it's more like, I think you'd call it community pressure. Constable Gumis acts as a reminder to the rest of us, but mostly we follow the rules because we want to. Because,' she cleared her throat, 'we agree with them. They make Ar Ramas what it is: a fine place to live.'

Ree watched her sidelong. 'And Anri, the hunter?'

Tiny spots of colour on her cheeks. 'What about him?'

'His lack of observance is pretty flagrant, isn't it? He seems to march about the place with his weapon out for all to see.' Ree waited to see if she'd react to the double entendre, but Mariam was preoccupied.

'Anri's different, he is. He chooses to live outside the settlement, and live apart from its laws.'

'How far outside?'

Her mouth twisted, not quite a grimace, but definitely an uncomfortable answer. 'Not that far. Edge of the timber yards.' She knows, Ree thought, she knows how flimsy this all is. She and Vida aren't stupid. They're going along with all this because everyone else is, because Camellia and Keretan and the rest of the Council can pronounce grandly on the merits of living in harmony without a sharp edge in sight, but the truth is that Constable Gumis can't even make Anri take his bow off his shoulder when he comes wandering through the village. What chance do these people have facing down armed bandits?

Her throat felt suddenly tight. Have I made things worse for them after all?

Flaming piss of the gods, was Camellia right?

Ree woke once in the night, roused from the warm, if ripe, comfort of their nest in the stables by the mournful howling of the wind. Checking the kid slept on, along with countless sheep, goats, mules and their three ponies, she limped painfully to the nearby doorway of the low, recessed building, and stood for a moment at the foot of the steps that led up to the terrace, a thick woollen blanket draped over her shoulders. The night was dark, thick cloud burying the moon behind a blanket of its own, leaving her with only the sounds of the storm – the wind's forlorn groaning, the rustle and swish of the trees dragged by its flurries, the patter and blast of the driving sheets of rain. Fat drops plopped from the awning above her head, splashing into unseen mud.

And there, on the far side of the valley, a cluster of timid flickers of light, barely visible through wind, rain and forest, but impossible to miss when all else was shades of midnight. So that was the bandit camp.

On the whole, Ree was not given to copious self-reflection. Her life had been, by her standards and expectations at least, long and interesting, but hardly packed with moments of joy. The list of things she looked back on with any particular jubilation was short – sometimes it included the kid, sometimes it did not – and dwarfed by the second list, which would no doubt be headed 'regrets'. The imbalance had, by necessity of emotional self-preservation, made her more forward-looking than the reverse. Why dwell on the past when it was little more than a source of pain and shame?

But staring out across the black valley, watching the feeble glimmer of the campfires through the fury of an invisible gale, she found herself overcome by unbidden memories. Once before, she had been stranded behind walls of stone, watching the approach of a vast and hostile force, and she had known that her supposed refuge was doomed. She had fled, leaving others to face the battle to come, and she had survived when so many had not. She told herself she'd done it for the kid, she'd done it for the right reasons – it had been the right decision, the prudent decision. But in the years that had followed, the doubts had trailed her like hounds. And it had been a long time since she'd felt anything like the bonds of family, even with the kid in tow.

Watching the distant fires brought all those feelings rushing back, their intensity undimmed by the intervening time. Tomorrow, thanks to the generosity of the citizens of Ar Ramas – however reluctant – she and the kid would leave, continuing their journey west over the last of these interminable mountains to their promised new life in Arestan, and in their wake, they would leave . . . what?

She stood beneath the dripping awning until her teeth began to chatter, then silently returned to her bed.

THIRTEEN

If there was one thing Manatas had learned about life in the valley, it was that morning brought mist, and the new day was no exception. The sky was so overcast it was impossible to tell where mist ended and cloud began. The forest had been hammered by the storm overnight, and great dumps of ruddy and amber leaves lay piled beneath newly bald and spindly trees.

The camp was, somehow, in an even worse state than the previous day. Manatas surveyed the state of the place with one hand on his ever-more-stubbly jaw, the bristles of his chin rough against the callused skin of his palm and fingers.

'Arkadas.'

'Captain?'

'By my reckoning, Sun's Night will soon be upon us, and we have little more than a few days to get this place into some semblance of military professionalism before the travelling circus arrives. Perhaps with Ioseb recuperating, we may finally achieve it.' He cast his gaze upwards at the slate-grey sky. The morning was bitterly cold, even close to the smoking cook-fire. The wood was wet, of course – getting anyone to do anything properly in the accursed camp was seemingly impossible, but that was going to change, and it was going to change that very morning. 'I would like you to take charge of the clean-up here, while I return to the village. There's still an outside chance that one of the farmers sees reason and we put this whole sorry affair to bed before escalation is required. A renegotiation, indeed.'

He rubbed at his eyes with cracked and chilly fingers. 'Everyone is on duty, Ioseb excepted. If those Sink-rats present even the shadow of a problem, I want them on punishment duty. Don't even blink. The latrines need moving, and they're as fit as any.' If everyone did their bit, they might yet salvage things before Ridderhof and his retinue arrived. He could hand over a smartly turned-out camp and a full accounting of stores and payments, and be out of the Ashadi before there were more days like this one. 'How is the patient this morning?'

Arkadas adjusted the heavy cloak on his shoulders, tucking it closed. Manatas knew he was another who preferred the warmer climes, like every right-thinking person. 'Improving, I'd say. Wound looks clean, the omens are good that it heals well.' He maintained a scrupulously blank expression. 'Not that it would be obvious from his remonstrations.'

Manatas's chuckle was mirthless. 'Keep an eye on him. If his recovery continues, perhaps he can play some part in redeeming his hand in this mess. In the meantime— Tauras, what in the name of all the gods are you doing?'

The big man was standing, feet wide and braced, with a cartwheel in his hands, arms extended, slowly lifting it up and down. The cartwheel was all that was left of one of the original shipments of the early days, the rest long since rotted or burned as firewood.

'Staying strong, cap,' came the strained reply.

Manatas nodded Arkadas to his duties and approached Tauras, whose attention was fixed somewhere beyond the mountains. His arms were still bare, despite the fierce chill of the morning, and veins stood proud along them like snakes beneath his skin. Manatas watched the cartwheel rise and fall once more, trying to estimate its weight. Solid oak, iron-rimmed, half his height in diameter, and soaked by the overnight rain. Manatas would not have volunteered to pick it up once, let alone heft it repeatedly.

'Tauras? Tauras, please put the wheel down for a moment. Thank you.' Manatas stepped smartly to one side as the wheel splattered down among the dead leaves. 'While I appreciate, uh, whatever endeavour this is, we must focus on our priorities. The end of our tour is nigh. In the next few days, the captain-general and his staff will be arriving here with our relief, and – *all being well* – someone new will be taking command of this chapter, and you, I and those among us whose service is complete for this turn will be on the road to sunnier times.' He saw Tauras's brows lower, and worried he'd used too many words. It was a perennial failing. He skipped to the command. 'For that to happen, we need this place looking like a camp should. I want you to stick close to Lieutenant Arkadas, and do what he orders, understand? Once we have this camp in order, then you can go back to, uh, whatever this is.'

Tauras saluted. 'Yes, cap.'

'Good man, Tauras. Remember we only have a few days, so we need to work fast. I'm going to . . .' He trailed off, his skin prickling. He could *hear* something. 'What is that noise?'

Tauras turned alongside him. 'Sounds like singing, cap. Like people singing the company song.'

Manatas's heart plunged through his diaphragm, ending up somewhere in one of his boots. 'It can't be,' he stammered, 'it's too soon . . .'

But from down the winding path came the unmistakable sound of boots, horses and marching voices. The travelling circus had arrived.

Breakfast was thick, sour yoghurt with lashings of honey – honey! Javani could scarcely believe it. She'd seen barely a sniff of the stuff in the last few years; as they'd moved further and further north, it had become either impossible to get or ruinously expensive, carried by a handful of caravans, guarded as tightly as they did the shipments of ore and precious stones that travelled the other way. It almost made up for the lingering stink of goat that seemed to cling to her, despite a fairly thorough (for her at least) scrub in a basin of freezing water.

The valley had lost a lot of its charm in the morning's cold grey light. A storm had torn at the hillsides overnight, sloughing away much of the foliage from the undulating forests, leaving them looking oddly bare and spacious, and a lot less pretty. It was also far colder than she'd been prepared for. Ree had been right about the warmth in the stables – she'd slept like a baby, curled under layers of fleece, and stepping into the morning air had been like being slapped round the face by an ice giant. The fireplace in the smiths' hut was already crackling, and she made sure she claimed the nearest stool as they sat down to eat.

'I'll get your shoe done first thing,' Vida said, taking a swig of buttermilk. There had been no discussion; Ree and Javani had walked straight from the stables over the rise and down to the forge, and been welcomed in without a word, breakfast already laid out for them. They'd made a point not to see anyone else. What would be the point anyway, Javani reasoned. They'd be on the road again by mid-morning. 'It'll mean going to the store.'

Javani looked up, her mouth crammed with yoghurt. 'My shoe?' she mumbled.

'The horseshoe, kid,' Ree supplied with a jaded twitch of her eyebrow. 'You have a store?'

'She's on about her stash,' Mariam said with a pointed smirk at her wife. 'Her secret hoard.'

Vida's face hardened, her brows lowering and jaw clenched, but she could hold it only for a moment before cracking a half-smile. 'Not sensible to leave it all out to rust,' she grunted. 'Especially over winter.'

'I knew it,' Javani crowed. 'I said you had too little metal in the smithy.'

Vida gave her a dispassionate look. 'You did,' was all she said. The 'And?' was unspoken, but Javani's jubilation deflated all the same.

'Tea's ready!' Mariam was back on her feet, despite Vida's protests, moving to where the gleaming samovar lurked. Ree had finally remembered to bring the last of their leaves with them, and Javani could tell from the hungry look in her mother's eyes that she had been looking forward to what was coming a near-inhuman amount.

'I know I said it before, but that samovar is extraordinary,' Ree said, trying to mask her anticipation. 'You really made that, Vida?'

'I did.'

'Even all those little twirly bits, the filigree?'

Vida's head tilted dangerously. 'You find that hard to believe?'

'Not at all,' Ree replied with a smile that was almost as sweet as the honey, and reached out to take her little tea mug from Mariam.

'Not too much colour?'

'Looks great.'

'Chuck in a bit more honey if you want it sweeter.'

Javani watched the cords of her mother's neck flex, the flash of her tongue on her parted lips, her eyes wide and nostrils flaring as she lifted the cup towards her mouth, and felt a sudden mortal and profound embarrassment, as if she were watching her in a moment of intimacy. By the gods, she thought, staring up at the roof beams, she's really missed a good cup of tea.

'By the gods.' Ree leaned back with a sigh. 'I've really missed a good cup of tea.'

Javani nodded thanks to Mariam as she took her own cup. It tasted off to her.

Vida downed her tea with minimal ceremony and jumped to her feet. 'Right. I'll get that pony shod and you can be off.' The suddenness of it shocked Javani – were they to leave so soon? She wasn't ready, she was nowhere near ready. There was so much more yoghurt and honey.

Vida pulled on her jerkin, then swung a heavy woollen cloak around her shoulders. Ree was up, too, moving gingerly towards the door, fishing for her own cloak. 'We'll come with you. That way we can leave as soon as it's done.'

Vida glanced down at her bad leg. 'You're sure? I'll be moving fast.'

'It'll ease once I stretch it. Besides, I want to see these stores. Come on, kid.'

'Do I have to? There's still—'

'Thank Mariam for breakfast, kid, and get moving.' Ree followed Vida out of the door and into the grey morning.

'Thank you, Mariam.'

'You're welcome, my dear. I'll make you up some packages to take with you now. You know, some say yoghurt and honey are the food of the gods, but really all you need are bees and lactobacillus, so perhaps the gods aren't so powerful after all, eh?'

'Bees and what?'

Mariam gave a weary sigh. 'So much I could have done for your education, so much! Go on, off with you – keep that mam of yours out of trouble.'

* * *

'Chapter Captain Manatas.'

'Captain-General Ridderhof.'

Manatas stood back as the man slid down from his horse. He was enormous, swollen in his armoured shell, his pale southern complexion ruddy and bloodshot. He was sweating despite the cold, what remained of his sandy hair plastered to his head. 'Just "commander" will do, captain.'

'Commander. You remember my lieutenant, Arkadas.'

'Of course not.'

His accent remained as ridiculous as ever, and Manatas forced himself not to smirk. His words sounded like he was gargling them. Manatas knew he was from far away, one of the small nations beyond the Sink, beyond even the fabled Clyden, yet somehow he had made it to the plains, and now commanded the most effective mercenary company outside the protectorate. In its glory days, at least. He was looking around the camp, and from the way his moustache twitched it was clear he was not impressed. That was hardly surprising; there had been scarcely enough time to do much more than brush leaves over the worst of the chaos. The circus had evidently been marching double-time since before dawn, all four dozen of them.

Manatas could feel the silence growing, and his furious shame with it. Another two days and he'd have got the place in order, that was all he'd needed. Just another couple of days.

'You're, uh, somewhat advanced in schedule, commander.'

Ridderhof removed his gauntlets and tucked them under his arm, then blew on his pink and stained fingers. 'We thought it prudent to hurry, captain, when we received your message.'

'My message.' Manatas's throat was dry, his tongue sticking to his mouth.

'Yes, the runner you sent.' He called back over his garishly decorated pauldron, 'Botrys! The message! We brought your man back with us, you'll be pleased to hear.'

Manatas could feel the weakness of his smile, and knew that he, too, was sweating, the air stinging his skin. 'I am, commander. So pleased.'

The captain-general's adjutant came shuffling around his commander's horse, a squat and surly figure, unflattered by the armour he insisted on wearing despite his administrative role. A face that could almost have been handsome were it not for its perpetually sour demeanour glared at Manatas with undisguised scorn, which melted to obsequious amenability as it turned to Ridderhof.

Botrys spoke in a monotone. 'Winter payment refused, men ambushed, one serious casualty. Threat of outright contractual default. Suspicion of planning an armed insurrection.'

Manatas goggled. 'Armed insurrection?'

The adjutant consulted his notes. 'Something about a "secret army" in the woods, was it?'

Manatas felt his jaw hanging loose, and closed it. There seemed little more he could do.

Ridderhof thumped his gauntlets against the chapter captain's shoulder. 'Needless to say, we hurried, captain. A serious message, for what I can see is a serious situation.' He strode away before Manatas could formulate a reply, barking orders to his subordinates as the column began to disperse around the camp. Botrys remained, studying his ledger.

Manatas took a swing at ameliorating. 'Pleasant to see you again, Botrys. Are you well?'

The adjutant did not look up. 'You will address me as "lord adjutant", or simply "my lord", captain.'

I damned-by-gods will not, Manatas vowed to himself, mumbling something noncommittal and nodding for Arkadas to follow. He waited until they were safely at the camp's edge before speaking.

'You sent a runner, Arkadas? To the captain-general?'

Arkadas met his glare with surprise. 'I did, captain – the company needed to know.'

'But why in the name of the gods didn't you ask me?'

'I thought I did, captain. We were discussing Ioseb's cousin, and I asked . . . It is no matter. I will volunteer myself for punishment duty.'

Manatas waved an irritable hand, his brow creased with the agony of realisation. His lieutenant had indeed asked, and he'd been too distracted by the antics of the Vistirlari to notice what he'd agreed to. 'Don't be absurd, lieutenant. You have the right of the matter.' He rubbed the heel of his hand against his throbbing temple. 'I just needed another couple of days.' He took a long, cold breath. 'And you also sent a runner to notify Ioseb's cousin?'

'I did, captain.'

'My cousin! Is he coming?' Ioseb of Cstethia was up and hobbling towards them, pale and unsteady but seemingly much improved. 'He'll tear fucking strips from those pissy little shitballs.'

'Ioseb, I am in private conference with my lieutenant. I'd thank you not to listen in or interject.'

'You should keep your fucking voices down, then. Is he coming? Is he here?' Ioseb surveyed the milling throng of the newly arrived column. 'I tell you, the place is in a pretty fucking sore state for a captain-general to arrive, eh? You must be feeling a right sorry shit-head, captain.'

'Thank you, Ioseb.'

'Wouldn't look like this with me in charge. And I'll tell you something else, we'd have a thrice-damned sight more in food stores if it weren't for your boy Tauras guzzling enough for four men every day. How are you going to square that one with the copper-counters?'

Arkadas gave a warning growl. 'Ioseb, enough.'

'That's your thing, though, innit? Always had a soft spot for lumbering animals—'

Manatas could feel the heat rising through him, the day's cold blasted away by its force. His fists were clenched and trembling. He had two knives at his belt and one more in each sleeve. It would be a shameful thing indeed to cut the throat of one of his men directly in front of his company commander, but perhaps it was time an example was made. Perhaps this was what it took to get things done. And where could they send him this time? He was already exiled.

But Arkadas was there just ahead of him. He bodily blocked Ioseb, one hand clamped over his mouth, the other wrapped around his back to stop him falling. 'Soldier, you need to save your strength for your recovery. Return to your sick-bed this instant, and remain there until you are given leave to depart. Your cousin is not here, but should he arrive you will be informed. When I release you, move silently away and do not come back, lest your return to health take a sudden step to the retrograde. Do you understand?'

Ioseb nodded. He looked a lot paler all of a sudden.

'Then go.' Arkadas pushed the man away, and he hobbled unsteadily back towards what passed for the medical tent. To his credit, while he clearly considered a parting shot, he decided against it.

Manatas released a hot, tight breath. 'Thank you, Arkadas.'

'Scant recompense, captain.'

But a smile was already pulling at the chapter captain's lips. 'Ioseb's cousin may not be among our new arrivals,' he said, feeling a weight lift from within his chest, 'but I see someone who is.'

She nearly smiled when she saw him, that slight curve of her mouth that was, in his experience, the closest thing Keds had to expressing outward mirth.

'Kediras!' Manatas called. 'You are a ray of light in a time of darkness.'

'Inaï.' She slung down her pack and weapons, removed her wide-brimmed hat and ran her hands through her long braids, beaded and ringed, shaking them out in a clatter. 'You look bad.'

'I have indeed seen sunnier days,' he sighed, then extended his arms for her embrace. She felt thin. 'Tour over? Are you travelling alone, or with comrades?'

She nodded back over her shoulder to where three tired-looking mercenaries had cleared brush and dead leaves and were erecting a line of tents with what Manatas had no choice but to call military precision. He felt another uncomfortable prickle of embarrassment at the state of his chapter.

Keds seemed to read his thoughts. 'Place looks like dogshit, Inaï. It's said a camp's appearance reflects the state of its commander.' She flicked another gaze over him. 'Seems about right.' She shivered, making her hair clatter again. 'And it's cold up here.'

'I swear the downturn in temperature is a recent development. It was quite clement in these parts until only yesterday.' He blew on his hands. 'How was the tour? You were missed here, I can say without embellishment.'

He'd hoped for a half-smile or a flicker of recognition, but she only stared out over the mist-wreathed valley. The tips of denuded trees stuck up like thorns from the sea of grey fog. 'Hard,' she said at length.

Manatas waited for more. He was prepared to wait for a while. She folded her legs and sat down beside her pack, then withdrew the slim velvet bag from it that Manatas knew contained her flute. She slid out the instrument, blew off the dust, cleaned it, polished it with the inside of the bag, then put it back away. He had not expected her to play it. She never did.

'Something stirred up the Guild down there,' she said as she tucked away the flute, as if the intervening time hadn't passed, and he hadn't been standing there feeling the warmth leaching through his toes into the black earth. 'We were running protection for a string of small settlements, way past the treeline. They came anyway.' She tightened the thong of her pack with a blank grimace. 'It got . . . bleak.'

'The Miners' Guild came into the hills? Into our hills?'

She nodded, still staring off at something only she could see. Manatas shivered. Keds had always been distracted, but now she seemed almost untethered.

'But why?' he asked, half trying to draw her back, half genuinely curious. 'There are no mining operations past the treeline. Are they to leave us no territory at all? Gods, was there contact?'

She nodded again, then twisted to look back at the three tents now erected behind her. 'My chapter,' she said with a voice like a tomb.

He put a hand on her shoulder. 'This is dark, Keds. My sympathies, it should never have come to this. I can only imagine . . .' He closed his eyes a moment, willing positivity. 'But you're away from it now, this place is the back of beyond – far from any encroaching diggers' associations. And tomorrow we can get on the road, resume the circuit. Warm places and comfort await, my friend.'

She looked up at him, a slight crinkle at the corner of her mouth. She looked so tired. 'Once you clean up your shit?'

'Once I clean up my . . . situation. And on that note, I think I see our captain-general calling me over. Wish me luck.'

She patted his hand as he moved away. 'Too late for luck, Inaï.'

'Never too late, Keds,' he replied with more conviction than he felt. 'Never too late.'

FOURTEEN

The captain-general was still rubicund, his strands of pale hair now floating on the breeze above his head. His armour gleamed with condensation. 'You're saying we were misinformed?'

Manatas could hear the trap in his question, absurd accent or not. 'Not at all, commander. But we're no strangers to the occasional garbling of communication in times of stress and upheaval. It's possible that the message you received appeared more, uh, emphatic than it needed to be.'

'Your man was not gravely injured after all?'

'He is up and about already, commander. With a spring in his step.'

'And the contractual situation with . . .' He peered at the ledger in Botrys's hands. The adjutant proffered it with unctuous zeal. '. . . Ar Ramas is not in doubt?'

Manatas steeled himself. Say it like you mean it, say it like it's true, and the rest may just follow. 'I'll have the delayed payment squared away this very day, commander, and we can be on our way tomorrow. I am, in fact, about to pay a visit to our clients, to see about making the final arrangements.'

'Excellent!' Ridderhof snapped the ledger shut and tossed it back to Botrys. 'Perhaps I will accompany you and see how the place is coming on. It's been some time since my last visit.'

'An excellent idea, commander, of course.' Manatas could hear his voice sweating. 'But my visit this morning will be short and to the point, barely worth the effort of your travel – after you are so soon arrived from such an exacting march. Why not come along later, to supervise the exchange?'

Ridderhof appeared to mull, his moustache twisting beneath his bulbous nose like a lamb's tail. Manatas ploughed on. 'My lieutenant will see that you are taken care of until I return. Arkadas!'

He pulled the lieutenant to one side and kept his voice low. 'Do whatever you can to keep Ridderhof and, gods help us, *especially* Botrys, from coming up to the village until I can get this mess cleared up. You understand? We get the payment agreed and arranged today, we are out of the mountains for winter, yes? You, me, Tauras, Keds, the whole crew. Like the old days. We'll winter at the lake, eat that breaded fish you like. The one with the crumbs.'

Tight lines showed beneath Arkadas's eyes, his mouth pursed. 'I'll occupy them for as long as I can, captain. But I will not lie. I will not deceive my company commander, nor his staff.'

'Of course not, Arkadas, nor would I ask you to. Nor would I countenance the same myself, of course.' Of course. 'Now I must away before matters overtake me once more.' He pulled the document wallet from his coat and checked the contents.

Arkadas followed his eye. 'What's that, captain?'

'Just something I prepared for the "negotiation", at our aggressor's request. Do you know where my razor is? I swear someone has appropriated it from my effects.'

'You're shaving, captain? Now?'

Manatas covered the darkening of his cheeks by slapping his hands against his face and rubbing. 'The, uh, company commander is present, lieutenant. We should look the part.'

Ree limped hard to keep pace with Vida, who seemed determined to reach the stores before the sun was much over the north-eastern peaks. Ree tried to keep the strain from her voice.

'No warmer than before breakfast.'

'No.' Vida glanced briefly in her direction. 'Your leg any better?'

'It's fine,' Ree lied, locking her face so the winces wouldn't show.

They topped the narrow rise, the cliff falling away to their left, the sheer grey face of the Grandfathers, as the villagers called the wall of rock, to their right, and began their descent into the village proper, which to Ree's disappointment was only marginally easier on her leg. Ahead, in the square before the Council House, Ree saw what from size alone could only be Keretan, horsing around with at least three children of varying sizes – although none, of course, as massive as he. She squinted. Younger than she'd have expected for a man of his age, but it was quite likely they were his. Beyond Keretan and his tumbling offspring, she made out Gumis in the shadow of the Council House, his baton of office in hand, apparently engaged in some kind of . . . ritual dance?

She almost pulled up short. Sword forms, he was doing sword forms, but with a short wooden stick, and very, very badly. The word amateurish barely did it justice; this was a level of practice somehow multiple levels below 'enthusiastic debutant'. Yet, as they made their pained way down the slope, she could see the rictus of effort on his face, the gleam of sweat on his brow and arms. He was taking it enormously seriously. Mani was off to one side, sitting on what would be a pitch for a stall on market days, not so much beaming with pride as offering indulgent encouragement. Ree didn't see Camellia, or the other one, Volkan, the one who seemed to look down his nose at everything. She realised she was relieved by their absence.

'Well,' Vida grunted, 'I'm going to the stores.' She gestured to the winding path that led up the sheer rockface that loomed over the village. 'Coming? Might take a little while.'

Ree craned her neck, taking in the dark zigzags carved into the rock, the handful of thick ledges and plateaus, and dark openings that might have been caves. There was that mechanism at the top of the uppermost, featuring plenty of dangling ropes. 'Your stores are up there?'

'High places are safe places,' Vida replied. 'I'll be back with your shoe. Don't wander off.' She set off towards the base of the cliff without looking back, her assumption that Ree wouldn't follow stark and, it turned out, well-founded.

Ree cast around for somewhere to wait, and found Mani had spotted her, and was waving her over. At least someone was pleased to see her. Gumis grunted and swished on before him.

'Come on, kid,' she said, and only then realised that she was alone.

Javani had been within a few paces of her mother and the others when she'd spotted Anri. He emerged from the thick foliage at the pasture's edge, bow slung over his shoulder, quiver at his back, an armful of what looked like snares over one arm. Without consciously meaning to, she diverted towards him, her boots kicking up spray from the waterlogged grasses.

'You,' she said as she closed on him. He gave no indication of noticing her approach, but she knew that he knew she was there. 'You owe me an apology.'

At last he deigned to notice her, a slight inclination of his head as he strode straight past her and carried on up the rise, arrows bobbing in his quiver.

She hurried to catch up. 'I said, you owe me an apology.'

He barely looked down. 'Oh, do I, now?'

'You do.'

'And why's that, then?'

'Because you were a dick to me yesterday!'

He laughed, a short, harsh bark, the mirth never reaching his hooded eyes. 'Oh no,' he said, increasing the length of his stride.

Javani had to break into a trot to keep pace. 'You could have been polite, or considerate, or even just—'

'Polite and considerate to the child who nicked my bow and lost my arrows, is it? Who's supposed to be apologising here?'

They crested the rise and descended the narrow trail to the village, but instead of following the others down towards the square, Anri went wide around the village perimeter, heading down the path towards the stables and the lower terraces and, eventually, around to the waterfall. Javani stuck with him.

'Those your snares? Are you going to set them somewhere new?'

'No, these are blessed artefacts these, gifts from the heavens, fallen from the sky. I'm taking them to the temple, I am, so pilgrims can come and worship in their radiance.' He rolled his eyes. 'Of course they're bloody snares.'

'You're a very unpleasant person.'

His smile was bright and toothless. 'So people keep telling me.'

'How did you get so good with a bow?'

'It's the strangest thing, right, I'd never picked up a bow before but one day a child started following me around asking daft questions and I found suddenly I could put an arrow in anything I wanted. Apart, perhaps, from said bloody child, mind.' He mimed being struck by sudden inspiration. 'Unless . . .'

'You practised a lot, is that it?'

'Of course it is, you sheep's fart. How else does anyone improve at anything? Meditation on a hilltop? Finding meaning in the soulless grind of existence? Pig shit.'

They descended to the next terrace down slippery steps, Javani doing her best not to stick out her arms to keep balance. 'You say that, but teaching helps, doesn't it? Before the practising. Someone must have taught you how to hold a bow, nock an arrow, how to—how to stand right!'

His eyes narrowed, although he still didn't look at her, and he grunted.

She pressed what she considered to be her advantage. 'How long are you going to be out with the snares? Vida's got to shoe one of our ponies, it'll be a while before we leave. You could give me a quick lesson, just, you know, one . . . for the road?'

He came up short and rounded on her, jabbing a grubby finger into her face with his free hand. 'Now listen to me, clever girl: I want nothing to do with you. You are not my bloody problem.' He swept the hand around. 'None of this is. So stop following me around and bother someone else. Leave me alone.'

He turned on his heel and marched away, leaving her at the base of the terrace steps, alone but for the whispering rush of the waterfall. She watched him striding off towards the rope bridge, towards the thick forest on the south-western slope, some of which still had a reasonable covering of leaves.

'No,' said Javani.

'What's he doing?' Ree whispered to Mani, as they watched Gumis flex and grunt. She already knew the answer, but wanted someone to confirm it, to admit what this absurd pantomime amounted to.

'Training,' the old man replied with a bristly smile. 'Constable Gumis believes it is his duty to keep himself fit and ready at all times.'

'Ready for what?'

He wouldn't be drawn. 'For whatever Ar Ramas requires.'

Ree watched the constable whirl and swing, sweat flying from his stocky frame. Keretan and his brawling brood had packed up and dispersed, and Mani and Ree sat alone in the square but for the occasional preoccupied villager, sole witnesses to the 'training'. 'Gumis is the law around here, then? For the whole settlement?'

Mani frowned, his brilliant white brows meeting like amorous caterpillars. 'The law, such as it is, comes from the Council, and the Council comes from the people.'

'The Council are elected?'

'We are.' He paused for a moment, one gnarled hand pulling at the ends of his moustache. 'Although, in truth, elections are infrequent, and there has been little interest in change. We've had mostly the same Council body for years, barring absences.'

Ree thought of the two empty seats in the Council House. 'Nobody's stood to replace them?'

He spread his hands, his stick resting between his knees. 'People have been happy with how things are.'

'And now?'

'Who can say?' He pulled a sad smile, his hands returning to the stick to rest. 'Life's only constant is change.'

'You mentioned before, about not harming animals. Is that a common sentiment around here?'

'It's true, I will not hurt a sentient creature, or have one hurt in my name. There are a few of us who adhere in Ar Ramas. But it is not a law, just an outlook, and we have no quarrel with those who act according to their own outlook, to their own needs.'

'So no meat?'

His smile redoubled in the face of her doubt. 'No meat. And little of the milk that is owed to kids and lambs. We have more than enough to eat without causing suffering.'

She nodded at his robes and cloak. 'You still wear wool, though.'

He laughed, and ruffled the cloak around him. 'Indeed. But the animals need shearing, or they struggle beneath the weight of their coats. And in skilled hands, it hurts them no more than a haircut would me.' He patted his hairless dome. 'In days past, at least.'

'And you really get enough nutrition?'

'I'm still here, am I not?'

'Incontrovertibly so. I don't know how, though.'

His laugh was squeaky and scratchy, like his voice. 'The same as with all things. Lead with love, and love widely. Treat all you meet as friend and sibling. You can change the world with hard work and with love.' Her expression gave her away. 'You're sceptical.'

'I've seen the world changed by a lot of things – cunning, treachery, violence, greed, certainly lust . . . but rarely love.'

His eyes were steady and kind. 'And what kind of change did those things produce?'

Gumis had apparently finished his training. Without acknowledging his audience, he wiped himself down with his kaftan, then shrugged it on and belted it, before swaggering off in the direction of the rope bridge, the baton at his belt. Ree watched him go with one eyebrow raised. Across that bridge lay the bandits. Somehow the ridiculous Gumis was the settlement's only line of defence.

'Mani, you're a wise man; what do you truly think of the situation with these supposed mercenaries?'

'I'm an old man, Just Ree – don't confuse being old with being wise. Volkan is a younger man than me, and the gods know he's far wiser.'

'Is he, really? He seemed like kind of a prick.'

Mani chuckled. 'A wise prick, perhaps. His heart is in the right place.'

'Perhaps his autopsy will one day prove definitive on that.'

Sweeper came running past, from the direction of the bridge. He dashed past them and went straight into the Council House, his blank-eyed face giving nothing away.

Ree felt the slightest uptick in her pulse. 'Well, that's unlikely to be good.'

Mani just sighed and stretched out his shoulders, preparing to stand.

A moment later, Keretan came surging out of the Council House, as impossibly vast as ever, Sweeper in his shadow. He marched straight to where Ree and Mani sat. 'Looks like you're needed,' Ree murmured to the old man as Keretan loomed over them. Once more, she found herself glad of Camellia's absence.

Mani's smile was persistent if strained. 'Keretan, what tidings?'

'An emissary from the company is at the bridge,' the big man replied in his booming voice. 'He has come to . . . renegotiate.' He seemed almost surprised to be saying the words out loud.

Ree did her best to keep her smile to herself as Mani pushed himself upright with his stick. 'Shall we see what he proposes?'

Sweeper coughed, in a nervous but insistent way, and Keretan swung his heavy gaze on Ree. 'He is expecting our . . . representative.'

Mani's mouth was an O, his moustache drooping. 'Our what?'

'"The vociferant lady with the white hair, and the fair countenance,"' Sweeper recited, in an impressive rendition of the mercenary captain's drawl.

All their eyes were on Ree.

She pushed herself upright beside Mani. 'Shall we see what he proposes?' she said with a bright smile.

FIFTEEN

Keretan kept easy pace with Ree's limp as they approached the rope bridge. For a man who seemed habitually confident and unruffled, a clear note of uncertainty had crept into his manner – at least in Ree's opinion.

'I'll admit, I am surprised,' he rumbled as they neared the waterfall and its ravine. Ree saw a cloaked figure waiting at the bridge's far end, seemingly alone, obviously pacing. 'I had thought your actions had created needless friction and distress, but the man seems genuinely . . .' Keretan paused, mulling his words, '. . . enthusiastic. There may be a pleasant outcome to all this after all.'

Ree said nothing, but her mind was working like a wind-driver in a gale. An enthusiastic negotiator? What games were they playing? One last desperate attempt to weasel supplies from the village before they all fled the mountains for winter? She shivered under her cloak. The air had a particular bite that morning.

'I don't expect you to understand our ways,' Keretan went on, 'but I hope you will respect them, as we respect you and your daughter in turn. I don't know why this man is so insistent on dealing with you, but I hope you will keep the needs of Ar Ramas, and its people, uppermost in your mind when you talk.'

Ree stopped. 'You're not coming?'

He looked down on her with grave grey eyes. 'It would be improper. He has come alone, and requested you as our representative. We should, of course, be gathering the Council, deliberating on the right course of action, but . . . if we can conclude this unpleasantness swiftly, why risk the delay?' He released a heavy breath. 'Your daughter mentioned that you were once a diplomat. If you were able to improve our lot through negotiation, well, you would have the gratitude of all in Ar Ramas.'

Ree met the force of his gaze, and found herself feeling somehow ashamed. 'I'll see what I can do,' she muttered, and made for the bridge.

Anri slipped through the forest, and Javani followed. She might not be a skilled hunter, or tracker, or any cop with a bow, or indeed much of a forest person in any respect, but all the weeks of travelling into the mountains with her mother had forced her to learn a few things through a combination of necessity and sheer osmosis, and while she knew she'd never match Ree in any number of other skills, she could at least move quietly and smoothly through the brush in pursuit of her quarry. He'd crossed the rope bridge and headed up the slope into the trees, travelling what looked a fairly well-worn trail, and hadn't looked back once. Javani smiled to herself. He had no idea she was tailing him.

What did she want from him? It was simple, although it took her a little digging into her own thoughts before she'd turned over a mental rock and found her answer. She'd told him the truth – a short, sharp lesson with the gloomy sod could probably improve her archery no end, or at least give her something to think about should she ever get a chance to practise again once they moved on.

But why did it matter? That was the key, and the answer had surprised her, and chilled her a little too. She knew Ree outmatched her in competence on every conceivable level; her existence had posed many challenges from her earliest days of consciousness, but Ree's unflappable confidence and varied expertise had left her with a curious mixture of pride and insecurity, even back when Ree had merely been Javani's Adult, and not her ma. Ree seemed to know everything, both factually and historically, and had travelled widely, with the linguistic skills to match. She read people as easily as books and asked difficult questions. And, to Javani's horrified fascination, her mother was also highly skilled with both blades and crossbows, and had little compunction about using them if she considered herself, or her daughter, threatened.

If there was one area where she came up short, though – aside, these days, from tact, which seemed bleakly ironic for a former diplomat – it was as a teacher. Javani wasn't sure if it was a broader failing, or the specific nature of imparting wisdom to her own daughter, but when it came to direct instruction on practical skills, she was dreadful. Not that Javani wasn't an equally dreadful student, of course, but that was to be expected: she was young and wilful, after all.

The end result of this was a competent but frustrated Ree, and a perennially incompetent and frustrated Javani. It didn't help that Ree wasn't much of an archer herself (add that to the list of her mother's faults), not that she'd admit it (and that one). But here was a chance to get some tutelage from someone with no relationship to her, no fraught and exasperated history, and someone who could most definitely shoot. A chance to learn, and finally excel.

It was a chance to surpass Ree at something.

And that was the part that had brought her up short, one hand against a damp trunk. Even before they'd been mother and daughter, Javani had kept Ree on some kind of figurative pedestal, if only to lob imaginary stones at. She'd known Ree was skilful, resourceful, hard-working (and hard work) and resolute. But since what had happened in Kazeraz, Ree's panic and slapdash revelations, and her injury, Javani had suddenly begun to see her in a different light – and not just as her mother. Ree was fallible, and she was getting old.

Not very, it was true – she was *barely* middle-aged, and had always had great skin – but from her grumbles about her leg, the weather, her breathless struggles with the steeper climbs, that faultless aura had tarnished, and been ebbing since. Her hair had always been white, although Javani had faint memories of Ree dying it different colours for a time, but whereas once it had looked incongruous with her striking vitality, nowadays it seemed . . . unremarkable.

As someone had suggested to her not that long ago, but before she was ready to recognise the notion, Javani had started to imagine a world without Ree – or at least a world without the Ree she'd known all her life thus far. A different, diminished Ree, who might all of a sudden start needing Javani's help and support, instead of the other way around.

Javani wasn't completely oblivious. From what she knew, from second-hand experience as well as anecdote, people her age could transform into adults with shocking suddenness, just at a time when their progenitors were losing the lustre of their own prime. Well, she was ready, and had been for a while. Sudden adulthood couldn't arrive fast enough, as far as she was concerned. She could do with a growth spurt for starters.

But in the meantime, she was going to get better than her mother at something. And if that meant breaking this cantankerous hunter to her will . . . so be it.

Anri had reached a clearing, striding past stumps and torn roots towards a row of huts at the far side. This must be one of the timber works she'd heard mention of. Javani paused in the cover of the trees, then began skirting around the near side of the clearing towards the huts. They really weren't that far from the waterfall and the rope bridge; the path had wound its way up the hillside to this relative plateau (presumably to make it easier to get the logs down), but she thought she could probably bellow from here and be heard by Gumis, assuming he was back on duty – Sweeper had been minding the bridge when she'd crossed in Anri's shadow, unresponsive to her cheery wave. Maybe he'd forgotten who she was. He had taken a fair few blows to the head. It was like he'd looked right through her.

She kept low, sliding from trunk to trunk at the clearing's edge, watching Anri as he approached the huts. Now she looked at them, she noted that most were fairly rough and ready – labourers' temporary shelters, maybe, when felling and sawing up here and caught in a storm – but the one at the end, standing apart, was a far more substantial construction. Strong beams and thick walls, a ribbon of smoke rising from its verdant roof, drying pelts on racks outside. It was to this hut Anri walked, still without a backwards look, without any hint he was aware of his pursuer. Javani was almost glowing with self-satisfaction.

He stopped at the low door, took a long, slow breath, then rapped on the frame with a curious, off-beat rhythm. A moment later, the door opened and a smiling woman appeared, definitely someone Javani recognised from the village but couldn't name. Anri mumbled something to her, and Javani couldn't catch her reply as she scuttled further forward, but she saw Anri reach into one of his satchels and pass the woman the drooping form of an ex-rabbit, a presumed victim of one of his snares. The woman bobbed her thanks, called something back inside the door, then set off across the clearing the way Anri had come, fastening her cloak (thick, woollen, inevitably) around her shoulders as she went.

Javani shuffled closer. Curious.

There was a rough window in the hut's side facing her, its thick-cut shutters hanging open to let in what little light the grey day could offer. Holding her breath, Javani scuttled the last dash to the hut's wall, huddling below the window, just as Anri ducked inside the door and closed it behind him.

'Hello, love,' she heard him say, 'how are you keeping?'

She listened breathlessly for a reply, but made nothing out.

'Not a bad haul, for the time of year,' Anri went on. 'Two animals, although one has gone straight to Sara for her pot. I'll go out again later and reset the loops. Further out, this time, things are getting a mite busy downslope, they are.'

Javani strained her ears. She could hear nothing beyond the sound of him moving around the hut, unpacking his gear, arranging furniture. She wondered if she dared peek in through the window. On a dim, grey day like this, she'd be silhouetted but wouldn't cast that much of a shadow.

'Oh,' Anri's baritone rolled out again, 'there's someone you should meet.' He raised his voice. 'Are you going to skulk out there all day, you little pest?'

Javani's mouth fell open, her cheeks already burning.

Shit.

'My lady Ree,' the mercenary called as she stepped off the slippery bridge and placed a grateful foot on the oozing mud of the promontory. 'As you requested.'

He extended a long-fingered hand, holding a single sheet of parchment.

Ree didn't take it. 'What's this?'

He took in a short breath, his head dipping, arm still extended.

'When last we spoke, you made a point of requesting – in writing, no less – an itemised account of the services rendered by my company for the people of this place, over the term of what I will consent to call our former contract.'

'Huh.' Ree tweaked the parchment from his grip. The writing was not the professional script of the contract; this was spidery, rushed, littered with crossings-out and misspellings. Somehow this tickled her.

She scanned the list. 'Most of this is just the same thing written different ways: protection.'

He nodded, hard. Ree noted he was freshly shaved, with only one small nick at his jawline. 'That is, after all, the primary service of my outfit.'

'But protection from what? What conceivable threat is there to these people, this high in the mountains, so far from anyone and anywhere else, other than yourselves? Not even the bastard Guild can trouble them.'

He raised a warning finger, glaring at her over its mottled tip. 'There's worse than us in these hills, I can tell you that for a fact. These mountains are about swarming with bandits and deserters, vagabonds and hoodlums, any and all of whom could pose a vile threat to this place and its people.'

Ree folded her arms, one eyebrow raised. 'I mean, you're just describing yourselves there.'

He sniffed again with a small, rigid shake of his head. 'Not two summers back, a chapter from my company rooted out a bandit gang that were preying on travellers along the southern trade road, ran them off and has protected all comers since.' He began counting on his fingers. 'Just this year, a dear friend of mine and her chapter suffered terrible losses fighting back the encroachment of said Miners' Guild on these free lands.' He bounced to the next finger. 'It's common knowledge that there are hidden bands of deserters holed up in the remotest parts of the Ashadi, even this high, survivors of the slaughter at Flywater, where ten thousand died and the river ran red for a week.'

He gripped his last finger tightly and locked eyes with her. 'And the whereabouts of the notorious Copperhand, the assassin of Nishak, are still unknown, but he and his gang were last seen travelling west into these mountains. Who's to say they didn't come this way, and all that kept them from slaughtering the inhabitants of this place – just as they did every man in the fortified camp at Helia – was the presence of my company?'

'Yeah, sure, who's to say,' Ree sighed. 'Just like my tiger-repelling brooch.' She rattled the clasp of her cloak. 'It must be working, I haven't been attacked by a single tiger.'

He twitched, taking half a step back. 'Don't joke about tigers,' he reproached her.

'Listen— What was your name? Mandlebras?'

'Manatas. Inaï Manatas.'

'Ah, that's right, your mother was Tabashti.'

A measure of the reproach faded from his expression. 'That she was.'

'Manatas.' Ree took a deep breath. 'You're clearly an intelligent man, at least as far as I can tell.'

He looked back through narrowed eyes. 'Thank you, I guess.'

She waved the parchment. 'You know this is nonsense. I know this is nonsense. Tell your buddies to pack up their stuff and get out of here. Leave these poor people alone.'

He didn't waver, meeting her gaze with clear, steady eyes. 'My lady Ree—'

'Just Ree.'

'—You're clearly an intelligent woman, and someone who can appreciate the nuances of a situation that is growing more complex as we speak. I will, in light of the frank tenor of our conversation thus far, continue to speak with candour, in the hope that through this expanded understanding you will gain an appreciation of the gravity of the position I advance.'

'You're not one to end a sentence on a whim, are you?'

'That I am not, my lady, but sometimes the expression of an idea in its most accurate form requires the most accurate vocabulary, and I will not apologise for applying studious effort in service of the noble art of communication.'

'I'll take your word for it.'

'Then do me the courtesy of listening closely.' He placed one hand on his mailed chest, and pointed with the other into the mist across the valley. 'This morning, the captain-general of my company, Elco Ridderhof, the very man I spoke of at our last meeting, arrived at my camp. He did so in the company of his staff, his private guard, his officer cadre, and all the associated hangers-on that make up a military column and its baggage. In addition, the relieved remains of several other chapters are his fellow travellers. My camp has swelled threefold at a stroke.'

Ree wrapped the cloak around herself as tightly as she could, hugging her body beneath it, and showed nothing on her face. 'Go on.'

'He was not due to arrive for days yet, but – for reasons not worth dwelling on – news reached him of our, uh, situation here, and he has proceeded with alacrity, and an intent to remedy matters in a direct and forthright fashion. If I return to him now, and I mean now, and tell him that the contract stands, that payment will be made as agreed, and this afternoon at the latest, then these travellers, these hardened, hungry soldiers, will not settle here. They will take the payment, and they will move on, and I will go with them. Do you understand? If the payment is made today, in full, or . . .' he winced, flashing white teeth in a grimace, '. . . or as close as will make no odds on the counting, then *everyone's* troubles are over.'

He gazed at her with dark, wide eyes beneath raised brows, imploring, exhorting her to understand.

'Troubles of your making,' she growled. 'You know this is extortion. Cut through the bilious cloud of your words and the threat lies plain beneath. I owe it to these people not to cave to your tomfoolery.'

'I do not recognise that assessment. And while others may be charmed by your constant insults and belittlings, I am afraid they leave me cold. This is your chance to deal with me – I meant what I said when first we met, I am a fair man – before others step in. Do you know how my commander got his nickname?'

'I don't, and nor do I care.'

He twisted his hands together, jaw clenched tight. 'You are a frustrating person to negotiate with.' He seemed to remember something, and a note of accusation entered his tone, his brows lowered.

'Are you . . . Are you working for someone? Are you a provocateur, sent here to make trouble?'

'What in the name of the gods would make you think that?'

'That little bolt . . . I am aware that the Guild seeks to spread its malign influence ever further from the plains, and only they are—'

'No. We can agree on a mutual antipathy to the Guild in general, but, on this, consider me solely the voice of your conscience.'

'Then what—'

'Give up. Go back and tell your commander and your "company" there will be no agreement, so you can all leave together.' She stepped closer, offering back the parchment. He took it without looking. 'That's what you want, isn't it? To get out of here? To go home? Do you have a home, somewhere, Inaï Manatas?'

She hadn't expected his cheeks to darken, or the sudden look away. She'd hit something there with the mercenary captain, something wholly unexpected. She filed it away for later, as necessary.

He cleared his throat and made a show of stuffing the parchment back into his document pouch. 'I cannot go back to them with nothing. It will not be accepted.'

'What, you need the supplies as rations? Then I advise you and your colleagues take up farming, the soil is apparently very fertile up here.'

'That is not—'

'You said this captain-general does things by the letter. The letter of the contract allows for renegotiation, and this is our position: no further agreement. He, and you, can respect that, or you can admit that this arrangement has no weight without the implicit threat of violence from those on your side to those on this side. And that,' she said, tapping her finger on the cold mail of his chest, 'is extortion.'

He gazed back at her with hurt in his eyes. 'Why are you treating me like this? I wanted to talk to you because I thought if I told you everything, you'd . . . Can't you see I'm trying to help these people?'

'You have a unique way of showing it.' She thought of Keretan's words. *The needs of the people of Ar Ramas*. What they needed was to be left the hells alone. 'Still, they're more generous than me back there, so how about a pity payment to clear off. Ten per cent should get you on the road. Don't look back.'

His hands were pressed to the sides of his head. 'You don't know what you're doing.'

Ree offered him a sad smile. 'You're not the first man to say that to me. Yet here I am.'

It was about then they heard the horse coming up the road behind him.

SIXTEEN

Anri met Javani at the hut's door, holding it open for her with a sarcastic flourish. 'What's wrong with you?' he muttered as she slunk towards him. 'Made myself clear, didn't I? You might as well come in out of the cold, then, last thing I want is your frigid corpse stinking the place up.'

The hut was small, warm and solidly built. A modest fire burned in a tidy fireplace, where a blackened iron pot of something bubbled on a hook. Most of the wall opposite the window was taken up by a raised bed with a straw mattress, piled with fleeces. A cot bed lay beside it on the floor, thin and low in comparison.

'This is nice,' Javani said, in an attempt at pretending she was a proper visitor. 'Good joinery.'

'Should think so and all,' Anri grumbled as he moved to the fireplace and stirred the pot. 'Built it myself, didn't I?'

Javani wasn't sure it was a question. 'Did you?'

He gave her a flat look, head tilted. 'Yes, you ghastly little afterbirth.'

She pursed her lips and looked around. 'Bit uncalled for,' she murmured, then came to a sudden stop. There was another person in the room with them.

In the corner beyond the fireplace, someone was sitting in a rough-timbered rocking chair, gazing in the direction of the open window. It was a woman, small and impassive, her legs wrapped in thick-woven blankets. She had to be around Anri's age, perhaps younger – the hair that crept from beneath her knotted scarf shone black and silver in the firelight – but her face had a perfect stillness to it, devoid of the pits and furrows that weathered the hunter's features.

'Gods, hello,' Javani stammered. So that was who he'd been talking to. To her surprised annoyance, she'd forgotten all about the one-sided conversation in her shock at being caught. The woman wasn't looking at her, hadn't reacted to her presence at all. 'I'm sorry, I didn't, uh, see you.'

The woman didn't reply. She was nearly motionless, but for the slightest rocking of the chair, her gaze lost somewhere through the open window, into the grey mists beyond. Javani was beginning to get the impression that this behaviour was a permanent state of affairs. Her eyes still on the woman, she turned towards Anri.

'Aren't you going to introduce us, Anri?'

He gave the pot another stir, deliberately not answering her promptly. Eventually satisfied, he banged the spoon against the pot a couple of times for good measure.

'This is Tanith,' he said at last. 'Tanith, this is an idiot child that won't stop following me.'

Tanith gave no reaction, rocking gently, eyes on the view through the window. Anri bustled over to a polished wooden table where he'd laid his pack and satchels, and set about clearing it.

Javani was trying not to stare at Tanith. She was breathing, and rocking, and blinked periodically, but that was about it.

'Who is she?' she said quietly. It seemed disrespectful to raise her voice, as if the woman were sleeping, despite her wide-open eyes.

Anri let out a sharp, angry breath through his nose, a snort of pestered exasperation, which Javani thought was pretty rude considering he'd invited her into the hut and must have expected she'd have questions about the silent woman in the corner.

He didn't answer for a moment, still busy with his pack. 'She's my wife.'

Javani inclined her head in acknowledgement. 'What's wrong with her?'

He stiffened, his back still to her. She briefly considered a pre-emptive apology, then discarded the thought. He had little enough respect for her already, why blow what was left?

He turned fast, one finger raised. 'Nothing's wrong with her, you chopsy shit! Now make yourself useful, crumble this cheese into one of those.' The pointed finger gestured to a fat block of hard, white cheese, and a stack of wooden bowls on a shelf beside the fire.

Javani retrieved a bowl and joined him at the table, where he was softening dried flatbreads with water from a clay pitcher. She stood her ground. 'You say that, but she's sitting in the corner in the middle of the day doing not a lot but rocking on that chair, and she doesn't seem to know that either of us are here—'

'She knows,' he growled. 'She knows.'

Javani crumbled the cheese. It came apart in pungent clods. 'That's as may be, but she's hardly joining in our lively banter, is she?' She tried to meet his eye. 'Come on, Anri. What ails her?'

'Nothing that concerns you. Finished with that cheese?'

She passed him the bowl by way of an affirmative.

'Good, now get out.'

'What?'

'Go on, off you piss. You should be warm enough to make it back to the village without carking it from here, although I'd stake nothing on it I'd care to see again. Now begone.'

Surprised, baffled, and more than a little hurt, Javani wandered to the door. He'd not even offered her any food.

'Bye, Tanith, it was nice to meet you.'

'Begone!' Anri bellowed, and with his shout ringing in her ears, she left.

Manatas stared at Ridderhof as he dismounted his horse once more, then remembered himself and saluted. The captain-general had removed some of his armour, but was still puffed and rotund beneath his cloak and padded outer garb.

'Excellent,' he barked in his ridiculous accent, 'we are not too late for the negotiations.' He came striding over, and Manatas realised with horror that Botrys was riding up behind him, along with half a dozen others.

Ree shrank back as the commander approached, easing back towards the bridge with evidently uncomfortable steps. There was something wrong with her lower leg, Manatas had noticed, an old injury perhaps. She always seemed to lean to one side.

Ridderhof came to a halt beside Manatas, his hands on his hips, surveying the spread of the village across the ravine. 'Botrys,' he called, 'you were right. You were absolutely right.'

Manatas cleared his throat. 'About what, was the adjutant right, commander?'

The captain-general leaned in and spoke with what he presumably considered a low voice. It was clear he had not yet had time to wash since his arrival at the camp. 'This place, its size, its wealth! They have grown so much since my last visit, and look at the size of the grain stores, the stables. Look beyond to the cultivated land, the trees cleared for timber, the scale of their works. This place is fat, and ripe, captain.' He glanced at Ree, who lingered by the bridge, her eyes darting between the new arrivals and Manatas. 'This is their representative?'

'It is, commander.'

'Excellent. Botrys!'

The loathsome adjutant strutted over and handed a sheaf of documents to Ridderhof with a smirk of great pride. Ridderhof slapped them straight against Manatas's chest. 'These are the new terms. Present them. They have until sundown to accept.'

'Or what?'

'Or our protection expires.'

'Meaning what, commander?'

'We care for those under our protection, captain. Once our shield is removed, who knows?'

Manatas swallowed, sentences suddenly hard to form. 'Commander, they're, that is, a payment will be forthcoming this very day.' He glared meaningfully at Ree as he spoke, his words loud enough to carry. 'There's no need to—'

Ridderhof stepped into his line of sight, his watery blue eyes blood-shot but magnetic. 'Present the new terms, captain,' he said quietly. 'They can afford very much more, so we take what they can pay.'

Manatas could feel the tension in his brow, like someone had knotted a rope around it and was winding it tight. 'But, commander, isn't that . . . extortion?'

The corners of Ridderhof's moustache fluttered as he smiled. 'It's commerce, captain: supply and demand. They have the supplies, we make the demands.' Botrys laughed despicably loud at that, but Ridderhof was already speaking again, this time without mirth. 'There's a clause in the new contract that allows for the stationing of a full winter garrison here, along with associated extra costs. I suggest that you see this new arrangement proceeds smoothly, captain, or you may find yourself cutting latrines from frozen turf in the hills over winter. Am I understood?'

It took all of Manatas's strength to ignore Botrys's leer.

'You are, commander.'

Ree followed them all back to the Council House with furious steps, the stabs of pain in her calf the feather on that particular cap full of shit. That had been an ambush, a fucking ambush, and for all that preening fop's talk of honesty and helping each other out, his pink, round commander had rolled over the pair of them like a fallen oak. She'd overheard enough of their conversation to know that it was a waste of time reading the new terms; if she'd found the initial contract insulting, this one had the potential to burst every vein in her head.

She walked in Keretan's enormous shadow, inasmuch as he had a shadow on the drab, cold day, and seethed. It wasn't her business, of course. She and the kid would be off soon, once Vida had finally shod that pony, and they'd filled their packs and saddlebags with fresh supplies, as Keretan had promised.

A small, nasty thought occurred, jabbing her sharp enough to falter her stride: what if Keretan and the Council gave away all their surplus to the bandits? What if they had nothing left to honour his promise to her and the kid? What would they do then? Push on, without enough food or fodder? Turn back? Unthinkable. Or . . . She swallowed. Stay in this place? After what had just happened? She glanced up at Keretan, whose face looked like it could have been hewn from granite. He'd studied the contract. He was taking the contract back to the rest of the Council. He'd said nothing to Ree at all.

Staying was unlikely to be an option. She was sure they'd honour their promise. They were desperate to be rid of her, after all – especially after this fiasco.

She trudged on, furious, frustrated and, beneath it all, ashamed. She was the one who'd demanded renegotiation, who'd stirred things up. But instead of upping sticks, the so-called mercenaries had doubled down. The fucking gall of them! She and the kid needed to get out of here before things got any worse.

Camellia was waiting on the Council House steps, her face a picture of taut anxiety. Ree avoided her eye, easing to a halt as Keretan continued. She bent to rub at her aching calf as the big man handed the bundled contract to Camellia, but she heard clearly the woman's sigh of relief. Relief?

'A contract? This is agreed?'

'We have until sundown,' Keretan rumbled.

Camellia was flicking through pages, scarcely reading their contents. 'We must tell them yes. We must tell them we agree, right away.'

Nine hells, woman, Ree muttered to herself, do you not even want to see what you're signing away?

'The terms are,' Keretan paused for a moment, 'aggressive. Live animals for festival slaughter among them.'

'Equilibrium,' was all she replied. 'A return to peace.'

Ree's eyes were shut very tight beneath her palms as she stood, trying to fight down her every instinct.

'Peace,' Keretan grunted in return. Her eyes still shut, Ree thought she detected a note of reproach in the word. She thought of the gleaming but mangled armour that hung inside the Council House, some kind of monument to battles fought, and, presumably, won? Keretan had been a lancer, and from the state of that armour he'd known battle, and survived. He couldn't be delighted at the prospect of being taxed out of existence by a bunch of brigands with a tame notary.

'Thank you, Ree.' Camellia was addressing her. She opened her eyes. 'Keretan tells me you negotiated this resolution. I am grateful that matters didn't escalate further. Thank you for putting pride aside.'

That was too much. 'Now hold on a moment,' Ree began, one fist clenching before her face. Keretan raised a slab-like hand.

'I know this is not the outcome you wanted.' His voice rolled over her like a boulder. 'It is, in truth, an outcome that none of us wanted here.' Camellia squawked at that, and went to speak, but Keretan rolled over her too. 'We are a fortunate community, rich in soil, in animals and climate. We cherish our families, our friends, and a chance to simply . . . be. That is what matters most.' Ree thought of the large children she'd seen him horsing around with earlier that morning. When he spoke of cherished family, she knew he meant it. That made her think of the kid, and not entirely unhappily. Come to think of it, where was she? She'd been behind them when they left the smithy . . .

'We must be allowed to live in peace,' Keretan finished, and Camellia nodded her emphatic agreement.

Ree ran her hands down her cheeks, dragging her features southwards. 'You're going to agree these terms? These odious, punishing, noxious terms? You're going to hand over the fruits of your labour, of your cherished families' labour, to these *pirates*, who do nothing but sit on a hillside and scratch themselves?'

'Peace must be preserved,' Camellia affirmed in a tone that she might use to a particularly slow child. Ree could feel the vein at her temple throbbing, the one beneath the old scar.

'Whatever they take, we'll produce more,' Keretan added. 'We will endure, and we will grow, and we will flourish.'

Ree tried to keep the pitch of her voice within acceptable bounds. 'And then what happens? You grow more, they take more. That's exactly what happened this morning! They saw you were thriving, they increased their demands accordingly. This has nothing to do with payment for services.' She noticed others gathering in her periphery, that girl Lali who acted as scribe to the Council and a handful of others she'd been introduced to along the way, Farrad and Solheil and Yasha, their disapproving stares impossible to ignore. She tried to lower her voice further, her words coming in an angry hiss. 'They are stealing from you, and you are getting nothing in return.'

'You're wrong.' Camellia's voice was quiet but firm, her eyes limpid. 'We get to live in peace. We get to live.'

Ree held her gaze, feeling the heat of her breath in her chest. 'At least you acknowledge the truth beneath,' she muttered. 'If you'll excuse me, I need to see a smith about a horseshoe.'

SEVENTEEN

Somehow, in the time Manatas had been away, the camp had transformed itself. Walking in the captain-general and his adjutant's wake, he passed picket guards at a marked perimeter, then crossed a wide area of cleared brush. A crew had taken down a handful of stout trees already, and were working on others with axes and saws, while the felled trunks were split into stakes by another crew. They'd begun earthworks, too, marked out in pegged rope lines with coloured flags. Tents formed even ranks either side of the camp's centre, and the grand pavilion of the captain-general, looming out of the thinning mist. The survivors of Keds's chapter had been subsumed, as had the shabby effort where Ioseb was continuing his convalescence. Manatas's own tent, he noted, had been moved, cleared away from the rise he'd set it on. He could only hope it hadn't been relocated close to the latrines.

Heartening as it was to see a real camp again, he wished the contrast with its previous state under his command wasn't so stark. He scratched at the collar of his mail. It didn't look like a temporary encampment, but maybe this was just how the circus travelled. He'd heard stories of the troops of the old Taneru empire of the distant south, constructing something akin to a fortress every time they stopped for the night, but it had always sounded like a lot of effort to him.

'Commander?' He quickened his pace to catch Ridderhof's horse as what looked like the camp's new gateposts approached. 'How long do you expect we will be staying here, before we commence our onward journey?'

The captain-general glanced down from his swaying perch. 'That depends, captain, on how long it takes to put matters to rest with the villagers. If they pay promptly, we will depart promptly.'

Manatas kept as close to his commander's mount as he dared without being kicked by the man's boots, trying to leave the chasing Botrys well out of the conversation. 'And if they don't, commander, and our, uh, protection expires?' He swallowed, his voice a fraction above a whisper. 'We're not really going to attack them, are we?'

Ridderhof barked a laugh, sending up a flutter of grey-feathered birds that Manatas didn't recognise from the balding trees around them. The commander leaned over in his saddle, matching Manatas's murmur with a hoarse stage whisper of his own. 'No, captain, we will not murder a village of innocents for their winter stores.' He righted himself in the saddle. 'Of course, they may not see it that way, and feel inclined to disburse to us from caution, and we will have no complaints.' He tapped the side of his bulbous nose. 'It would certainly be in our interest to give them that impression, yes?'

Manatas matched the man's mirth with a weak smile, his breathing suddenly a little easier. 'Yes, commander.'

'We will take what we can, and be off, captain, very soon. Don't wrestle with your undergarments. It makes marching difficult.'

They passed into the camp, and sentries Manatas didn't recognise saluted them. Ridderhof trotted his horse towards the grand pavilion without another word, Botrys at his heel, who gave Manatas a look of deep suspicion as he passed.

'Have you inflamed the lord adjutant's displeasure, captain?' Arkadas was at his shoulder. He must have been waiting for Manatas's return.

'That fool sees conspiracy everywhere,' Manatas sighed, watching the adjutant and his commander dismount before the tent and hand their reins to waiting grooms. 'Too stupefied to follow the workings of the world, he assumes others connive behind his back to arrive at pre-agreed conclusions, instead of working things out as they go.'

Arkadas inclined his head. 'Why do you suppose that is, captain?'

Manatas blew air through his teeth. 'My guess, it's what he'd do, were the chance to present itself. Only the gods know why Ridderhof keeps him so close.'

Arkadas shuffled, uncomfortable. 'I'm sure he does good work for the company, captain.'

'You're right, Arkadas, I shame myself. It's unworthy to snipe.' He waved a hand around the camp. 'I see our new arrivals have been busy.'

'Indeed they have, captain. I took the liberty of relocating our tents to flank the commander's.'

'It's not downwind of the latrines, it'll do nicely. Is it my imagination, or do there seem to be more people here than there were this morning?'

'Inaï!' Keds was striding towards them from the direction of her tent, her face tight, the knuckles of her fists pale.

'Keds, what's the commotion? Arkadas was about to explain to me why there seem to be ever more people in my camp.' He looked at her again. 'What is it?'

The lines around her mouth were deep, her eyes wide. 'Catastrophe.'

Vida was making to leave the forge as Ree reached it, her leg throbbing. 'My apologies, I have the iron for your shoe but it will have to wait a time.' She had the decency to look a little pained. 'I'm needed for the exchange.'

Ree stared skywards. It was still murky overhead, and a cold wind blew through her cloak and stung her cheeks. 'They're doing it now?'

'Preparing. Everything was dispersed after yesterday's affair. I don't know when the exchange is planned for, but the Council voted to accept the terms without delay.' She gave a narrow, rueful smile. 'Sweeper was just here.'

Ree interlaced her fingers and squeezed. So much for taking the long way around to clear her head; the rage had come roaring right back.

Vida cleared her throat. 'I will shoe your pony as soon as I can.' For a moment, she looked like she was going to pat Ree on the arm, but abandoned the effort. She nodded, once, then resumed her preparations.

The kid stuck her head out of the hut's doorway. 'Ma? Where have you been?'

'I could ask you the same question. Get over here.'

'Do I have to? It's warm in here.'

'Now, kid. My leg is too sore for kicking through any more horseshit.'

The kid slunk out of the doorway, a cloak borrowed from Mariam draped over her skinny shoulders. 'What?'

Ree raised a finger that was not quite trembling with suppressed fury. Calm, she told herself, you're not angry at the kid, you're angry at the short-sighted cowards who run this place, and you're leaving this very day. Although she was a little angry at the kid.

'Kid, I'm all for you having your independence and following your instincts and all that, but I think we need to recognise a few things.'

Surly eyes looked back, the merest hint of bottom lip projection. 'Like what?'

'Like the fact that a lot of your instincts are going to stink like an abattoir in summertime. Like the fact this valley is swarming with ever-greater numbers of murderous bandits, who may very well not be above hostage-taking, or worse. Like don't go fucking wandering off into the woods without telling me where you're going!'

Her chin jutted. 'What? You wandered off too, I didn't know where you were either.'

'Because you weren't there to tell! And I am a grown adult woman, rich in years and experience, and still, as we have seen, not immune to making cock-eyed miscalculations. You don't even have the benefit of experience.'

The kid inflated, her eyes balling. 'What happened to partners, Ree? What happened to taking decisions together, treating each other as equals?'

Her finger was up again, and now it was wagging. 'I never said equals, kid, and it should be abundantly clear as to why.'

Vida cleared her throat. 'I can, ah, come back,' she said, edging towards the hut door.

Ree put up a hand, forcing the ire out with her breath. 'It's fine. Sorry, Vida.'

The kid gave her a lopsided look. 'This isn't really about my behaviour, is it?'

Ree's return glance was emphatic. 'It is a bit.' Her stern look faded, and she gave a regretful chuckle. 'But I think it's fair to say I've found a rich source of frustrations this morning.'

'Then we both have,' the kid added, and Ree made a mental note to follow that up. For now, her attention was back on Vida, who seemed about ready to leave.

'Tell me something,' she said. 'Do you support the Council's decision?'

The shutters came down on Vida's face, her expression immediately neutral. 'It's not for a simple smith to second-guess the Council.'

'And Mariam? What does she think?'

'We're of a mind. We just want to work our craft and get things done. We stay out of Council business.'

Craft. Ree thought of what the kid had found, the bow and the bundle of arrows. 'So. We know you can make weapons. What's stopping you making more? Just a lack of materials?'

Vida said nothing for a moment, her features still blank but her eyes calculating. The smith was shrewd, despite what she might call herself. Would she deny it? Demand to know how Ree knew about the weapons? No, Ree thought, she'll jump straight to—

'We like it here,' Vida said, 'and it's against the rules.' She sniffed, rubbed at her chin. 'The odd arrow for Anri they'll overlook. More than that, well . . .'

The kid was leaning forward. 'You'd be punished?'

'Excommunicated. I doubt we'd be overtly exiled, but we'd certainly be marked, ostracised. And that would be no good for Mari.' She coughed, rubbed her hands together. '"Exclusion for warmongers and weaponsmiths, those who would threaten our children and bring violence to our homes,"' she murmured.

Ree gave her an appraising look, her brows tight. 'The wording of the law? Or a direct quote from someone?'

Vida met the look with seeming indifference. 'You should relent a little on Camellia. She's the heart of this place. You don't know her history.'

Ree affected a shrug. 'And she doesn't know mine.'

'Speaking of history,' chirped the kid, 'what's wrong with Anri's wife? Is her condition why he's so unpleasant?'

Ree flicked her attention back to the kid. 'What *is* wrong with Anri's wife?'

'That's what I want to know.'

Vida made a face, halfway between a polite smile and a grimace, her blunt features scrunched. 'I'm late. I'll see to the shoe later.' She set off from the forge.

'What about Anri?' the kid called after her, and Vida paused for a moment.

'Mariam will be back soon,' she said with a heavy sigh. 'She hates to gossip, hates to.' Then Vida turned and resumed her march.

The kid stared blankly at Ree. 'What good is someone who hates to gossip?'

'When they can't help themselves anyway?' Ree said with a grim little smile. 'Pretty good indeed.'

Under the pretext of inspecting the new location for his tent, Keds led Manatas and his lieutenant up the slope to the rear of the camp, overlooking the commander's pavilion and the ranks of tents spreading away from it. A couple of unfamiliar sentries nodded at them from what would soon, it seemed, be the new perimeter. In the distance, Manatas could see Tauras helping erect a palisade, probably without being asked.

'There.' Keds gestured with little more than her eyes, her voice a low growl. Weak sun pawed at the thick cloud overhead, its wan light just enough to draw the lines on her face in deep relief. She looked so tired.

Manatas followed her instruction. A cluster of new figures were at the camp's far edge, five or so, their clothes and armour dark against the golden leaf carpet beyond them, their cloaks the colour of ash. No pack animals that he could see, definitely not part of the circus; he'd have remembered them if they'd arrived with Ridderhof and company that morning. They carried satchels and tall packs, and many, many weapons, most of which they were in the process of racking and unpacking in their new quarters.

'Who are they?' he whispered. The men had an aura to them, or perhaps a demeanour: there was no levity in their movements or grunted communication, no joking or joshing, or even smiles at completing what must have been a long march. Instead, they simply focused on the task at hand, whether it was erecting tents or inspecting and cleaning a set of wide-bladed hand-axes, with sour expressions and thousand-yard stares.

'Seventh Chapter,' Keds replied, looking away up the slope, anywhere but at the new arrivals. 'We had some . . . dealings. A lot of them are Pashani.'

'Pashani? As in, Pashan Eren?'

She nodded, the rings in her braids tinkling softly.

'I thought they were all wiped out.'

'Sadly not,' she growled. He tutted, and she shot him a look. 'You know what Pashani did to my family, Inaï.'

'Doesn't mean what was done to them was right.'

'You think it's a coincidence that those who escaped were the worst of all?' She jerked her chin, jaw tight. 'See who approaches your commander.'

'He's your commander too, Keds,' Manatas admonished, looking past her shoulder at where Ridderhof was barking instructions at Botrys and his cadre of notaries. A man was walking towards him, from the direction of the Pashani. He was dressed in similar fashion, dark mail, grey cloak wrapped twice and drooping. He had a sort of sideways walk, head down, eyes looking up through strings of lank hair, his face half-obscured. Something about his shuffling walk made Manatas uncomfortable. It was as if he was approaching the commander and his staff without anyone noticing him, slipping through their vision. Manatas felt increasingly compelled to shout a warning.

'Who is that?' he said instead.

Keds had bared her teeth.

'A fucking demon.'

EIGHTEEN

Manatas reached the commander's pavilion just after Keds's demon. He'd skidded around the corner and slowed to a brisk walk, trying to disguise the urgency of his arrival as he trotted past the guards at the entryway.

'Lado, commander, reporting,' the man was saying with a flourishing salute. He was talking through his hair, but Ridderhof seemed indifferent, his eye on a sheaf of documents, his ample frame propped in a tall-backed chair and boots stretched out on a revolting bearskin. Manatas did not look at it. 'Of the Seventh.'

'Ah, our comrades in the east,' Ridderhof barked, not looking up. 'We were expecting to come to you, not the other way around.'

'We've been travelling this way for a time, commander. We have been forced to roam by tactical necessity, most recently into the mountains.' Lado's accent was urban, from somewhere beyond the plains, nasal with short vowels, but he had a Vistirlari cast to his features. Manatas's brain caught up as the man went on. 'The lads and I are here early, it must be acknowledged. We were notified of a serious wounding to my cousin, Ioseb. Do you know of his condition?'

Ridderhof looked up at this, finally taking in the wiry, travel-stained man before him. He managed to keep all but the barest flicker of distaste to himself. 'For that, we will require his chapter captain, who I believe cannot be far— ah, Captain Manatas.'

Manatas saluted as he stepped forward, less ostentatiously than Lado, but at a level he considered decorous. 'I am happy to report that Ioseb's wound is minor, and his recovery continues apace.'

'Such news gladdens my heart.' Lado's face, hard as it was to read through the drooping hair, suggested otherwise. His voice was quiet, strained almost, and it set Manatas on edge. Everything about the man set him on edge, his lopsided stance, the long-handled blades at his belt, the coil of his fingers beside them, the way the filthy tail of his cloak dragged through the mud. Gods damn Keds, she'd primed him to dislike the man before they'd even been introduced.

'Chapter Captain Inaï Manatas,' he said, one fist to his chest. 'Of the Ninth.'

Lado nodded, hair swaying before his pallid face. 'Lado of Cstethia. No noble chapter captain, I. Just a humble man-at-arms, grateful for the honour of his tour.'

Ridderhof sniffed. 'Where is your captain? Will those on rotation be coming to us, or shall we meet them on our descent?'

'It grieves me greatly, captain-general,' Lado said in his whispery voice, hand on his heart, 'to report that our captain has perished, and two lieutenants with him. Formal notification will be incoming, and I'm sure your capable staff will appoint successors in due course.' As the captain-general huffed in surprise, Lado reached up and swept a swathe of his hair behind one ear, and Manatas saw deep scars down the man's cheeks. They looked too regular to be from battle, but a moment later the hair fell back into place, and his view was lost. 'Others, however, will definitely be joining us.'

Ridderhof puffed out his cheeks. 'Very well. We will await official notification before acting. Concerning your comrades, we will be here a day or two longer, after which we must try to meet them en route.' Ridderhof sniffed again, and wiped his nose on the back of his hand. The morning was still sharply cold, even in the close air of the pavilion. 'Was there anything else, man of the Seventh, before you are dismissed?'

Lado bowed his head, the hand back at his mailed chest, the very picture of a humble supplicant. 'Only, captain-general, on where the matter of restitution has come to rest.'

'Restitution, soldier?'

'I was notified that my cousin was grievously wounded, and while it cheers the soul to hear of his fortuitous recovery, I feel bound by my familial bond to ensure he is well cared for in his convalescence.

I hope you can forgive my impertinence, captain-general, but what will be the nature of his compensation?'

Ridderhof's moustache twitched. 'His pension will be adjusted, no doubt, albeit an amount befitting the nature of the injury. I will leave the details to Botrys and his staff. Was there anything else?' The angle of his wiry brows made it clear the captain-general had much to do, and Lado was encroaching on his valuable time.

'Only to know the fate of the perpetrator of this crime upon my cousin's person.' Lado's eyes were tight with constrained passion behind his dangling hair, or at least so it appeared. 'I assume punishment was swift and fair, and the redress was paid promptly, or perhaps added to the outstanding tally?'

'The redress.' The captain-general seemed struck by the notion, his lips pursed in thought. 'Captain Manatas, the redress?'

Manatas swallowed, acutely aware of the attention of all of the company's senior staff. 'Given the, uh, minor nature of Ioseb's injury, and the manner in which it was suffered—'

Lado's hooded gaze was on him immediately. 'Manner, captain? What was the manner of his mauling?'

'Don't interrupt an officer,' Ridderhof murmured with a half-hearted wave of his hand. 'What was this manner, captain?'

Traps, traps everywhere. There was no way Manatas could confess to his commander that discipline in his chapter was so lax that Ioseb had brought his wounding on himself, but a failure to protect his troops and an indifference to diligent finance would make him look no better. He chose his words carefully. 'Given that the injury in question was sustained at a delicate time, vis-à-vis our contractual arrangements with the clients, and that subsequent negotiations proved fruitful with,' he glanced at Ridderhof, 'more favourable terms, I took the decision to waive redress in this instance.'

The captain-general grunted, apparently satisfied, but Manatas could feel the burning gaze of Lado's half-hidden eyes. He had no wish to make an enemy of Keds's demon, not when they could all be gone from this place the next day, and he need never see Ioseb or his cousin again. 'Again, commander,' he added, 'as the wound has proved shallow, and Ioseb has,' Lado's eyes hadn't moved, 'impressive powers of recovery, it seemed imprudent to make an issue of what happened in the face of our other, positive, outcomes.'

Ridderhof clapped his hands. 'There. Satisfied, man of the Seventh?'

Lado bowed his head again. 'How could I be otherwise, captain-general? My thanks to you and your capable staff.'

The captain-general gave a half-nod and a vague wave. 'Dismissed. You too, Manatas. See to your camp.'

'Yes, commander. Thank you, commander.' Manatas cursed himself. Lado's obsequious manner was contagious. Still, at least he'd got away with the Ioseb Inquiry. He was ready to breathe a sigh of relief as he left the pavilion.

Lado was waiting for him outside, his head tilted to one side, hair hanging loose. Manatas saw his scars clearly in the grey daylight, two deep grooves from cheekbone to jaw that flexed like a crescent moon when he offered Manatas a dreamy smile.

'Captain Inaï Manatas,' he said. There were flecks of silver in the dark of his eyes, and the corners of his teeth were filed. 'I've heard of you.'

Manatas held himself straight. 'Only good things, I trust.'

Lado held the smile. 'Friend to mindless animals, but no friend to his men. Be seeing you, Captain Inaï Manatas.' Then he was away with his shuffling, swaying walk, sliding through the camp, like a blade between ribs. Manatas shuddered.

'Arkadas!'

His lieutenant was not far. 'Captain?'

'How is Ioseb? His recovery continues?'

'I've not checked in on him since dawn, but he seemed well enough then. For Ioseb.' Arkadas's brow furrowed with concern. 'Is all well, captain?'

'I have no idea, Arkadas. I have no idea.'

Javani took the seat closest to the fire while Mariam prepared the last of the tea. For dried dung, the fire didn't smell too bad. Tarfellian seemed to approve; the enormous dog was laid out beside it like a sandy barrel with legs.

'There's more food on the counter,' Mariam said, her attention on the gleaming samovar, 'help yourself if you're hungry.'

Javani helped herself, pointedly ignoring Ree's disbelieving headshake. She was a growing girl, after all.

'You said you had questions, did you?' Mariam was still focused on the tea, her long hair tied back well out of harm's way. Javani noticed pale scars on her forearms, bumps and lines. Probably burns from crafting or cooking; Javani had known one woman in Kazeraz who seemed to burn herself every time she used the great clay oven in the square, no matter how she tried. Her forearms had been a lattice of angry scars, but she'd persevered. At the time, Javani had wondered why she didn't just ask someone else to handle her baking for her, but now it made her think of her own attempts at archery. Some things were a matter of pride.

'We hoped you might provide some insight,' Ree began, leaning back on her stool to rest her leg, 'on a few matters of interest.'

'We're after gossip,' Javani clarified brightly. One of Ree's eyebrows was up at the corner, her mouth a thin, peevish line. Javani continued to ignore her.

Mariam laughed as she passed over the tea cups. 'Clearly you've been talking to Vida, then. What gossip would it be?'

Javani folded her arms before her on the table, palms down, and leaned forward. No point prevaricating around the thingy. 'What's wrong with Anri's wife?'

Mariam seated herself neatly opposite, her steaming tea cup in both hands. 'Ah, Tanith.' She drew her mouth tight, and for a moment Javani thought that for all Vida's proclamations, Mariam would tell them nothing. 'Well, you'll be leaving soon, so I suppose it can't hurt.' She leaned incrementally forward, and from the corner of her eye Javani spotted Ree doing the same. Secrets were about to be shared. The hairs on Javani's arms were standing up, and her skin tingled.

'Well, the truth is,' Mariam began, then took a slow breath as if readying herself for a gruelling feat of endurance, 'I've got no idea what's wrong with her. Nobody does.'

'Not Anri?' Javani wondered at the heat of his retort – *Nothing's wrong with her*. Was it that he just couldn't answer the question?

'Not Anri, not Camellia, not Mani, not anyone in the settlement. We have a few folk with knowledge of the healing arts in Ar Ramas, but her affliction is beyond any of us.'

Ree cleared her throat. 'Catch me up here, what is her affliction?'

Mariam gave a puzzled laugh. 'Didn't you hear? I just said nobody knows.'

Javani turned to her mother. 'She sits in a chair all day, staring at nothing. At least, as far as I could tell. Didn't seem to know what was going on.'

'Like, confused?'

'No, like, I dunno, indifferent. No reaction to anything, just staring. Anri had someone from the village looking after her when he was out.'

'That'll be Sara,' Mariam provided. 'She and her family live up near the bridge. Nice girl, prone to tall stories, mind.'

Ree was chewing her lower lip, brows lowered. 'She's catatonic?'

Javani shrugged. 'You tell me.'

Mariam was nodding. 'Aye, that's the word for it. Not much spark to her, like.'

'For how long? Continuous, or in spells?'

Mariam made a face, her mouth pulled down, her free hand raised. 'Anri claims he has conversations with her, and I know in the early days she had good days and bad, but I reckon it's only got worse. I'm not sure she's been, you know, with us, for a good spell now.'

Ree sat back again, stretching out her leg. Tarfellian gave a happy huff from beside the fire. 'And no one knows what caused it? She just . . . dropped down, one day?'

'I know they travelled here together, but as it was told to me, she fell ill during the journey. Short spells at first, then more prolonged. He was near carrying her when they arrived.'

Javani rested her chin on her hands. 'Is her illness the reason he's, you know, how he is?'

Mariam gave her an even look, brows raised, eyes steady. 'And how's that, then?'

'A dick.'

Her laugh woke Tarfellian, who huffed and replaced his giant head on his paws. 'Between you and me, I reckon that's just Anri. I don't think he's changed much.' She leaned back with a sigh. 'He's never really been one for the community, always preferred to be outside, unbound.'

'Did you know him before?' Javani asked. 'You have similar accents, I wondered . . .'

'Not really,' she sighed. 'We took different paths. He's a cousin, maybe, or a cousin of a cousin . . . one of the few who came when Vida and I sent word.'

Ree sipped at her tea. 'And you and Vida keep him supplied with arrows and the odd bow?'

Mariam's cheeks darkened, but she didn't look away. 'Know about that, do you? He's outside the village, so it's not like we're really breaking the rules, and he hunts and snares more than he could ever use himself, so as I see it—'

Ree's hands were up. 'No need to convince us, truly.' She bent forward and massaged her leg. 'What about Camellia, though? What's her story? Does she have family here?'

A hint of reproach entered Mariam's eyes. 'I think you could say that Ar Ramas is her family – some of the younger folk call her Mother Camellia, but she's got no children here. I heard talk of a spouse, long ago, but no, she's by herself. Well, apart from the Council, and the weaving and spinning, and the planning, and the new building work and all, the water mill was her idea – she's busier than anyone here, and we're grateful for her.'

'Vida called her the heart of this place.'

Mariam folded her arms, her tea resting on her elbow. 'And I agree with Vida.'

'And this new agreement with the bandits? What do you think of that?'

'I wouldn't know.'

'You're not moved by their offer? Protection from bears, birds, and the dreaded Copperhand?'

'That's not nothing,' the kid murmured. 'Didn't he and his gang kill a hundred men in a night?'

'I heard it was a thousand,' Mariam declared, momentarily distracted. 'In absolute silence, so the story goes.'

'And is the story worth what you're paying?' Ree said quietly.

'I think,' Mariam replied, her arms now tight across her, 'that it is Council business, and me and Vida keep out of that.'

Ree was leaning forward again, her dreadful wagging finger on the rise. 'And that's something I wanted to ask about, because—'

A rap came from the door, followed by Sweeper's muffled voice. 'Mistress Mariam? Vida said to tell you they're going ahead with the exchange.'

Mariam rose to her feet, cup still in hand. 'Now? Vida's not taking it out, is she?'

'I hope to the gods Sweeper's nowhere near it this time,' muttered Ree, twisting towards the door.

Javani, the least encumbered, opened the door to reveal the battered and downcast form of the village dogsbody. He barely seemed to register her, his eyes somewhere on the threshold – although one was still so swollen it was unlikely he was seeing much with it. In the grey daylight, he seemed older than she remembered. She'd pegged him as a young adult, but – and perhaps it was the effects of his wounds, the pained shamble of his walk – on fresh inspection he seemed closer to Ree's age, deep lines around his unswollen eye, silver strands winking from his hair in the feeble, cloud-choked sun.

'No one's taking it out,' he said to the floor. 'They're at the bridge. They've come to collect.'

NINETEEN

Manatas had been surprised that Keds came with them to the exchange. He'd left Arkadas in charge of the suddenly expanded camp and its burgeoning population, and, once more in Ridderhof's mounted shadow, he, Tauras and a small crew that he, if not exactly trusted, then certainly didn't distrust as much as he distrusted the others in his chapter, had set off for the bridge.

Keds had fallen in beside him without a word, marching in step like the old days, her stride matching his. For a while he'd just enjoyed the comforting familiarity of her presence, reminding him of a simpler time, or at least one where he'd awoken each day without a sharp throbbing in his temples and a crushing sense of inevitable doom. He'd missed Keds. He'd missed her company, her humour, her insight, and of course her skills and capabilities. It was with a rare sense of hope that Manatas found himself walking: Keds had returned, the exchange, with ever-richer terms, was imminent, and would be followed in short order by his departure from this distant, isolated place. For the first time in a while, things were looking up.

Then she spoke.

'We need to kill him.'

She kept her voice low, her face forward, her expression fixed and neutral. She ignored his startled reaction, and his uneasy glance at the commander's armoured back, a few paces ahead of them.

'You mean, presumably . . .' Lado, Keds's demon.

'I do.'

He spoke at a little above a whisper. Not only was the captain-general riding directly in front of them, but Tauras was close behind and liable to request clarification at high volume of anything he overheard and didn't follow. 'Kediras, we can't just kill the man. He's a contracted soldier of the company, for a start. We'd be in breach of half a dozen of our own by-laws, duty-bound to hunt ourselves down and deliver ourselves for judgement and restitution.'

This time her eyes did flicker towards him, her passive mask marred by the slightest curl of her lip. 'I'm not suggesting we do it in public, Inaï. But that man cannot stay here. He is poison. He will taint this place with his presence, and the longer he stays, the worse it will be.'

From the corner of his eye, he could see the tension in her brow, the muscles working at her jaw. Keds rarely displayed outward emotion; the same intensity in Tauras would have resulted in bellowing and possibly ripping the arms off something. 'What did he do, Keds? Why is he your demon? I found his manner to be both fawning yet oddly aggressive, but he said nothing out of turn, nor did he act untoward. And he's no son of Pashan Eren.'

'He and his Pashani comrades are the reason that my chapter is dead.' She was near spitting now, growling each word like a death-curse. 'He brought the Guild on us all, and fled in their path, led them straight to us.'

Manatas nearly pulled up short. 'Wha— how? By intention?' He rubbed at an eye, still trying to keep his voice under control. 'Keds, to call this serious would be to understate to an egregious degree. We could take this to Ridderhof, have him—'

'There's no proof, Inaï. Nothing to convince, or convict. Just my own intuition.'

'Even so, with a clear declaration—'

'You've seen how he is. He makes them like him, those who command.' Her teeth were locked in a grimace. 'Until he doesn't need them any more.'

Manatas thought of Lado's report. His chapter's captain perished, along with two lieutenants. 'How do you know this, Keds? How can you be sure it was—'

Her voice was as heavy as a tomb. 'Where do you think he was stationed before I chased him out? He knew exactly where we were.'

They walked on in silence. They were not far from the village now, he could hear the rush of the waterfall. 'Perhaps we could—'

She took a short breath through her nose. 'It's the only way. He cannot be allowed to stay here, this close to the company commander.'

Manatas could feel a muscle below his eyelid twitching, and pressed a finger to it. 'He came to check on the well-being of his cousin, and should now be satisfied that the man lives, and will be well. There's no reason for him to stay beyond there. Let's get this exchange over and done with, then tomorrow we can all go our separate ways, and never lay eyes on the man again.'

Keds sniffed. 'We'll call that Plan B.'

Ree was surprised to see half the village already turned out before the bridge, or at least what she assumed to be half. The weak sun lit several dozen wool-clad folk clustered around a growing pile of sacks and bags, wreathed in the creeping spray from the fall. She saw chickens and geese in barred crates, and even a sheep and a goat, held by tethers. At the bridge's far side, Sweeper had joined two other, smaller figures, fussing over the same four mules they'd encountered on the morning of the ambush, each now, if anything, more heavily laden than before. Gumis watched over the proceedings from the bridge's far end, his arms folded across his ample chest, the baton of office standing proud from his grip. The mercenaries had not yet appeared across the ravine, but the bubbling anticipation of those present suggested their arrival was expected imminently.

'Ree, how kind of you to join us.' Keretan loomed over those around him, impossible to miss, impossible to ignore. 'You'll find Mani excellent company for the proceedings, no doubt.' With a giant hand, he indicated the stacked timber where she and Mani had sat before, and where the old man was already ensconced, his stick balanced between his knees. He gave her a broad, bristly smile and a cheery nod. Ree sucked at her lip. The implication was clear.

She was gracious enough to assent without argument, and nodded to the kid to follow as she parked herself, one leg extended, beside the old councilman.

'Ordered out of the way?' he asked in his scratchy, jolly voice, and she inclined her head. 'Try to take some solace in the outcome.

When today's affair is completed, the clouds of uncertainty will part, and the light of peace will bathe us all once more – even you, Just Ree. And that's got to be worth celebrating, hasn't it?'

She offered him a tight, grim smile. 'I'd love to believe it, Mani.'

His eyes were guileless. 'Then do.'

Javani spotted him skulking towards the back of the crowd around the supply pile, his bow and quiver not in evidence for once. She sidled up to him, trying to cover her approach with the bodies of the assembled village folk, until she was close enough to surprise him. She stepped carefully into his blind spot and opened her mouth.

'It's you again, is it?' he muttered, not even looking in her direction. 'Not a moment's respite from your pestering to be had, you're a fucking pouch rash.'

She glowered at him. 'What's a pouch rash?'

He snorted and glanced at the silvery sky. 'A rash of the pouch, you gormless moppet. Like you, a scrotal irritation.'

'Who's minding your wife?'

'Who's minding your business?'

Javani stood in furious silence for a moment, breathing hard through her nose. 'How did you know I was coming? You can't possibly have seen me.'

He flicked his gaze at her sidelong. 'The smell, wasn't it?'

She felt herself swelling with rage. 'How dare you—'

'Gods, child, I'm serious. Slept in the stables last night, didn't you. You picked up a healthy dose of ruminant.'

Surreptitiously, Javani pinched a wad of shirt and sniffed it. There was, perhaps, a slight hint of goat. 'I had a bath yesterday and everything,' she muttered. 'It's so unfair.'

'Two in a year won't kill you, mind,' he replied, his attention back on the mustering before them. 'Three might, you'd dissolve.'

She turned to look up at him. 'What are you doing here? I thought you stayed out of all this.' She gave a vague wave of her hand to illustrate her vague point.

He pulled down the corners of his mouth, his peppered beard flexing. 'I do. Just passing through, stopped for a look.'

'You don't have an opinion on all this mercenary stuff?'

He gave an exaggerated sweep of his head. 'No.'

'Come on, seriously. What do you think?'

'What do I think?' He glanced momentarily skywards. 'I think you're the most annoying person I've ever met, your skill with a bow is inversely proportional to your irritating nature, and none of *this*,' he waved his hand in a sarcastic imitation of her own gesture, 'has anything to do with me. Clear enough, or what?'

Without waiting for an answer, he turned and stalked away, stomping over the bridge hard enough to set it trembling. He cuffed Gumis on the back of the head as he passed, just enough to tip the man's woollen cap over his eyes. By the time the furious Gumis had freed himself and determined the culprit, Anri was halfway towards the trees and not looking back.

Javani realised she was smiling.

This time, Ridderhof did not dismount. He stayed perched on his saddle, imperious in the thin afternoon light, wrapped in his layers of armour and sweeping riding cloak. Manatas, two paces behind him and three to the right, was shivering in his mail.

'You're jingling, Inaï,' Keds muttered.

'Undoubtedly from the crispness of the mountain air.'

'It's not that cold, Inaï.'

'Chapter captain,' the captain-general called from on high, 'make the count, sign off the payment, and let us return to camp. We're due a festival feast tonight.'

'We're a little early for Sun's Night, aren't we, commander?'

'No shame in paying our seasonal respects a little early ahead of our departure, captain. See to it.'

'Immediately, commander.'

Four mules and three men were waiting on the near side of the bridge, the former cropping at the thick, wiry grass that grew between the rocks beside the path. Manatas vaguely recognised the first of the mule wranglers, stooped and scrawny as he was, but the livid wounds on the man's face would have made a definitive identification a challenge in normal circumstances. Manatas thought once again of Ioseb and his Vistirlari hoodlums, and clenched his jaw so hard it hurt. Deep breaths, Inaï. We are nearly free of this place.

'Halt!' The screech came from the head of the bridge, where the self-styled village constable was brandishing his baton. 'Come no closer to Ar Ramas until you are officially invited.'

Deep breaths, Inaï.

'If it please you, I am here to make collection and sign off the payment agreed with my company commander. Captain Inaï Manatas? We met already?'

Ree shook her head, incredulous. The skinny captain wasn't meeting her eye, or had not yet noticed her on her vantage beside Mani on the timber pile. She nudged the old man, gently, and nodded towards where Keretan and Camellia stood at the near end of the bridge, as silent and immobile as pillars of stone. 'Why are they letting Gumis handle this? Isn't he going to inflame things every bit as much as . . .' she hesitated, '. . . others might?'

'Gumis is a member of the Council as much as they are,' Mani admonished, then chuckled. 'He may make a lot of noise, but anyone with a functioning mind can see he's harmless. A bit of theatre like this should make them feel like they've earned their pay, don't you think? Honour satisfied on both sides.'

'If you say so,' she replied, one brow arched. She looked around. Where had the kid got to now?

Manatas returned to the captain-general, keeping his pace steady, mindful of all the eyes on him from both sides of the ravine. 'The payment is assembled in sufficient quantity, commander, but there remains a practical obstacle.'

Ridderhof tilted his head forward, moustache flaring. 'Which is, captain?'

'They have only four mules, and it's too much for them to carry all at once. There's also the matter of the live animals, which will not cross the bridge and must be herded across the valley floor.' He gestured with cold fingers towards the secondary pile at the bridge's far side, around which a cluster of chilly and ambivalent villagers were gathered. 'Now we could make two trips, but given the hour and the time required to unload and return, we'd not be finished before dark, so . . .'

The captain-general followed the implication: no feast. 'Indeed. That would be unacceptable, as would returning tomorrow.'

Manatas felt a little of the weight lift from his chest. 'I am in complete agreement, commander. I think if we were to load some of the excess onto your horse, were you to dismount it, we—'

'Out of the question.'

'Commander?'

Ridderhof pointed to where Tauras stood, along with the small detachment Manatas had brought out with them. 'That man looks large enough to carry the animals across. The rest of you will split the remainder between yourselves.'

'Commander, are you sure? We could—'

'You have your orders, captain, and the light is beginning to wane.'

'Yes, commander. Tauras!'

Javani watched the huge mercenary approaching the bridge, and thought she saw genuine fear in his eyes. He wasn't huge like Keretan, a towering obelisk of a man; he was huge across, great thick arms and legs, a barrel chest and stout gut, topped by his fascinating half-shaved head. The idea that he could somehow be afraid of the slick and swaying rope bridge tickled her no end.

'This man will be collecting the additional goods,' the drawling captain called across. 'If you'd be so kind as to assist him, there's a chance we could be finished with this endeavour a little sooner.'

The villagers shuffled back from the pile of sacks and the tethered animals. Apparently not everyone was delighted at the quantity of their yield going to the mercenaries.

'Just one man is permitted. Is he armed?' That was Camellia. Javani rolled her eyes.

'He has relinquished all of his primary armaments, in deference to your customs,' the captain called back. Javani was convinced she could see at least one knife strapped beneath the mercenary's arm, but she wasn't going to draw attention to it. She wanted this nonsense over as much as Ree did; with this unpleasantness resolved, they could finally be on their way.

Although, when she thought about their onward journey, somehow it no longer filled her with the same excitement as before. The notion of finally crossing the last of the Ashadi into Arestan, land of balmy summers and plentiful harvests, and starting their new life at last seemed less appealing than it had. She scratched at her arm. She knew they couldn't stay here, of course. She and Ree had made themselves borderline pariahs in less than two days' stay. But if the people of Ar Ramas just got to *know* her and Ree, they'd like them, she was sure of it. They'd just got off to a bad start. Even people like Lali or Anri, she could win them over. She had faith in herself. She even had faith in her mother.

They just needed this nonsense with the mercenaries over and done with.

Manatas watched Tauras inching his way over the bridge, a leaden feeling in his chest. This was going to take forever. He had no doubt that the bridge would hold Tauras's considerable mass – it looked solidly built, and he was aware that the settlement possessed a surprising number of skilled artisans – nor would it buckle when he returned fully laden. The limiting factor was the big man's own unease concerning heights, no doubt exacerbated by the attentions of what must be half the population of the settlement upon him, rendering his progress little faster than a crawl. But Ridderhof had been explicit. He had his orders: Tauras was the man to go. And the rest of them might just die of exposure or senescence while they awaited his return.

He became aware of sounds behind him, footsteps and muttered voices. He turned, but Keds was faster. He felt her go rigid beside him, and knew.

Sauntering up the path towards them, two of the saturnine Pashani at his heel, came Lado of Cstethia.

TWENTY

Ree caught the sudden movement among the mercenaries from the corner of her eye, some vigilant instinct never completely dropping them from her attention. New figures arriving, a burly, well-armed pair, grey-cloaked, and someone ahead of them, slightly hunched, almost apologetic in his approach. A subordinate making an improper arrival? But the reaction of Manatas and the spare woman next to him implied something else entirely. Something wholly concerning.

Ree slid forward on her timber seat.

'What the fuck is he doing here, Inaï?'

'I am as in the dark as you are here, Kediras.'

'Don't let him near the civilians!'

'On that front, we are in firm accord.' Manatas was already striding to intercept the incoming Vistirlari and his escort. 'Soldier Lado, what brings you out of camp in such unexpected fashion?'

The man's smile was ingratiation itself through the curtains of his hair. 'Chapter captain, I can only offer my apologies for intruding at this delicate juncture, but I fear this news cannot be delayed.'

'News? What news would that be?'

Ridderhof had noticed Lado, and half-wheeled his horse around for a better look. 'Captain Manatas, why are these men here? They are not part of this operation.'

Lado spoke past him, drowning out Manatas's attempted deflection. 'With your permission, captain-general, and with great regret, I fear duty-bound to interrupt, for the facts of this exchange have been altered.'

He put up a hand, his shaggy head bowed. 'If I overstep, forgive me. I will return to the camp without delay, and recommence duties.'

'Speak of these changed facts, man.' Ridderhof nudged his mount closer. Past him, Manatas spotted that Tauras had at last reached the bridge's far side, and was being given a wide berth by the assembled villagers as he trundled towards the mound of sacks and animals. In the meantime, his chapter had taken possession of the mules, and the former herders had scuttled across the bridge in Tauras's shadow.

Lado tipped his head upwards a fraction, while remaining a picture of unctuous deference. 'Once again, captain-general, and with the greatest sadness, I must raise the spectre of restitution.' He straightened another inch, walking slowly towards the commander. 'In the name of the company, we must ensure that the transgressor faces justice, and amends are made.'

He'd raised his voice as he spoke, his words carrying clearly over the ravine to the waiting villagers. Manatas could already hear their whispered reactions, a growing susurration of disquiet.

Manatas risked a reprimand for pre-empting his commander. 'What is this transgression you speak of? For what crime are you seeking redress?'

Lado addressed him, but once again his words were clear, projected for the benefit of their secondary audience.

'What other crime could require such a level of reparation? I speak of murder, Captain Manatas. The murder of my cousin Ioseb of Cstethia. Under the contractual terms agreed, and the company charter, I demand satisfaction.'

'Ioseb is dead? That's . . . He was getting better!'

Lado's shrouded eyes gave nothing back. 'Poison of the blood can kill a man days after a scratch. A tragedy for my family, and for the company.'

The susurration across the bridge had become a hubbub. Somewhere within it, Tauras was picking up bundled sacks, attempting to balance them across his shoulders.

Keds caught Manatas's eye. Her gaze burned with a single message: *I told you so.*

* * *

Javani heard the words from the other side of the ravine, heard the snarl of *murder*, but it took several moments for her to connect the panicky reaction of the villagers with her own actions, and in large part that was only because all of a sudden everyone was looking at Ree.

Javani's neck felt unexpectedly hot, and her throat was so tight. Shit, thought Javani. Shit, shit, shit.

Lado was level with Ridderhof, ostensibly speaking to the commander, but in practice addressing his words to those on the other side. He knows exactly what he's doing, Manatas thought. This is another turn of the screw. But to what end? We're already taking more from them than is prudent – how much more can he demand?

And then he heard it.

'In addition to the punitive measures endorsed in the contract, captain-general, we must insist that the offender be turned over to the custody of the company to face trial.' He softened his voice again, recovering that nasal whine that Manatas had first heard at the commander's pavilion. 'For what sort of company would we be if we did not enforce the peace of mutual protection?'

'Indeed,' replied the captain-general. 'Indeed.'

Ree knew the eyes were on her, all but the ones that mattered most. Keretan and Camellia were still at their post on the bridge's near side, just beyond where the enormous mercenary toiled, apparently fruitlessly, in attempting to carry every one of the extra sacks simultaneously, as well as at least one medium-sized animal. An idle part of her brain wondered if he'd been ordered to bring it all back in one go, or simply thought he had. She felt an element of pity for him either way.

Still no reaction from the Council leaders. Better they think Ree responsible than the kid, of course, but they'd acceded to every demand made by the mercenaries so far without argument – at least with those making the demands. Would they fold in the face of this, and turn her over without a squeak?

Probably.

Shit, thought Ree. Shit, shit, shit.

Then Camellia surprised her. 'You may calculate the cost of your injury, your lost life, and we will pay it,' she called out across the ravine, 'but we will give you no one. Our people are no part of our contract.' Beside her, Keretan stood tall and broad, underlining her words with his presence.

Oh, thought Ree. She was even a little ashamed.

Manatas was thinking as fast as he could, the wheels of his mind spinning, but his thoughts were blurred and useless. Lado had taken the villagers' rebuff in his stride; in fact, he'd likely expected it. He advanced now, wide of Ridderhof, who seemed perfectly content to sit back and watch, wide of the bridge's end and the puffed-up little constable who supposedly guarded it, to where he could address the two village elders directly.

'If you will not identify the culprit to us, nor turn them over to our custody to face trial for the crimes of which they are accused, then I must warn you that the by-laws of our company charter are clear. As a representative of the injured party, I am empowered to enter this place of settlement with sufficient reinforcement to ensure the completion of our task, and conduct investigations to my own satisfaction. Is that not right, captain-general?'

Ridderhof started, sitting upright in his saddle. 'The precise terms are . . . a little hazy in my recollection,' he hazarded. 'If Botrys were here . . .'

'Rest assured, captain-general, that before daring to interrupt your operation, I conferred with the lord adjutant.' Lado had dropped his voice again, once more dripping with deference and barely contained admiration. 'He assured me of the particular sections of the charter, and even furnished me with copies.' Lado patted a satchel at his belt.

'I see.' To Manatas's disgust, Ridderhof looked impressed. 'Then continue, soldier.'

Lado saluted to a servile degree, but the edge to his words was clear to Manatas. 'That I shall, captain-general.'

Ree was watching intently as the newcomer straightened, turned, and began sidling towards the bridge, his previously passive comrades moving to join him. Her palms were sweating. Only Gumis barred their way, his gleaming baton of office gripped in both hands.

'This is bad,' she murmured, for her own benefit as much as Mani's. 'This is very bad.'

'We will not surrender you to them,' the old man replied, his eyes kind but searching. 'Surely you know this?'

She watched the new man's crosswise swagger, the tilt of his head, the wiggle of his fingers, and knew in an instant that this was a man who enjoyed the anticipation of causing pain almost as much as the act itself. They were witnessing a performance, and this was only the first act.

'And what happens then?' she breathed.

The enormous mercenary was still balancing sacks in his arms; he'd now managed to tie several together and draped them over his shoulders, but couldn't seem to keep one set on as he reached for the other. Ree spotted the long-handled knife strapped beneath one of his beefy arms. If he dropped the sacks and started swinging, he could probably kill or maim every one of the assembled village folk without even tiring.

There had to be something she could do.

'You will never enter this place,' the little constable squeaked, his face flushed dark. 'You are uninvited.'

'Oh, I very much doubt that,' Lado replied, continuing his crab-wise advance towards the bridge.

'Come no closer! Another step and you will feel the force of my authority!' The constable hefted the stick in his hand, a thin sort of cudgel, polished smooth. It looked utterly impractical. Manatas thought of the wicked knife he'd seen at Lado's belt, the long, straight swords that the Pashani carried on their hips.

'Keds, we need to do something.'

Her eyes said *You think?* but she was already moving, sliding with quick steps between the Pashani and Lado, one hand on the hilt of her gently curved long-blade. Manatas made for the space between the constable and Lado, marching upright and direct, as if tacitly ordered by the captain-general. As he reached Lado, he spoke quick and low. 'Soldier, while I appreciate your urge for justice and mourn the sudden loss of your cousin, I currently have a man on the far side of this bridge who is midway to ensuring that every one of us in that camp eats well for the winter months, and it is my strenuous inclination that this restorative action be delayed until that man and his haul are returned to us. Do you understand me?'

Lado's eyes sparkled behind his drooping fringe. 'Unless you have orders to that effect from the man on the horse behind us, chapter captain, it is my strenuous inclination that you get out of the way, before an unfortunate misunderstanding occurs.'

Manatas's lips stretched in a grimace of frustration. 'Now, see here—'

'No,' the man replied, and took a step back, then looked past him to where the constable lurked, huffing and sweating. 'While I am glad of the offer, captain,' he called out, his voice echoing from the cliffs beyond, 'I will have no trouble removing this little pig without your assistance. You may step away.'

'How dare you!' came the constable's shriek from over Manatas's shoulder. 'You will show *respect*—' Warning shouts followed, calls from the village side for the constable to retreat across the bridge, but they sounded likely to go unheeded. Manatas kept his eyes locked on Lado. The man's smile beneath his hair was tremulous and growing.

'Throw down your stick and run, little pig,' Lado jeered over Manatas's shoulder. 'Run squealing back to your sty, and let men work.' His hand moved to his belt, resting on the hilt of the wicked knife Manatas had seen earlier. It had a little skull moulded in the steel of its pommel.

Manatas kept his body between Lado and the little constable. 'Listen—'

'Inaï!' Keds's voice was a warning, but without panic. Speeding footsteps behind him, barking breath. Manatas turned sharply, and caught the constable's wrist as he took a wild swing at Lado. The man was huffing and snarling, and Manatas had to sway to one side to dodge a blow from his off-hand.

'That's enough, friend,' he cautioned but, teeth bared, the man grabbed for the baton with his free hand, trying to wrestle himself from Manatas's grip. Manatas felt a profound anger growing within him, not just at the man's temerity at laying hands on him, nor at the stupidity of his actions when all Manatas was trying to do was prevent an incident they'd all regret. No, it was Lado's sneering face in his mind's eye, not two paces behind him as he grappled with the constable, the way he'd stared him down, the quiet contempt of his simple 'No.'

'Sit *down*!' Manatas snarled, delivering a precise punch to the man's abdomen and possibly bruising a kidney. The constable doubled over with a gasp, and Manatas stepped to one side, swivelling the man's wrist around with him until he yelped and dropped the baton. Manatas placed a heavy foot on it, then let the man fall to the turf. He sat groaning and clutching his midriff, his breathing coming in halting gasps, interrupted by sporadic retching.

'I apologise for the roughness of my actions,' Manatas growled through gritted teeth, 'but your ardour left me little choice. Kindly remain where you are for a few moments, and I believe we may yet achieve understanding.' His primary concern was now a rush of angry villagers across the bridge seeking vengeance of their own. He turned towards the bridge. 'People of Ar Ramas,' he called, '—'

'Another murder attempted on our company!' Lado bawled. 'First by bow, now by battery. Their crimes compound! The charter is clear, and this time, justice will be swift.' He closed on the sitting constable in a single stride, the wicked knife already half-cleared from his sheath.

Manatas was reaching for his own blade, seeing Keds in his periphery with her narrow sword leaving its scabbard, when Ridderhof barked, 'Captains!'

They froze, Manatas forced to tear his gaze away from the gurning Lado to his mounted captain-general. 'Commander.'

Ridderhof nudged his horse forward, waiting until he was almost on top of them before speaking again, his voice a little above a murmur. 'In the case that there is some confusion, we do not draw on fellow soldiers of the company. Is that understood? It would be a terrible shame if our clients were left with the impression that we are an ill-disciplined rabble, prone to infighting, yes?'

'Yes, commander.'

'Weapons away, and step back. Now.'

Breathing hard, Keds and Manatas sheathed their blades, then shuffled back from Lado and his Pashani.

Lado still had the gasping constable around the neck, one hand on his half-proud knife. 'And our assailant, captain-general? As you so wisely declared, our laws must be sacrosanct.'

Ridderhof's moustache twitched, and he pulled on the reins, turning the horse away from them. 'Indeed they must,' he said. 'Carry on.'

Manatas was certain he was the only person in the valley to hear Lado whisper, 'At last,' as he pulled the knife clear and held it up to the sky, its fearsome blade glinting dully in the weak sunlight. The constable was kicking and gasping in his grasp, but Lado had an iron grip for such a wiry man. Already, Manatas could hear shrieks and cries from across the ravine as it became clear what was about to happen. Beneath the drooping screen of his hair, Lado's mouth was stretched wide in a rictus of delight.

To his shame, Manatas said nothing, looked away, trying to block the terrified mumbling and frantic, desperate struggles from his mind, doing his best to ignore the plaintive howling from across the bridge. They might be notorious for their lack of armament, but fifty irate labourers could overwhelm the handful of mercenaries that remained with him if the mood took them, which when Lado slaughtered the constable it just might. And Ridderhof would gallop back to the camp, raise the remainder of the company, then come charging back to return the favour. The entire valley would be bathed in blood by sundown, and all because he couldn't stop Lado of Cstethia pulling the wings off this particular fly.

'Stop or he dies!'

Now *that* voice carried above the panicky hubbub. The mercenaries turned as one, looking across the ravine to where Tauras stood, draped in sacks, looking very uncomfortable indeed. Perched on his back, with her legs wrapping around him and his own blade pressed against his throat, was Ree.

TWENTY-ONE

'Huh,' Lado said, then brought the knife in an arc towards the constable's neck.

'Stop!' Manatas bellowed. 'Commander!'

Ridderhof was by now clearly bored of this palaver, thinking only of the feast to come and itching to get away. 'Yes, stop, soldier. While they have a hostage, we should do nothing to imperil his well-being, of course.' He waved an irritated hand.

Lado bowed his head, and the knife disappeared with a sweep of his hand. 'Of course, captain-general. The well-being of our confederates must always be paramount. On your feet, little pig.' He yanked the gasping constable upright.

'Yours for ours,' came the shout across the ravine.

Manatas released a slow breath. A quick exchange of Tauras for the stupid little man with the stick, and they could get back to camp before sunset. Maybe there really would be a feast tonight.

'The captain-general speaks nothing but wisdom,' Lado went on, seizing the man by one arm and twisting it up his back until he squealed. 'We are civilised people after all. We do not exact summary punishment when there can be a trial. Let justice be served for all to see.'

Manatas's breath caught in his throat. 'Commander?' he spluttered. 'What trial? We must return this man to the village immediately, and secure my man's release! Commander!'

'While I would never dream of speaking for the commander,' Lado said, speaking for the commander, 'he is doubtless aware that the pursuit of justice for its own sake is both noble and vital for the continued good order of a company, and that this man has committed a crime against us – you, Captain Manatas, are both witness and victim. He is a reckless danger, and must be confined for the safety of others. As for the man they have taken,' he gestured towards the village, where a host of distressed faces peered back, 'which is, in turn, another crime that will not be forgotten, well . . . Let them try and contain him. If he escapes and returns to us, he is a true soldier, worthy of his contract. If not . . .' Lado shrugged, one-sided. '. . . Perhaps he was unworthy of serving after all.'

Manatas looked weakly to the captain-general. 'Commander, you can't be proposing . . .'

Ridderhof sniffed and gathered his reins. 'The man-at-arms makes a good point. Your man is a professional, and should be able to take care of himself, especially against a village of unarmed farmers. In the meantime, we shall arrange the first of what I expect shall be many trials. But first, it is time to feast!'

With that, he geed his mare and cantered off down the track, lost in the fading light between the trees before Manatas could formulate another thought, let alone a meaningful sentence. Lado didn't even acknowledge him as he and his Pashani comrades dragged the whimpering constable away in the captain-general's wake. Only Keds met his eye.

'I need to . . .' he began, taking a step towards the bridge. 'I have to say something—'

'There's nothing to say,' she said firmly, gripping his arm.

'But Tauras—'

Her gaze was bleak but unwavering. 'They'll probably take better care of him there than in the camp, Inaï.' She pulled him away. 'Come. Now there's nothing left to do but drink.'

Ree watched them go, incredulous, as the mercenaries slunk back into the forest, one by one. The last to go was Manatas, one pointless look over his shoulder before he was lost to the trees. A moment later, the promontory was bare.

'Cap?' the brawny man in her grip said plaintively. He sounded all too much like a lost child. He was trembling a little, and she hoped it was from the day's deepening cold. She wondered how long she should stay wrapped around him. The knife in her hand was getting very heavy, and now the mercenaries had gone, everyone was looking at her again.

'I'm going to climb off you,' she murmured into his well-ringed ear, 'but the knife is staying with me. Don't try and run, don't try and fight – there are archers in the woods, they'll bring you down. Understand?'

'The secret army,' he breathed, and Ree felt her eyebrows climbing. 'Fingers was telling the truth!'

'Yes, exactly that,' she said, and carefully slid from his back. Good as his word, he stayed exactly where he was, fat sacks dangling and swaying from his shoulders. She massaged her arms and aching leg while he stood there; she was not accustomed to manoeuvres like that, not these days. 'Stay there, understand?'

'Yes, c— Yes.'

She blinked. He had definitely been about to call her captain. She took in a long, slow breath, and turned to face the villagers.

The villagers looked more or less exactly as Ree had expected, their expressions a mixture of shock and disbelief, tinged with an anxiety that clearly bordered on the shores of absolute terror for more than a couple. She recognised ever more faces – Asherah and Parvin, Yasha, Farrad, the muscular Solheil behind. Their urgent conversations were impossible to ignore – 'They took Gumis! Took him away!' 'What did he think he was doing, charging like that?' 'Defending the sanctity of Ar Ramas!' 'Defending the outsider, the one who stirred them up in the first place – we should have handed them over to face trial, not one of our own. What if they come back for him?'

That last speaker had been Lali, the girl who took notes for the Council, the one who always seemed to look at Ree as if she were guilty of an unforgivable faux pas, such as farting at prayers with malice aforethought. She had the same look on her face now, glaring sidelong at Ree with a mouth like she was chewing nettles. Gods save me from the baseless ire of fifteen-year-olds, Ree muttered to herself. She caught sight of the kid skulking behind the crowd, peeking from one of the timber piles. And twelve-year-olds, she added, grateful at least that the girl was on the right side of the bridge this time.

Mani was doing his best to calm the assembled villagers, a hunched and wizened one-man defensive wall between her and their ire. He spoke of the need to treat strangers as friends and brothers or sisters, and that mutual affection would bring benefit to all. 'Don't give in to despair, my friends,' he said in his creaky, squeaky voice. 'All of us working together can build a better world.'

Although nobody seemed to have the heart to contradict him openly, it wasn't until Camellia spoke that the dark looks began to settle. She didn't look at Ree, nor at her well-built captive; she seemed to glide straight past them to speak to the worried crowd, which was swelling as news spread across the settlement. She spoke to them in a low, soothing voice, her words hard to pick out, and Ree didn't fancy making an obvious attempt to overhear.

'Mistress Ree.' Keretan was beside her, a dark outline against the silvery sky. The temperature had really dropped now, and with her adrenaline draining away, Ree could feel her jaw beginning to tremble. Perfect timing, just as she was about to receive a roasting from the councillor – he'd think she was on the verge of tears. She tried to clamp her jaw shut, and gripped the long, borrowed knife tight to keep her hands from shaking.

'Master Keretan,' she replied through gritted teeth. Here we go, exile had to be moments away.

'Thank you,' he rumbled, his voice deep enough to rattle gravel, 'for trying to save Gumis. I appreciate what you did, even if it didn't work.'

Ree could only nod and offer a flicker of a smile. Twice now she'd underestimated the councillors, but she didn't want to get her hopes up beyond that. 'He's alive, that's something. Thanks for not turning me and the kid over to them.'

She was relieved to see Vida muscling her way to the front of the crowd, then striding to join them. Mariam was behind her, had spotted the kid and was moving to intercept her before she squirrelled off somewhere again.

Vida kept her voice low, her question aimed at Keretan. 'What should we do with him?'

Keretan lifted his block-like chin towards the captured mercenary, who stood immobile with his back to them, still slung with sacks of produce. 'Why is he still standing there? He could make a run for it if he chose, he's big enough to free himself without anyone here stopping him.'

Ree pulled at her lower lip with her top teeth. At least the shivers were subsiding. 'I, uh, told him there were archers in the forests, with bows on him, and he'd be shot to bits if he moved.'

Keretan's eyes narrowed, his brows tight. 'He believed you?'

She pulled a face. 'He's afraid of the secret army. Besides, your friend Anri is out there somewhere, right?'

One of Keretan's eyebrows twitched. 'Anri may be out there, but he'll not involve himself in this.' He pursed his considerable lips. 'As for what we should do with our new guest, perhaps the ram enclosure—'

'We must release him immediately.' Camellia had joined them, floating over in her long robes as some of the crowd began to disperse. Ree worked hard to not let her reaction show. 'We will not imprison anyone!'

Ree could feel her nostrils flaring, something she'd never been aware of before. It made her think of Anashe, and she hoped the lanky hunter was safe and happy. She'd gone south with the White Spear, perhaps all the way back to Arowan, back to her prospects, both personal and professional. Ree hoped she'd found success. 'Do you want to bring your constable home? That man behind us is about your only hope of seeing him again with all his limbs connected.'

Camellia waved her hands as if chasing away a stinging insect. 'How can you say such a thing? Gumis is our brother—'

'And if you want to secure his release, your best chance is by exchanging him for that bandit.' Ree kept her voice level, her eyes wide and steady. 'Free him, send him back to them now, and you'll have nothing left to bargain with.'

Camellia said nothing, but seemed on the verge of tears. At length she flexed her hands once more, saying nothing, no longer arguing but far from in accord.

Vida cleared her throat. 'The ram enclosure, Keretan?'

The big man nodded. 'It's half under cover, he can keep warm in the stables, and everyone can see him. Do you still have that length of chain? His fear of invisible archers may not hold him forever, and as our guest says, until we can arrange another exchange, we'll need to keep him secure if we're to bring our constable home safely.'

Vida grunted in acknowledgement. 'I still have some chain in the store.'

Ree realised she was still gripping the knife. Her fingers were cold and sore. 'What about this? I assume I won't be allowed to keep it.'

Vida extended her hand. 'I'll put it with the others.'

Ree kept her face neutral as she passed the knife carefully to the smith. Others plural, eh?

Keretan released a mighty sigh as Vida escorted their compliant captive away. 'The people of Ar Ramas deserve to know what's going on, and not from half-heard rumour. I propose an open meeting at the Council House. Camellia?'

The woman nodded vaguely, her gaze blank, deep lines cast in her cheeks by the fading winter sun, then her eyes came into focus. 'It's getting dark. People should be with their families tonight.'

Keretan clapped his hands together and blew on them. 'Tomorrow, then, after prayers. I'll put out word.'

Ree folded her own hands into her armpits for warmth. 'I don't know exactly what those in the camp across the valley are planning, but you might want to consider stationing a watch at the bridge, and at the edges of the village. In the, uh, constable's absence.'

Keretan inclined his head. 'We'll consider it, indeed. Good evening to you, Mistress Ree.'

Camellia went to follow him, then paused and turned back to Ree, who had taken the moment to work some life back into her aching calf.

'Camellia? Was there something else?'

Her eyes were red and glistening. 'I mourn the wind that blew you to our threshold,' she whispered, her voice cracked and tight, then turned and hurried after Keretan.

Ree watched her go in the twilight. 'You're welcome,' she muttered.

TWENTY-TWO

Manatas awoke with a thudding pain in his temple like his skull was being trampled by a cavalcade, and an unshakable sense of deep foreboding. He was the wrong way around in his tent, his head downslope, his boots nestled at the drooping flaps, which had no doubt helped along his headache like a marching drum. He was cold, and sore, and upside down, and somehow the morning seemed far too bright.

Fractured memories of the night before filtered through the fog of his mind as he contemplated how best to extricate himself without a) an embarrassing rear-first exit from the tent in sight of his troops and b) any exertion whatsoever, given the volatile state of his cranium. He blamed Keds, but in the end, she'd been right: there had been nothing left to do but drink.

They'd returned to the camp to find Ioseb already burning on his pyre, Lado leading in the solemn remembrance that followed, while not three paces behind him their prisoner kicked and hissed against his bonds. The Pashani had lashed the man to a tree at the camp's edge, gagged and blindfolded, and largely ignored from there on, aside from being occasionally pelted with food he could neither see nor reach. Manatas hoped someone had moved him closer to a fire before the night watch; given how cold his own tent was, the man might have frozen to death overnight, and the chances of a salvageable outcome would have gone with him.

Ridderhof had had his feast, though; Botrys had seen to that, and the two of them had held court outside the pavilion as the ever-expanding camp of mercenaries gorged themselves on both the proceeds of their payment from the village and the contents of their combined baggage trains. The captain-general had been scooped from his armour at last, and sat florid and sweating in the raucous firelight, Botrys simpering at his every quip.

There were more Pashani than he'd remembered at Ioseb's pyre, and a couple of new Vistirlari too, friendly with Zurab and Rostom, deferential to Lado. Manatas had kept out of the way, drinking with Keds and the remains of her chapter up at their own campfire upslope of the pavilion, Arkadas watchful beside them, and tried not to worry about Tauras.

From there, the memories became increasingly blurred. He remembered Keds, brooding in silence with her sister's flute across her knees, polishing it reflexively. He remembered the whispers, the rumours that seemed to hop spontaneously from group to carousing group without any member appearing to move. Whispers that the village was rich and fat and ripe for the taking, whispers that the company would decamp in the morning and Tauras would be left to his fate, whispers that the captain-general had squandered the company's treasury chasing the blunders of his doltish son and nobody would be paid what they were owed. Dark, swirling talk around the dark, swirling camp.

The knuckles of his right hand were sore. Had he punched someone who'd raised the bear? He hoped not, not again. It was an ugly thing to—

'Captain? Are you rising today?'

'While it is my square intention to become vertical, Arkadas,' Manatas called as firmly as he dared, 'I am currently circumscribed by malicious circumstance. If you would care to both keep your voice to a dulcet minimum and advise on the current level of observation of my predicament, I would be in your debt.'

'Coast is clear, captain,' came Arkadas's whispered reply.

Feeling every thud of his pulse hammered into his forebrain, Manatas shuffled backwards out of the tent into the glaring day. The air was bitterly cold, and his knees felt slick with moisture the moment they cleared the heavy canvas. A few painful moments later, one hand clamped across his eyes, massaging his rebellious temples, Manatas was upright and outside.

'It snowed, then.' His breath was a white plume in his narrow strip of vision. The day's grey dawnlight, meagre as it was, reflected from the soft blanket of snow with fierce intent. He once again cursed Keds and her limitless aquavit.

'It did, captain.'

'Cold enough to slaughter hogs,' came Keds's gravelly voice from somewhere nearby. Gingerly, Manatas removed his protective hand. She was right where he'd left her the night before, perched before the fire, a skin still in her hand. She was alone.

'You're up early, Kediras.'

Arkadas leaned close enough to whisper. 'She has not, as yet, retired to bed, captain.'

'Ah.' Manatas shuffled over to the fire, grateful for the warmth, and squatted down beside her, waving away her offer of the skin with a pained frown. 'What news in the camp?' This was an old company saying, intended to ask after a comrade's general health and well-being, but Keds took it literally, possibly out of obtuse spite.

'Snowy, Inaï.' She took another long drink from the skin. 'We should kill him today. Early. I heard the new Vistirlari talking last night – more from his chapter are coming, and others besides.'

'Kediras!' he hissed, then lowered his voice. 'Truthfully? How many?'

She shrugged with her mouth. 'There are already more than there were when he arrived. I'm not inclined to wait for more to join us for our trip east.'

He pressed his sore knuckles to his mouth, feeling them cool in the chill air, and looked to see if Arkadas had overseen some breakfast. 'I am more concerned with ensuring the safe return of our absent comrade, and the welfare of our unexpected prisoner. Have you seen anything of him this morning?'

Keds waved a dismissive hand, but Arkadas nodded. 'He's alive, captain. Someone was kind enough to put him inside a tent overnight, but I imagine he's far from comfortable.'

Manatas nodded with relief. 'Alive is the important thing. As long as that's the case, we can return him to the village and see Tauras returned—'

'Tauras is in no danger, Inaï!' Keds was staring at him with wide and furious eyes, her teeth bared. 'The farmers won't hurt him, he'll eat better than we do.' She lowered her voice to a growl. 'Worry about us.'

'If we don't see to their man's return, they may exact their frustrations upon Tauras, or come seeking their confederate themselves, and there are many more of them than of us, recent arrivals or not.'

'They're farmers, Inaï. And cowards at that – how else could they have arrived at this plight?'

'Everyone has limits, Kediras, and I have no interest in finding theirs. They don't want to fight us, and I don't want to fight them, and we should endeavour to keep matters to that state.' He stood, massaging his thumping temples. 'As soon as Ridderhof rises, I'll seek an audience. I don't exactly understand his thinking of yesterday, but after sleeping on the matter, I'm sure reason will prevail. That strange little constable hurt nobody, and a trial is a farcical notion. Lado is seeking vengeance for his lost kin, a natural impulse, but he remains a man-at-arms in this endeavour, not a man of rank. Ridderhof can order him to stand down, and stand down he must, however much it pains him.' He rubbed a hand over his re-bristled chin. 'And that being said, I'd have liked a closer look at the departed Ioseb before he was consigned to the lands beyond. That pyre was awful swift—'

'We must kill him, Inaï.' The anger hadn't left her voice. 'We are men of violence, and must be curbed with the necessary means.'

'Don't quote me back to me, Keds.'

'Then get a new catchphrase.'

'I will retire my refrain when it ceases to hold true.'

'*Either we kill him,*' Keds sighed, swirling the last of the liquid in her skin. 'Or he kills us. One way or another. He won't respect the rules – why should you?'

'And what would be the difference between us then? Let me talk to Ridderhof. I'm the ranking captain in the camp. I'm sure in the clear light of day . . .'

He trailed off as the dinner bell began to ring across the camp, an insistent, piercing clanging, not the simple rhythm that called out mealtimes. Already mercenaries were milling around the camp in urgent whirls, converging on the captain-general's grand pavilion. Botrys stood in the entryway, his face ashen, and – to Manatas's horror but somehow no great surprise – his palms rusty with blood.

TWENTY-THREE

There were too many wool-clad people to fit in the Council House, and the meeting had spilled out into the square. There had to be nearly two hundred, their murmured words rising and falling with an anxious edge; they milled fearful, wide-eyed and whispering, swift glances over shoulders to the far side of the valley, which was still veiled in morning mist.

It had snowed in the night, not a huge amount, but enough to crust the ground and squelch underfoot as it thawed, and the valley had a sudden stark, wintry feel that seemed totally at odds with the mellow amber forests Ree and the kid had stumbled through in the preceding weeks. Mist and snow weaved between black, empty trunks, dark slashes against the grey. Ree's toes were cold in her boots, and her breath drifted up before her face in stout puffs. The kid had, once again, wandered off.

It took some time for the Council to decide that enough of the settlement's population had arrived to commence their address. Ree was unsurprised that it came from Keretan – his great booming voice carried easily over the square. Ree could almost feel it coming up through the ground. It was a voice, in her view, accustomed to command. With the rest of the Council flanking him, Mani leaning lopsided on his stick, Keretan did his best to reassure the hundreds of people in earshot.

Yes, their constable had been taken away by the mercenaries, but they expected he would return shortly. Yes, there was now an apparently terrifying professional soldier chained up in the ram pen, but he would likewise be returning to his people in short order. Yes, despite agreeing to new and slightly more onerous terms of protection, the outstanding payment had yet to be made in full, but Keretan and the Council had resolved to put the matter to rest as soon as the meeting was concluded.

The villagers listened in uneasy silence, Ree suspected largely because if they began talking they'd doubtless miss the next alarming admission. When Keretan finished his address and asked for their patience and understanding, the inevitable hubbub began, growing in pitch and volume as people worked their way through the implications of what they'd been told, and added in a dollop of opinion or conjecture as they verbalised their thoughts.

The first questions were muttered between knots of conversation, loud enough to hope for an answer from the councillors on the steps, and then repeated with greater force when none was forthcoming. Ree had total sympathy for the villagers, but was nonetheless glad that she stood between Mariam and Vida towards the back of the press.

'Who will protect us without Gumis standing guard?' That could have been Yasha.

Keretan raised a slab-like palm. 'We have no need of protection within the village – that is the purpose of our agreement with the mercenaries, after all.'

'But they took him!' came the retort.

'And you said the agreement wasn't in force until the last of the payment was made,' added someone else, perhaps Parvin, with a definite edge of reproach. 'What if someone attacks us?'

'What if *they* attack us? I hear they were going to come into the village, before Gumis stopped him – that's why they took him.'

Voices were rising on all sides.

'They were going to kill him, weren't they? Until the visitor stopped them.'

'She made it worse! She attacked that man first.'

Ree clenched her jaw. Part of her had been waiting for this, but she was by no means thrilled by its arrival. 'Mariam, Vida? Are you going to say anything? These people are frightened and bewildered, and your friends on the steps are doing a lousy job of managing the situation.' And if this continues, she added to herself, it likely won't be long before they start turning on each other, or – more likely – outsiders . . .

'We stay out of Council business,' Vida muttered, although Mariam looked pained, her face tight.

'This is beyond Council business,' Ree hissed. 'This is everyone's business! Your people need honesty, not platitudes. They want to know what's being done to keep them safe.'

'Gumis was taken because he made a mistake,' Camellia called over the clamour, 'but we shall have him returned shortly, and with him, peace.'

'Oh, come on,' Ree cried, unable to contain herself. 'You're saying he brought it on himself?'

She became aware of a sudden hush, and once again the eyes of the settlement upon her, followed by undulant whispers as her identity and significance were spread across the crowd.

'Thank you, Mistress Ree,' Camellia said with a face of stone, 'but your contribution has already sufficed.'

Keretan placed a heavy hand on her arm. 'If our visitor has something to add, perhaps we should hear her out,' he intoned. 'Let all voices be heard – in an orderly manner – and perhaps we can reach a common understanding.'

Camellia glowered, but said nothing more, and gestured with one dismissive hand for Ree to speak.

'Thank you, Camellia, Keretan, members of the Council.' Vida and Mariam had shuffled slightly away from her, she hoped to give her space to express herself, and not because they were reluctant to be associated. She hefted the walking stick that Mariam had found for her, a close replica in form and function of the one Mani used. With Gumis no longer in attendance, she was comfortable that she was unlikely to be challenged for carrying something that could be used as a weapon. 'I'll be short: there are people across the valley who mean you harm. The man who came late to the meeting, who almost cut Gumis then took him away, that man and his confederates have no interest in peaceful coexistence. You need to prepare yourselves for two possibilities: that Gumis does not come back, and that that man does.'

The voice of Volkan, Mani's narrow counterpart, was sharp across the square. 'He only threatened to come into the village to search for you.'

'And while I'm grateful the Council denied him, that was only a pretext. He'll find another.'

'What would you have us do? Take up weapons of war and cut his head from his shoulders at his approach?'

Ree put up her palms – this was an old dance by now. 'I suggest only defensive measures. Fortifications, gates, care around your points of entry. There's nothing aggressive or violent about that.' She gestured with her empty hand towards the bridge and the lower terraces, where the timber stacks lay powdered with snow. 'You have plenty of good, strong wood to hand – why not use some of it as walls and gates, a lookout post, anything that comes to mind?'

Volkan was shaking his head with a disdainful sneer. 'And how will that look to them? If we commit labour and resources to fortification, it will provoke a response – how could it not? It is provocation in its purest form, a manifestation of ill-trust.' He folded his spindly arms. 'Any such action increases the likelihood of escalation, and the chance of peaceful dialogue recedes.'

'That's backwards,' said someone in the crowd, Ree couldn't see who, maybe Parvin again, and she was grateful for their intervention. For a moment, she felt less alone. 'Building up walls should put them off attacking, not encourage it.'

Volkan gave a weary sigh. 'But the act of erection is far from atomic, yes? To wit, it will take longer for the walls to be useful than it will for their construction to be noticed, and, in turn, acted upon.'

'That's conjecture,' Ree responded, when the voice in the crowd didn't, 'and is an abdication of your duty of care.' He went to reply, but she shouted over him, one hand pointing across the misty valley with furious jabs. 'If the people in that camp so chose, they could flatten this place, and even if they spare your lives they will take your food and your shelter and if you're *lucky*, you won't end up enslaved, just homeless and starving. Do you understand? You are at the mercy of the better natures of pirates.'

Already she could hear voices raised around her, consternation and alarm, but she ploughed on, forestalling the retorts. 'You call them professional soldiers, but they look like shabby bandits. For once, call a thing what it is. You've been lucky so far that all they've done is tax you through a pretence of contract, but what we saw yesterday is a flaming beacon, announcing that your luck is spent. They have no obligation to you, they are not of you, they are not your people. They are strangers, who owe you nothing, and look at all that you have with avaricious eyes.'

It had gone quiet again, quiet enough to hear Camellia mutter to Keretan, 'Do you believe we've arrived at common understanding?'

Volkan wasn't ready to concede. 'Let them come,' he cried with an expansive sweep of one arm. 'Let them take our empty structures, or fallow fields. They are not worth our lives – we will fall away, move on, and start afresh elsewhere. Ar Ramas is not a place, but an ideal!'

'Move on?' came the voice from the crowd again, or perhaps a different voice. 'Strike out into the mountains, at the threshold of winter? With no shelter or supplies beyond what we can carry? What of our animals, our crops – our *children?*'

That got the arguing going again, but one thing became clear to Ree's ears: the people of Ar Ramas were not keen on either freezing or starving, and cared very much for the health of both their elders and infants. Volkan had the audacity to look disappointed by their complaints.

Camellia intervened. She took charge not with bellowing or frantic gesturing, but with a single step forward, her head tilted, her eyes soft and sorrowful. The shouts and grumbling fell away.

'My people,' she said in a voice laden with regret. 'My friends. We have all known suffering. We have all known war, or famine, or plague, or all of these things and more. Each of us is here because we wanted a better life, a life of peace, a life away from the horrors of the plains and the lands beyond. When my friend Volkan says that Ar Ramas is an ideal, he is not wrong. Ar Ramas stands for many things, but chief among them is the right to live without fear. The right to be left alone, to make a life of your choosing among those who feel the same. The right to leave behind the misery and privations we have known first-hand, and never look back.' Her eyes were red, and Ree was astonished to see tears tracking unremarked down her cheeks. 'The right not to repeat the mistakes of the past.'

Camellia took a slow breath, but made no move to wipe at her eyes. 'There must be no escalation, no retaliation. We cannot embrace the disgraceful ways of war at the first hint of hardship. If we took up arms, how much blood would be shed, how many children would lose their families anew? Who would till the fields, thresh the grain, milk the goats, churn the yoghurt?' She gave a weary, mournful sigh. 'What good does all this talk of battle do?'

Only Ree seemed unconvinced. She waited a breath to see if anyone would respond, but heard only shuffling silence. 'No one is talking of battle,' she replied, cutting through the muffled introspection. 'But your people need to be protected, Camellia. You want the right to live without fear, but what are you doing to secure that right?' She scratched around for an image, and thought of the noble Tarfellian. 'Where is your mastiff, your sheepdog? You'd never leave a flock unguarded, why would you do the same with the people who trust you to lead?'

The woman at the top of the steps seemed shocked by her impudence, her red-rimmed eyes wide, mouth working. 'We protect our flocks from the dangers of the natural world, which is wild and unpredictable—'

'It's the same world you're living in, Camellia,' came Ree's bullish reply. She gave her half a breath to speak, then aimed low. 'Or was I wrong to think you cared about your people?'

That got some serious disquiet, and Ree knew she'd overstepped. Free hand raised, she was already turning, heading in the direction of the stables. 'Do what you want,' she called as she went, 'by noon you'll no longer need to count me among your problems.'

Vida was a pace behind, not quite an obvious bodyguard in the face of a hostile crowd. Ree hissed to her as she limped away, 'You'll have the shoe done by noon, right?'

The smith nodded. 'I'll get to it as soon as the vote is done.'

'The vote?'

'You advanced an argument, on Keretan's behalf. Whether to start building fortifications and such.'

'And the village will vote?'

'No. The Council.'

'Ah.'

'Indeed.'

Ree eased up on her pace. The stick was hard on her palm. 'Well, it's the thought that counts, right?'

'No,' said Vida.

TWENTY-FOUR

Javani had wandered around the edge of the square for nearly a whole minute before deciding she was bored by Council business on principle. Inexorably, her feet took her towards the stables, and the ram pen that projected from one side, most of it open to the elements, its far end beneath the awning of this corner of the stable building. Below the awning sat the immense figure of the mercenary that Ree had captured, a steel collar around his neck, chained to the wall behind him. He was extraordinary to look at, a mass of muscle, his bare skin whorled with tattoos she assumed were significant and his head shaved but for the two tight, waving braids. He looked cold.

Tarfellian was on watch, and came lumbering over to greet her as she approached, snuffling her hand and thudding his enormous body against her by way of hello. She greeted him in turn with a determined scritch behind his ears, which elicited a huff of approval and a thumping wag of his curling tail. She and Ree had spent the night at the smithy; while Javani had been happy to sleep in the stables again, Ree thought it imprudent, given the enormous mercenary chained in the ram pen. Instead, they'd bedded down on old fleeces around the fireplace of the hut (Anri would no doubt mock her for a residual sheepy aroma when she saw him), and she'd been delighted when Tarfellian had thumped over to where she lay and flopped down beside her like a very warm, very heavy blanket that occasionally huffed, sighed and farted. No worse than Ree, she'd remarked, and just ducked the clout that had followed.

'Excuse me, mistress.'

The voice had come from the ram pen. It had come from the hulking mercenary.

'Excuse me, mistress?'

It was an unexpected voice. Not the grizzled, raw growl his appearance suggested, not Keretan's booming baritone, just a, well, normal man's voice, mid-pitched, young, with a hint of a south-eastern accent.

He was talking to her.

Javani, never one to shy from potential peril, leaned her arms against the top timber of the ram pen and estimated his distance from her compared with the length of the chain that held him. It was probably fine. That said, he looked like he could rip the chain from its moorings if he put his mind to it, and it was probably for the best that he'd not yet attempted it. He'd made no attempt to free himself or escape at all, which had puzzled Javani, given his size and obvious strength; Ree had only smiled and muttered something about her 'secret army'.

'Can I help you?' she said, which in retrospect was an odd choice of words, but she'd committed to it now.

He shuffled a little forward, then cast a furtive look towards the nearest patch of forest and stopped. 'Do you, er, do you know if there's any more food?'

Beyond him lay an empty bowl and platter, evidently scraped so clean that Tarfellian wouldn't have bothered licking them.

'I don't, sorry.' And then, because she saw the look in his eyes, 'I could ask someone, though.'

'Thank you, mistress. Thank you.'

Gods, something about him reminded her of Moosh. It seemed impossible, he was utterly different in every respect she could name, but the way his eyes broadcast his every thought . . .

'Are you cold? There's a big pile of fleeces just inside the doorway there, you could probably reach it without, you know . . .'

His eyes lit up at that, and he clambered slowly inside the outer door of the stable, mindful of the length of his chain, then returned a moment later with an armful of the fleeces that Javani and Ree had slept under on their first night. She felt immediately better seeing his bare arms covered; the poor lad must have been freezing.

'Thank you, mistress.'

'You're, uh, welcome. If you keep moving, you'll stay warmer, too.' She watched him for a moment, settling himself beneath the wool, his glances frequent towards both the forest and the opposite side of the valley, still half-lost in the mist and snow. 'What's your name?'

'Tauras, mistress. Ninth Chapter, Company of the Wolf, under the command of Captain Inaï Manatas.'

'What's the Company of the Wolf?'

'Free company, mistress. The cream of professional soldiery, operating all across the protectorate.'

'We're not really in the protectorate here, though, are we? I mean, that's rather the point.' She waved a general hand at their surroundings, which were a long way from the fort line or the machinery of the Serican state.

'We were forced to relocate, mistress, by the hostile actions of the Miners' Guild, and their western encroachment. Captain says they squeezed us out, mistress, forced us up into these, er, accursed hills.'

'I see. I'm Javani, by the way. You can call me Javani. You don't have to say mistress.'

'It's polite, mistress, to say mistress. Important to be polite. Shows good discipline. Good discipline is at the heart of an effective fighting force.'

'Did your captain teach you that?'

'He did, mistress.'

'Is he the thin-looking one with the . . .' She imitated streaks at her temple. 'Takes ages to finish his sentences?'

She realised he was speaking slightly past her, his eyes not quite meeting hers. Was this deference? 'Captain Manatas is a firm believer in using the right word at the right time, mistress.'

'As well as any others that come to hand? No, never mind.' He was still looking past her, watching the forest as if he expected something to leap out of it. 'Are you looking for something?'

His gaze on the trees was unwavering. 'Lots of dangers in the forest, mistress.'

'Oh? Anything I should know about?'

'It's not just the secret army. Captain says there are still War Criminals in the hills.' She could hear the capital letters in his speech.

'Not bloody Copperhand again?' she sighed.

He nodded firmly, eyeline still nailed to the surrounding trees. 'Lots of dangers in the forest, mistress.'

'Um. Right. It was, uh, nice talking to you, Tauras.' She gestured back over her shoulder towards the upper terrace and the muted clamour of the Council meeting. 'You should be home soon, anyway.'

The hope was so raw in his eyes. 'We're going back to Mahavrik? When?'

'No, sorry, I meant, back, uh, in your camp. When your friends give Ar Ramas back their constable.'

She watched the hope die, and felt a terrible twist in her gut. 'Oh. I see. Thank you, mistress.'

'Can I get you anything?' She'd had to say something. She couldn't have left it like that.

'Can I have a razor, or a very sharp blade?'

She rocked back on her heels, astonished at her misjudgement. 'Are you—'

'It's my scalp, you see?' He pointed with a thick finger at the shaved swathe of dome between his braids. 'It starts to grow back fast, and I don't have my knife to keep it short.' His gaze dropped to the snow-streaked mud before him. 'I usually do it every morning after turning out.'

'You're worried about your haircut?'

He looked back up, meeting her look with earnest eyes. 'I have to keep it like this, it's very important. Otherwise people won't be afraid of me, you see? They have to know I'm scary, it's important.'

She managed not to goggle. Surely he'd remain physically imposing even with a bit of pate-stubble. 'Why is it important?'

'Because if people think you're scary, you don't have to fight them,' he said in a small voice.

'Kid!'

Ree's voice cut through the morning mist like a scythe. Javani turned to see her mother marching down the terrace steps towards her, her gait with the stick still uncomfortable, her face dark with displeasure.

'I'd better go,' she said to the man in the ram pen. 'Look after yourself, Tauras.'

'Thank you, mistress. I will.'

'And Tarfellian will keep an eye on you, won't you, boy?'

'Kid! Get over here!'

Javani went.

For a moment, Manatas considered the possibility that Keds was responsible, but her expression, even through a haze of sleepless alcohol, confirmed she was every bit as wrong-footed as him.

They descended the slope in a tumbling mass, scrabbling to reach the huddle outside the pavilion. Already Botrys had gathered Ridderhof's personal guard close around him, then disappeared back inside the tasselled flap. Two of the guard remained before the entryway, wide, armoured and sweating despite the morning's biting chill. Their haunted faces told Manatas all he needed to know, but he asked it anyway.

'What is it? What's happened? Let me inside, by the gods.'

The guards did not move, barring his path with their rigid bulk. 'Nobody goes inside. Lord adjutant's orders.'

'Don't be absurd. I'm captain of this chapter, and this is my camp.'

'Nobody inside, captain.'

'Where is the captain-general?'

'Nobody. Inside.' Thick drops of sweat were rolling from the rim of the man's helmet, his teeth gritted.

Commotion from behind drew his attention. Another group had reached the camp, waved through the new gate by the sentries, a column of at least two dozen leading pack animals or pulling single-wheeled barrows laden with kit and provisions. The man at their head was shaven-headed and scarred, and after pausing to direct his men to pitch camp in one of the few clear spaces of the new perimeter, he advanced on the pavilion, one hand resting on the straight sword at his hip.

'Hannu Jebel reporting, captain of the Eleventh.'

'The unloved Eleventh,' Keds muttered, her words slurred, and Manatas hoped to the gods that the new man hadn't heard. He was of a similar age, perhaps older – the shaved head made it hard to be certain – silver stubble at his chin, old nicks and gouges decorating his head like stripes of pale paint.

'Manatas, captain of the Ninth. This is Kediras of the Third.'

Keds flopped a hand up in salute. It still contained her aquavit.

'What brings your chapter to our encampment, captain? We were not expecting the Eleventh to join us here.'

Jebel ran a hand over the ridges of his scalp. 'We reached the rendezvous early and set up, but then a group of Pashani came through, informed us the circus was setting up camp here. We were tired of waiting.'

'Pashani? Of the Seventh?'

The grizzled captain nodded once. 'I believe so. They travelled with us. Dour bunch of fuckers, but they can hunt and they can drink. Where's Ridderhof? Are the rumours true?'

Manatas felt his neck hair rise. It was impossible, surely, unless somehow . . . 'Rumours? What rumours are these?'

'That he's hocked us all. Pissed away the treasury bailing out his idiot son, then sanctioned an off-book chapter to go raiding Guild caravans to try to make it back.' He hawked and spat. 'With predictable consequences.'

From the corner of his eye, Manatas saw Keds's knuckles whiten.

'Well?' Jebel's tone was aggressive, impatient. 'Where is the old fool?'

'He's fucking dead,' Keds spat.

'What?'

'Now, Keds, we know nothing for certain—'

Jebel was glaring at him through narrowed eyes, one finger raised. 'Is she drunk?'

Manatas let his hands fall to his sides. 'Not enough to make her wrong.'

'Hm.' The impatience had left Jebel's gaze. 'When's the election? Wait until we're back at the fortress, presumably, gather the captains.' He was rubbing his chin with one hand, looking off into the mist across the valley.

'We don't yet know for certain what's happened,' Manatas ventured. 'We don't even know that he's dead.'

Botrys burst from the pavilion behind them. 'The captain-general is dead!' he howled.

'Well, that'll do it,' said Inaï Manatas with a weary sigh.

TWENTY-FIVE

And then, somehow, Lado was there, sliding from the shadows of the pavilion as if he'd been part of them all along. He slipped behind the guards to Botrys's side, and nobody seemed to pay him the slightest mind.

'Jebel, captain of the Eleventh, reporting. How did the commander die?'

Botrys was doing a very good impression of someone stricken with grief, Manatas mused. It was certainly possible that he was distraught at the captain-general's passing – Ridderhof had possessed a distinct fondness for his adjutant that Manatas had found unfathomable, and it was possible that something between them had amounted to amity – but it was more likely that Botrys had realised his time in the sun was up. The inevitable election would usher in a new captain-general, and with them their choice of staff, and only someone in questionable command of their faculties would keep Botrys around. A return to the administrative pool beckoned for the self-styled lord adjutant, or perhaps even a very, very early retirement. There was a pension house, it was said, somewhere in the outskirts of Astarvan, a walled estate where old mercenaries saw out their last days in peace and comfort. Or would, if any lived long enough to see it. Botrys had a one-way trip squarely in his future.

The lord adjutant sniffed and summoned his breath. 'It seems he climbed into his bath and opened his wrists.'

'A Livarnian suicide?' Jebel was rubbing his chin again, eyes narrow.

'He seemed in such high spirits last night,' Manatas said weakly.

'Are you fucking fools?' Keds roared. '*He* did this!' Her half-blade was in her hand, extended towards Lado, who seemed to slither between Botrys and the house guards. His head was tilted, his mouth half-open in apparent confusion. 'Lado of Cstethia murdered the captain-general.'

Botrys seemed irked by the disruption to his moment of drama. 'That is a grave accusation to level, captain.'

'She is drunk, disregard her,' Jebel added, to Manatas's ire.

'No, no, let her have her say.' Lado spoke from the gloom beneath his dangling hair. 'Let her vent her frustrations. We are all of us upset by the sudden passing of our beloved commander.'

Keds was swaying on her feet, her eyes balls of fury. 'Livarnian suicides are the stuff of sagas, no man can kill himself that way. I've known some try, and they all . . . needed . . . assistance.' Her blade swung back to Lado. 'That man is poison, he has murdered Ridderhof, he will damn us all—'

Botrys waved his hand. 'Guards, remove the captain, she is drunk.'

'I'll take her.' Manatas stepped forward, swaying to the side of Keds's waving blade, and put one arm across her. 'Kediras,' he whispered, 'you have to stop this now. Even if you're right. We can't win this here.'

Her eyes found his, bloodshot and afraid. 'Then we can't win it anywhere.' She stepped from his grasp and turned away. 'I'll remove myself. Fuck you all.'

'Keds—'

'Fuck you too, Inaï.'

Lado waited a breath after her departure before speaking. 'I wouldn't dare speak for everyone here, but I think we can forgive Captain Kediras her outburst – it's been a shock for us all, especially after such an exhilarating evening. Some of us are evidently not ready to let go.'

'I apologise for the bluntness of my confederate.' Manatas could feel the thud of his pulse in his neck, the strange queasy anger lurking beneath his veneer of calm. 'But surely none could object to a thorough investigation? The captain-general of our company is dead. I can think of no matter more grave, and more deserving of our full attention.'

Lado's spread fingers were back at his mailed chest. 'If the lord adjutant will permit, then I must burden you all with my confession. I fear that our blunt-tongued comrade spoke the truth after all.'

Botrys started, seeming to come awake with a splutter. 'Confession? What are you talking about, soldier?'

Manatas could only stare, his mouth forming unvoiced syllables. After all that, he was going to confess?

Lado took a sidling step forward, his head still inclined, hand on his chest, looking every bit the penitent sinner. 'I had forgotten this matter, but the harsh words of the departed captain stirred my memory. I had intended to bring a concern to the captain-general's attention when first my chapter and I arrived at this encampment, but such was the grave state of my dear cousin, and the emotional upheaval from his sudden, unexpected departure, that it slipped my mind completely. Until last night.'

Botrys's dark brows were a thick line, his eyes darting. He licked at his lips. 'What matter was this?' he croaked. Manatas and Jebel remained silent and watchful. To Manatas's eye, the adjutant was radiating guilt like a beacon on a cloudless night.

'On our serpentine journey into these mountains, my chapter and I came across a bundle of correspondence, hopelessly mislaid. We took it upon ourselves, in the name of our duty to the company, to reunite these missives with their intended recipients. Unfortunately, their outer seals had been damaged, and to my eternal shame I caught sight of some of the contents.' He took a long sniff, his head shaking with the weight of remorse. 'Some of the messages were intended for the captain-general, and it is a further regret that I did not deliver them at the moment of my arrival. It was only at the feast last night that the thought reoccurred, curse the weakness of my memory.' He knuckled one greasy temple.

'These letters to the commander,' Jebel growled, a gaze like steel on Lado, 'what was in them?'

Lado raised a pair of pale, scarred palms. 'Little I could fathom, chapter captain. It all related to matters of accounting and expenditure, the upkeep of the winter fortress, and perhaps . . . something relating to his son? I knew I should not have even spared a glimpse, and it is my shame to bear that I did.'

Jebel had one hand on the pommel of his hefty-looking sword.

He was by far the heaviest-armed and -armoured among the informal gathering, even accounting for the house guards at the mouth of the pavilion. When he spoke, his tone remained as weighty as his sword. 'And why is it you think you're responsible for his death, man-at-arms? What did you do with these letters?'

Lado bowed his head, his stringy hair draping like a curtain. 'Merely presented them to the captain-general, chapter captain, as he was returning to the pavilion. It was only then that I had remembered them.'

Oh, I am sure, Manatas thought to himself, but said nothing. He had a modicum more self-control than Keds, or at least a measure less of a thirst for oblivion.

Jebel wheeled his scrutiny on Botrys. 'Adjutant? You saw these letters? Were you aware of their contents?'

The adjutant licked his lips again and clasped his hands, his eyes flicking from corner to corner, searching for a way out. The feeble silver morning light glistened from a single bead of sweat standing proud from his brow. But before he could stammer a reply, Lado spoke for him. 'Though I would never dare speak for the lord adjutant, I can confirm that the captain-general was alone when he received the bundle, and there is no reason to suppose the lord adjutant would have knowledge of the private correspondence of the commander.' His tone was so reasonable, so smooth, so oily. Of course Ridderhof was alone, Manatas heard Keds growl in his head, that's when you killed him. He once again left his concern unvoiced.

'Where are these letters now?' Jebel no longer sounded angry, or even suspicious. More . . . hungry.

'I believe he placed them in the travelling chest in his sleeping quarters. Perhaps, with the lord adjutant's permission, you could investigate them.' For the briefest moment his eyes flicked to Manatas. 'Thoroughly.'

Manatas cleared his throat. 'Now is it your contention that the content of this so-called lost correspondence caused the captain-general to take his own life?'

Lado's eyes were wide and guileless behind the curtain of hair. 'I could not say, chapter captain, only that the one happened before the other.' He slid a hand along his temple, tucking a lank swathe of his hair behind one ear, displaying the deep scars of his chin to Manatas in what he felt had to be some kind of gesture of contempt. 'But I would describe his mood at the time as somewhat mournful.'

'And he'd been in such high spirits,' Botrys echoed.

'So the rumours were true after all,' Jebel mused to himself, 'and Ridderhof took the coward's way out.' He took a step towards the pavilion entrance. 'I'll see to these letters.'

Lado was somehow in front of him without seeming to move, just there by pure coincidence. 'Forgive me once more, chapter captain,' he said, his face twisted in a grimace as if the words caused him physical pain, 'with the captain-general deceased, the lord adjutant has command of the company, and the encampment. At least until a replacement is appointed.'

Jebel paused, teeth not bared but waiting in reserve. 'Well hold on,' Manatas broke in, 'the most senior captain present should take acting command until the next election.'

'But who is the most senior, captain?' Lado asked innocently. 'We are blessed with three chapter captains in our number, their stature prodigious. Someone must decide who takes acting command.'

Jebel seemed indifferent to prolonging Botrys's sunny moment. 'With your permission, lord adjutant?'

Botrys was beginning to swell again, near glowing with what Manatas took to be relief. Whatever it was he was afraid of, Lado had deflected it. Which meant Lado probably knew what it was, and that meant new problems. 'I shall consider your request, chapter captain,' Botrys replied with a level of haughtiness Manatas found to be entirely without foundation, 'and give my decision later this morning, once matters have settled. Let us begin preparations for Captain-General Ridderhof's pyre.'

'That's it?' Manatas looked from Jebel to Botrys to the guards, ignoring Lado. 'That's our investigation? We haven't even established that these letters exist, let alone caused the commander's demise. We can't burn him before we've—'

'The lord adjutant has spoken,' Lado said in a quiet, menacing way, 'and he commands the company, and the camp.'

'Then perhaps we should discuss the election,' Manatas snapped. 'Or the selection of an acting commander—'

Lado talked over him. 'Although the chapter captain makes a good point, lord adjutant – a sinister possibility has occurred.' His eyes were wide, brows drawn, the hand returned to his matted armour. 'It could yet be that the letters are a distraction, that the perpetrators came in fact from the village across the valley in the dead of night, bent on assassination, to weaken us and sow dissension in our ranks!' His voice was rising, the centre of attention to everyone in earshot, which, by now, was half the camp.

'That's preposterous,' Manatas exclaimed. 'We have rings of sentries, palisade walls, guards around the tent—'

'I believe the chapter captain stated the need for a thorough investigation,' Lado countered, his eyes on Botrys. Even Jebel was nodding along to his words, and Manatas felt his respect for the man ebbing away. 'Who knows what evidence we might discover if we look closely.' This with a knowing glance at Manatas, who realised with sinking certainty that evidence in the captain-general's quarters would be plentiful and varied, and would paint whatever picture Lado wished. His own words to Keds came back to him: we can't win this here.

He tried anyway. 'Botrys, are you seriously—?'

Once more Lado was talking over him, and none of the other officers said a word. 'Lord adjutant, with your permission, I will begin interrogating the prisoner immediately? He surely knows the depths of their plans.'

Botrys waved his assent, and Lado sprang away, two Pashani materialising from behind the pavilion to join him as he went. Manatas remained, waiting to be dismissed in a daze. Ridderhof dead, Botrys in charge, and to Lado he was a puppet.

One imperious dismissal later, he climbed back up the slope to where Arkadas stood, one disapproving eye on the now-retching Keds.

She sat up, wiped her mouth, then took another swig from her skin. Finding it empty, she threw it over her shoulder towards the line of the new wall.

Arkadas gave him a grim nod. 'Captain.'

'Arkadas. Ridderhof is dead. It's a stark likelihood that Lado of Cstethia was his killer.'

Keds spat something nasty into the fire. It hissed. Her voice sounded raw as a wound. 'What excuse did he give?'

'That he and his chapter, uh, "intercepted" some of the commander's correspondence, which was so incriminating in its nature that the old man was forced to end his life or face professional disgrace.'

Arkadas grunted. 'Think there's any truth to it, captain?'

'It's far from impossible that Lado has robbed messengers, and likewise that Ridderhof did in fact drain the company's treasury chasing his son's folly.'

'But?'

'But, Arkadas.'

A shriek pierced the grey morning, echoing from the snowbound hills and setting Manatas's teeth on edge. Arkadas scanned the upper slopes, eyes wide. 'What in the name of the gods—'

Manatas rubbed at his eyes with numb, cracked fingers. 'Lado's other inspiration – that assailants from the village murdered the captain-general. He's . . . interrogating yesterday's prisoner. To see what he knows of this nefarious plot.'

Arkadas's mouth said nothing, but his eyes did all the talking required.

'Now do you see?' Keds growled. She was poking the fire with a stick, furious jabs sending up sprays of ash. 'Either we take care of him now, or we run. That's the choice, Inaï.'

'Captain, desertion is a death sentence.' Arkadas's tight tone betrayed his disquiet.

'I'm aware of that, *lieutenant*,' she snarled back. 'But so is staying here. Well, Inaï?'

'I hear you, Keds. I hear you.' Manatas took a long, frosty breath. 'I like precisely none of this. I must ponder.'

TWENTY-SIX

Her mother was leaning hard on Javani as they crossed the pasture towards the forge. 'What's the hurry, Ma?' she cried plaintively. Despite herself, she'd enjoyed talking to Tauras, the giant, boyish mercenary.

'We need to get our baggage together, kid, then we are leaving this place. We've stayed more than long enough.'

'What about the shoe? Vida said—'

'*Fuck* the shoe! That pony can hobble, and rue its foolishness in losing it in the first place.'

Javani looked at her mother sidelong. Her limp was no better, and she was sweating from the speed of their walk, her words bitten and breathy. So much for rest and recovery, once more. 'Are you sure you're fit to travel?' She nodded back at the sheet of grey rock that loomed over the village. 'There could be a lot more climbing to come.'

'I'm fine.'

'And aren't you worried about the mercenaries? What if they're prowling the woods? We could blunder straight into them—' like last time.

Ree pulled up short, her face flushed, yanking Javani to a halt beside her. 'What's got into you, kid? Why are you fighting me on this? We need to leave, it's not safe here.'

They faced each other, knee-deep in snow-topped wiry grass, a fierce wind blowing down the valley towards them, snapping at their cloaks, stinging their cheeks and ears. 'That doesn't mean it's safe out there,' Javani retorted.

Ree jabbed a finger into her chest. 'Listen up, kid. You say you want to be treated as an adult, an equal partner in decision-making? Then you need to act like an adult, and you need to think like an adult. However much you might think you like the folks who live here, and don't misunderstand me, they're not all without charm, they are led by blockheads with a death-wish, and they are going to get all these lovely people either dead or destitute before Sun's Night. If we stay, we will be among them, understand?' She ducked her head from side to side, staring into each of Javani's eyes in turn, searching for acknowledgement. 'Understand, kid? We need to leave. Today.'

'But it's not fair!'

Ree recoiled, her hands rising, one holding her stick. 'What did I just—'

'It's not fair to leave them in this mess, when it's my fault! I found the men in the woods, I shouted at them, I shot one. That's what started all this, isn't it? And now we've created all this, this chaos, we're just going to leave them to face it without us?'

Ree had recovered, her finger back to wagging. 'None of this is your fault, kid – none of it. The Council of this place invited bandits into their valley, and they've been too cowardly to face them ever since. All we did is walk into a mess that they made for themselves. And now we're walking out.'

'But we could make a difference, couldn't we?'

Javani watched her mother rehearse several answers in her head within a second, her lips moving, eyes distant, and she pressed home her point before Ree could find the right one.

'We could have left a bunch of times already. If you'd made enough fuss, Vida would have got that shoe done, and we'd have been on our way with all those supplies Keretan promised.'

'Now, kid, that's—'

'But we haven't, because you like it here.'

'That is not—'

'Not *living* here, *arguing* here.' Javani folded her arms, stuffing her freezing hands beneath her cloak. 'You love telling them what they should be doing and, what's more, you know they've started to listen. Some of them have, anyway. And if we stayed, maybe you could get them all to listen. Maybe we could clear up the mess after all.'

Ree's lips were tight, her eyes wide and burning. 'It's a nice idea, kid, but I'm afraid your aim's as bad as your archery on this one. They won't listen to a thrice-damned thing I say.'

'Ah, Ree, Javani, hold up!'

Mariam was coming over the rise behind them, loping through the thin snow with long, elegant strides. Ree jerked a thumb at her. 'Witness,' she muttered, then, 'Mariam, have the Council voted?'

'They have, yes,' she said as she reached them, only slightly out of breath from her speedy pursuit. 'Very quick, it was.'

Ree's eyebrow was arched like a bow. 'And did they choose to undertake any fortification measures?'

'They did not, no.'

Ree turned back to Javani, her own arms folded. 'See, kid, not a thrice-damned thing.'

'They *did* vote to set up a citizens' watch, though.' Mariam could just about keep the smile from her voice. 'Just a few people, mind, at the borders of the village. Not armed, of course, but perhaps . . . each with a walking stick or two?'

Javani cackled as her mother's mouth fell open. 'Did Camellia . . . ?'

'Outvoted. Mani tipped it. Said there was nothing violent about people out walking who needed a little assistance.'

'See, Ma? Maybe one or two thrice-damned things.'

'Watch your mouth, kid, or – do you smell burning?'

Mariam was already swivelling on her heel. 'There, across the valley. Another one.'

Ree rubbed her jaw with her hand. 'Now who's dead this time?'

And then the screaming began.

Manatas was sure there'd been a priest somewhere among the circus, some kind of cleric or holy man, but it was Botrys who addressed the assembled company before Ridderhof's roaring pyre. To his shame, Manatas was glad of its warmth. The day was grey and bitter, the scattered snow now churned slush beneath their feet.

Botrys began speaking, his smug voice barely audible over the stinking crackle of their burning commander. They'd got the pyre up even faster than Ioseb's; apparently the work party had been able to reuse some of yesterday's unburned wood. Manatas realised he couldn't see Lado. He wasn't with Botrys or the house guards, nor was he visible in the Pashani contingent who stood, heads bowed, as grim-faced as ever; at least this time their demeanour matched the occasion.

'Where's Lado?' he whispered to Keds, who stood between him and the rest of her squad.

'He'll show up,' was all she replied. She seemed unconcerned, disaffected. Manatas tried to be, too.

'. . . which is why, later today, I will be appointing an acting captain-general,' Botrys announced in his reedy, complacent voice, 'who will serve until a full election is held at a conclave of the captains.'

Manatas stood straighter. 'Hear that?'

'It changes nothing.'

'I am disinclined to agree, Keds. I am surely next in line, in seniority and in stature. If Botrys names me acting commander, even for a day—'

'He's not going to do that, Inaï.'

'What? How could he not? Hells, even if it's Jebel, at least he'll follow the rules. Then we can finally get out of this place, finish our tour and winter in comfort at the lake—'

'He's not going to do that, Inaï.'

He could feel the hope within him struggling against the leaden certainty of her words. How could Botrys not name him or Jebel? He would hardly name Keds, of course – she was by far the most junior captain, her previous outburst notwithstanding. But Botrys was bound by the company's charter as much as the rest of them. An acting captain-general from among the captains present, then a full election once they were returned to their winter quarters. The by-laws were clear.

Then he saw Lado. The man was sauntering between the knots of pyre-watchers, his bandy-legged walk seeing him slip seemingly unnoticed through ranks of mercenaries, raising little more than a ripple of curiosity. Botrys acknowledged him as he closed, and beckoned him over. Manatas could not hear their conversation, but he did not care for the look on Botrys's face: a paranoid eagerness, lips licked, eyes flitting. He noted that Lado's hands were stained very dark indeed.

Botrys gave a firm nod, and then cried, 'Bring forth the prisoner.'

Manatas was immediately on edge. Were they about to throw the hapless village constable onto Ridderhof's pyre?

The Pashani who followed were dragging not the rotund constable, but someone Manatas recognised only vaguely, bloodied and beaten as he was: one of the clerks from Ridderhof's entourage, an accountant perhaps, or a notary; Manatas had no idea which. He'd seen the man only peripherally since the circus's arrival, and could think of no reason for Lado and his Pashani enforcers to have taken such exception to the fellow.

'Brothers- and sisters-in-arms,' Botrys declared, his voice as ill-suited to clamorous address as ever, 'it is only right that you should hear of the shocking revelations we have uncovered in our thorough investigation of the captain-general's passing.'

Keds and Manatas exchanged looks.

'Our treasury has been defrauded, comrades. False accounting and trickery have diverted funds that should have refilled your bonus hoard for the successful completion of your tours – the money is lost! Our winter quarters have been mortgaged and sold!' He was nearly screeching now, trying to shout over the rising outrage of the assembled mercenaries. 'But all is not lost, comrades! This man, this corrupted wretch, has confessed his part in the crimes, and we will reclaim what is ours. But, it saddens me greatly to say that your bonus payments for your tours will not be forthcoming this year.'

Only the fierce looks of the Pashani either side of the unfortunate clerk kept the mercenary body from tearing the man apart. Manatas was unsure of which way to veer – the man could be a scapegoat, but he might very well also have been Ridderhof's pet coin-swerver. And might very well know the extent of the lord adjutant's involvement in the scheme . . .

'Ridderhof killed himself over this?' It was Jebel, chapter captain of the unloved Eleventh, still looking fearsome and dissatisfied. 'This was what was in the letters?'

'It was,' Botrys averred.

'Then let us hear this man's confession,' Manatas was shocked by how clearly his voice carried. 'Let us hear the depths of this affair.'

Botrys swallowed, but Lado slid forward, placing one blood-dappled hand on the kneeling clerk's battered chin. 'Do you confess to these crimes, here and now, before your brothers- and sisters-in-arms?'

The man's eyes were wide, their whites sharp against the darkened ruin of his face. 'Yes,' he croaked, trying to nod and wincing. 'Yes!'

Lado released his chin, then turned towards Manatas, not quite looking at him, head as angled as ever. 'There you are, lads. He confesses. Boys, the gallows.'

'Wait!' shrieked the clerk as the Pashani hoisted him up by his armpits. 'Wait! You said if I—'

'Silence him,' Lado commanded, and a Pashani hand clamped down over the man's protestations. 'It would be a ghastly thing to submit our assembled brethren to his piteous squeals for mercy, given the gravity of his crimes.' Botrys seemed disappointed the man had been silenced. He seemed to enjoy the pleas for mercy, almost mouthing along with moist lips and hunger in his eyes. Lado bowed his head. 'How wretched to be forced to execute one of our own, but the laws of our company are clear. And without adherence to law, how are we more than animals?' He was definitely looking at Manatas as he said it.

The man was dragged away, kicking, struggling and producing muffled screams, his efforts fruitless in the rigid grip of the Pashani. At the top of the new wall, one of the work groups had slung a rope over a new timber frame. Manatas realised he was growling.

Botrys was now extolling the virtues of the successful investigation into the missing funds, praising himself above all, with some reflected glory for Lado. It became clear that the lord adjutant's grand plan for compensating the company was simple: take the difference from the villagers. Mathematically speaking, it was nonsense.

'In the meantime, I shall appoint an acting captain-general, but I will leave it to you, brothers- and sisters-in-arms, to choose your preferred candidate. We shall perform the poll at dusk.'

With that, Botrys exchanged a nod with Lado, and he and the

house guards strode back to the pavilion. Lado and his Pashani got to work on the assembled mercenaries immediately, perhaps eighty in number. Manatas saw the man smile for the first time, as he was suddenly charm personified, clapping soldiers on the back and introducing himself.

'Did you see that?' Keds murmured.

'Which part? I found no shortage of material to witness.'

'He's paying them. Probably Guild coin from the caravans. Fuck.'

'He's bribing our comrades?'

'I imagine he and Lord Blundershit have come to a tidy agreement on division of spoils. Fuck!'

Manatas felt lost. 'For the vote? But who . . . He's not even a captain! He can't stand for election.'

Her gaze was furious melancholy. 'But it's not a full election, Inaï, just a temporary arrangement. I don't see the organising adjutant objecting.' She bared her teeth and spat. 'He does that. It's what he does.'

'What is?'

'Plays by the rules; the letter, not the spirit. And he never lies, not properly. Instead he presents a monstrous vision of the truth, so twisted it's worse than deceit.'

Manatas's throat felt thick, his head light. 'Do you still intend his death?'

'I do, but it won't be now. He's not going to leave the camp before dusk. And you can bet the moment he's announced as acting commander, he's going to have some commands of his own.'

Manatas swallowed. 'What do we do?'

'The only thing we can.'

She turned and strode away into the mist.

TWENTY-SEVEN

Sweeper and two other villagers were at the top of the winding path that led down to the river and the valley floor, little more than long branches in their hands, when Ree, Javani and Mariam arrived. The rest of the settlement had dispersed to their daily tasks after the meeting, but Ree could see them clustered in bunches around the nearest terrace, some evidently comforting others.

'Sweeper,' Mariam barked as they reached him. 'Was that what I think it was?'

'Can't say for sure, mistress,' he mumbled, eyes downcast. He was rubbing his hands together. He seemed to do that a lot.

'And you two, can you say? You three were closest when it started, yes?'

Ree was surprised by Mariam's fierce animation, and a little impressed. Until this point, she'd seemed content to play the garrulous and supportive wife to her taciturn partner, but there was steel here. The two other proto-guards shrank back a little in the face of her questioning, before blurting that the eventual consensus on the screaming was Gumis, although a few people thought there had been two different voices at least.

'We also saw, um, people moving, mistress. On the valley floor, by the river, in the brush,' Sweeper added. His wounds were not improved. He looked like he'd been kicked by a horse.

Mariam wheeled on him. 'How many? Doing what? Travelling in which direction?'

It took effort for Ree to keep her eyebrow from rising. Exactly the questions she'd have asked, in almost the same order.

'Hard to say, mistress, between us we counted three but, um, could have missed some. Dressed like bushes, they were. Moving along the far bank, towards the falls then back.'

'Scouts?' Ree hazarded. 'Scouting for what, I wonder?'

'Maybe they're hunting or foraging?' the kid piped up. 'Lots of them over there now, wonder how much food they've got between them.'

'Maybe,' Ree replied, but the look on Mariam's face told her they'd reached the same conclusion. The mercenaries were scouting crossing places to the river, meaning they were engaged in Planning. Gumis's screams suggested they'd asked for his opinion on a few things, too. Things were in danger of getting out of hand.

'We need to know what they're up to,' she said. 'We need to scout them back, confirm their numbers and activities. Find out what they're burning, what they've done with Gumis . . .'

'And what they're planning to do next?' Mariam finished.

'Something like that.'

The kid stuck her oar in again. 'Anri could scout them,' she declared, 'he gets around the forest pretty well, can move quietly, and he's, uh, *pretty* good with a bow.'

Mariam gave a sour laugh. 'Good luck getting Anri to do anything for anyone else. He's not going to stick his neck out on this, he's not.'

The kid frowned, her little face scrunched up like a balled leaf. 'But, but, it's for the safety of the village!'

'Which he reckons he has no part in,' Mariam sighed, running her hands through her great swathes of hair and retying it at her neck.

'I could go, mistress?' Sweeper volunteered, and Ree had to do her best not to laugh.

'A noble offer, Sweeper,' Ree said, 'but I think we're going to need someone with a bit more . . .'

'Killer instinct?' Mariam supplied, her head to one side. 'I suppose you'll be wanting some of your weapons back, will you?'

Ree flicked a glance at Sweeper's branch. 'If I'm going out there, I'm going to want more than a walking stick. Unless you wanted to go, Mariam . . . ?'

Her reaction was measured. 'Wouldn't know what I was looking for, would I?'

'I could really go—' Sweeper repeated, but the kid squawked over him.

'Wait, what?' She was having trouble keeping up, which Ree found disappointing. 'You're going out whe— You can't scout!'

'And why's that, small person?'

'Well your leg for a start! You still can't walk properly on it. And, and, and—'

'I won't get close, and I'll wait until after sundown when it's nice and dark in the forest.' She cast an eye out over the valley, much of it still silvery with snow, the watery sun casting faint shadows through blankets of cloud. 'That ridge, see it? Above where the road runs down from the bridge. I should be able to climb up on this side, out of sight of the camp, and get a good view on them from above.'

'Can't someone else go?'

'These people aren't fighters, kid.'

'Nor are you, remember? You left all that behind, right?'

Ree gave her a meaningful look, that said equally clearly *Not now, kid*.

The kid gave her an equally meaningful look, which said very clearly *Well, very soon, then*.

'Come on,' Mariam said, extending an arm, 'let's go and find Vida, then maybe between us we'll convince Camellia to let you have your gear back, eh?'

'I'll go up and get it, mistress,' said Sweeper, turning to follow. Ree went to wave him back but remembered Mani's words: he likes to help, let him help.

'I'd be grateful, Sweeper, thanks.'

The kid fell in step with her as she clomped off behind Mariam towards the terrace steps that led up towards the square. 'We're not leaving, then?' she murmured sidelong as they walked. 'Wasn't that long ago you were ordering me to stuff my unmentionables in a sack and ride out of here on a half-shod pony.'

'We're still leaving,' Ree growled back, trying to keep her voice low. 'Just not yet.'

'Right. Just not yet.'

'That's what I said. We fix this, then we go.'

'You should let Anri do the scouting, he'll be much better at it.'

'Shut up, kid.'

Javani grew bored, inevitably, with the tedious discussions over whether Ree should be allowed her sword back, and drifted away once again, alone but for her thoughts. She was, on the whole, delighted at Ree's sudden change of heart. The screams echoing through the valley had galvanised something in Ree's core, and she'd flipped seamlessly from charging off into the mountains, demons take the cowards, to volunteering herself to go off alone on a probably-not-suicidal-but-definitely-very-risky scouting mission. And while Javani was proud and a little touched that her ma would do such a thing for people she seemed to, for the most part, despise, it wasn't hard to wish that there was another, safer way for Ree to demonstrate her adjusted attitude.

She was wandering aimlessly, cloak wrapped tight around her against the bleak chill of the day, looking this way and that as she walked. She realised she was looking out for Anri. Not that she particularly wanted to exchange words with him – the man was a cast-iron bastard, she was certain of that much – but she'd meant what she said: he'd be a far better candidate to go skulking silently through the woods at nightfall, and, if she were truly honest, someone she wouldn't shed *that* many tears over should something nasty occur.

She chided herself. That was beneath her, and she knew it. Anri might have many flaws, many, many flaws indeed, but she'd still be upset if he was murdered by bandits doing something she'd asked him to do. Not that he'd do it, Mariam was right there. She couldn't even find him to ask him anyway. She guessed that when Anri didn't want to be seen, he wasn't, which just wound her up all the more.

'Mistress? Did you ask someone about the food?'

Tauras. She'd walked all the way to the stables. He was sitting under a pile of fleeces against the outer wall, his chain snaking through the frozen mud into the open doorway and the darkness within. His bowl and platter were unmoved from her last visit. Tarfellian was still on guard, curled up a safe distance from Tauras on the other side of the fence and producing great huffing snores.

'Sorry, Tauras, I got, uh, side-tracked. I'll go and find someone now.' And then, reflexively, 'Was there anything else you needed?'

His face brightened like a small child offered sweet ice. 'Do you know if there are any cartwheels around? Or maybe a small boulder, or something the size of a small boulder?'

'Why in the name of the gods do you want anything like that?'

He seemed puzzled by the question, thick brows knotting. 'To lift up.'

She waited for the rest of the answer, but that seemed to be it. 'And then what?'

'Then . . . put down.'

'And then?' she asked, dreading what was coming.

'Lift up again!' he beamed.

She scratched at her temple with cold fingers. 'But why?'

'To keep me strong! So I can lift other heavy things!'

'Like small boulders?'

'Or something of a similar size, yes, mistress.' He was nodding eagerly, elated that she understood so perfectly. She already wanted to release him. If anything, she wanted to send him home to his own ma.

'How did you become a bandit, Tauras?'

The excitement left his face, replaced with a frown that bordered on hurt. 'I'm not a bandit. I'm a professional soldier, mistress. Man-at-arms, Ninth Chapter, Company of the Wolf, under Captain Inaï Manatas.'

Her hands were up. 'I know, I know, you told me. Sorry. I forgot.'

'That's all right.' All was forgiven in an instant.

'How many chapters does your company have, Tauras?'

'I don't know, mistress. At least six.'

'Didn't you say you're the Ninth Chapter?'

'They're given odd numbers. Captain says it's to make the company seem bigger, mistress.'

'Huh. How many people in your average chapter?'

'Thirty fighters, plus ancillary staff. It's supposed to be, anyway, but captain says we're under-personned, mistress.'

She leaned on the top timber of the ram pen's fence again. 'What does your company do, Tauras?'

'We protect people. But only people who pay. Otherwise we'd never have enough to eat, as we couldn't buy food. So people who need protecting, they hire us with a contract, and then,' he paused for a moment, 'we eat!'

'What do you protect them from?'

'Being hurt. Being afraid. There are bad people in the mountains, actual War Criminals.' She could still hear the capital letters when he said it. Gods damn the myth of Copperhand and his silent killers. 'Lots of dangers in the forest,' he repeated, his eyes drifting to the treeline.

'Do you think the people in this village are afraid now?'

He looked slowly around, although there weren't many villagers in view from where they were, then nodded.

'Why do you think that is?'

He thought for a moment, chewing his lip. 'They stopped paying to be protected, didn't they? And now they're afraid.'

Oh well, she'd tried. 'What's going on in your camp, Tauras?'

'I don't know, mistress. I'm not there.'

From anyone else it would have seemed sarcastic.

'I'll see you later, Tauras. I won't forget to ask about your food this time.'

'Yes, mistress. Thank you, mistress.'

It was not yet dusk, but it seemed the election had taken place already. Word passed quickly across the camp, the votes were counted, Lado of Cstethia was taking acting command. Manatas didn't even remember being asked to vote. Botrys was playing fast and loose with the by-laws to keep himself in a position of power; as Lado was not a captain, Botrys could dismiss him at any time and return him to the ranks. He probably thought he was being devious, but Manatas had no doubt that the scheme itself had come from Lado.

'And now we answer to a demon,' he sighed, folding shut his ledger of records – Botrys had ordered all the captains to turn in their numbers, fully up to date. The light was nearly gone now, and his eyes were not what they used to be.

He ducked out of his tent into the fading gloom and almost went head-first into Arkadas. 'Lieutenant? What's the commotion?'

'Captain,' Arkadas looked flushed and sweaty, 'have you seen Captain Kediras anywhere?'

'You can still call her Keds, Arkadas,' Manatas replied, but something cold had seized his gut. 'Why? What is the commotion?'

'Her chapter, they packed up and left,' he gestured to where the neat row of tents had been earlier that day. Keds's tent remained. 'You'd . . . you'd better come and see.'

'Come and see what? Come and see what, Arkadas?'

He couldn't reply, just jerked his head for Manatas to follow.

He followed.

TWENTY-EIGHT

Outside the camp, the trees were little more than looming dark strips in the late afternoon gloom. The sun was lost behind the mountain to their back, only a thin stripe of watery red sunlight still visible at the crest of the great grey bluff across the valley that backed the village of Ar Ramas. The mist was up again, seething from the valley floor, cool and moist against his cheek, leaving a stinging burn as Manatas hurried after his lieutenant. Arkadas didn't flap easily, but he was flapping now.

Arkadas pulled up a short way from the picket line, as the beaten trail of the camp led down to the established road that cut along the slope in the direction of the waterfall and the village beyond. The trees were spread thinly here, apart from a bunched cluster at the path-side, thin brown trunks still dusted with last night's snow. Figures were gathered around the trunks, some carrying torches, one or two with official company lanterns, their oily smoke thick and noxious on the bitter wind. Snow was falling again, tiny flakes drifting through the skeletal oaks, gleaming in the lantern-light.

'Why is everyone out here, Arkadas?'

He could only respond with a gesture. *Up.*

The upper branches of the wiry trunks bowed under the weight of four figures, suspended and swaying. Manatas recognised the unfortunate clerk immediately, the man whose confession had been so public and so fatal. It took him a moment more for his eyes to adjust, to register the shapes and identity of the other three. Their limbs were still, no twitches, no struggles, only a soft swing on the wind's caprice.

Manatas swallowed hard. The light was faint, but the colours were unmistakable. 'Arkadas, am I looking at the Third Chapter?'

Arkadas only nodded.

Keds's chapter. Keds's survivors. But Keds was not among them. Where was she?

The gathered men at the base of the trees shifted, opening their circle to include the newcomers. There, at the heart of it, stood Lado of Cstethia, bathed in lamplight, the strings of his fringe casting shadows like dancing fingers across his face.

'Ah, chapter captain, your timing is impeccable – you've saved us the burden of dispatching a man to fetch you.'

Manatas was aware of footsteps behind him, the crinkle and crunch of thin snow on frozen leaves, and knew he was surrounded. Surrounded by members of his own company, thrice damn it, people who should be his allies and comrades-in-arms. Arkadas looked pale and sweaty in the flickering torchlight. Will he hang us, too? Conspirators in a plan never enacted? He looked up again at the hanged mercenaries, their drifting feet a good three paces clear of his head. He couldn't even remember their names. Keds had told him, introduced them – a tired, haunted trio, but steadfast and professional – and they'd drunk together on the night of the feast. They hadn't been talkative, but he hadn't felt like talking. Now he felt a great burning nausea rising within him.

'Brave soldiers of the Company of the Wolf!' Lado called to the gathering assembly, still obsequious even in command, 'I have summoned you from your duties for the gravest of reasons: treachery.'

Manatas swallowed. From the corners of his eyes he guessed that half of the company were out of the camp already, spreading across the trail and the churned underbrush, shuffling between snow-bleached trunks. Perhaps more than that now. Dozens of professional soldiers, battle-hardened and ruthless, cold and restive. He was one of them, after all, for the sake of the gods. He tried to calculate his chances of escape, if he and Arkadas could somehow muscle free of arrest and make it to the road. Ridderhof's horse was still tied up beneath the stable awning one of the work groups had erected. Maybe if he . . .

He knew he was fooling himself. Perhaps as an officer he could demand beheading over hanging. But did he trust Lado to accomplish the act with a single stroke? Or would Botrys demand the honours? Gods save him, the thought of Botrys hacking away at his neck like a drunken butcher filled him with more dread than anything. Where in hells was Keds?

Lado took one of the lanterns from the man next to him, one of the Pashani in their pale, drab cloaks, and held it above his head, casting his scarred face into deep vertical lines. Snowflakes drifted around him like a twisted halo.

'I speak of the disappointing treachery of desertion,' Lado proclaimed. 'Those you see above us, who danced their last at the rope's end this very afternoon, attempted to betray us all. They turned their backs on the company, on our brotherhood, our family, and cast us aside. They broke their contracts, but more than that, they broke their sacred duty. Their fate was inevitable, for the gods loathe those who abandon their families the most. I hope, one day, we can find the strength of spirit to forgive them for the hurt they have done to us.'

He hoisted the lantern higher, and now Manatas could make out the sweeping lines of blood that marked the legs of the hanging crew, the obvious wounds. They'd been hunted, then: brought down by arrows and dragged back to the camp, strung over branches and hoisted, wounded and bleeding, to dangle and strangle as Lado and his Pashani sadists watched. All while Manatas had been updating his damned-by-gods ledger.

Where was Keds?

'I regret that these are not the last we shall be hanging this day,' Lado continued, affecting great hurt and sadness in his voice. His eyes sparkled in the lantern-light, greasy tendrils of smoke coiling around him like pet serpents. 'Others have tried to abandon us. They have been found. They will soon be joining their fellows here, kicking out one final jig. But my soldiers, such waste and treachery shames us all. I understand that doubt and apprehension can dog even the surest minds in times of great upheaval. I understand that even the strongest among us can feel lost and afraid.' He placed his hand back on his chest, a movement that made Manatas reflexively grit his teeth. 'I understand.

'But we are the Company of the Wolf! Wolves are pack animals, we must stick together. Deviation or separation hurts us all. Do not agonise over our absent pay or levels of supply – all is in hand. I give you my word as your acting commander that you will all receive more than you ever hoped for, and soon. So steel your nerves, gird your loins, and prepare. Our time is coming.'

He moved the lantern in a slow arc, illuminating dozens and dozens of armoured mercenaries, standing watchful in the frozen forest.

'We are wolves. Don't make us hunt you down like dogs.' He tossed his empty hand. 'Dismissed.'

The host began to disperse, and Manatas felt the tension that had wrapped his chest and throat disperse with it, an incredible feeling of lightness flooding through him, leaving him almost giddy.

Lado was looking right at him.

'Chapter Captain Manatas, a word.'

Anri was waiting for Javani as she wandered back up the terraces, as she'd suspected he might be. He'd have spotted her looking for him and hidden out of the way, then met her on his own terms. The dick.

'After me, were you?'

'No.' She concentrated on climbing the terrace stairs, cut into the earth and lined with thick timber and river stone from the valley floor. Three sets in a row were robbing her of both breath and the mood for conversation.

'Saw you talking to the big monster, I did,' he said, falling in loping step beside her, bow slung casually over one shoulder. 'Lucky he didn't try and eat you up, not that there's bugger all of you but gristle.'

'Thank you, I guess?'

'Another big hoo-ha your mother's made with the Council, I see. You two cursed by an ancient sorceress of popularity, were you?'

She pulled up short one step from the top, her chest heaving. 'You want to know why I was looking for you? Really?'

He rubbed his nails against his jerkin. 'Actually, I'm not all that fussed.'

'My ma is about to go wandering off into the woods, risking her neck, to find out what's going on in the mercenary camp, what they're up to, and whether your constable is still healthy.'

'Not *my* bloody constable,' he muttered.

'When it's obvious to every bastard in the village, not to mention the whole mountain range, that the best person to be doing something like that is you.'

'And that's why you were after me, was it? To do your mother's dirty work? Wiping your little arse for you next, is it?'

She jabbed a finger into his chest, pushing him half a step backwards. '*Fuck* you, Anri. She's doing this for you, for all of you. We could have left already but I wanted her to . . .' She trailed off, shaking her head, then sighed with exasperation.

He wasn't moved. The dick. 'Now listen here,' he said, his eyes wide and intent, 'don't include me with the rest of them. I'm not a part of this village. I'm not a part of their stupid little rules, their stupid little politics. I just happen to live nearby, that's all. Daft bastards would have starved and frozen without me to watch out for them – Anri, hunt us some game, would you? Anri, kill that wolf that's been stalking the flock, would you? Anri, bring us some furs for winter, as all we have is shit-caked wool that smells worse than we do. Gods, I never wanted to come to this piss-riddled outpost in the first place, did I. I'd have moved on long ago if it weren't for—' He stopped suddenly, clamping his jaw shut.

Javani glared at him, her arms folded, her breathing slowing. 'Yes? If it weren't for what? Tanith, your wife? Was that what you were going to say?'

'It's none—'

'Oh, give it a rest! You found me, you started talking to me. If it was just to make yourself feel better, talking down to a girl, then I'm sorry it didn't work out for you the way you hoped.'

His whiskered jaw was clenched. 'You don't understand anything, clever girl.'

'Then help me to. Tell me what I don't know. How else am I going to gain this divine understanding? Inspired guesswork?'

He sniffed and looked away, nostrils flaring.

'It was Tanith's idea to come to Ar Ramas, wasn't it?' Javani took a step closer. He didn't move away. She tried to remember what Mariam had told her and Ree. 'But she fell ill on the way, and when you arrived here, you couldn't move any further, right? You had some kind of agreement with her, but her illness meant you could never get your side, and never leave. How's that for inspired guess-work?'

One corner of his mouth gave the slightest twitch. 'Could be you're not as pig-thick as you look, pest. Still wrong, mind,' he went on, 'but a better class of wrong, at least.'

'Will you go scouting in the forest? With my ma, if not instead of her?'

He laughed.

'Fuck, no.'

TWENTY-NINE

Up close, within the glow of torch and lantern-light, Manatas could see the splatters of fallen blood clearly against the churned leaves and snow beneath the hanged figures. He did not look up. He would not.

'Chapter captain.' Lado was chewing, Manatas couldn't see what. He had the lantern in one hand by his waist, casting strange and unsettling shadows over his ravaged features. Small flakes of snow drifted between them like dying insects, catching the light for a moment before tumbling into darkness. Manatas could feel the press of his Pashani confederates either side of him, behind him. He wondered if all the looming figures were Pashani of the Seventh, or if others were only too eager to join Lado's own particular house guard. Botrys was keeping Ridderhof's old guard wrapped around him like a blanket; Lado seemed perfectly happy to form his own cadre. 'I wanted to pick your brain about something.'

His choice of words seemed far from incidental. There was no sign of Botrys or Jebel, and Manatas had lost sight of Arkadas, but he hoped his lieutenant had retreated to a safe distance and was at this moment preparing his escape. He would not be, of course. Arkadas had always cared so much about following the rules.

'What service might I render, acting commander?'

Lado's eyebrow twitched, very faintly, behind his hair when Manatas used the word 'acting'. It felt a small, pointless victory. He was going to ask about Keds, that much was obvious. He was going to ask if Manatas had known anything of her plot. And when he protested ignorance, he'd be strung and gasping beside the last of the Third Chapter who dripped above his head – assuming he was lucky. There were plenty of worse ways to make your exit from the mortal realm, and he had no doubt that Lado was a man who had familiarised himself with many of them.

'We find ourselves short of intelligence, Chapter Captain Manatas.' He pulled his mouth wide in a facsimile of a smile, showing sharp, clean teeth. 'Not, of course, in terms of mental acuity, you understand. We are all keen thinkers here. I am referring to detailed information of the actions of our foes.'

'Our foes?'

Lado swung up the lantern in the direction of the valley's far side, where a crescent of prickles of light glimmered in the gathering dusk. 'Our delinquent clients, who have challenged us so boldly, who have maimed and murdered our troops, who conspired to end the life of our own beloved captain-general. Our foes, chapter captain.'

Manatas couldn't help himself. 'I thought Ridderhof took his own life after his fraud was discovered?'

Lado didn't even blink, didn't acknowledge that he'd spoken, ploughing forward with his discourse. 'We know now that they plot and conspire, but we do not yet know their depths. They are secretive and false, chapter captain, they hide themselves and make plans that would see us break and perish.' This did not sound like the villagers he'd known over the past few months, and Manatas almost laughed. Almost. But then he thought of Ree, the new arrival, and that punchy little hand-bow that had wounded Ioseb. The notion near-sickened him, but perhaps Lado had a point after all.

'Did the constable provide anything useful?' Manatas had not seen the man for some time. He hoped there would be enough of him left to exchange for Tauras.

Lado flicked his fingers away, dismissive, disgusted. 'Nothing, of course. He's as steeped in their lies as any.' He rounded on Manatas, seemed to swell in the lantern-light. 'And this is where you come in, chapter captain. As our resident expert on the locality, and friend of the natural world and its creatures,' Lado couldn't keep the smirk off his face, 'your company requires you to perform some reconnaissance.'

'Reconnaissance, acting commander?'

'You're going to scout the village. Mark its perimeter, its defences, its points of access. Its guards and their patterns, its food and animal stores, the sleeping locations of its inhabitants. A very detailed report, chapter captain, as befits a man of your rank. But most important of all,' Lado leaned forward over the lamp, plunging his curtained face into darkness, 'you're going to make sure that none of our lost siblings have made worse choices than we feared.'

Manatas resisted the urge to scratch his head. 'You mean, watch to see if any deserters are in the village?' Keds! Keds had escaped him and he didn't know where she was, and he was disquieted by the prospect of her being in Ar Ramas. Manatas hoped the relief hadn't shown on his face.

Lado nodded, slowly, resuming his chewing without visibly putting anything into his mouth. 'Something like that. We shall expect a great deal of intelligence from you, chapter captain.'

He risked it. 'It would be of benefit to know the parameters of those I'm scouting for, acting commander – earlier you mentioned other deserters had already been recaptured. Anyone of note? Who else is out there?'

Lado sucked gently at his lip, his eyes narrow, the lantern flickering beneath him. 'No one important,' he said after a moment. 'We brought home some jittery clerks who had tried to steal away with what remained of the working treasury.' He shook his head, wearily. 'We suspect they were party to my predecessor's fraud. Their confessions will no doubt confirm it.'

Manatas kept his face neutral through sheer force of will. 'Nobody else?'

'None I can recall, no.' Keds had escaped him, and Lado was presenting him with an opportunity to abscond himself. All he needed to do was find Arkadas and . . . but what about Tauras? 'You have your orders, chapter captain. Be about them now, and we shall expect your detailed account at dawn.'

Manatas was already turning, his mind racing away to schemes and escapes, when Lado spoke again. 'Oh, and chapter captain, it's important that we share our expertise around the company, don't you think? We don't want to be reliant on one or two specialists for crucial operations, especially given how risky life can be out here. To that end, Mantenu and Antulu here will be accompanying you on your assignment.' He flashed a quick, false smile. 'To keep you honest, as the old saying goes.'

For the first time in many years, Manatas came close to swearing. He nodded his understanding with a single, sharp dip of his head. Two of the Pashani slid from the circle to his side, torchless and brooding.

'Will that be all, acting commander?'

Lado passed the lantern to the man beside him, who to his disappointment Manatas recognised as Zurab, Ioseb's Vistirlari accomplice, then began rummaging for something in the satchel that hung from his shoulder. 'Yes, chapter captain, you are dismissed.'

He'd gone three paces, the Pashani marching in lockstep at his elbow, when he heard the high, timid note play out. He did not stop. He did not look round. He did not adjust his stride. He kept his gaze fixed on a point a thousand yards in the distance as he walked away at a measured pace, while behind him Lado found his first few notes on Keds's sister's flute.

'I need all my gear, not just my sword.' Ree managed not to snatch the proffered scabbard, but it took effort. For days she'd had nothing more menacing on her person than a withering stare, and the thought that she was armed once more was both comforting and oddly disturbing. What if she hurt someone?

She shook off the thought, as Sweeper looked to Camellia for confirmation. Behind them, the waterfall churned on in the twilight, its drifting mist sparkling as it caught the light from the braziers that burned along the village's pathways and the narrow shafts of warm light that escaped through gaps in the shutters of the nearest huts. Gentle snow was falling, half-hearted and damp.

With evident reluctance, Camellia nodded, and Sweeper scampered off back towards whichever hidden store they'd been keeping her ordnance in. Her sword belted, Ree waited, resisting the urge to tap her foot. It had been a cold day, and now what passed for daylight had gone the temperature had dropped like a stone. Standing around in the freezing evening was not going to get her off to the most auspicious start on an evening that promised a greater than zero quantity of crawling through dirt.

'Someone should go with you,' Camellia said. Her face was tight, lines beneath her eyes, a convincing expression of concern. Behind her, Volkan – the other half of the Council's official delegation – snorted with derision.

'I'll say,' he muttered.

Ree gave a weary shake of her head, and tried to look casual leaning on her stick. 'Two people means twice as much to go wrong.'

'You mean, two people means someone will be there to keep an eye on you,' Volkan snapped. 'How do we know she won't tell us any old story on her return? She has her own agenda, always does,' he sniffed.

Ree controlled her breath. 'I've never been anything but straight with you,' she retorted, not looking directly at him. 'I'm doing this as a favour, because you need to know what's coming, and clearly nobody in this place feels up to the task. Consider it a parting gift.'

Volkan snorted again.

Sweeper reappeared at last with a bundle in his arms, and Ree saw the length of her unstrung bow poking from each end. No need for that, but the hand-bow, that was coming, as were her knives. Let's see, belt-knife, trail-knife, surprise-knife . . .

'One of my knives is missing.'

Sweeper blurted immediate apologies, his head bobbing. 'Should I go back and look for it, mistress?'

'No, don't bother. We can find it later. I have enough for now.'

Volkan couldn't keep the sneer from his voice as Ree tucked her blades around her person. 'Are we to start carrying weapons around the village now, Camellia? Is this where you would have us end?'

'No!' Camellia near-shrieked. Her eyes gleamed wet with unshed tears in the twinkling light. 'Not inside the village. At its edges if we must, but never within. Nearly three hundred souls call Ar Ramas their home, and we quarrel and fight and drink like any other congregation, and I will *not* have arguments become murderous violence through proximity to tools of death, do you understand? I will not!'

Ree flexed her mouth in acknowledgement. Camellia wasn't always wrong.

The kid and Anri emerged from the shadows, each walking as if they had nothing to do with the other. She ought to have a word with the kid about that. There was something untoward about a girl her age hanging around with a socially maladjusted middle-aged man, but this wasn't the time.

'You're going, then?' The kid just sounded weary.

'I am.'

'Be careful.'

'I will.'

'I'm not going to come looking for you if you trip over your stick and can't get up.'

Ree snorted and gave a disbelieving shake of her head.

'I'd expect nothing less.'

Her knuckles white, Javani watched her mother cross the slick, gloomy bridge, then disappear into the murk of the twilight forest beyond. She watched a moment longer, just in case Ree came tearing back out with a herd of bandits at her heels, but she did not reappear. Well, she wasn't going to stand around in the cold all night. Mariam was expecting her back at the smithy, along with a mountain of food.

As she turned to leave, she realised she couldn't see Anri. But that, of course, proved nothing.

Manatas trod quietly through the darkened forest, and tried not to cry. He was not by nature a weeper – though the gods knew he'd encountered a few in his tours, and he would never judge a man for showing the profundity of his emotions – but right now everything was just too much. There were plenty of reasonable explanations for why Lado might have come into possession of Keds's flute, of course there were. But she'd never have willingly left it behind. He knew that with graveyard certainty. She was gone but not gone, fled but not deserted, presumed dead without a body. The uncertainty gnawed at him. At least he knew Tauras was alive, and probably safer than the rest of them.

He blinked his eyes in the dregs of lingering daylight that filtered through the thick denuded trunks around him, retaking the tears that threatened to betray him. What kind of monster was Lado, to toy with him so, to play lethal games? What was this current adventure, traipsing around a frozen forest in darkness for the man's amusement? Was it some kind of test, or just a way for Lado to keep Manatas out of camp while he rifled through his belongings, or made Arkadas disappear? Keds had been right, he was a demon. He should have let her kill the man the moment they saw him.

But would that really have been better?

He paused, one hand against an icy trunk, and squinted up at the escarpment that loomed overhead, a dark mess against the dull silver of the cloud above. They weren't far from the river now, he could hear it, at least, if not see it. Who scouts in darkness?

The village was exactly as he'd known it would be. Above him, over the crest of the escarpment, the centre, with its rings of huts, square and Council building, its grain stores, barns and workshops. Behind it, the wall of grey rock, riddled with caves and goat-trails. To his left, the jut of the promontory and the waterfall beyond, and the rope bridge to which he'd made so many trips in the past. To his right, the winding, narrow trail cut up into the escarpment that the villagers used to descend to the river to fish, or for pack animals that found crossing the rope bridge to be a task up with which they would not put. And beyond the climbing terraces, the narrow rise at the shoulder of the cliff that led around the peak towards the goat pasture and the dwellings beyond, the overspill.

Three ways in, three ways out: the rope bridge, the cliff path, the pasture. For a bunch of peace-focused agronomists, they'd unwittingly picked an excellent redoubt, rich in both covered approaches and natural fortifications. Of course, they'd done nothing to augment those fortifications, and rarely posted a guard of any sort. Why would they, so far into the wilderness?

Why would they, when they paid a mercenary company to protect them?

He cast an eye back at the two Pashani, who lurked a few paces behind, their drab cloaks merging with the twilit woods. They'd said nothing to him for the duration of their trip around the valley floor, fading in and out of his vision, keeping their distance constant. He wondered if they'd fall back if he tried to approach.

'Friends,' he whispered. What had been their names? Pashani names all sounded the same to him. 'Mantelu? Antenu?'

'Mantenu,' said one.

'Antulu,' said the other.

'Noted. Soldiers, I think we've seen enough, for one night, yes?' He patted the ledger in his satchel, which had doubled as a notebook for his observations. 'Shall we return to camp? I, for one, have not yet eaten.'

'No,' one of them said.

'No?'

'Commander is expecting full night's report.'

Manatas took a breath to speak, then another. 'Are you telling me we're expected to spend the night out here? Doing what, exactly, beyond losing touch with our extremities?'

'Scouting,' said one.

'Watching,' said the other.

'Ah, I see, I see. As long as there are clear, military objectives to be observed, who am I to quibble?' Jaw clenched, in part to stop it chattering, he scanned the slope around them, the winding neck of the valley to his left. 'Well, if it's watching I'm to do, I'm going to seek a place of height and coverage.' He gestured to a prominent ridge that projected from the sweep of the hillside above them. 'I take it you'll be coming too?'

In unison, they craned their necks to scan the ridge.

'We watch from here,' one said, unslinging his bow from his shoulder.

'We watch you. We watch out for you,' the other added, his own bow loose in his hands, an arrow already nocked.

'Message received,' Manatas sighed, and began his climb.

Manatas was three agonised paces from the ridge's barren crest, sweating and panting in the night air, when a voice said, very clearly, 'One more step and you die.'

THIRTY

Inaï Manatas, Captain of the Ninth Chapter, Free Company of the Wolf, stood just below the crest of the barren rise with burning thighs and one foot hovering, his breath coming in ragged gasps, and tried to work out what in hells to do next.

'If you'll permit,' he said between gulps of air, 'I'm going to need to replace this foot on solid earth in the coming moments, or I'm liable to lose what little strength remains in my standing leg, and go pitching backwards down this sharp descent, which would in turn cause me no small amount of hurt, in both the sense physical, and to an additional emotional degree, given that I just spent the better part of the evening clambering up the accursed thing, and I have not yet eaten.'

'Oh, it's you,' the voice replied. 'Captain Verbose.'

He squinted in the faint light. The night was overcast but the moon was strong, sending veins of silver through the thick cloud and offering an undulating glow across the landscape. The snow had stopped and he hadn't even noticed. 'Manatas, Inaï Manatas.'

'Inay, was it?'

'Inaï. I have a diaeresis.'

'Sorry to hear that. Try rice and stewed apple, and drink a lot of water.'

'May I put my foot down?'

'You may, but come no closer.'

With relief, he returned his boot to the scrabble of the hillside and leaned forward, hands on his aching thighs. He looked past himself, down to the foot of the slope, where he knew two figures in drab cloaks would be lurking, watching, with arrows nocked.

'If it please you, I may need to approach the peak of this ridge all the same.'

'Try it and I will shoot you dead.'

'If I don't, there are two fellows at the base of this climb who might very well do the same, and, without the intention of disrespect, I'm well familiar with their capability and intent, whereas yours, invisible speaker, remains a mystery to me; therefore, being a student of odds, albeit at an amateur level, I find myself inclined to assume a prone position and crawl to the cusp of this hogback, and take my chances as to what follows.'

There was a pause, possibly one of comprehension. At length, the voice said, 'There are two men at the bottom of the hill who will shoot you if you don't reach the top?'

Manatas grimaced. 'While that omits a body of the situation's nuance, I feel you have seized the meat of the question, yes.'

'Are you running from them?'

'Gods, no – they would pursue me if I tried, and after my recent exertions I would not care to wager on my chances of escape.'

'You just need to reach the top, and stay in view? What manner of game is this?'

'If it please you, it is no game, and the longer spent in this hissed conversation some paces short of my intended destination, the greater the likelihood of one or both of my attendants taking it upon themselves to investigate. I can only appear to be catching my breath for so long. May I please approach?'

The voice was quiet for another moment, then grunted. 'You can come up to the ridge, but if you make any sudden movements, I will put a bolt through your eyeball and lodge it in what passes for your brain.'

'You have my gracious thanks, for the former at least.' Manatas flopped forward and on knees and elbows covered the remaining distance to the frost-pitted stone that marked the narrow highpoint before the ground fell away once more on the far side. He peered over, seeing the twinkling lights of the village through the sweep of wavering trunks, far below and across the gentle hush of the falls. His best guess was that the voice was coming from behind a goat-tattered but hardy-looking shrub that stuck out from the ridge-top, still thick with dark and bitter-looking leaves.

His breath restored, the ground cold and uncomfortable beneath him, but his rising tide of panic momentarily receded, he said, 'May I ask, have we met?'

The voice didn't respond.

Manatas could feel his heart beating against the rough and frigid ground. 'The negotiator, from the village, the newcomer. It's you, isn't it? Ree.'

'Maybe,' came the reply.

He felt the corners of his mouth pulling in an incongruous smile. 'Well, by the gods, this is a coincidence, is it not?'

The shrub scoffed. 'Hardly. This ugly chunk of rock offers the best vantage in each direction. In retrospect, it was only a matter of time.'

His eyes narrowed. The wind was getting up, sending a low moan through the valley. 'You were watching the camp?'

No reply for a moment, then, 'I'm the one with the weapon on you, you're the one who does the talking.' He thought he heard a little chuckle. 'Should come naturally enough.'

'You're truly armed? They returned to you the weapon that killed Ioseb?'

This time, he heard granite in her voice. 'That bolt no more killed your man than it did convert him to monotheism or cure his warts. Tend to your own camp before you cast accusations of murder at mine.'

He raised one hand from the wretched earth in acknowledgement. 'Your words are heeded.'

'Good.'

'Tell me, my man Tauras, is he safe?'

'You first: Gumis, the constable. What state is he in? We heard . . . We heard a lot.'

Manatas bowed his head. The ground was sharply cold against his skin, and he pulled it straight back. 'Truly, I do not know. I have not seen him for some time. If it's anything by way of consolation, not all of those screams belonged to your constable; there was another man, a notary . . .'

'What in the name of the gods is going on in your camp?'

Manatas took a long, slow breath. 'I am loyal to my company, and I will not divulge information that could be used in any sense military or operational against us.'

'Not even if I threaten to put a bolt through your scrotum and pin you to the mountainside for the goats to fuck?'

'Now, why would you say a thing like that to me?'

'Because we're at odds, Chapter Captain Mantilas.'

'Manatas!'

'Your man Tauras is fine, by the way. He can surely eat.'

'He surely can.' He had not permitted himself to worry, especially given Keds's uncertain fate, but hearing that Tauras was alive and voracious cheered him. 'I am glad.'

'Why are there men wearing the colours of your company threatening you with death if you don't climb this hill and spy on us, Inaï Manatas?'

'That would, again, be considered a matter confidential.'

'Doesn't sound good, though, does it?'

The voice – Ree – was quiet again, and he heard shuffling from behind the shrub, as if she were making herself comfortable. He wished he'd thought to wrap his cloak beneath himself before he'd collapsed. The cold of the ground was seeping into him, his mail jammed into his thinning undershirt by the coarse rock.

'It does not,' he sighed at length.

'How long are they going to make you wait up here?'

'That would—'

'Come on, I could sit up here and watch you if I wished. I already know you're here, what are you risking?'

He sighed again. 'I am not expected to report until dawn.'

'Hm.'

He heard the scrabble of loose rock, then the shrub shivered as something slid out from behind it and disappeared into the darkness beyond. He squinted, but the thin moonlight had been swallowed by cloud, and the mountainside was little more than inky stripes.

'Hello?' he said, after a moment.

The moan of the wind was his only reply.

Javani was woken by Sweeper's hand on her shoulder. She hadn't even realised she'd nodded off. She looked up from her nest of fleeces, bunched as close to his watch-fire as she'd dared, into his battered, swollen, earnest face.

'Your ma's back, mistress.'

She was tickled that he called her mistress, but then he called everyone mistress. Except Mani and Keretan, presumably, and the other men. Gendered terms were an oddity, weren't they, said her half-asleep mind, while the rest of her got round to examining what he'd just told her.

'Already?' She leaped up from the fleece-nest, feeling the instant sting of the night air, and pulled her cloak around her. 'Where is she?'

'Gone to see the Council. Went right by you, mistress.'

'Rude.'

Teeth gritted against the sudden cold, Javani chucked an extra fleece over her shoulders and marched.

They were inside the Council House, the building shockingly warm from its roaring fireplaces at each side, the room smelling of sweat and fear. Javani saw her mother at the room's centre, leaning on her stick as she held court. The councillors were not on their stump-chairs but standing around her, expressions intent, their reactions to her words ranging from disbelief to abject terror.

'There's been some kind of coup in the camp – that man, Manatas, that we were dealing with, he's lost control and is in fear of his life. They've hanged several of their own troops out the front of the camp, I saw it from the crest. I'm not sure for what but it could be related to the power-shift. They're actively scouting the village now, they fully intend to attack.'

Keretan was grim-faced. 'You're sure of this? There's no chance of further negotiation?'

'What would they negotiate for, beyond your surrender?'

Camellia was pinched and drawn, deep lines down her face in the firelight. 'And Gumis?'

Ree shook her head. 'Uncertain. But,' she let out a tight breath, 'the omens are not good.'

'Should we threaten their man in return?' Keretan rumbled. 'As a means of bargaining, nothing more,' he added, to the horrified looks of his companions.

'I doubt it would achieve a thing.' Ree ran a hand through her thick white hair, pulling it back from her eyes. 'You know I don't want to tell you your business but, as things stand, your business is beginning to overlap a great deal with mine.'

'What would you have us do?' Mani asked, his moustache drooping, his eyes clouded with sadness.

'You need a hard perimeter, and you need everyone inside it. That means the foresters, the goat-herds, the folk at the timber yard, all of them – they're not safe. Fortify, build up walls where you can, make it as hard as possible for them to pick people – or materials – off. Stand by to cut the bridge. And,' she sighed again, 'you should consider arming your guards. Properly. I know you have a store of weapons hidden away.' Keretan and Camellia exchanged wide-eyed looks at this.

'Unthinkable!' Volkan hissed. 'What manner of message would that send? It's an outright declaration of hostilities, a challenge to belligerence!'

Ree rubbed at her eyes. 'They are determined to assault you regardless. A show of force could act as a deterrent, not an invitation.'

Mariam appeared behind Javani, walking straight past her with a sack over her shoulder. 'Not interrupting, am I?' she queried.

Ree shook her head. 'I think we've done what we can.' She waved her stick at the Council, making Volkan flinch. 'Get everyone inside the perimeter, and make it as hard as possible for them to breach it. They're in the forests now, and they're going to move from sniffing around to probing for weaknesses very soon.'

Mariam held out the sack for inspection. 'As requested, flatbreads, three types of cheese, a skin of *kipir*, some fruit, and a little pot of yoghurt with honey. Please mind the pot, it's one of mine and I am rather proud of it, like.'

Ree took the sack as Javani wandered over. 'Thank you, Mariam. This will do nicely.'

'Ma? I know you missed dinner, but that's a lot for you, isn't it?'

Ree slung the sack gently over her shoulder, then reached over and ruffled Javani's hair. 'Ah, perfect.' She plucked the fleece from across Javani's back, ignoring her protesting squeal, and slung it over her other shoulder. 'Get yourself to bed, kid.'

She set off again, marching towards the exterior door with the sack over one shoulder, fleece over the other, stick tapping against the packed earth as she went.

'Ree? Ma? Where are you going?'

'Back out. Don't wait up.'

THIRTY-ONE

Manatas was on the verge of nodding off, the freezing, rugged ground beneath him no longer enough to keep him wakeful, when he saw the shadow move. He watched for it to move again, and in short order, it did. Nonetheless, he was impressed. A woman who used a stick to walk had got within fifty paces of him before he'd spotted her. For a moment, he pondered whether that should concern him: was age catching up with him? His hair was more and more silver every day, he saw the streaks at his temples had become great swathes in the reflection in his shaving bowl. Would his eyesight be the next thing to diminish, or would it be his concentration? He'd never been much of a bow-shot, but his vision at distance had served him well on several campaigns, when the faint sight of a Mawn standard could mean the difference between—

The bush next to him shook and rustled as the woman thumped down beneath it. 'Captain Maranas,' she said, by way of greeting.

'Manatas.' He had to catch himself and remove the smile from his voice. 'You came back.'

Her reply was the sound of rummaging, then something heavy and soft flopped down onto the ground beside him, hanging over the lip of the ridge. 'Here.'

He reached out a cautious hand. For a moment he thought it was a sheep carcass, but it was only a wrapping. 'Thought you might be chilly, stuck on the mountainside all night,' she said.

'That's neighbourly of you.' A dozen reasons sprang to mind for leaving the offering well alone, not accepting this woman's charity, not leaving himself beholden to her. But his fingers and toes were numb and his teeth were chattering. He slid the fleece over himself, wrapping it around his body, at last some level of cushioning from the jabbing rocks below.

'Your two friends still at the bottom of the hill?' She sounded like she was chewing.

'While I have not looked of late, it would be imprudent to assume otherwise. They are skilled at concealment, and the cloud is thick.'

'You'd better keep your head down when you're eating, then.'

A sack slid from beneath the bush, its open neck offering a waft of pungent goats' cheese. He reluctantly withdrew a hand from the warmth of the fleece and teased it open. 'This is for me?'

'Not all of it. We're sharing.'

His mouth was dry, then suddenly wet with saliva. He'd ignored the growling of his stomach like a true professional, but the sight and smell of actual food was like being kicked in the gut by a horse. He found himself fighting back urgent cramps as he pulled out a hunk of bread and set about smearing cheese on it.

'There's yoghurt, too, but I'm keeping that separate. The pot's an heirloom.'

'That is understood.' His hand was shaking as he brought the food to his mouth. At the last moment, the thought flashed across his mind: this is a trap, this could be poisoned or drugged, you should fling it into the valley and bellow an alarm.

He didn't care. He bit. He chewed.

It was magnificent.

'Are you all right, captain?' She sounded amused. 'You made a noise like you'd soiled yourself.'

He swallowed, and resisted the urge to refill his mouth immediately. 'You can rest easy on that score, my lady Ree – unless you had the foresight to bring a spare set of breeches as well?'

'Sorry, cap, you shit yourself, you're on your own.' She was chewing again, and a moment later, so was he. The chill on his skin and the ache of his bones were forgotten. The cheese wasn't even that good, the bread old, but he didn't care.

'Why?' he said when his mouth was empty again.

'Why do you think?'

'You're trying to turn me, and you think bribery will get you what you want.'

She murmured something, her mouth full, then tried again. 'It's more credible than feeling sorry for a poor bastard stuck up a mountain with no food and no warm clothes, isn't it?'

'It is.' Yet he wondered. 'And what is it you want from me, my lady Ree?'

'The same thing any woman wants from a man who has the power to give it: information.' He could hear the smile in her voice. He tried to picture her. He'd seen her from a distance, the bridge between them, then closer at their second meeting, and now, with only a thick and bristly shrub between them and two Pashani killers their heedless chaperons. A fair countenance, tough as leather, large dark eyes and a still-strong jaw. A forked scar on one side of her face, between eye and ear. A thick shock of white hair, whiter than he'd have expected for her age, which had to be in the same bracket as his own. A fair countenance.

'Aren't you going to ask what I'm after, captain?'

'Hmm?'

'The information. I thought we had a little bit of jousting on the go.'

He shifted on the fleece, tucking it further underneath. Sadly it lacked the magical qualities required to warm him from beneath, but it had eased the freezing of his nethers. 'I regret that, grateful as I am for your hospitality, I remain unable to share information that might materially impact the operational effectiveness of my company.'

'The same company that made you sit on a mountainside and watch a village in the dark?'

'The very same.'

'Are you sure it's still your company?'

He kept his hesitation to less than a blink. 'I am in no doubt.'

'Well, you're no fucking fun, then, are you?'

Manatas pursed his lips. 'I do not care for the use of such language. There are plenty of words a person can use that need not cause offence to the listener.'

Her cackle made the shrub shake, and for a moment he feared

her laughter would echo from the peaks and bring the Pashani sprinting to his location. His panic passed. His chagrin did not. 'Why are you laughing at me?' he hissed. 'Does my propriety amuse you?'

'Aren't you fucking precious,' she chuckled. 'Inaï Manatas, you are a professional soldier, a hired killer, a man who commits sanctified murder for coin. Your "propriety" is as incongruous as a nun on a battlefield.'

'I have seen sisters in combat,' he muttered, 'tending to the needs of—'

'I think you're missing the point there, captain.'

For a moment, eating was forgotten, and he felt heat rising in his once-chapped cheeks. 'You are, it strikes me, a hostile person by nature, seeking primarily to provoke as a means of interaction.'

'It's best to see someone's true character up front, don't you think?'

He aimed a stern frown at the midnight shrub. 'That is limited justification for the inflicting of verbal misery on all whose paths you cross.' He released a hot breath, near invisible in the moonless gloom. 'I am none of those things you called me.'

'You're not a professional soldier?'

'Very well, I am one of the things you called me.'

'What were you before?'

The silence hung between them for a moment, punctuated by the cloistered hooting of a distant owl. It was a question not asked on the plains, and, until now, the mountains too.

'I was a ranger. At the edge of the protectorate, beyond the fort line. Protecting the settlers there from Mawn raids, keeping the trade routes safe, that kind of thing.'

'What happened?'

He tried to shrug, prone and wrapped in his cloak and the fleece. 'The collapse. The siege of Arowan, the chaos that followed, well . . . The whole Serican state kind of . . . fell in on itself, curled up like a dying spider. Everything stopped. Our wages about came to an end overnight, and the systems that kept us riding went with them. We still had to eat.'

'We?'

'I had some comrades, stuck with me all this time.' For the most part. 'We ran cows down by the lake for a time . . .'

'Hence the rawhide?'

'. . . But the herds moved on, and left us in their wake.'

'So you became bandits?'

'Hey, now!' This time he was the one who'd risked bringing the Pashani. 'I told you,' he continued in a controlled and lowered voice, 'we are contracted operatives of a registered free company, and our enterprise is legal.'

Somehow, he could *hear* her raised eyebrow. 'A lot of stuff gets called legal out here at the fringes. Doesn't mean it's right.'

'Well, I sleep just fine,' he lied.

'You have a family somewhere?'

He cleared his throat, softly, then took another bite to cover his thinking time. 'I did.'

'Oh. I'm sorry to hear that.'

'They— They're not dead. I feel I should state that upfront, lest you be inadvertently misled. They are merely no longer, as such, mine.'

She said nothing, and the silence weighed, pressing on him to continue. A small voice at the back of his mind, the same that had been convinced he was about to be poisoned, was screaming at him to clam up, to scrabble back, to put as much distance between himself and this sly and treacherous woman as possible. He ignored it.

'I was away a lot, even before. I sent money. After the collapse, for a time, I wandered, before finding gainful employment once more. I tried to return to what I'd thought of as home. I was, uh, disabused of that notion. The money was welcome, but I was not.' He cleared his throat again. 'Some time after that, not even the money was welcome.'

'Do you miss them?'

He rolled over, staring up at the moonlight-mottled blankets of black cloud that drifted overhead. Small stones dug into his shoulder blades. 'I think about them, sometimes. I wonder. We had some children, some that lived, but they were very small. A young man spoke to me, on that last visit, but in truth I could not say which he was, who he was, and that, in itself, tells me that his words were well-spoken and deserved.'

'You'll never go back?'

'There is nothing to go back to. Only the lake house remains.'

He heard her shuffling around beneath the shrub. When she spoke next, her voice sounded closer. 'What's the lake house?'

He could feel himself smiling at the thought, lips cracking against the cold. 'A place barely deserving of the name. We spent some time there, my comrades and I, on the shore of a lake at the foot of the southern spur, on the route to Pasaj. We've been back a few times since, between tours, between contracts. It's a fine place to winter – clement weather, good food, fine fishing, and all the benefits that proximity to a major trade route can bring, especially to those flush with demob coin.' He sighed.

'It sounds nice,' she said softly. It sounded like she was only a hand's span from his own head.

'And you?' he said, some long-buried instinct insisting that reciprocity was the soul of politeness.

She puffed silvery air into the darkness. 'My story is long, and tedious, and of little interest to anyone beyond its protagonist.'

'I find that challenging to believe.'

'Kind of you, but wrong.'

'How did you come to this place? That at least has the intrigue of relevance.'

She sighed, sounding not sleepy but tired. He'd lost track of the hour, the moon lost behind clouds, the night still but for the whisper of the wind through the naked forest, the creaking of the trunks, the soft calls of night-time things. 'We came from the north. Tried to cross into Arestan, but the peaks were too high. We've been shuffling southwards since, moving like crabs, weeks of travel and no closer to our destination.'

'People speak highly of Arestan, in my limited experience.' He paused. 'Although the one fellow I know of who travelled there for sure did not much care for it.'

'Oh?'

'Disliked the humidity, as I recall. Claimed the air steamed from mid-spring to autumn.'

'Maybe our wasted efforts have been for the best, then, hm?'

He put one hand behind his head, shifted in search of relative comfort. 'And who is your "we", here?'

'Me and the kid. My, well, daughter, I suppose.'

'You suppose?'

'It's complicated.'

'Again, the boundaries of my credence are tested, but I'm sure you know your business best.'

'I do.'

'How old?'

'Twelve. Nearly thirteen, gods – we must be within a few weeks now.'

'A dangerous age, I'm told.'

She snorted. 'That kid would be dangerous at any age.'

'And as for how you came to be engaged in the attempt of crossing into Arestan from so far out in mining country . . . ?'

He saw movement in his periphery, the waving of her hand, dismissing the notion. They were so close now, lying flat, one each side of the ridge's crest, almost close enough to bump heads. She'd not threatened to shoot him again since her return. 'Enough nonsense to fill a book.'

'And how you came to be in the region in the first place? Your accent doesn't mark you as a native of the plains.'

'Thank you. I've changed it a few times, just in case.'

He wasn't sure if she meant it. 'And your life before?'

'Two more books. At least. But don't expect a happy ending.'

He mused. 'Tales end, but life goes on. We're not yet at any kind of ending.'

'Not yet,' she said, but left the rest unvoiced.

They lay in silence, for a while.

THIRTY-TWO

Javani had watched her mother collect her weapons from Sweeper's colleagues by the watch-fire at the bridge, then lumber off once again into the dark of the woods. Cloak wrapped tight around her in the face of the cheek-slapping cold, she'd waited until Ree was long gone from her sight before making her way to the bridge herself. She gave Sweeper's friends a nod as she passed, but didn't even slow her pace. She figured they were there to watch for people trying to come into the village unobserved; they should have no interest in people travelling in the other direction.

She made her way across the frigid, swaying bridge as fast as she dared, which was to say, not very, one hand gripping the side rope, the other holding the lantern she'd pilfered from outside the Council House. They'd had scores there, one wouldn't be missed. Once blessedly aground on the far side, she scampered up the winding trail that, even in near darkness, was becoming ever more familiar.

By the time she was in sight of the clearing, she was expecting to hear Anri's voice at any moment, braced against some sudden caustic quip. The timber yard was dark, the stacked piles of felled trunks little more than a range of miniature blue mountains, as were most of the foresters' huts beyond them, but cracks of light spilled from gaps in the shutters of the endmost – Anri's. Tanith's.

She wondered how close he'd let her get. She was still wondering by the time she stood at the threshold, her breath a glowing golden plume before her face in the warm light that sneaked from the door-frame, and raised her hand to knock.

Javani hesitated. She could hear talking coming through the door, low tones of conversation. Was Tanith having one of her lucid moments? Would it be unforgivable to interrupt? She swallowed. This was important. If she was, well, whatever the right word for escaping her catatonia was, then she should hear it, too. Javani knocked.

The door was wrenched open an instant later, filled with Anri's bullish form. He was cast in silhouette by the light behind him, but Javani had enough light to see the passing of whatever great excitement he'd had on hearing her knock. His shoulders dipped, his head drooping. 'It's you, is it?'

'It is.' She clung tight to the importance of her mission, unwilling to let his attitude wear her. 'Is your wife, uh . . . here?'

'What? Course she is.'

'I mean, is she . . . with us?'

'Just come in, then, pest. I didn't spend all that time banking a fire to have you piss my warm air into the night sky, did I.'

Inside was as she remembered, if dimmer, the mellow glow that had seemed so bright and welcoming from across the clearing in fact the result of three fat and smoky tallow candles and a fire that was far from roaring. She looked around, peering into shadows as her eyes adjusted, trying to locate the talkative Tanith.

Anri's wife was in the bed by the window, lying beneath blankets, staring blankly up at the smoke-wreathed beams above.

'Who were you talking to?' Javani asked without thinking. The words spoken, she finally cohered the notion: he talks to himself, or at least to her with no expectation of a reply. She wondered if it was that or go mad, sitting in silence for day after day, night after night, with someone who was supposed to be your partner for life, and was now little more than furniture. She cursed herself for the thought.

Anri's brows, already low, dipped to a dangerous level. 'Eavesdropping, is it?'

'No, I, uh. Your voice carries, that's all.'

He leaned back against the sturdy table. 'What is it, pest? You're interrupting my dinner.' Javani couldn't see any food in evidence. Ree had clearly not come visiting with her little feast on her way to wherever.

'My ma – Ree – has been scouting the mercenaries.'

He folded his arms. 'And? So have I.'

'Well, she's been watching them tonight, and she thinks they're building up to an attack. Soon. They're checking the, uh, paths of approach, and, uh, looking for ways across the river.'

'So? They're always doing that. There's a bunch of new boys with them, haven't worked it out yet.'

She clenched her fists, her fingers still barely thawed in the hut's warmth. 'Listen, all right? Ree told the Council that they should get everyone back inside the village, not leave anyone fending for themselves.' Her eyes scrunched with the effort of remembering Ree's words. '"The foresters, the goat-herds, the folk at the timber yard." That's you. You're at the timber yard.'

His beard bristled as he scowled. 'No, I'm not.'

'Yes, you are,' she said, waving her hands around in a circle. 'This is the timber yard, you're in it!'

'I'm not. This by here is a clearing, where I chose to live and build a house, which others subsequently elected to expand by means of felling and stripping the trees around it, and fill with the proceeds of said expansion.' He thumbed his chest. 'But I was here first.'

'I don't think that matters—'

'Well, it does to me, right?'

What would Ree say? No, not that. She tried sounding reasonable instead. 'Anri, they were talking about cutting the bridge. There will be no way into the village from this side, and if the mercenaries start to lay siege, or something—'

'So?' His bellow should have been loud enough to wake the dead. Tanith gave no reaction. Anri stood up from the table, suddenly towering over Javani, plunging her into his shadow. 'You're not listening to me, pest, so I'm going to use small words, yes? Tanith and me, we are not part of the village. We are not part of anything, yes? And the Council, the *Council*—' the word sounded filthy on his lips, '—can make whatever edicts they bloody well choose, and boss around anyone who lets them, but not me. Yes? Not. Me.'

'But don't you want to—'

'And you know what?' He was pacing now, throwing multiple half-shadows from the candles as he walked. 'I never signed up to their cock-eyed notions of peace over sense, did I, and I never signed a contract with a mercenary company, or reneged on my side. I never agreed to hand over my only means of self-preservation to anyone. Me and mine are staying out of this.'

'Is this about Tanith? I understand you don't want to leave her, but couldn't she be moved? Wouldn't she be better off in . . . the . . . village?' She could tell from the shade of his face that she'd made a terrible, terrible error.

'Leave us the fuck alone,' he growled, his hands making fists.

Her hands were up; she was already backing towards the door. 'Fine, it's fine, I'll do that. But Anri, the mercenaries won't.'

'Get *out*!'

Ree had her hands behind her head, resting on the folded hood of her cloak. The night was cold, and sharply so, but the ridge was out of the wind and she'd at least dressed and packed for the conditions. Maybe it was the two cloaks, maybe it was the *kipir*, but she'd long ago stopped worrying about the temperature. Overhead, great rents had appeared in the thick cloud, revealing patches of indigo sky prickled with the gleam of distant stars. The closer she looked, the more stars she saw, dots between dots between dots, until the next wall of silver-etched cloud rolled over and obscured her view.

The easy breathing of the mercenary on the crest's other side was the only thing she could hear in the night's depths; all else was stillness.

'Mistress Ree? Are you sleeping?' His voice was little more than a whisper, clearly not intended to wake her had she been planning to answer in the affirmative.

'I am not, captain. Just watching the stars.'

'As am I, I must confess. It is a boon to see them, if only briefly – such is the vapour that haunts these valleys.' He sighed. 'So far we travel, yet the stars stay the same. On any night, in any place, we can look upon the stars of home.'

'Can we, though?' She adjusted her hands. 'I've gone south a fair way, and north a fair way, and those little buggers shifted in the sky, I'll tell you that much. I'd hazard that if we crossed the girdle of the earth and travelled norther still, we'd be looking at an alien night.'

'That would be something.'

They'd talked, and talked a lot, and Ree felt the hours wearing on her, the draw of sleep against even the sharp and lumpen mattress of the hillside. But despite the pleasant diversion of his conversation, she had not yet achieved her aims, and dawn would not be far away. The gaps in their chatting had grown longer as their minds and bodies slowed, and she needed to give matters a firm prod in the proverbial.

'You know,' she said, stifling a yawn, 'the real shame of it, as I see it, is that there's a genuine proposition for your crew here.'

'Excuse me?' He sounded sleepy, but rousing.

'This place is expanding, and needs to trade. They've hidden themselves away but obscurity is not security, as we used to say in my old line of work.'

'Would I wish to know the nature of said line—?'

'In short, they need protecting. It's not enough to declare yourselves peaceful and expect the rest of the world to play along. And what about internal discipline? As that place grows, it's going to get too big for everyone to know each other. Then you need proper laws, and proper enforcement, because you're not one big family at that point, you're a town, you're a collection of individuals, living their lives, making their choices, and acting as humans do. And humans need to know that there are rules, and that everyone's going to stick to them, or things are going to come apart pretty swiftly.'

'You mean, a watch? Law-men? Notwithstanding the passing insult you paid to my company a moment ago, that is exactly the kind of work at which we excel.'

She rolled over, the rocks hard against her elbows. 'But that's it, captain, that's the crux, the rub. You can't police civilians with military men, especially outsiders. The enforcement must come from within, do you understand? It must be part of the social fabric, and understood to be in service to the people, not commanding or intimidating them into obedience. Otherwise, you're not the law, you're little more than occupiers.'

She heard him click his tongue in irritation. 'But you would deign to have us at the fringes, out of sight and mind? To fight battles where they might not upset the sensibilities of the paying populace?'

'I'm not here to debate the function or ethics of professional soldiery, Mantlebrass, it's far too late for that.'

He'd rolled over, too. The top of his head poked over the ridge, his dark eyes gleaming in the scattered starlight. 'You talk of a genuine proposition, but all you describe is the arrangement that my company had with the village, before, well, things got all twisted up. There are threats in these mountains, I did not speak false when first we met, and the presence of my company, my chapter, is what has allowed these people to flourish in peace to their present size and wealth. Had we not been on hand, they could have been slaughtered in the night by any number of renegades, perhaps the Guild would not have thought twice about expanding their domain up into these hills.'

'The Guild? This far from trade routes and mining plunder? Be serious.'

'Not just them—'

'Ah, yes. The deserters of Flywater are up here somewhere, is that right? And the assassin Copperhand and his gang, lurking in the trees for years, awaiting their moment to strike. Tall tales, captain.'

The heat had not left his voice. 'I did not speak false. They went up into the forests and were not seen again, but that does not mean they ceased to be. There are worse things in these peaks than Lado of Cstethia.'

At last. 'Is he the man that now commands your company?'

She heard him pause, felt the weight of his resignation. 'No, that is Botrys, the lord adjutant.'

'Botrys? Sounds like a fungus, probably a poisonous one.'

He chuckled, but it was thick with sufferance. 'You may be right.'

'And Lado of, where was it? Stethica?'

'Cstethia.'

'He's the man who tried to enter the village, and took Gumis away?'

'He is. A wild man, a dangerous man, who seems to have taken control of the entire camp despite holding no rank and commanding no allegiance.'

She was leaning forward on her elbows, her face now separated from his only by loose stone. Part of her thrilled to the proximity, and she hushed it. 'Who were the pyres for?'

'The first was for Ioseb, the man you injured.'

'You said injured, not killed.'

'I did. The second was for the captain-general, who, we are told, took his own life to escape professional disgrace.'

'You think this Lado is responsible for both.'

'I know he is responsible for the hangings that have followed.' She heard the crack in his voice, the tension of his words. 'And he will be responsible for what comes next.'

'How soon will he attack?'

'I do not know. But I fear it will be soon. He has promised the men-at-arms plunder in place of absent pay, and the camp is hungry.'

'Can you run? To the village, into the hills?'

She realised she could see him shaking his head. The ambient light was growing, blacks becoming blues, blues becoming tinged with violet. To the east, the faintest yellow glimmer lit the sky above the jagged peaks. 'The Pashani would take me before I made it halfway there, and they'd take you with me. Others have had the same idea, and now they swing before the camp. And I still have people I care about down there.' He swallowed. 'My path is set.'

'Hey, we're a long way from an ending yet.' She thought of a sermon Mani had given at the temple before the meeting that morning. 'Work hard, and you can change your fate.'

'I fear there are limits to my capabilities on that score,' he sighed, 'but I appreciate the sentiment.' He sat back on his haunches and stretched. 'Dawn's not far away, and I must make my descent. It would probably be best if you weren't still around when I did so.'

'Agreed.' She began to pack everything back into the sack, taking care over Mariam's yoghurt pot.

'Your fleece.' He'd unwrapped himself.

'You know what? I'm going to leave it here, under the bush. Just in case we get to scouting again soon.'

The light was good enough to see the flicker of smile that cracked his features. He wasn't *all* bad-looking.

'Be seeing you, my lady Ree.'

'Be seeing you, Captain Manatas.'

'Wait – before you go, a favour. I have a friend—'

'We'll look after your man Tauras, don't worry.'

'No, another friend. She's, she's no longer in the camp, and I hope to the gods that she may yet appear elsewhere. She has experience of living in forests, but . . .'

'You think she may come to the village? What's her name?'

'Kediras. Goes by Keds. She's very dear to me.' She saw pleading in his eyes.

'I'll watch out for her, and let the others know. Although it seems unlikely any of your company would aim to escape to the village, knowing what's coming.'

'I know.' His head hung. 'I am sorry.'

'It's not over yet. Until next time, captain.'

'Until next time.'

THIRTY-THREE

Manatas descended the mountainside with as much caution as he could muster, in between yawns. His back, neck and shoulders ached, he was cold and stiff, and the furthermost parts of his body were numb, but he felt a flicker of something hopeful, something almost cheerful. He nurtured it as he made his painful way down, concentrating on the thought of his bedroll and tent, and the hours of oblivious sleep that would soon be his.

As he reached the foot of the ridge, the Pashani faded into view from wherever they had been lurking among the trees. It seemed impossible that they had been tucked behind the trunks themselves; the men were wider than the span of each, it would not have been feasible to hide them behind without folding them in half.

'Dawn's fortune to you, comrades,' he said as he stepped between them, and they fell in behind him as before without a word. 'I trust you had a comfortable night?'

One of them, possibly Antulu, grunted. They began making their way back to the camp in the pre-dawn gloom, its torches and watch-fires twinkling distantly through the trees. When they were roughly halfway across the valley in the thick of the woods, the other Pashani, possibly Mantenu, said, 'We heard you talking.'

Manatas felt a clench of sudden cold, but heat burned his cheeks. The hopeful flicker he'd been carrying since leaving the ridge blew out. They were close to him, too close, behind and to each side, the heavy knives at their belts within easy reach. He would not evade them, and he would not best them. 'You did,' he said slowly, his tongue thick in his mouth.

Possibly-Mantenu continued, 'You talk to yourself often, on watch? Antulu does same. For wakefulness.'

Definitely-Antulu grunted again. 'Is true. For wakefulness.'

Manatas could feel his pulse in his ears, feel the sweat at his back despite the cold that soaked his bones. 'I do indeed find that it helps, in that way. Uh-huh.'

Apparently satisfied, the men did not speak again, and they crossed the valley in silence.

Manatas had to wait to report. Botrys had dragged one of the fancy chairs from inside the commander's pavilion and positioned it beneath an awning, and now sat in it beside a brazier, draped in furs and dozing. Ridderhof's revolting bearskin drooped from the chair's crest, sightless eyes gazing at the forest's wintry gloom. At one of the clerks' tables before him, Lado sat hunched, apparently concerned with nothing more than paperwork by the light of the single candle fixed to its corner. It was still not quite dawn, and Manatas did his best to stand at attention, when every part of his body ached and cried out for sleep. By this stage, it was probably only his fitful shivering that was keeping him awake.

At last Lado looked up from the documents before him and cleared his throat. 'Chapter Captain Manatas, I see you are safely returned. And a little early.'

Botrys started and snuffled awake, slow-blinking eyes eventually landing on Manatas. 'Ah, you're back. From, uh . . .'

Lado spoke smoothly. 'The scouting of the adversary, as you requested, lord adjutant.'

'Indeed. Yes. Well?'

Manatas delivered his report in dry terms, fighting to keep yawns and chattering teeth at bay. There was, ultimately, little to say – there had been no deserters in view, and he was not inclined to make mention of his encounter with the counter-scout, nor of the extent of their conversations. His mind wandered as he spoke, thinking again of the woman with whom he'd talked the night through, and felt that strange, fluttery feeling return. Had he been starved of meaningful conversation for so long?

'Well?' Botrys was looking at him.

'Perhaps the chapter captain has overtaxed himself in the delivery of his duties, lord adjutant,' Lado suggested, those dead eyes glinting behind his hair.

'My apologies, I was momentarily distracted. What was the question?'

Botrys sniffed. 'Your apologies, what?'

Manatas chewed his tongue for a moment, then replied. 'Lord adjutant.'

'Better. Acting commander, repeat the question.'

'Chapter captain, would you agree that the defensive readiness of the adversary remains low, and that as yet they are making few efforts to remedy this?'

There had to be a correct answer here, something to delay whatever action they planned. Should he agree, and risk them moving immediately? Or would a response in the negative spur them on? He was too tired to think it through, his mind already half-asleep and imploring the other half to join it.

'I would, lord adjutant.'

Botrys nodded several times, one hand on his chin, making hmming noises. 'And, acting commander, my second question?'

'Chapter captain, would you agree that the command structure of the adversary consists of a single executive body, and the ability to self-organise of its remainder is minimal?'

Again, there had to be a correct answer here, but he just couldn't see it. 'I suppose I would, lord adjutant.'

'Good, good. Dismissed.'

Lado cleared his throat again as Manatas saluted and turned to go, drawn by the near-gravitational pull of his bed.

'Oh, yes,' Botrys roused himself once more. 'Stay close, Manatas, you'll be needed again shortly.'

'May I retire to my tent for a brief—'

'The lord adjutant has given his order, chapter captain.' Lado's tone had that hurt surprise he did so well, so injured by the very notion of insubordination.

Manatas could feel himself swaying, his vision coming in and out of focus. 'I will remain close, lord adjutant.'

They were back to ignoring him. Lado shuffled his documents once more, then turned to Botrys. 'I'd say that with this information, coupled with Chapter Captain Jebel's report, the operation you ordered was a wise one, lord adjutant.'

Botrys settled back into his furs. 'Of course it was.'

Manatas blinked from his trance. 'Jebel made a report? What operation has been ordered?'

Lado didn't look up. 'You have been dismissed, chapter captain.'

Somnolence forgotten, Manatas stood, stranded in the netherworld of his orders, and began to fret.

Ree crossed the hated bridge slower than she'd have liked, but the light was poor and her leg was aching. A night spent on a hillside in winter's early stages had not been the best rest and recuperation for her injury, and already she could hear the kid's barracking in her mind, her little face snippy with righteous indignation, telling her off for not letting herself recover. She was smiling as she left the bridge.

The smile faded as she reached the far side. No guards, the fires burned out, the torches and lanterns with them. She was going to have serious words with whoever was supposed to be maintaining this watch effort. The village was still and dark, wreathed in pre-dawn mist, the cockerel not yet crowed and the denizens still happily abed. She envied them that, at least – she'd happily bed down on the pile of old fleeces in the stables after her night on the mountain, never mind the smell. Or the giant mercenary, chained in the ram pen. At least the kid had taken herself away somewhere, she'd have had stern words herself if the girl had still been wrapped up by a burned-out fire at this hour.

The nearest hut to the bridge contained the chest for confiscated and surrendered weapons, and she made for it from habit, catching herself as she reached the door. Gumis was gone, and nobody stood in his place, nobody to demand she hand over her only means of self-defence. She could keep her sword at her hip and march through the village as Anri did, and who would stop her?

But she thought of Camellia, her tearful outburst when Volkan had intemperately suggested the villagers start carrying weapons. *I will* not *have arguments become murderous violence through proximity to tools of death*. With a sigh, she stowed her weapons, including all of the knives. She still had her walking stick, at least. Small victories.

Yawning and sore, she set off for the Council House where a few lights still burned, and prepared to tell those within that they might not live to see sunset.

Despite the guttering lanterns at the doors, the Council House was empty. Ree gave a heavy sigh. She should not have been surprised, the day had not yet truly begun and she could hardly blame them for taking rest where they could. Still, the thought of dragging herself to the stables, or worse yet over the rise to the smithy, and then back again to address the Council when they woke was overwhelming. She'd wait for them inside, and take a nap while she could.

She clomped inside the thick darkness of the Council House, which was broken only by the wan dawnlight that crept through the gaps in its shutters and the stretched, wavering rectangle of lantern-light of the doorway. Her leg was aching and her body was making an irrefutable declaration that she was too old to camp on rocks. The hearths were cold but there were rugs before each of them. She'd roll one up and use the other as a blanket, and bollocks to anyone who complained later.

Ten paces in from the door, she knew the air was wrong. The building was empty, lightless, dormant – its air should have been still and heavy. But the air in there *moved*.

Ree was not alone.

She turned in time to see the man detach from the shadows beside the door, little more than a silhouette outlined by fading amber lantern-light. Too surprised, too dull-witted with fatigue to shout, or scream, or do anything that required critical thought, Ree flung up her stick to catch the man's silent swipe of what looked to be a full-length sabre. It bit deep into the wood and wrenched it from her hand, and she stumbled backwards on weak legs as the silhouette advanced. Stupid, stupid, stupid to leave her weapons like that. Had she been concerned for Camellia's fucking feelings? After the way she'd behaved? And now she'd die for it, and the ghastly woman wouldn't even know why.

A second man was in there, sliding from the door's other side where he'd been waiting, the thin light from the doorway catching the gleam of the sword in his hand. Fifteen years ago almost no one had had a sword of a decent size and quality, and now every fucking bandit from here to the salt desert had one. And her own sword sat in a box, beautiful, useless. She vowed that if she survived, she would never remove the thrice-damned thing again.

The shadows advanced on her as she took unsteady backwards steps, trying to count in her head how many remained until she'd tumble over the stump-chairs and crash into Keretan's glorious, mangled armour before she died. Beautiful, useless.

'This one of them?' the first silhouette said. He had a Vistirlari accent.

'Don't suppose it matters now,' the other replied, and Ree felt the back of her foot meet the spreading wood of a chair.

The light in the doorway grew, just a touch, not the pale wash of dawn but something like candle-light. Ree edged her way around the wide chair, knowing now that she had maybe two paces left before she hit the back wall, and tried not to let the certainty of her impending death distract her. The men would have to negotiate the chairs themselves, and when they did, if she could time it right, she might spring—

Who was she kidding? On this leg? In this state? She might as well kneel down now and present her neck. At least it would save everyone some time.

Was that . . . whistling?

A shadow in the doorway, a flickering shape, then a person, a person was there. A moment of hope.

Sweeper. Come to refill the lanterns.

Her face curdled with bitterness. Oh, he *so* likes to help. Of all the useless fuckers in this place, it had to be the—

She saw the moment he turned, the moment he saw the shapes moving in the gloom within, the moment he changed.

The man she thought of as Sweeper vanished into the darkness, but as he did so, something gleamed in his hand.

They were almost on her, one stepping between the chairs, the other circling, blocking her escape the other way.

'Wait,' she croaked. She'd lost Sweeper, and couldn't look for him. 'Wait.'

'Waiting's not going to do it,' one of the silhouettes replied. They were close enough to swing now, close enough to thrust, the heat of their breath brushing her skin.

'I think, this time,' she said, her voice tight, 'it might.'

She ducked.

As the man's sword whipped over her head, something *blurred* in the darkness. She heard a sound like a sigh, and felt droplets splatter her face. Blinking furiously, when she cleared her vision the silhouette before her had vanished. She didn't need to look at her hands to know what had stained her. All she had to do was keep her distance now.

'Rostom?' said the first silhouette. 'Rostom, where'd you go?'

This time, she was watching for it, far enough back to see the pool of darkness rise from behind her stranded assailant, see it fold itself around him, clamping his mouth, pinning his arm, then the flash across his helpless throat. The darkness held him, pulsing, gasping, until the last of the life ran from his body and he slumped, his body hitting the dirt floor with a thud that seemed to echo in Ree's bones.

She could see him, standing framed in the doorway's feeble light, she could see him because he let her. He stood alert, poised, his hands loose at his sides, from one of them dangling the dull blade. It dripped. Two breaths, then three and she watched his shoulders droop, his head drop, the shuffling deference of Sweeper return. She wasn't buying it any more.

'Light the fires and the lamps, then let's see how much cleaning up we're dealing with,' she snapped, her voice still unsteady, her breath not yet calmed. She could feel the gallop of her pulse beneath her ribs. 'And *you* have a lot of explaining to do.'

THIRTY-FOUR

She wouldn't let him open the shutters; it seemed imprudent, given the carnage on the floor of the Council House. The chance of someone looking in and seeing the rich carmine redecoration that Sweeper had wrought upon the place was one problem too many for Ree, who was already somewhat oversubscribed, problem-wise.

Sweeper. So handy with a broom, a keen polisher of pots and refiller of lamps. Shuffling around with quiet steps, never noticed, never missed. Sweeper, a man who could, without hesitation, vanish into darkness and murder two armoured, heavily armed men with a single, small blade, and not make a sound doing it.

Sweeper. He likes to help.

'That's my knife, isn't it?'

He was back to his apologetic best as they laboured to roll the first man up in a rug. 'Sorry, mistress, I'll clean it off and give it right back.'

'You know what, you can keep that one. I have others.'

'Sorry, mistress.'

'Drop the humble horseshit, will you? I know who you are.'

He paused, their victim half-rolled. Ree had insisted they do their best to clean up before the Council arrived – it was one thing to deliver bad news, it was another to do it when surrounded by exsanguinated corpses and their vivid splatters. They'd need to dig the floor out to get rid of the worst of it, and the beautifully woven rugs were beyond a lost cause. At least they'd be able to wipe down Keretan's armour. From the look of it, it had seen worse. Something had been bothering her about its construction, but this wasn't the time.

'You know who I am?'

'Keep pushing, you daft sod, he's rolling back. If he and his pal go into rigor before we get them packed away they're going to be even less fun to deal with.' She blew a sweaty strand of hair from her face. Fatigue was creeping back into her muscles, her mind getting woolly. It had been a long night. 'Yes, I know who you are. Who else could you be, after a display like that, Copperhand?'

He hung his head. 'I don't like that name.' His voice sounded different, his pitch and timbre unchanged, but the intonation, the inflection, stripped of its submission. He no longer seemed meek and withdrawn. He seemed quiet and dangerous.

'I can see why you call yourself something else. Quite a reputation you left in your wake, and that's coming from someone who knows a thing or two on the subject.' She blew at the strand of hair again, but it was stuck to her forehead. 'Come on, let's get him rolled beside his friend and see what we can do about the—'

'By the gods!'

Camellia was in the doorway. It had to be Camellia, didn't it, Ree mused. She tried to raise her hands to calm the woman, but couldn't risk their load unbundling itself again. 'Listen, Camellia, I know this looks bad—'

Her pitch could have knocked bats from the sky. 'By the *gods*!'

It was going to be a long day.

Javani ran faster than Vida, and was lighter on her feet than Mariam. She skipped past the waiting crowd and behind Keretan's ring of what might have been called guards anywhere else – some of the younger farmers and labourers, the ones who moved heavy things around for much of their days, and now gripped items that weren't far away from Gumis's baton or Ree's walking stick in their sweaty hands – and into the wide-open doorway of the Council House.

She stood, panting, one hand on the carved oak frame, and took in the scene within. The blood was impossible to miss: in swathes and splatters, it painted an extraordinarily vivid scene in the otherwise modest interior. Just before the semicircle of stump-chairs, it was as if something had burst. A huge dark pool marked the matted floor, two slick trails pulled across it towards the fireplaces, their ornate rugs now missing, bare, pale reeds beneath.

Ree stood between the splatter-marks, leaning hard on her stick, while Camellia whimpered and gasped before her. Sweeper was sitting in the far corner by his pots, his head in his hands. 'Not here, not here,' Camellia burbled, pacing before Ree, hands pressed to her face.

Javani ploughed straight in between them. 'Ma, Ma! Are you all right?' Camellia went to say something, looked at Javani and her face crumpled, and she turned and staggered away without a word. Volkan had entered, and stood, hands on hips, pinched face lemon-sour.

'I'm whole, kid, if that's what you're asking.'

'Is Camellia all right?'

'Who can say? Right now all I want is a seat.'

The only place to sit that wasn't the floor was one of the Council's stump-chairs. They both stared at them for a moment. 'I'll stand for now,' Ree said.

Javani kept her voice low. 'Is it true you killed two assassins?'

'I didn't kill anyone, kid, and that's the gods' truth.'

Javani scoffed. 'Oh, right. Camellia killed them, did she?' She looked around the dawnlit chamber. 'Or Sweeper, was it?'

Something about her mother's reaction washed the smirk from her face. 'Ma?'

'I'll tell you later, kid. Right now, we need to get the Council together. Our visitors this morning were just the first little taste of what's coming, and these people need to organise themselves.' She stood straight, cricking her back and neck. 'Ten years ago, kid, I'd have seen them off without a scratch, without even—'

'You've got to stop doing that, Ma.'

'Stop what?'

'Saying "ten years ago" this and "fifteen years ago" that. You're not that person any more. You've got to get used to who you are now, and start living as that person, right?'

'That's easy for you to say, kid – a decade is a thrice-damned sight longer for you than it is for me. I've had four of them and the last one *really* galloped by.'

'I don't know what to tell you. I'm living as who I am, and I'm looking forward to who I'm going to be, when I get there.'

Her mother's face softened. She had streaked brown lines across her cheeks, but Javani didn't let it bother her. 'You know what, kid? Me too.'

Keretan ducked inside the Council House, the nervous crowd outside apparently under control for now. He conferred with Camellia and Volkan, then the three of them approached.

'Might be time to make yourself scarce, kid.'

'I'm not leaving you.'

'Then don't get in the way.'

'Rude.'

Keretan cleared his throat. His dome wasn't far off brushing the ceiling at the building's edge, but he looked nervous. 'Mistress Ree.'

'Keretan. Sorry about the mess.'

'I understand you were trying to clean it up.'

Ree scratched at her cheek. 'It's all I've ever been doing.'

Volkan jabbed a curling finger past Keretan. 'It's your mess, brought to our shores, our houses. Let's be in no doubt: those men came here last night for you! It is your aggression, your criminal behaviour, that has so inflamed this situation, that has brought murder and devastation to our threshold!'

Ree held his gaze, still leaning heavily on her stick. 'No. One of the men asked his friend if I was "one of them". Who do you think "them" might be, given where they were hiding?' She gestured to the Council House around them.

Volkan was unmoved, but Javani saw Camellia look to Keretan with alarm in her wavering eyes. 'Once again, we're forced to accept your word on something that exonerates your reckless behaviour,' Volkan said. 'Will these coincidences ever cease, I wonder?'

'And wasn't there supposed to be someone watching the bridge? What happened there?'

'They came for you, and you alone, and you have shed blood in our Council chamber. Your lack of respect for us and our ways has never been in doubt, but after this savagery we would be justified in turning you over to the mercenaries to face their justice!'

Keretan put up a warning hand. 'Volkan—'

'Just look at what you have done to poor Sweeper, rendered an imbecile by your—'

'You want to talk about Sweeper?' Ree's finger was up before the old man's face. 'Well!' Javani leaned forward, all ears. Ree paused for a moment, as if deliberating. 'Just think about what you were happy for others to do to him before we arrived,' she finished, which struck Javani as an anti-climax.

'Please, both of you,' Keretan rumbled. 'This serves nobody but those who wish us harm.' He took a long, slow breath, possibly in the hope that others would, too. 'Mistress Ree, did you learn anything more, last night?'

Ree pursed her lips and worked her jaw for a moment, the spattered lines across her face clearer now as the light grew. 'I did, and the arrival of our late visitors confirmed it.'

'And?'

'Where's Mani? We need the whole Council here.'

'Taking prayers, for those who can. Please, tell us now.'

'Their commander is dead and a madman is in charge. He's telling them they won't get paid in coin but instead in spoils, and they mean to take Ar Ramas, and soon. They're beginning preparations to attack, and clearly removing the Council was their first step. They don't yet know they've failed, so I'd say you have a narrow window to take some steps before something else happens.' Ree took a breath, then looked up at Keretan. 'Things are going to start happening pretty fast from here.'

'You can't possibly know this,' Volkan snapped. 'Have you been inside their camp? Have you—'

'Volkan!' Keretan's shout was loud enough to stir Sweeper in his corner and give Javani's heart a jolt. Camellia put one hand on his arm. 'I apologise.'

'What "steps" would you have us take, now?' Camellia's voice was little more than a whisper. 'You have told us to take up arms, to build walls, to drag everyone inside our bounds. Will that save us, from what you say is to come? Will anything?'

Despite the clear fatigue weighing on her, Ree stared Camellia down. 'That's for the village to decide. But they need to know what's going on first. Convene the Council, and tell your people, and do it quickly, before rumour and panic overtake you and set this place ablaze well before the bandits do.'

'You would have us fight them!' Camellia's eyes were already wet, her voice cracking. 'You would have slaughter in our streets.'

'I want none of these things, Camellia, you halfwit!' Anger had taken hold of Ree now, pulling her upright, her knuckles white around the head of her chipped walking stick. 'But you cannot deny people the chance to make their own choice, just as you cannot demand they give up their lives and their property without fighting for it.'

Camellia's head was shaking, her long braids flying from side to side. 'No, no, no! It should never have come to this.'

'We can only face what is, not what should be! Wishing things were otherwise is the sport of children, not governors – no offence, kid.'

'None taken,' Javani murmured, still trying to keep a low profile.

Ree took a step forward, filling Camellia's tear-streaked gaze. 'The people of this place chose you to lead them, all of you, and agreed to live by the rules that you set. But there's a contract that you made with them, one never written or signed, but that exists nonetheless: you agreed to protect them from harm. You're in charge, that is your duty.'

Her head was still shaking, small tremors now. 'We must try talking, we must—'

'Camellia.' Ree's voice was soft now, almost caring. 'There are people in this world who cannot be reasoned with, cannot be deterred, except by force. One of those people has found you, and he wants what you have, he wants your land, your food, your herds, and more, and he has promised as much to a group of professional soldiers who haven't been paid for a long time and have nowhere else to go.

'Winter is here, and conflict is inevitable. But there are still more of you than there are of them, and you have high ground and natural defences. You can run, probably starve, maybe be hunted down, or you can fight for what's yours. That's the choice you need to make, and you need to make it as a community.'

Camellia's gaze was lost in the blood-wrecked floor. 'You have brought ruin—'

'Camellia, I am so *fucking* tired of this. What was your plan to keep everyone safe forever? Hide away in the mountains and try not to attract attention? We're a social species – you can't isolate yourselves forever, not without stagnation and decay. You say we brought this to your door, but the worst we ever did was move up the schedule. This day was *always* coming, and if you'd hoped to dodge it by dying first and leaving your children to face the wolf at your door, you're a bigger coward than I thought.' She didn't wait for a response. 'Keretan, once again, I am sorry about the rugs.' With that, she turned and clomped off towards the door. 'Kid, come.'

Camellia was staring after her, the sharp-edged pain in her eyes the closest thing to a weapon Javani had seen in her vicinity. 'You don't know a thing about me,' she whispered, and the teariness was gone from her voice, her gaze hard as steel.

'Then prove me wrong,' Ree called over her shoulder as she reached the doorway.

'Very well,' Camellia said. 'Volkan, put out the word. We're convening the Council immediately.'

THIRTY-FIVE

Javani followed her mother back out into the press, towards where Vida and Mariam loitered at the square's edge, but as she made her standard sweep for Anri, someone else caught her eye at the fringe of the ring of not-guards: Lali, her ink-stained fingers crammed in her mouth, her eyes wide, doing her best to peer through the crowd outside the Council House without appearing to stare. Their eyes met.

Javani steeled herself to look away before Lali's anxiety veered into the inevitable disdain, but the other girl's expression barely changed. If anything, for a moment, Javani thought she saw a flash of . . . hope? in her eyes. Without really thinking about it, she diverted her course.

A moment later, she stood before the other girl at the corner of the building, one hand on the damp wood, her mouth open and her treacherous mind suddenly empty of what to say. *A perfect time to run out of words, Javani.* The silence began to grow.

Lali saved her. Fingers still lingering near her mouth, she lowered her eyes then raised them again, and there was that little optimistic flicker. 'What happened in the Council House?' she said, not with burning curiosity but with barely contained terror; that sliver of hope was that she might have heard wrong. 'Is it true?'

Is what true, Javani went to retort, but they were past that now. 'It probably is.'

Lali swallowed, hard. She resumed chewing her nails, eyes glazed. It made her look so much younger. 'They won't really attack the village, though, will they? They won't actually attack,' she mumbled.

Hope still wavered in her eyes. 'Lali,' Javani said with the weariest tone she could muster, 'they already did. They sent men to kill the Council.'

'But she stopped them, right?' She swallowed again. 'Your mother. Did she . . . did she kill them?'

Javani thought of the look Ree had given Sweeper, the mud-brown streaks that had criss-crossed her face. 'They're definitely dead.'

'Do you . . . do you think they'll try again?'

'I don't know. Maybe not like that again.' Javani scratched at her neck with the hand that wasn't resting on wet timber. Her fingers were getting cold, her cheeks hot. 'But they're not going to give up now. It might be something different next time, but it's coming.' Just saying the words made her stomach burn.

'But Volkan says—'

'Lali,' Javani said, trying to keep her voice gentle, trying to learn from her mother's own diplomatic shortcomings. She risked putting a hand on the older girl's arm. 'They're making ridiculous demands because they mean to attack no matter what. All that's left to decide is what your people are going to do about it.'

The girl's eyes, already wide, positively boggled, her brows lifted in terrified pleading. 'But . . . but . . . but . . .' Tears began to roll down her cheeks, and she swallowed once more, her voice thick. 'They really mean us harm?'

Javani tried to remember Ree's words to the Council. 'They want what Ar Ramas has, its food and shelter, and they don't want to trade for it. Not when they can just take it by force.'

'But it's so unfair! We worked for everything we have! We only want peace!'

Javani's shoulders lifted in sympathy. 'No argument here.'

Lali was looking around now, those big eyes searching near and far. 'Can we, can we flee? Can we hide somewhere? Where can we go? How can we go?'

Javani's shoulders had not yet lowered. 'From what Ree said, it doesn't sound like that will work.'

Lali's eyes locked onto hers, transfixing her with a gaze of alarming intensity. 'Can she save us? Your mother? Can she?'

Well, this is quite a turnaround, said the snippy little voice in

Javani's head, what happened to all plains-folk are instinctive murderers? Or is it that now we can be useful, you're willing to overlook our savage faults, hmm? Manufacturing what she hoped was a confident, composed expression, Javani gave the most considered and helpful reply she could formulate.

'Maybe?'

'Kid, stop fucking dawdling! Get over here.'

Javani broke from Lali's gaze. 'Sorry. Duty calls.'

But Lali was no longer listening. Her thoughts had turned inward, the eyelid-stretching terror replaced by a lowered brow and downturned mouth. It was hard to shake the feeling that she was plotting something.

'Sorry, Ma, I was looking for—'

'Never mind your bollocks, run and find Mani, will you? Someone said he's by the stables. We need the whole Council here as quick as possible, word is spreading and people are beginning to lose their shit.'

Javani looked around. Villagers were moving quickly, expressions gaunt and harried, congregating in knots or moving with alacrity away from the square, presumably to spread word of the attack on the Council House. The air had a definite whiff of panic. She still couldn't see Anri, and was angry with herself for being disappointed.

'*Now*, kid!'

'I'm going, I'm going!'

Manatas realised he was awake, which meant that until a moment ago he had not been. He'd fallen asleep standing up, something he'd not managed in over a decade. Something he'd not needed to even attempt for over a decade. He did not feel better for it. Refreshment remained at a distance.

He blinked until his eyes could focus. Harsh grey daylight filtered through the stripped woods around him, the frozen, rutted ground still dusted with glaring snow. It was hard to say how long he'd been standing at the fringe of the pavilion, beyond that dawn had come and gone and the day felt no warmer. Feeling had entirely left his feet.

Botrys and Lado were where he remembered them, the former

now dressed and shaved but still in the grand chair beneath the pavilion's awning, the latter still at his low table piled with documents, his candle long since burned to a nub. Manatas wondered if Lado slept. He had that reptilian quality that suggested he merely rested without ever releasing his grip on consciousness. And where was Keds? Perhaps Arkadas had word. He needed to find Arkadas.

Someone came shuffling past him, hunched against the cold, and Manatas started to recognise Zurab, the late Ioseb's erstwhile henchman, someone he'd never have credited with the necessary backbone to approach the vicious double-act now running the company.

Lado didn't look up, but had clearly spotted him coming some way off. 'Yes, soldier? Do you have business with the lord adjutant?'

'Commander, lord adjutant,' Zurab said, saluting without confidence. Manatas felt his lip curl at seeing the man show such deference to superiors, given how he'd behaved when Manatas had been his commanding officer. 'Is there news on the, uh, advance party?'

Now Lado was looking up, considering the Vistirlari from beneath his lank curtain of hair. 'News, soldier?'

'It's just that . . . Rostom hasn't returned, commander. And it's his turn on prep duty, commander.'

Lado watched, narrow-eyed beneath his veil, while Botrys merely stared at the man blank-faced, as if he had no idea what he was talking about. It was quite likely, Manatas considered, that he didn't.

Without warning, Lado stood, the sharpness of his movement sending Zurab a step back. 'Lord adjutant,' he said, the wheedle back in his voice, 'the man-at-arms raises a stark and unwanted spectre, to wit: our aggressors may be more cunning and more ruthless than we surmised.'

Botrys gazed at him blankly, but made no move to interrupt.

'Grievous and unlikely as it sounds, it is possible that our operation has failed. That it should do so is tragedy indeed, for it means only the prolongation of this unfortunate, damaging situation. You were truly foresighted, lord adjutant, when you made your contingency plans,' Botrys nodded along at this, and Manatas wondered if he'd have been able to name his contingency plans with a knife to his spleen, 'and I agree that now is the time to advance them.'

Lado inclined his head towards the man in the great chair. 'With your approval, lord adjutant?'

'Yes, yes, absolutely,' came Botrys's complacent response. 'Put my plan into action.'

Lado beckoned over several of the runners from the adjutant's staff. 'Fetch Chapter Captain Jebel while I make preparations.' He seemed to look directly at Manatas as he ran a red tongue over colourless lips. 'All the captains will have a role to play.'

Jebel appeared not long after, his armour glinting dully in the light, as Manatas was still shaking life into his limbs. Botrys had retreated into the pavilion for a meal and Lado was gone from his table, his Pashani minders likewise. That Manatas could not see the man reassured him not at all.

Beyond the sweep of the pavilion, he barely recognised the camp in daylight. The neat organisation that had sprung up in the wake of Ridderhof and the circus's arrival had, for want of a better word, tumesced. Things had shifted and expanded, the lines less clear, the rigour blurred. Everything seemed to be at an angle, in echo of Lado's slanting walk, perhaps.

'Manatas. What news in the camp?'

'Captain Jebel.' Manatas rubbed at an eye. Just an hour of sleep, prone this time, and he'd have the strength to face this. 'My report was well-received.' He coughed. 'Yours?'

Jebel only grunted. So much for a subtle enquiry.

'I was, uh, covering the—'

'Know why I was summoned? Word around camp is we lost men in some botched endeavour.'

Manatas sensed an opening, the word 'botched' nectar in his ear. 'Something is indeed awry, captain. Time is moving on and our supplies are dwindling, a situation unimproved by our unexpected new arrivals and the ludicrous waste of the feast. We are not equipped for a winter campaign, we lack the requisite furs, gear and provisions. You must agree that it is past time we were on the road as a company – were we to depart today, we could yet ration our—'

Jebel was staring at him, and his eyes were not kind. 'Why would we do that?'

Manatas blinked hard, trying to clear his head. 'For the reasons aforestated, captain, the increasing lack of food being paramount among them.'

Jebel shrugged, light gleaming from his scarred and shaven dome. 'There's plenty of food in the valley. More than enough to sustain the company, plus any more who arrive.'

'There is?' Manatas scratched at his brow, his throat tight. 'Is it possible that one of us is mistaken, or am I misinformed on the nature and volume of our supplies? Perhaps there is another—'

'Not in the camp.' Jebel inclined his head towards the other side of the valley, where Ar Ramas was lost in wreaths of mist. 'Over there.'

'That is the village,' Manatas said, redundantly.

'So it is,' Jebel replied, without mirth or inflection. 'A weak, soft village, with stores and shelter enough to see us through the winter in comfort.'

'But it is not ours.'

Jebel's lip was curling, the top of one scarred cheek almost covering one eye. 'Today, maybe. Let's see what tomorrow brings. I'd say our need was greater, wouldn't you, *captain*?' This time, the sneer in his words was impossible to miss.

Manatas swallowed, his throat unfathomably dry. It was too hot beneath his mail, despite the day's bitter chill. Surely it was worth one last attempt at persuasion, one last try to make Jebel see that reason could win out? That making for the foothills at a canter was the only rational path, the only *fair* path . . . but even as he formed the thought, he knew the battle was lost.

Then the mournful, mangled dinner bell began to ring, and the summons began.

THIRTY-SIX

Mani was at the edge of the ram pen, and he was not alone.

'Please, friends,' the old man called in his scratchy voice to the dozen or so villagers who were congregating with fierce aspect around the pen. 'Still the passion of your hearts, the clamour of your thoughts, and breathe with me. Long and slow, that's it.' He took a deep breath in and out through his nose, his moustache whiffling. 'Long and slow. Let your minds settle, and let them rest on what matters most to you, and to us all.'

He turned in a slow arc, arms wide, walking stick dangling, the attention of the gathering throng diverted his way. Beyond him, through the bars of the pen, Javani saw Tauras sitting beneath the shelter of the stable roof, wrapped in fleeces, watching with rapt attention to see what the old man might say next. Javani was not surprised that he appeared to have no idea that the people who'd collected around the pen might have intended him harm. But then, she supposed, he was built like a tree, with several smaller trees attached to it; what did he have to fear from panicked farmers and craftspeople? They had little more than sticks like Mani's between them, and from the way they'd abandoned their attempts at menace to listen to the squeaky old fellow, their hearts hadn't really been in it. Maybe it was a self-image thing, she pondered, letting them feel like they were Doing Something about the unnerving situation in the valley, but not exactly putting up resistance to being talked around. She could see the appeal in that.

'That's it, my friends. Think of only love – the love we have for our families, for our children, for our friends, and the love we have for our fellow people, recognising our shared humanity, our shared need for something greater than ourselves. That is love, my friends, the greatest experience, the greatest gift we can give, the greatest gift we can receive. We must lead with love, no matter our struggles. It will be love that binds us.'

Mumbles and nods from the people around the pen, their eyes downcast. Javani felt the tension leaving the air. It was definitely not the time to remind anyone that the mercenaries who had set their minds to sacking Ar Ramas would likely not be deterred by the offer of a hug. She frowned. The thought made her ashamed. Who's to say, after all? Maybe if they'd had loving families and communities, they wouldn't have ended up menacing peaceful villagers in the mountains. Loving families like her and Ree? Oh, shit, Ree.

'Um, Mani?' She cleared her throat. 'You're needed up at the Council House. A bit urgently.'

'Of course, my dear.' His eyes sparkled beneath snow-white brows. 'I'll head there as fast as my poor old legs will carry me. Would you mind checking on our friend here in my absence?' He nodded back towards Tauras, who was regarding proceedings from beneath his fleeces with guileless but optimistic incomprehension.

'Sure.'

Mani set off for the Council House, his stick crunching on the frozen ground, and the crowd dispersed, many going with him. A couple of villagers lingered.

'I'm telling you,' said one, a man she recognised as Solheil, 'he was doing something to that sheep. Picking it up, putting it down, picking it up again. It's not natural, whatever it is he's doing.'

Javani leaned over. 'Don't worry,' she said with a bright smile, 'he does that. Not enough cartwheels around, you see.'

They were too baffled to respond, and, after a moment's hesitation, turned to follow after Mani.

'We are blessed,' called Lado of Cstethia to the assembled mercenary company, from a raised mound outside the walls of the camp, 'that we have the wise head of the lord adjutant at our company's command. Lesser commanders might have steered us wrong in the face of such defiance, such hostility, such calculating and underhanded malice. But not Lord Adjutant Botrys. In the early hours, the lord adjutant dispatched two of our best and brightest men into the heart of the aggressors' nest, in the hope of bringing this sorry and miserable affair to a swift end.'

He bowed his head, affecting to blink away tears. Beside him, Botrys preened, his armour shining like a second sun. 'It grieves me to say that those men were lost, and we believe them murdered. This is our sacrifice to bear, for trying to do what was right. All we wished to do was bring an early end to the suffering of this valley, but . . . well, some people just can't be reasoned with, I suppose.'

Snow was falling again, small flakes, each one a bitter kiss of ice against Manatas's frozen skin. Fatigue dragged at him, hanging off his limbs, fighting to haul him to the frosted ground. Each gust of wind blew through him like knives. Only the presence of Arkadas (who had had little to report beyond keeping his head down and following orders, to Manatas's pained approval) at his elbow kept him from collapsing to the snow-streaked dirt; he would not force his lieutenant to carry him back to the tent.

'We have tried everything that we can to resolve this situation, and our hand, extended in peace, has been slapped away at every turn. There is nothing left, now, but to meet violence with violence, no matter the hurt it causes our noble hearts.'

Manatas would have laughed, but he was just too tired.

'The lord adjutant has made his plan, but he is a wise man, and a fair man. He knows there are those within this camp whose reservations linger, even in the face of such provocation from the aggressors. It is to those he speaks now, with these words:

'It is time to decide, soldiers of the Company of the Wolf, whether you are truly wolves. On the other side of that valley is all you have worked for, all that has been taken from you, all you deserve. And standing in your way are nothing more than insolent peasants, unfit to wash the mud from your boots.'

Even half-asleep, Manatas marvelled at the rhetoric: the insolent peasants were somehow both worthless and beneath contempt, yet also a terrible threat to the company. He wondered how many in the audience would notice. He missed Keds. He missed Tauras.

Lado was still talking, his voice rising in pitch and volume. 'Soldiers, it is time! Time to take what is yours by right! Time to take what you need. Time for sustenance, shelter and . . . support.'

Manatas couldn't decide if that final 's' was intended to be 'sex' or 'slaves'; either way the notion repelled him. His sidelong looks into the assembly did not find many other faces that showed an element of distaste; most seemed . . . well, hungry.

'And what of the rules? What of the laws?' Lado's voice had dropped now, and the mercenaries as one craned forward to catch his words. He tilted his head again, speaking up through his hair, his tone at once intimate, heartfelt. Manatas wondered whether these were still supposed to be the words of Lord Botrys. He wondered if any of them had been.

'Have you ever seen a city fall?' Lado asked, a wistful note creeping into his words, a hint of memory and shared wonder. 'I was there when Ozuri fell, when the walls came down. I smelled the panic in the streets, and for all that followed . . . I saw it, I touched it, I *tasted* it. And I realised the one true constant of this world.'

The clearing fell silent but for the creak and jingle of mercenaries craning forward.

'There are no rules,' said Lado of Cstethia in a voice of jubilant revelation. 'There is only what you do.'

They cheered. The company cheered.

Manatas had never felt so alone.

Lado summoned the senior officers after the assembly. Botrys was present, lurking at the fringes, but the pretence that any of this had originated in his own mind had long since shrivelled away. Lado, pacing as he spoke, was by turns exultant and wounded, praising the bravery and cohesion of the company while lambasting the murderous treachery of the villagers. Manatas would have found it exhausting had he been fresh. As it was, he concentrated only on staying upright and keeping his eyes more open than not.

'Through sheer luck,' Lado spat, sweeping his hair past his ear, 'they find themselves in a strong position, with regards to defence. We'll need to work around it. But we must remind ourselves, our aggressors are little more than impertinent farmers. They have not the strength nor the discipline, the training or equipment of this company, and they will fall to us.' His smile stretched the scars beneath his dangling hair. 'Panic will be our friend. Gather all our weapons of range, bows and crossbows, assess and count them and ensure their maintenance.' He gestured towards the only structure of any permanence in the camp, the abandoned half-built food store. 'Assemble them there, dry the strings, count the missiles. When the time comes, we will fell their best before they even know we have arrived.

'In the meantime,' he continued, the grin falling away like dead leaves, 'we shall continue to sow the seeds of a successful outcome. I will speak to each of you with your orders.'

Manatas's body chose that moment to betray him, forcing a yawn between his clamped jaws, and Lado's gaze seized on him like a snake.

'Ah, Chapter Captain Manatas, we once more find ourselves in need of . . . intelligence.' He wafted a hand towards the sweep of the valley. 'Our Pashani comrades stand ready to accompany you on your next reconnaissance endeavour. Off you go.'

With only a hooded look to Arkadas, whose reciprocal expression was a masterwork of neutrality, Manatas went.

The Council had convened, the Council House's doors and shutters thrown wide, the place as opened out to the throng in the square beyond as was logistically possible. They'd even dragged the chairs closer to the doorway. Ree leaned back against the wall beside one of the fireplaces, eyes closed, feeling the fire's warmth lapping at her aching legs, no longer fighting to stay awake against the exhaustion that weighed on her. Mariam had taken a wash-cloth to her and removed the worst of the second-hand blood in a bid to make her presentable, in defiance of her feeble protestations; the smiths now stood a pace or so on each side of her, either as a protective screen or in the hope of preventing her doing something else reckless. She'd lost sight of Sweeper. Somehow that made her uncomfortable.

She barely stirred when Keretan called on the Council to prepare themselves, peering between half-closed lids at the four occupied stump-chairs, Gumis's empty seat at one end, the girl Lali seated before the two perennially empty seats at the other. Now she'd had a moment to ponder, to deduce, it was time to do something about those seats. It took a lot of effort to push herself up off the wall, one hand rubbing at her gritty eyes, and get her mind back up to speed.

'Are we ready?' Keretan rumbled. He looked sweaty, and he wasn't even that close to the fires. Beyond the doors, the gathering on the terrace looked to have reached a hundred or more of Ar Ramas's population, and was still growing. One eye on the burgeoning crowd, Keretan briefed the Council members on what he would say: thanks, praise, attempts to reassure, and then confirmation: Gumis was likely dead, and the mercenaries had attacked in the night. It was possible that they would attack again, in numbers, and attempt to plunder the village. At this, Volkan audibly scoffed, but Keretan pushed on. It was time for the Council to vote: should they capitulate to the mercenaries, or abandon their peaceful way of life?

'Hold on,' Ree called, and heard groans when she spoke. Camellia had her head in her hands, even Vida was holding her expression rigid. 'A decision like this should be made by all the right people, don't you think?'

'She'd have us deposed,' sneered Volkan. 'Replace the Council with the rule of the mob! Abandon the principles of—'

'No.' Ree didn't raise her voice, but he stopped anyway, as if he'd been waiting for the cue. She wondered if he really believed half the things he said. It was like he was forever seeking the most contrary thing to say at every point, like it was a game to him. He pretended to positions of great wisdom, but in reality he seemed little more than a contrarian, incapable of scratching beneath the reflexive and superficial. She met him head-on, her foggy mind be damned.

'I am saying,' Ree growled, 'that the people of this village elected a Council they trusted to make decisions, so let *all* of them decide.' She gestured towards the two furthest seats, the ones that always sat empty during meetings, then turned and stared hard at Mariam and Vida.

Mariam looked at the floor and shuffled her feet. Vida coughed and would not meet her eye.

'Come on, smiths,' Ree said in a low voice, 'your village needs you.'

'We stay out of Council—' Vida began.

'I know you blame yourself for the mercenaries arriving. But one fuck-up doesn't mean you give up on making decisions, Vida,' Ree growled, 'it just gives you perspective. Camellia's been fucking up all along and she's still there, doing, I guess, the best she can.' She didn't look to see if the other woman had overheard. 'Do what they elected you to do: guide the village, take the hard decisions. They need you. Both of you.'

The smiths exchanged a look of great meaning and history, then without a word, went to take their seats.

Keretan cleared his throat. 'Very well,' he said, and called the meeting to order, his great voice booming out over the terrace as he reeled through his introduction. 'To the motion in question: are we to change our laws?' He cleared his throat again, perhaps to hide the crack in his voice. 'Are we to resist?'

THIRTY-SEVEN

By the time Javani was satisfied that Tauras was in no danger in the ram pen, beyond possibly being sniffed a little too enthusiastically by the loitering Tarfellian, and made it back to the Council House, it was all but impossible to get in. The residents of Ar Ramas were crowded around the terrace, packed in against the day's bitter cold, and not even her most piteous slithering attempts through the press got her anywhere. She could hear the voices of the Council over the anxious murmurs of the crowd, Keretan's booming bass most of all, but the content of their words was lost to her.

Eventually she gave up, huffing with frustration, and looked for a spot at the crowd's edge where she might at least be able to see over some heads and into the building. And there, as if fated, she saw a familiar figure, off to one side by itself.

'Good morning, Anri.'

He only sighed, his eyes swept up and around as if with great suffering.

'How's Tanith?'

'She's fine, thank you.' The words emerged reflexively, yet still with bad grace.

'What have I missed?'

He sucked in his hollow cheeks. 'Where do I start? You've clearly missed the most basic instruction in manners—'

'With the Council, I meant. Have they voted?'

He raised a scathing eyebrow. 'If they'd already voted, you think the great unwashed would still be hovering around like flies on shit?'

'Oh.'

He sniffed. 'Motion's been advanced, hasn't it, we've had opening statements and questions from the floor, now we're in summing up.'

'You can hear them from here?'

His cheek twitched, maybe in mirth, maybe disgust. 'Don't need to hear them to see what they're saying.' He was a fair bit taller; seeing over the crowd was not the problem it was for her.

'I'm surprised they let Ree speak, after everything that's happened so far.'

'Your mam? She's kept right out of it, she has. Maybe she's finally learned something.'

'What? Then who's been arguing in favour of defending the village?' Her mouth went dry. 'Has anyone?'

'Oh yes. Big man's been all in on this, hasn't he.'

'Keretan?'

'The same. Fancies a recapturing of his glory days in the cavalry, no doubt.'

'What's he been saying?'

'Does it really matter? You know the steps of this dance by now.'

Javani puffed out her cheeks, watching her breath plume before her. 'I suppose not.' She rubbed her hands and blew on them. 'Which way do you think they'll vote?'

He sniffed again, then spat down into the mud. 'You know what they're like. Frightened of their own bloody shadows, this lot. They'll just shut their eyes and hope it all goes away, same as with everything else.' He rounded on her, animation in the dark wells of his eyes. 'You and your mam should be counting your lucky stars that you can ride out of this mess and off into the hills. This bunch are going to get themselves pillaged out of existence.'

'But aren't you in danger, too?'

'Their problems are their own.'

Javani chewed at her lip and wrapped herself tight in her cloak. 'I know it wasn't your idea to come here, Anri, and I get why it's important to you that you're not part of the village, but, well, you are, aren't you? You and Tanith. I mean, you can't keep away from the place, for a start, can you?' She gestured to encompass his presence on the terrace.

He waved a calloused and grimy finger. 'Not the same thing at all, though, is it. For a start—'

'What was the deal you made with Tanith?' She spoke quietly, but he fell silent, finger still raised. 'Before she got ill? She wanted to come here, what was your side?'

'None, of your, *fucking*—' He looked up and past her. 'Oh. Voting started.'

'What? When?'

'While you were pissing grease in my ear. Now stop up your orifice and let me concentrate.' He narrowed his eyes, already dark creases in his weathered face, while Javani glanced from him to the backs of the heads of the crowd in front and behind. 'No surprises so far. Volkan's against, Camellia's against. It's Keretan's proposal, so he'd count if the other votes are equal.'

'How do you know—'

'Hush, gods take your tongue. No Gumis,' and for a moment he looked pained, and Javani wondered if, for all his gleeful bullying of the unfortunate constable, Anri had genuinely cared for the man, 'and bugger me, who got the smiths out of retirement, then? I thought they'd vowed never to return, come the floods of world's end.'

Javani buffed her nails against her cloak. 'My ma can be pretty persuasive. When she puts her mind to it.'

Anri sniffed again. 'They're in favour, both of them, though Vida looks like she's swallowed a mule. So two for, two against.'

Hope lit Javani's ribcage. 'So Keretan's vote carries it? The laws are changed?'

'No.' His voice was lead. 'Mani remains.'

The hope in her chest burned out like a tinder flame. Gods, Mani would never vote for anything that risked hurting others. He'd made it limpidly clear that his preferred method of dealing with the encroaching mercenaries was showering them with affection in the hope that, what, they'd change their ways? She was clenching her fists so hard they shook.

'Huh,' said Anri.

'Huh? What huh?' she demanded. A great sigh went through the crowd before them, but of relief or horror?

'Well, bugger me,' he muttered. Ahead of them, people on the terrace had begun to mill, breaking off in knots, dissipating. The meeting was ending.

'What happened? Answer me!'

He flashed her that impertinent gap-toothed grin. 'No.' He shouldered his bow and turned on his heel. 'Be seeing you, pest. Or not, with any luck.'

'Wait, Anri, wait! Ugh!' She shook her head in outrage. '*Dick!*'

The press eased, Javani found her mother loitering outside the doors to the Council House, leaning on her stick not far from where Javani had attempted to reassure Lali earlier that morning. The look on her face told its own story, but even had Javani lacked the experience and acumen to read Ree's moods, however disguised, Camellia's arrival just before her own would have provided a definitive answer.

'So,' the councillor said, her face ashen. 'You got what you wanted.'

Ree raised a weary hand. 'Camellia, I didn't want any of this. I've tried to explain this in more ways than I can count, but you seem impervious to the notions I'm trying to describe.'

Camellia clenched her eyes shut, and Javani saw the trickle of tears from their corners. Ree was gazing up the sky again, her exasperation overpowering her diplomatic intentions. 'That it came to this,' Camellia whispered, then with her fingertips pressed against her eyelids she turned and marched away, robes swishing as she went.

'You know, Ma, I don't think you and Camellia are going to be best friends any time soon.'

Ree reached out an arm and dragged Javani into an awkward hug, which she didn't fight too hard, despite her lingering ire at Anri. She seemed pleased. 'Ah, she's just upset because she lost. I think my friend Camellia has had the running of the Council to her liking for years, and all of a sudden she's not getting her way.'

Javani thought of the woman's anguished expression, her silent tears. 'I don't *think* it's that, Ma. Or maybe not just that.' She scratched at her nose. 'How *did* you win? I missed it all.'

Ree released her from the half-hug. 'Mani.'

'He voted for violence?' It was nearly a shriek.

'Well, no. He abstained. Cast no vote.' Ree looked momentarily wistful. 'Keretan summed it up as "we must be prepared to kill or be killed", in so many words, but Mani said something quite temperate in response. "Should the bonds of love be exhausted, I would rather suffer injustice than act unjustly. But what is just? Such a decision must be a personal one – I cannot ask everyone to follow me and my path. May we choose to choose love, and be found by love in return." And with that, he abstained.'

Javani scratched at her nose again. It was getting cold and starting to run. 'Do you think he meant it? Dying over fighting back?'

Her mother gave an uncertain shake of her head. 'Who knows? He certainly wouldn't be much use in a battle. They've got some funny notions in this place.'

Something about the way she said it infuriated Javani. Her mother's knowing smugness, her superiority, Javani's own lingering frustration with Anri, suddenly it was all too much.

'It's tough being the only sensible, rational person sometimes, isn't it, Ma?'

'I'm not sure I care for your tone, kid.'

'You know you're as unreasonable as any of them. You've been calling them fools and cowards to their faces since we arrived.'

'But they are fools and cowards. Some of them, anyway.'

'Don't you wonder why they're like this, Ma?' Javani thought of Anri's unfulfilled bargain with Tanith, Keretan's battered armour, Camellia's abhorrence of bloodshed. 'Stop to ask some questions before judging them?'

'Where's this coming from?'

'They were all running from something when they came here. All trying to make a better life, start again – just like us. And they managed it. Can you really blame them for wanting to pretend that their perfect new life wasn't under threat?'

'You think I've been unfair.'

Javani didn't respond, holding her mother's stare, and after a moment, the flint left Ree's eyes. 'Maybe I have.'

'I'm glad we agree.' Javani put her hands on her hips, aiming for an authoritative stance, her anger still simmering. 'So are we leaving now? Anri thinks we should get out of here pronto, and Vida can probably fit the shoe pretty quickly if we ask her.'

Ree couldn't reply immediately, her mouth forming a series of soundless shapes. 'Well, kid, you see—'

'Yeah, that's what I thought.'

'No, but with all the escalation, and the bandits roaming the woods, it wouldn't be safe to travel . . . We'll get away yet, just—'

'Give it a rest, will you, Ma? I'm glad we're staying. It's the right thing to do. But will you please just admit that we're staying because you want to, too?'

'I have no love for this place and its nonsense,' Ree scoffed.

'But you love bossing them around, and they've finally started listening to you – come on, admit it! Admit you love being in charge, being that voice of reason, being the one who asks difficult questions and isn't afraid to ruffle some feathers.'

'Kid, I—'

Javani steamed right over her. 'You were a diplomat once, or so I keep hearing – don't tell me you couldn't have swallowed your pride on any one of fifteen occasions if you'd wanted to, and we'd have left already. But you didn't, you wanted to stay, you wanted to tell them how to live, that they were doing it all wrong, just like you do with me.'

'Gods, kid, is this about your archery?'

'No!'

'I wanted to fix something I saw was broken! Is that so bad?'

'Oh, I'm broken now?'

'Of course not, you're just . . . unfinished. But less and less so every day,' Ree hurried to add.

Javani folded her arms. 'Admit it, then. Admit you've wanted to stay.'

Ree's gaze was cold and hard, but beneath it was something else, something almost . . . appraising. Something appreciative. 'Fine. I wanted to stay, deep down.'

'Because?'

Ree sighed. 'Because I like being listened to.'

The heat of Javani's ire had faded, and as it cleared new thoughts came creeping out to occupy its space in her mind. 'It's not just that, is it, Ma?' A memory had surfaced, a memory of a memory. 'You told me once about the siege you were caught in. The one where you escaped, but your friends wouldn't come with you. Even though the odds were impossible.'

Ree didn't say anything, only watched her, perhaps wary of a new outburst.

'You said that escaping was,' she squeezed her mind for the words, 'the rational choice, the logical choice, but in the end it wasn't the right choice. That you thought afterwards you should have stayed.' Javani rubbed at her cold nose again, leaving a trail on her palm. 'Are you making up for that now? Trying to make the right choice this time?'

Ree was shaking her head again, this time in disbelief. 'How in the name of all the gods did you get so perceptive?'

Javani wrinkled her nose. 'Probably picked it up from one of the ponies. So?'

Ree rubbed a hand over her eye, and for a moment Javani half-wondered if she'd been wiping away a tear before discounting the thought as absurd. 'Well, my girl, you're half-right. I think.'

'Oh?'

'Maybe I did run from the biggest conflict of my life back then. Maybe I've been running ever since. And maybe now I'm looking at another conflict and knowing I should run again but . . . this time . . . This time I can do something about it.'

'So how am I only half-right?'

'Because this time I don't just want to be right, kid. I want to *win*.' Ree's eyes flashed in the dull morning light. 'Now help me round up a few people. It's time for a council of war.'

THIRTY-EIGHT

He was so tired, and the day so cold, but a small, treacherous part of Inaï Manatas was inwardly delighted that he was out of the camp and scouting again. He tried not to make his approach to the neutral ridge too direct, too obvious, mindful that Mantenu and Antulu might be taciturn but they were not fools nor likely to stay their blades.

'Friends,' he said as they made their painful way along the valley floor, the mush of dead leaves and scattered branches squelching beneath their boots, tough vegetation springing back as they passed. 'Might I ask your take on our current predicament, expressly, the position of the company in general, vis-à-vis its likely operations to come?'

Antulu grunted. Mantenu regarded him with sad, empty eyes. 'What?' he said.

Manatas came to a stop, resting one hand on the rough trunk of a young oak. 'I mean, comrades, to divine your feelings on the likelihood that we may soon be taking up arms, as a fighting force, and embarking on a campaign against our former clients, with the stated objective of seizing their property for ourselves.'

Antulu grunted again. Mantenu tilted his head to one side. 'Yes,' he said.

'Yes? To precisely what?'

'To the fighting.'

Manatas took a long breath through his nose, swaying back a little on his heels. 'And you don't worry yourselves that this is . . . improper? Obscene? To go to war on civilians in this way, with the intent only to plunder?' He shook his head, eyes tight. 'All because they refused to hand over that which they worked for willingly?'

'Yes.'

Thrice-damn Ree, her words sloshed around his head, inescapable, irrefutable. 'There is a word for such things.'

'Yes.'

He rubbed at his temples with his free hand. Keeping his eyes closed felt best. 'Are you telling me that this is how the famous warriors of Pashan Eren find their glory? Their honour?'

'No.'

He opened his eyes, peering over the webbing of his thumb. 'No?'

'Honour is lost to us. We are already dead,' Mantenu said. Beside him, Antulu shrugged.

Manatas blinked, several times. 'Would you kindly run that past me one more time? Am I, at present, conversing with spirits?'

'Pashan Eren is gone. Pashani are gone. We are . . .' Mantenu paused, searching for the right word.

'Late,' supplied Antulu.

'Late,' Mantenu agreed. 'Others gone ahead. We catch them soon.'

'The rest of your people? They're dead, and you're in a hurry to join them?'

Again, Mantenu shrugged with his face. 'Hurry, no hurry. No difference. Fate is written. Pashani are dead. We are Pashani. We are dead.'

'Soon,' Antulu added. 'Catch up.'

Manatas removed his hand from his face. 'And you don't think that perhaps making some different choices might help you avoid this fate? For example, renouncing arms, leaving the mountains, taking up peaceful pursuits?'

Antulu grunted again, this time incredulous. 'Cannot be avoided,' Mantenu clarified. 'Is written.' He nodded onward. 'Wasting time. Move.'

The smiths had not gone far, still locked in conversation with Mani just inside the Council House. Vida looked grim-faced, Mariam just looked tired, although Mani seemed to be chattering away quite cheerfully when Ree approached, leaning heavily on her stick.

'Just Ree,' he declared, 'you've not yet left us.'

'Funny,' Ree replied, 'the kid and I were just discussing our departure.'

'And?' Vida asked it, but all three looked in expectation, possibly for different motives.

'We'll be delaying it until the current unpleasantness is resolved – that is, if you don't mind hosting us a little longer?'

Mariam looked ready to burst with relief, and Mani beamed. Vida merely nodded. 'All right,' she said.

Ree addressed the smiths. 'You two feeling better for doing your civic duty again?' She nodded to the arc of Council seats.

'Yes,' Mariam replied with an earnest smile.

'We'll see,' was Vida's response.

'Careful, Just Ree,' Mani said with a bushy grin. 'Hang around here much longer, and you'll get roped into the Council one way or another – poor Gumis has left a seat open.' He put a hand on his heart when he said the constable's name.

Ree could hardly control her grimace. 'I don't think that would be in anyone's best interest,' she replied, her free hand raised.

'Who's to say?' Mani's eyes twinkled in reply.

Ree cleared her throat. 'If I may, time is a little against us. Mariam, Vida, who are the most capable in Ar Ramas, the best engineers and artisans? Is there anyone with military training?'

The smiths exchanged uncomfortable looks. 'Why?' Vida said.

'The vote is passed, the law is changed, correct?' Ree said. They nodded. 'Then Ar Ramas can start preparing its defence. And that means we need to assemble a council of, uh . . .' She caught Mani's guileless gaze.

'Of what, Just Ree?'

'A council of defence,' she finished, lamely. She could make a few concessions. 'Now, has anyone seen Sweeper?'

The council of war/defence ended up being only a smaller version of the village council: Vida, Mariam and Keretan joined Ree around a map that Lali had inked on the largest stretch of parchment in the settlement, the stretched and yellowed hide of a vast ram. Camellia and Volkan had removed themselves, and Mani pleaded infirmity.

The kid had insisted Anri would make a valuable contribution, but had still been outraged at being sent out to fetch him. Sweeper was there, though, hovering in the shadows, a broom in his hand, neither part of the Council nor apart from it. In light of her revelations, Ree found his skulking act considerably less endearing.

'I'll keep this short. Ar Ramas contains fewer than three hundred souls, many of whom are children or infirm. There could be as many as a hundred armed and armoured mercenaries across the valley from us, even discounting those deserted, hanged, or otherwise eliminated, and in a stand-up fight they will murder everyone in this place who raises a hand against them. Even in a siege, they'd likely kill or maim so many that the town would never recover.'

Keretan snorted in disbelief. 'Then Ar Ramas is doomed? Do you not think we should have mentioned this in advance of the vote, and perhaps some might have fled and survived after all?'

'She means,' Vida said in a firm voice, one blackened finger tracing the lines on Lali's map, 'that we need to avoid direct combat as much as possible.'

'Oh,' Keretan replied. 'That sounds correct. How do we do it?'

Ree's finger returned to the map. 'We need to get this place in good order as quickly as possible, in the ways that will make the most difference. Walls, obstacles, screens, barricades and traps. So many traps.' She raised a wry eyebrow. 'Three ways in, three choke-points: the bridge across the ravine by the waterfall, the river path down into the valley, and the neck of the rise on the pasture trail. Our job is half-done by the landscape.'

There was that look again, that uncomfortable exchange of glances between Keretan and the smiths.

'Traps?' Keretan said. 'Is that wise? If the gods smile on us and we're victorious, we'll still be living here. Our children will be playing here.' For a moment, he looked sickened by the thought, swallowing hard.

'Could probably build them to constrain, not kill,' Vida said, one hand on her chin. 'Or maim at most. You can't really sling a net over men armed with sharp weapons and expect them to stay put; they're not boars.'

Ree leaned in. 'What are you thinking?'

'Spike pits, mostly.' Vida traced a finger over the map. 'Dig trenches, line them with stakes. Places they'll be moving through, of course, but also anywhere they might be looking to take cover under barrage.'

'Barrage?' Keretan said, brows lifted.

'One pit next to another, recessed a little,' Mariam suggested. 'So anyone coming to help someone who falls in gets caught too.' Ree was delighted to hear a little glee in her voice.

'Is it too much to hope you have any blasting powder hidden around here?' Ree asked.

'Sorry,' Vida grunted. 'No saltpetre.'

Ree tapped the map. 'All the cut timber stacked here – we'll need most of it for barricades, but what do you think to some tripwires along the thoroughfares? Use the slope of the terraces to our advantage.'

Vida was nodding along, already sketching lines on the map with a narrow strip of charcoal. 'We can use logs, or maybe old wheels,' she mused. 'The heavier the better.'

'We can strip the water mill materials for ropes and pulleys,' Keretan suggested. 'If the gods indeed smile on us, we can always put it all back together.'

Vida was still gazing at the map. 'We should consider secondary traps on strategic locations – let them think they're through the perimeter, hit them with something unpleasant, then cut them off from behind.'

'What about pole traps?' Mariam suggested. 'You know like, bent staves, something nasty on the end, kept under tension – maybe they'd work with tripwires? There are plenty of saplings at the edge of the pasture that would do, there are.'

'What do we expect of their discipline?' Vida was looking to Ree now, her gaze grave but intent. 'Are they likely to concentrate on their objectives, or break off into looting? If the latter, we should plan some doorway drops on the closest houses. Something worse than skins of goat milk.'

'If there's time,' Ree countered. 'We should probably concentrate on the big things first.' She looked down at the lines Vida had drawn over Lali's map. 'If we use the pits right, we should be able make them wary enough to channel them into some other surprises.'

'We could put some bows under tension behind doors,' Mariam said, her eyes flashing. 'They pull open the door, it releases the string . . . sorry, I'm getting carried away, I am.'

'We don't have the bows, my dear,' Vida replied, giving her a kiss, 'but I love the enthusiasm.'

'On the subject of bows,' Ree said, 'they likely have far more than we do. We'll need to keep out of sight as much as possible.'

'Woodsmoke,' Keretan rumbled. 'We've gathered plenty of green wood to season – if we set it on top of some well-placed fires, it'll choke the valley.'

Ree nodded. 'It might also be time to ask people to start collecting rocks and stones. We may run out of things to throw.' She looked back at the map. 'The broad strokes are clear, I think,' she said, sweeping her finger over the parchment. 'Defence in depth, always falling back to the next ring, let the traps do the work and never, ever get caught in a stand-up fight with them.'

'Agreed,' said Keretan and Vida together.

Keretan cleared his throat. 'Should we be cutting the rope bridge?'

'It's too soon,' Vida countered. 'There's no shortage of timber in the forest, they'll likely build a temporary crossing if they have warning.'

'They may do that anyway,' Ree sighed, running one hand through her ever-grimier hair. 'There's a lot here, a lot to do, and our defenders are going to need drilling on top of it all. Are your people capable of this? We won't have long, and I know not everyone is keen on our proposals.' To say the least.

Keretan answered. 'Ar Ramas is a place of peace. The people who came here, the people who stayed, did so because they wanted to live without fear. And sometimes you can outrun your fear . . .' He trailed off, throat bobbing.

'. . . And sometimes you have to face it,' Vida finished. 'We have farmers and builders, labourers and carpenters, we have people who are fit, hardy and well-fed, many of whom had a life before this one . . . and while not everyone wants to fight, everyone can dig. We'll get it done.'

'What about,' Mariam said, her voice almost manic with possibility, 'doing something with *bees?*'

* * *

The plan was made, although in the end it featured few bees. It had been faster than Ree had expected, with no hint of argument or challenge, just objective-focused co-operation. She was almost disappointed. She gave a silent prayer of thanks to the gods who had kept Camellia and Volkan out of proceedings. She considered thanking the councillors themselves, but discounted the notion as ridiculous.

'What time is it?' she said, suppressing a yawn. 'I could murder a cup of tea.' And a nap, for that matter. The surge of adrenaline from the attack on the Council House and all that had followed was long since spent, and an hour spent poring over a map in a gloomy chamber hadn't helped.

'Not noon yet,' said Mariam, who was closest to the door. 'I think we might have used the last of your tea, though. Sorry.' She regarded Ree in the grey light that crept in through the open shutters. 'You look shattered. Why don't you get some sleep while we get started.'

Ree shook her head. It buzzed a little when she did so. 'No time. Time's the enemy now. Every moment we're unprepared they could launch an attack and take this place. What about bells for the perimeter? To raise the alarm?'

'We don't have many bells,' Mariam said.

'Any, in fact,' Vida added.

'We do have a lot of horns, though,' Mariam finished. 'Would they work?'

Keretan cleared his throat with a rumble. 'We've not yet discussed who goes to the caves.'

'The caves?' Ree raised an eyebrow.

'The very old and the very young, I'd say, and anyone who wants no part in the violence,' Vida said flatly. 'Unless you think differently?'

Keretan shook his head. Despite his size, he seemed almost meek in Vida's presence. Perhaps she just had that effect on people.

'Good. I'll get the apprentices together. Mari, gather who you can. We all know our tasks?'

Ree's brain was fogging. 'What am I doing?'

'Having a kip,' came Mariam's answer.

'Don't worry,' said Vida with that hint of a smile, 'we'll save you a trip to the stores.' She chuckled mirthlessly to herself. 'At least the old dispute about wasting storage space up there will be settled.'

'Wait, wait. Before we disperse, there's something we need to address.'

Vida paused, one foot towards the door. 'And what's that?'

She turned her head and called towards the back of the room. 'For the sake of the gods, Sweeper, stop skulking in the shadows. It's time to explain yourself.'

THIRTY-NINE

'So you're Copperhand,' Vida said, almost expressionless.

'He doesn't care for that name,' Ree supplied from her perch by the fire.

'You're a War Criminal!' Mariam exclaimed.

Sweeper stared at the ruined floor. His welts looked no better in the flickering light. 'I'm sorry.'

'Sorry for what, exactly?' Ree tilted her head, shrugging off her creeping lethargy. She'd sleep well tonight, of that she was certain, as long as the village wasn't burned to the ground in the meantime. 'What you did, or being revealed?'

He gave a small snort. 'Both, I suppose. But I am sorry I lied to you all.' He lifted his eyes for a moment, and in place of the customary deference, Ree saw something that approached frankness. 'I never intended any of this.'

'Did you really butcher an entire army as they slept?' Mariam's voice was breathy and hushed with wonder, and Ree detected a level of interest that bordered on unseemly. 'What happened to your gang?'

'There never was a gang,' he sighed. 'Just . . . I'll tell you now, all right? I'll tell you and you can decide what to do with me.'

'Go on,' Vida prompted, with eyes of stone.

'I grew up in . . . it doesn't matter. Borderlands, swallowed by the war in the early days. I was a tracker and a scout, but never professionally. Mostly I watched the herds.'

'You were a quiet step,' Ree suggested, and he nodded.

'We knew there was fighting, but it was always over the hills, until one day it wasn't. The first we knew was a group of soldiers, maybe a dozen, foraging I suppose, came tearing through our little settlement, stripping it bare.' He shook his head. 'I still don't know who they were fighting for – they wore no colours, showed only hunger.'

'And you slew them?' Mariam couldn't hide her disappointment. 'That's hardly an army, is it?'

He shook his head again. 'We hid. They took what they could, then, almost as an afterthought, they took a couple of people too.' He swallowed. 'Girls, they were. Daughters of men I worked beside. Dragged them away, bound over mule-back.'

The atmosphere had changed. 'Ah,' said Vida.

Sweeper ran his hands through his matted hair. 'We argued over what to do, and, in the end, some of us followed. Not enough, not nearly enough. But the sign was clear, we followed them back to their camp. And then we argued again, and it got dark.'

Ree was less sleepy now. 'And?'

'Desperation won out. In the morning they'd move on, and take our people with them. Someone had to get close to the camp, see if we could sneak in and make a rescue.' He gazed down at the floor again.

'You were chosen?' Keretan prompted.

'I volunteered. Fancied myself a *quiet step*.' He wrapped his narrow arms around himself, seeming to shiver despite the warmth of the fires. 'They were camped in a dip just below a rise. They'd gorged and drunk themselves stupid, I could hear the snores from down the slope. The moon was bright, the clouds scattered. I knew where the mules were, the two tents they'd bothered to raise, thought I knew where the girls would be.' He stopped, sniffed. 'In my head I was already making the rescue on my own, scouting be damned. I was going to be the hero. Then I tripped over the sentry.'

He was staring past them now, into the wavering flames of the fireplace beyond, their light dancing in his wet eyes. 'He'd been asleep, just as fed and boozed as the others. We stared at each other, side by side on the ground, and I watched the realisation reach him, who I was, what was happening. I saw him tense, prepare to shout a warning, rouse his comrades, and they'd have slaughtered us all.' His eyes dropped again. 'So . . . I killed him.'

Nobody spoke, although to Ree's eye Mariam was desperate to press for more. One killing was not yet an army, after all.

'I'd never killed anyone before.' Sweeper's voice was light, faint against the crackle of the fires and the noises of activity from outside. 'But I'd helped in butchering hogs and cattle, and my knife was sharp.' His eyes drifted, his tone with it. 'They used to say I was good with the animals, how there was no shrieking or struggling, how they'd stay quiet . . . calm, even. To the end. How I was a calm touch. Killing a man is a lot like killing a pig, especially if both are surprised.' He sighed, his gaze returning to the room. 'But I was too slow. Our scuffle had woken another supposed sentry, and he was coming to investigate. So I crept around behind him and killed him too.'

From the corner of her eye, Ree saw Mariam mouth 'Two.'

'After that,' Sweeper continued, 'all I could think about was that someone would wake, that they'd see the bodies of the sentries, that we'd be discovered and exterminated. I counted them all, asleep around their fire, guessed the others would be in the tents, so . . . so I made sure none around the fire would come after me.'

'How many were around the fire?' Mariam asked, unable to hold herself back.

'Seven,' he said simply, without looking at her. 'I had the knack for it, whether learned or innate it didn't matter. That first stumble had primed me, and now I was aware of every breathing thing around me, every lurking obstacle, the precise line of the cut needed to render them inactive and silent.' He rubbed at his arms again. 'So much like killing hogs . . .'

'Three more were in the tents, then, were they?' Mariam was doing her best to keep the impatience from her voice. 'With . . . with company?'

'Yes,' he replied softly, 'and no. Two men slept within. They were straightforward. But the girls from my settlement weren't there. I began to panic. Then I heard approaching steps from the top of the rise.'

'The last man?'

'I wasn't sure. I thought perhaps the other members of my band had circled around and were approaching for the far side – maybe they had found the girls already and were looking for me. I slipped back out into the night to see a man walking the crest, not one of my fellows, not even a man I recognised, although his armour marked him as the same bunch that had taken our people. So I crept up to the rise and killed him too.'

'How?' Mariam demanded, but Vida shushed her. Mariam still muttered 'Twelve' under her breath.

'And then I saw it.'

They waited to hear what he'd seen, Mariam near twitching with impatience.

'. . . The rest of the camp.'

'Ah,' Vida said again.

'They'd pitched right beside the main body of their force, laid out in neat little rows across the valley in the moonlight. All I knew was that the girls might be anywhere in there.' He rubbed at his thighs, as if trying to clean something off his palms. Ree supposed he was. 'There was nothing else in my head but finding them, and not being caught. So . . . I continued.'

Vida watched him with steady eyes. 'You continued?'

His throat bobbed as he swallowed. 'I knew I had to find the sentries first, any patrols . . . but there were so few. They were expecting nothing, least of all a lad with a butcher's knife creeping through the darkness.'

Ree shifted against the timber wall. 'How old were you?'

'Sixteen, maybe seventeen. Long time ago now.'

'Gods.'

'Then I . . . I went tent to tent, as fast as I could, even tents I thought were too small to hide them, just in case.'

'How many tents?' Keretan murmured.

'I don't know. Dozens. Maybe a hundred.'

'And those inside?'

'Ones, twos. Sometimes three. I had the knack. A calm touch.' He cracked a bitter smile. 'The gods were smiling on me that night, it seems, in their own perverse way.'

'Gods have mercy,' Vida murmured, but it seemed reflexive.

'And the kidnapped girls?' Mariam demanded. 'You found them?'

His bitter smile became a mirthless laugh, a barked breath of incredulous scorn. 'By the time I was finished, first light was in the east, and I was a creature of blood, my mind empty of purpose beyond killing. If I had stumbled over those poor girls in my trance, I'd probably have cut their throats too.'

'They weren't there?' Mariam's brows were rucked in outrage.

'I wasn't to know it, but they'd kicked their way clear long before we even set out, and were hiding out in the plains. The soldiers had given them up and carried on. They made it back to the settlement a little before we did – after the others dragged me back.' He took a long breath. 'There was no joy. They couldn't look at me. I saw the terror in their eyes, of what I'd done, of what might be coming in return, of what walked among them. When I came back to them, my hands were so stained they thought I was wearing gauntlets.'

'Copperhand,' Mariam whispered.

He didn't acknowledge her. 'We fled, all of us: the settlement, the farmers, even the local merchant. Some still travelled with me – those who'd not seen me walk out of that camp with dawn at my back, that knife so heavy in my hand. Those whose questions got only silence. But one by one they fell away.'

Mariam tilted her head in tentative sympathy. 'Did you have a family?'

'Nothing that could survive that.'

'And you went west?'

He nodded. 'My gang, as popular myth calls it, were little more than displaced farmhands who'd lost everything to my bloodlust, had they but known it. We went into the hills. I went over the Ashadi.'

Ree's throat was becoming dry. 'You really made it to Arestan?'

'I did.'

'And you came back? I thought it was paradise!'

He shrugged, battered face indifferent. 'Not my kind of place.' He nodded up through the roof beams. 'The climate up here is more pleasant.'

'Gods, don't tell the kid. You really came back for the climate?'

His eyes cast down once more. 'I became . . . agitated.'

'Guilt, then.'

A slow nod. 'I wanted to come back and check on those I'd left behind. To try to . . . atone, for what I'd done to them.' He spread gnarled hands. 'But it turns out the Ashadi are hard enough to cross once, near impossible a second time. I lost my way.'

'But you found Ar Ramas.'

Another nod. 'I hadn't been looking, but it seemed, well . . .'

Ree matched the nod. 'Yeah. A fitting place to atone.' She glanced sidelong at Vida, Mariam and Keretan. 'He likes to help,' she muttered.

'You're really Copperhand?' Vida said. 'That story is about you?'

Mariam was shaking her head, brows low, eyes alive with disquiet. 'It doesn't seem possible. A hundred . . . two hundred, all by yourself? Without discovery, without alarms . . . ?' She looked back to Sweeper. 'Do you remember them?'

'Some. Body shapes, some faces, the way their hair lay while they slept. The glow of moonlight on their necks.' He looked down again. 'I remember the necks most.' He clasped his hands to his chest. 'I'm sorry I lied to you. I'm sorry I pretended to be something I'm not. But honestly, after that night, I swore I'd never hurt anyone ever again, until . . .'

'Right,' Ree said. 'Until this morning.' She pushed herself up and away from the wall. 'Maybe it's not my place, but as far as I'm concerned you saved my life today, and the lives of many others in this village. I think that goes some way to atoning.'

Vida grunted, perhaps even in agreement.

'It's kind of you to say this,' Sweeper replied, still staring at the floor, 'although it still feels like I have a long way to go.'

'That we can discuss shortly.' Ree's chuckle was grim. 'I imagine we all have some pressing suggestions. For now, you stay close, and we'll decide your part in this in turn.'

'What's your real name, then?' Mariam asked, her hands on her hips. 'We can't keep calling you Sweeper, and I don't think anyone will relish calling the name Copperhand around the place.'

'If it's all the same,' he mumbled, 'could I remain as Sweeper? I've been happiest here, as that name.'

'Works for me,' Vida declared. 'Now, I believe we have important things to do, yes?'

The council of defence dispersed.

As soon as Keretan, Vida and Mariam had left, a shadow appeared in the doorway, looking flustered, and for an instant Ree thought one of the councillors had come back for her. They had not. 'There you are, kid. Did you bring your friend Anri?'

'Couldn't find him,' she griped. 'And he's not my friend. He's a dick.'

'You were the one who thought he should be part of this.'

'He should! He's the one who needs to understand that.'

'What is it with you and him, kid? What's the fixation?' Ree's eyes narrowed. 'Do I need to worry?'

The kid threw up her grubby paws in disgust, lip curled almost to her eyeballs. 'Gods, no, Ma, it's not like that. I just need . . . He and I have unfinished business, that's all.'

Ree nodded, fighting back another yawn. 'Well, he'd better show up soon.' She tapped the lined and annotated map. 'We'll be cutting the bridge at the first sign of trouble, and he and his wife will be stuck on the wrong side.'

The kid made a sour face. 'He'd probably say that's just how he likes it.'

Sweeper poked his head up from his work in the corner. 'Want me to go looking for him?'

'Go on, then. If you find him, warn him about the bridge and ask him to come in. Come straight back.' She paused for a moment. 'We can help move his wife, if that's worrying him.'

'That won't be it,' the kid muttered.

Sweeper went, scurrying out despite his obvious, livid injuries.

'What's going on, Ma?' The kid followed her out into the day's silvery light. Away from the fires of the Council House, it was bitterly cold outside. Shouts and calls filled the air, and already a team of labourers were setting up around the stacked timber beside the bridge. Someone jogged past with what looked like a bundle of shovels over one shoulder.

'Preparations. We need to move fast.' She turned to look up at the great cliff-face behind the village, the Grandfathers, where Vida was dishing out orders at the base and the great hoist at the summit of the rock shelf was spinning into action. Sacks of river stones went up, bundles of supplies came down. The stores were in the caves, and the stores were being broken open. What treasures would lie within?

'Vida and Mariam seem very capable, don't they?' the kid said.

'Yes, they do,' Ree replied, one finger tapping her lower lip. She scanned the edge of the terraces, the drop into the valley, the sweep of the opposite flank of the mountain. Something caught her eye, a grey tuft swaying in the breeze at the crest of a distant, familiar ridge-line. 'Huh.'

'What is it? What are you doing? You need to rest!'

'Stay here, kid, hold down the . . . you know. Stay in the village, don't go into the woods, understand?'

'Where are you going?'

Ree cracked half a smile. 'Into the woods. Relax, kid, you'll understand when you're older.'

Her bottom lip was jutting. 'That adults are hypocrites? I understand that just fine already.' The kid looked away, shoulders hunched. 'I can't believe you're doing this again.'

'What? Going somewhere without you?'

'Deciding things without me! How are we ever going to be partners if you never involve me in decisions? Never tell me when there *are* decisions?'

'Kid, I do not have time for this now.' Ree took a sharp breath through her nose, exhaled. 'We're crossing the mountains to Arestan like you always wanted, aren't we?'

She was still half-turned, arms wrapped around herself. 'Are we, though? Sometimes it feels like you only agreed to cross the Ashadi because we'd exhausted every other possibility. And now the *moment* an alternative comes up, we're doing that instead.'

'I thought you wanted to stay here longer—'

'Maybe I did, but it's not like you checked, is it?' The kid took a rattling sniff of her own, and her voice dropped, becoming almost pleading. 'How can I trust you when you won't trust me?'

'Don't be . . . We can talk later, all right? I have to go, and now.' Ree was already hobbling away, her stick thudding. 'Don't let them cut the bridge before I get back,' she called over her shoulder.

'No,' came the reply.

FORTY

Javani watched people engaged in energetic tasks for a while, waiting to see if anyone would order her to do something. When nobody did, not even Mariam, who buzzed past in a flurry of harmonious instructions to a group of people who really weren't that much older than Javani in, you know, a general sense, she felt a little disappointed. Not that she wanted to start humping coils of rope around or hacking out frosty turf, but it was the principle of the thing.

'Lots of activity going on, mistress.' Tauras was leaning on the near side of the ram pen, fleeces draped over his massive shoulders, his chain stretched about as far as it would go. He was watching the residents of Ar Ramas tearing past on the upper terraces with a fascinated look on his face. Javani was astonished, and a little upset, to see Tarfellian curled up against his legs like a giant, snoring, sandy mound. The dog glanced up at her approach and had the decency to look ashamed.

'Tarfellian,' she hissed, 'you're supposed to be guarding him!'

'Oh, he is, mistress,' Tauras replied with that bright, open expression. 'Kept me right safe, he has. And warm.' He reached down and gave the dog's belly an energetic rub, which produced a sigh of near-indecent approval from the ancient mastiff. Tauras gestured to the urgent frenzy on the terraces with his other hand. 'What's all the commotion?'

'Um. You know. Preparations.'

'Right, yeah. Preparations.' He nodded as if he understood, then wiped his nose on the back of his hand. 'Can I help? I'm good at lifting things.'

'And putting them down,' Javani replied without meaning to, but he only beamed with recognition. 'Uh, Tauras,' she said, feeling the need to clear her throat a lot, 'I think maybe your help wouldn't be . . . welcome, right now.'

His broad brows creased, a note of hurt in his eyes. She noticed that stubble was growing between his great braids, and it did make him just a little less intimidating. 'But why? I'm good at lifting things. And putting them down,' he added with a hopeful lift of his eyebrows, searching for that recognition.

She tried to think of a way to explain that wouldn't hurt his feelings, and, independently, marvelled at herself for doing so. 'You remember what you said, about looking scary? How it meant you don't have to fight people who are frightened of you?' He nodded with enthusiasm, back on familiar ground. 'Well, it's hard for people to accept help from people they're scared of, I guess.'

'Oh.'

'Sorry.'

'It's all right, mistress.'

'You don't have to call me mistress. You can call me Javani. That's my name.' She felt it was important to clarify that, just in case. He looked totally crestfallen, his eyes downcast, his mouth downturned, and she cast around for something to sweeten the sting of her words. 'But, you know, once people get to know you, they'll see you're not really that scary, right? Like, uh, like I did.'

Hope returned to his eyes. 'You think so?'

'I do. You just keep being, uh, you, and they won't find you scary for long.'

'I will do that, Javani. I'm good at it.'

She returned his giant smile without a jot of artifice. By his feet, Tarfellian snapped up his head, swivelled in the direction of the waterfall, and growled.

Javani turned to look. 'There are people by the bridge. There's something going on.' She swallowed.

'I need to go.'

* * *

Ree was almost all the way to the top of the ridge, huffing and sweating with her sword digging painfully into her hip, before she heard the first snore. She dropped to her hands and knees for the last part of the climb, mindful that she was a thrice-damned sight more visible in daylight than she'd been before dawn.

'Mantlepass! Are you fucking *asleep?*'

The snoring came to an abrupt and gasping halt. A moment later, a croaky voice came from the far side of the briar.

'Forgive me, for I have been somewhat deprived of opportunities for rest today.'

'Well, fucking likewise, chum, and you don't see me catching flies on a fucking hilltop.'

A pause followed, which matched something that sounded a lot like a yawn on the far side of the shrub. 'Am I to deduce from the aggression of your language that your mood has been afflicted by your somnolent deficiency?'

She flopped down beside the bush. 'Deduce away, chum.'

Neither spoke, while around them the trees creaked in the wintry breeze and somewhere a partridge called.

'Well?' she said at last.

'Well?' he responded, his speech still sluggish with lethargy.

'What do you want?'

'Want? What?'

'Piss of the gods, Mantelpiece, wake the fuck up, will you? Why did you signal me up here?'

'What signal?'

'The fleece! You strung it over the top of the bush, where I could see it from the village.'

He was quiet for another moment. 'Ah. I had not intended, that is, when I rearranged matters, it was purely to air the—'

Ree hissed like a snake into the brisk afternoon. 'Then why are you here? Your minders still keeping their bows on you?'

'I fear so. I was merely dispatched to gather further intelligence.' She heard him rub at a bristly chin.

'On what? For what purpose?'

'I could not rightly say.'

'Either they're keeping you out of the camp for some reason, or you're out here to witness something. Which do you think it is?'

'I could not rightly say.' This time he sounded truly dejected. 'In truth, it could be either, or both. Or something else.'

'This man who's taken control of your camp, the man who took Gumis—'

'Lado. Lado of Cstethia.'

'What do you know about him?'

He sighed, and she heard the crunch of shale as he shifted against the crest. 'In truth, I barely know the man, it was my confederate Kediras who identified him as a threat – she demanded that we kill him on his arrival. Perhaps she was right. She has not made herself known at the village?'

Ree shook her head, then realised he couldn't see her. 'No. Sorry.'

'Perhaps she will yet turn up.' He cleared his throat. 'As I say, I know little of the fellow, beyond his ability to worm himself into positions of authority as if greased by the gods. He has a manner, somehow unctuous yet possessed of snarling aggression, and wears victimhood like a mantle.'

'And he doesn't like you?'

'I would hazard he does not. He knows of me, that much I know, for he raised the bear twice already.'

Ree blinked. 'Raised the bear? Is that bandit code for something unspeakable?'

She heard him sniff, hard, as if tamping down an excess of emotion. 'It is for another time,' he muttered.

'What's he planning? This Lado.' She swallowed. 'How long do we have?'

'I could not rightly say. I cannot betray any information that might jeopardise—'

'Do better, chapter captain. Your narcoleptic scout no doubt observed that the folk of Ar Ramas are finally awakening to the notion that their lives and livelihoods are in danger, and are preparing to do something about it, but we need time if we're to do more than drag planks. Remind me, where do you stand on the wholesale slaughter of peaceful farming communities?'

'I am,' he said, a hard edge to his voice, 'opposed to such.'

'Then what binds you to this absurdity? Some crusted oath?'

He seemed to hiss, flinching at her words. 'It is not that, though I am a man who lays stock on his word by point of principle.'

'What, then? Why do you chain yourself to this madness still?'

The captain was quiet a moment, and she heard him shift against the scree. 'After I lost everything, it was the company that restored order, structure, to my existence. It gave me a family again, of sorts at least. One with rules. We must have rules, or all is chaos.'

'Do you feel those rules are holding up?'

'I . . . I cannot say.'

'Then do what you can, Mandolas. Delay, defer, deny – buy us time, any way you can.'

'I can yet do little from this vantage—'

'So descend!' she hissed. 'Find a basis for argument with those that watch you. Stay up here and you'll do nothing but watch us die. Does that sound like an agreeable afternoon to you?'

'It does not.'

'Then pull your fucking finger out, Captain Manatas, and maybe I'll see you again before long.' She began to slide away from the shrub, back down the slope.

'Wait! Before you go.' The top of his head poked over the crest of the ridge beside the bush's wiry expanse, only a few paces from her. In daylight he was, she admitted, not unattractive, if weathered, blocky, almost bland good looks were your thing. He was gazing at her with wide, shadowed eyes that burned with earnest uncertainty. 'He is hoarding weapons of range.' He swallowed, the creak returning to his voice. 'He intends to winnow any attempts at defence before battle can be joined.'

She held the gaze, fighting to keep her voice and expression under control.

'Where?'

This was it. It meant betraying his company. He was teetering. She exerted sheer will, keeping her eyes on him, keeping her face neutral, open, attentive but not demanding, no hint of the violent desperation that raged inside her.

He broke. 'The wooden shack, at the back of the camp. Closest thing we had to something permanent. The weapons and their missiles are laid out and wrapped to keep them from the elements.'

'Thank you, captain.' She resumed her retreat, then froze, shifting painfully to look down the slope. 'Do you smell . . . smoke?'

Anri was lurking not far from the bridge, behind the ring of what Javani supposed were now sentries, his bow slung over his shoulder and Sweeper in his shadow.

'Happy now, pest? Not content with dogging my footsteps yourself, now you're dragging old Shuffles by here in on your games?' He gave the forlorn Sweeper a contemptuous nod.

Javani ignored it, looking past him. 'What's going on across the bridge?' People lurked on the far side, but she couldn't see who through the brand-new, hastily erected barriers of loose timber and the nervous-looking villagers who stood around them.

Anri didn't even turn his head. 'Who gives two bedpost-sized shits? Now you've seen me, are you finally going to leave me in peace?'

She focused on him. 'That's exactly it, Anri – peace. There won't be any soon. The bandits are going to attack, do you understand? And before they do, the village will cut the bridge.' She peered into his blank eyes, looking for a sign he understood. 'You'll be cut off, on the wrong side.'

She found nothing.

'So? None of this is my quarrel. This bunch can settle their own affairs, I'm better off out of it.'

'But you won't be! You're part of the village, Anri, you and Tanith, whatever you tell yourself.'

He turned to leave. 'It's too cold to be standing around listening to this bollocks. They cut the bridge, fine, I'll just sling a rope over those mill fixings in the rock by the fall and swing across. Fucking doddle.'

She grabbed his arm. 'Wait!' She fixed him with her most fearsome stare. 'Do you think the mercenaries across the valley will give two bedpost-sized shits that you think you're not part of the village? Do you?'

He shook her off. 'Leave me alone,' he growled, and set off for the bridge, calling over his shoulder, 'I'll be just fine.'

For a moment, she hesitated. Should she simply let him go, leave him to his fate? What was her fixation, after all? Certainly nothing romantic, gods no – the thought near flipped her gizzard. He was more like . . . more like a problem, a project, a wobbly tooth she couldn't stop probing with her tongue. He was going to teach her archery so she could surpass Ree, on that she was adamant, but the more he tried to drive her away, the more she resolved to stick to him like horse glue. I'm the one in charge here, she vowed. I decide who my friends are. Friends? Acquaintances, then. He didn't make any effort to fit in with the rest of the village, wasn't expected to make friends with all the other children or make awkward small talk with Lali, was standoffish and caustic, often needlessly confrontational, quite a lot like . . .

Javani stopped the thought there.

She caught up with him as they reached the barriers, little more than some of the piles of timber rearranged, crewed by half a dozen people who wore thick wool and carried stout sticks, but whose wide, twitching eyes betrayed their shivering anxiety. Anri had come to a stop, and on reaching him, Javani saw why.

Across the bridge was a delegation from the mercenaries, but unlike on previous occasions when most had loitered at the edge of the trees while their emissary approached the bridge, this time they stood in a clear line, heavy armour glinting in the dull light, weapons proud and very, very real in their hands. At their head was the man who had taken Gumis, the man Ree had named as Lado. With cold shock, Javani realised that her mother was still the wrong side of the bridge. If this was the beginning of the siege, it was very bad timing indeed.

'People of Ar Ramas,' he called, his tone somewhere between outraged and scornful, 'I will be brief, as time is short. Summon your leaders if you must, but I will not wait.'

He shuffled closer, one hand resting on the hilt of a wicked-looking knife at his belt. Beside Javani, Anri muttered, 'Cross in a moment, won't I?'

Someone went dashing off in the direction of the Council House, but Lado was already speaking again.

'You are in breach, people of Ar Ramas. You harbour murderers, and have acted with naked aggression towards the members of my company. Your agents have assaulted and threatened, kidnapped and imprisoned, while reneging on an honest contract after long reaping its benefits. And now—' He gestured with the hand that was not on the knife towards the meagre fortifications. '—Now you build engines of war within your own domain, take up tools of violence in your hands, in defiance of what you claim as your own laws.' He took another step, now only a pace from the bridge's far end, and dropped his head in apparent sorrow. 'And when we sent our brightest, most pure-hearted envoys to make one last, desperate attempt to negotiate with you, they never returned. We can only assume they were murdered, as was my cousin, further compounding your crimes.'

'They tried to assassinate the Council!' Javani was a little shocked to realise the shout was hers, her voice shrill and thin in the clear air.

Lado shook his head as if pained by grief. 'Still, the lies. The lies and the deceit and the denial.' Javani heard people approaching, and a moment later Keretan's great shadow passed over her, followed by Camellia and Volkan.

'But!' Lado cried, lifting his head, his greasy hair falling in curtains across his scarred face. 'The gods smile on you yet, for despite the provocations, the Company of the Wolf remain reasonable. We remain pragmatic. We are willing to make a settlement at the last.'

'What is your offer?' This time, Keretan's baritone boomed from the slick rock of the falls. He sounded far from shrill and thin, which Javani considered somewhat unfair.

'Surrender yourselves to justice,' Lado said, barely keeping the malicious delight from his voice. 'Cease these activities, allow us to enter the village and conduct our investigations, identify and try the perpetrators of the crimes against our company, and collect the restitution owed. All debts will be settled.'

'And in return?' Keretan called.

'We are generous to our friends,' Lado replied, eyes glittering beneath his hair.

'Meaning what?' That time, it could have been Camellia.

Lado spread his hands, finally revealing the gleaming hilt of his knife, and dipped his head. 'You will all be spared.'

Javani swallowed. She might not be any sort of diplomat like her mother, but even she could interpret the implication of his words. He didn't need to clarify what they'd be spared from. Or not.

'Consider our offer,' Lado called, throwing his cloak around him and hiding the unspeakable knife. 'You have until sundown. Don't make us do something you'll regret.'

The line of mercenaries turned almost as one and set off down the road towards the trees. Lado lingered a moment longer, seeming to sniff the breeze. 'Lest we be misunderstood,' he said with a mock bow, then turned and followed his men.

Around Javani, the adults fell into an anxious babble. Lado's implication had not been lost on them, and multiple demands to cut the bridge immediately were not slow in arriving, though to her relief nobody proposed surrendering the village to Lado and his bandits. 'As if they'd stop at hanging one of us,' one of the sentries muttered, which would have pleased Ree to hear.

Beside her, Anri shouldered his bow again. 'Oily little prick, that one, isn't he? Be seeing you, pest. Good luck with this.' He made for the bridge, then came up short, sniffing the air as Lado had. Javani sniffed too.

'Is that . . . Is something burning?'

Then someone spotted the spreading plume of black smoke rising from upslope, at the top of the winding path that led to the timber yard . . . and Anri's house. And there, emerging from the trees with her hands raised in panic, was Sara, the woman who minded Anri's wife during the day.

Anri said nothing, just threw his bow and quiver to the ground and set off across the bridge at a run.

FORTY-ONE

The flames were bright through the trees well before Javani reached the clearing that was the timber yard. Anri was a blur ahead of her, a dark shape barrelling through the black stripes of trunks in the snow-dappled landscape. All Javani could hear was her rasping breath in her ears and the crushing splatter of frosted mulch beneath her boots.

By the time she reached the yard, it was already clear they would not be able to extinguish the fire. The line of lean-tos was burning fiercely, the raw heat from the flames warming Javani's skin from the yard's far side. Behind them, nearby trees charred and steamed as snow melted.

'Tanith!' Anri roared as he charged straight for his house. The lean-to beside it was already crackling with orange flames, the beams of its roof scorched and smouldering.

Maybe, Javani thought, as she slowed her pace a little in the face of the fearsome heat, maybe she's having a lucid spell, maybe the heat and the smoke will have sparked something in her, and she'll come staggering out at any moment . . .

But then she remembered the look of utter panic on Sara's face, and she knew there was no way Tanith was walking out.

'Tanith!'

Anri smashed open the door and charged inside, one arm over his nose and mouth against the sudden billow of dark smoke. Javani was only paces behind him, still not exactly sure what she was doing. The scene inside the house was infernal chaos, lit orange by flame and swirling with choking fumes. Javani blinked away acrid tears and tried to make sense of what she saw. Everything was in the wrong place, in the wrong shape. The back of the roof had fallen in, one heavy timber dropped right onto the raised bed beneath the window. Right where Tanith lay, motionless.

Anri was hunched over the timber, his arms wrapping it, grunting and straining between choking coughs. 'Help me!' he bellowed at Javani's approach. The heat inside the house was growing to uncomfortable levels, sweat drenched her and her skin felt like she was standing too close to an open oven. Shadows flickered across them from the gaping hole in the roof, the flames from the next building now peeking above the gap, their progress remorseless.

She had one go at shifting the timber with him, trying to ignore Tanith's peaceful, oblivious face beneath it, before both she and Anri realised it was useless. 'Get help!' he bawled, but she was already moving. She dashed out of the house into the sudden cold sting of dusk, finding a handful of villagers gathered outside, milling and uncertain.

'Help Anri!' she yelled, pointing at the house. 'There's a fallen timber, he can't move it.'

A couple started forward, hands up to shield themselves, already looking like their resolve had failed. Javani looked beyond them to see Ree arriving, hobbling out of the forest as fast as her stick would carry her.

'Ma!' she called. 'Anri's wife is stuck under a fallen timber. He needs help.'

One look at her mother's exhausted face told her she'd be no more use than Javani herself. The villagers were still trying to approach the house, but they were so tentative, so feeble. Anri needed serious strength.

'Kid!' Ree yelled as Javani set off at a run. 'Where are you going?'

'Get up, Tauras, I need you.'

He was on his feet in an instant, clearly on the verge of giving a salute. Tarfellian, displaced, gave a reproachful huff. 'Mistr—Javani?'

'I need help lifting something. How fast can you run?'

'Will the secret army—'

'They want you to help.'

One scarred hand went to the collar at his neck, and the chain that ran from it into the stables. 'What about the chain, Javani?'

'Oh. Bring it with you.'

It took him a single heave to wrench it from the wall.

A few more people had gathered in the burning timber yard, but they were achieving little more than warming themselves on the flames. A half-hearted attempt at a bucket chain to the stream at the clearing's edge had faltered from both a lack of buckets and a lack of participants; others had fallen back, concerned about the safety of the rest of the village and its other outlying structures. Only then did Javani think of the smithy and the schoolhouse, and felt a sudden stab of panic that they might also be burning. Horns were blowing across the village, a new, unnerving chorus that did nothing to reassure.

Everyone but Ree scattered as Javani and her new assistant came pelting into the clearing, his chain jangling like the approach of a mail-clad battalion. Javani ignored the looks and gasps and made straight for the open door of Anri's house, her breath already burning at the top of her chest before she'd sucked down her first lungful of smoke. Anri was still inside, somewhere in the choking murk, still labouring over the great timber. Javani saw others with him, a couple of struggling figures, bent double and gasping as they wrestled with the heavy wood.

'Everyone get back,' she barked into the smoke. 'Tauras, hold your breath and shut your eyes.'

'Yes, Javani!'

He seemed to use her name as punctuation, or possibly where he'd have been saying 'sir' or 'captain'. The thought was oddly pleasing, but it was hardly the time for self-administered back-pats.

Wet wool wrapped around their heads, she led Tauras on hands and knees across the room until they reached the bed. Anri was still there, coughing and hacking, straining at the barely shifted wood.

'Tauras, get your chain over the branch up there, then wrap it around this timber. Got it?'

His eyes open barely a crack, the big man nodded. And if there was one thing Tauras could do, Javani had learned, it was follow instructions.

'Ready? Anri, ready? Heave!'

Two breaths later, they were out, Javani leading Tauras, Tauras supporting Anri, Anri carrying Tanith. Tauras still had his eyes shut. They collapsed gasping to the brittle earth outside, feeling the blaze at their backs, as the side wall of Anri's house collapsed and the rest of the roof fell in with a noise like a dying man's groan. Beside her, soot-blackened and breathless, his hair and whiskers singed to stinking curls, Anri hunched over Tanith's inert form, whispering and whimpering to her between raw-throated coughs. Javani's eyes were still smoke-stung and streaming, but she couldn't be certain that Tanith was breathing.

Javani became aware of eyes on her, and the oversized mercenary sitting beside her on the crusted dirt, wiping at his eyes and neatly wrapping his chain back around himself. She looked up to see Camellia standing over them, gaunt features lit haggard by the glare of the flames behind them. She looked at Javani, then at Tauras, then at Javani again.

Standing did not come easy to Javani, her throat still raw and the beginning of a pounding headache vying with a lingering dizziness for brain-space, but Tauras offered an obliging hand from beside her and she made it upright reasonably quickly, one hand raised to forestall Camellia.

'I know what you're going to say – yes, I let the prisoner out – but he wanted to help! He did help! We saved Tanith!'

Behind her, Anri was repeating his wife's name with greater and greater urgency, near-bellowing at her to wake. Javani froze, then turned inch by inch. Tanith's features, below her shuddering, roaring husband, were waxy and frozen in death. Javani's words dried on her lips. 'But . . . but . . .' she mumbled, 'but we saved her . . .'

Ree was there, putting an arm around her, leading her away and declining to mention the smoking stink upon her. 'Come on, kid, you did what you could. You did a good thing. I'm sorry.'

Camellia remained, murmuring words of comfort to the hysterical hunter. As Ree led her from the clearing, Javani watched over her shoulder to see Camellia place her hands on the stricken man, who made no move to remonstrate or throw her off. A jingling beside her told her that Tauras was walking with them.

'Shall I go back to the stables, Javani? I can try and put the chain back in the wall.'

'Might as well,' she croaked back, still feeling a caustic sting in her lungs and throat.

'I'm sorry we couldn't save the lady, Javani.' He looked down at the lengthening shadows of the barren trees that surrounded them. 'She must have breathed too much smoke before we got there.'

'Yeah,' was all she could muster. Her eyes were still watering, but it was no longer from the smoke, and her words became suddenly difficult. 'I'm sorry . . . too.'

She buried her face in Ree's shoulder and wept.

FORTY-TWO

Javani and her mother were still explaining to Mariam and Vida what had happened, and to the crowd of not-quite-sentries gathered by the growing earthworks beyond the bridge, when Anri came storming across it. He was grim-faced and filthy with soot, but for the narrow spider-cracks where his tears had fallen. He marched past the uncertain bridge guards and over to where he'd thrown down his bow and quiver such a short time before. Something about the look in his eye spurred Javani to separate herself from Ree's calming embrace and move to intercept him.

'Anri?'

He didn't reply, merely snatched up his quiver, checked the arrows inside and put it over his shoulder.

'Anri, are you— How are you?'

He dusted grit and moisture from the bow, tested the string, and turned to look over the valley. Watch-fires were burning on the opposite slope, torches and cook-fires, streamers of smoke rising into the crisp silvery air, the sweeping spread of the mercenary camp now impossible to miss.

'Which fucker was it?' he growled, his voice raw and savage. 'That greasy little pig-bastard, was it?' He set off for the bridge again, bow swaying in his white-knuckled grip.

Javani thought she heard a warning shout from her mother, but she was already moving, scampering in the wake of his furious strides. 'Anri, wait, hold on.'

He marched straight over the bridge, deaf to her calls, the force of his tramp enough to set the boards bouncing beneath her feet and almost send her tumbling. She caught up with him at the roadside, as he stopped to shake the arrows in his quiver back to order.

'Anri! Will you just . . . Where are you going?'

The declining sun glowed gold and bloody through the streaked cloud above, relighting the fires in the hollow pits of his eyes. 'Where do you think?' he growled. He drew an arrow from the quiver and nocked it, his eyes never leaving hers.

'You can't just . . .' She floundered, trying to find words of comfort, words of warning, words of anything that might penetrate his wall of furious indifference. 'There are a hundred of them,' she finished, her voice little more than a girlish squeak.

He pulled back on the string, testing the draw, the fletching against his cheek. 'I'm only after one.'

'But—' Javani chanced putting a hand on his arm, and found herself shaken off with a venom she should have expected. 'Sentries, and patrols, and . . . They'll catch you!'

'You don't think I can hit him, is it?' His eyes were wide now, the light lost from them, whites brilliant against the soot that smeared his face. 'You don't think I can put a shaft through that pig-bastard's throat from outside their lines?' He shook his head with a wild sniff, and gnashed his teeth in the camp's direction. 'They won't see me coming. I could lance ten of the fuckers around a cook-fire from the other side of the valley, from this very spot by here.'

'And what then?' she shrieked back at him. 'What do you expect them to do when one, or ten of their number, drop dead in their camp with arrows in them? Hmm?' She took a step closer, demanding his attention with her gaze. 'Do you think they'll turn and run off down the valley?' She stepped right into him, glaring up at his bristly chin. He stank of smoke, but then, she supposed, so did she. 'Or will they grab their weapons and charge the village, and slaughter everyone in it?'

'Not my fucking problem, is it?' he roared back.

'Of course it is, you infant! You'd be responsible! At least give the villagers a chance to build their defences before you try for vengeance – we need to delay them, not spur them on!'

'You want to talk responsibility?' His voice had dropped now, back to the growl, the warning note of a cornered dog. 'You want to cover who's to blame for the fact my wife is dead and my home is ashes? Who brought this misery into the valley?' He shook his head again, face locked in a snarl, his breathing heavy. 'Camellia was right. This was you. You and your vile mother.'

'Oh, grow up!' Javani snapped back. 'Ree's many things, occasionally vile among them, but you *know* she's right about this. She's been right all along. You can pretend you're all isolated and self-sufficient, but without the village on your doorstep you'd have died out long ago. You're part of the village, and it's part of you. And if you go storming off now, all you'll do is get yourself killed, or everyone else, or both.' She took a wild swing, and aimed low. 'Is that what Tanith would have wanted?'

His face curdled. 'Oh, fuck off, you little fucker.'

'That wasn't very inventive, for you.' She noted his grip on the bow was a little looser.

Something that with sunlight and regular watering might have eventually become a smile twitched at his whiskery mouth. 'Plenty more where that came from, there is.'

'I'll be holding my breath.' She put her hand back on his arm and, with a lightness of touch that inwardly delighted her, she steered him around in the direction of the bridge. 'Let's go back, shall we? Lots to do before the light goes, I imagine.'

He only grunted. They walked slowly back to the bridge, where he stopped, one hand on the first post, and took a deep breath.

'Aren't you going to say it, then?' he muttered, his gaze on the drifting spray curling below. Now the fire of rage had burned itself out, he seemed smaller, diminished, and increasingly brittle.

'What?'

'"I told you so."'

She patted his back. 'I would never say such a thing.'

'That a fact, is it?' He resumed his walk across the swaying boards.

'Rest assured, though,' she murmured as she fell in behind him. 'I'll be thinking it. Loads.'

* * *

Ree had barely had time to register her relief at hearing the attack on the timber yard was a one-off, and the forge and pastures were as yet unscathed, before Volkan was holding forth.

'This is only the beginning,' he screeched at the gathered and fractious crowd. 'Do you see now what awaits us? They will burn the village to the ground if we defy them, they will enact great punishment upon us all – and for what? What have we to fear from the exercise of law, the pursuit of justice? Let them investigate the offences they allege in the manner they require, and let us settle our differences. We must seek peace, brothers and sisters! We must seek reconciliation.'

The afternoon was waning, and Ree had barely slept the night before; the thought of summoning the energy to take the old man apart was daunting, but she was willing to give it what she had. She leaned on her stick as she turned, already sucking in a breath to speak.

'Volkan, please.' It was Camellia, her voice quiet but enough to hush the assembly. Ree paused, her mouth half-open, her words held in check.

'Camellia.' Volkan spoke with his chin in the air, as if the only way he could focus on people was if he lined up along the slant of his nose. 'Do you not agree that it is incumbent upon us to pursue harmony? To—'

'Volkan.' Ree could hear the strain in Camellia's voice, her own fatigue lending her sensitivity to the tremor in the councillor's words. 'If we permit the mercenaries to enter the village in large numbers, do you expect them to leave once their investigations are complete? What form do you think these investigations will take?' She took a sharp breath through her nose, and Ree saw tears glisten at the corners of her eyes. 'When they deem their debts to be settled, what do you expect them to leave us for ourselves?'

'Come, now, they are reasonable people—' Volkan wheedled, one eye on the nervous expressions of their audience.

'No.' Camellia shook her head, braids swaying. 'They are not.' She met Ree's eye, only for a moment. 'Not any more. Come, my people, the hour is late and there is much yet to be done. Sentries remain, everyone else to their tasks.'

As the congregation broke up, Ree found Camellia passing her. 'Uh, Camellia, listen—'

The woman didn't break her stride. 'Do not talk to me. I have burials to arrange.'

Ree only nodded. It was all she had the strength for.

A polite throat-clearing beside her announced Vida's presence. The smith looked grave. 'We should talk,' she said.

Ree walked slowly at Vida's side along the terrace, her every step a rolling grumble. Around them, the sounds of activity filled the crisp late afternoon air, the scents of industry and baking mingling in confusion. Even the thought of the enterprise tired her. 'Well?'

'Not here,' the smith muttered, and nodded towards the Council House. She looked well-used, her hair darkened and sweat-slick, her fingers stained with earth. 'Out of the open.'

They walked another few ambling steps, Ree leaning harder on her stick than she'd have liked. 'It's nearly sundown,' Vida observed, possibly in an attempt to take Ree's mind off her huffing progress.

Ree grunted. Lado's deadline for surrender. 'It is.'

'If they attack now . . .' Vida released a heavy breath, shaking her head.

'Our defences aren't ready.'

'Not by a country mile. Even with every able body in the settlement, there's just too much to do, a day isn't enough. And that's before our fire-fighting in the timber yard. Not that we had the time or people to bring more timber down anyway.'

'It's been a busy day.' Ree took a heavy breath to match her laboured stride. 'And we're not done with it yet.'

The smith gave her an even look. 'Do you think they'll attack at dusk? Or wait for dawn?'

'Better we give them something to think about in advance,' Ree replied, her gaze fixed on the approaching doorway. 'And we can discuss that presently.'

Most of the blood was gone from the Council House, presumably – and ironically – at Sweeper's hands, but some of it would be part of the structure forever. Ree took up her now-favoured spot leaning against the wall beside one of the crackling fireplaces, savouring its warmth in her tired and aching limbs. Her eyes were already half-closed. 'Now what has you so exercised?'

Vida took a swift glance over her shoulder to the doorway, then stepped in close, her voice a little above a murmur. 'There's . . . oddness.'

Ree struggled against the waves of fatigue that rolled over her. 'Oddness?' she said, through a yawn.

'Irregularities,' Vida clarified, her manner still conspiratorial. 'With the equipment I retrieved from storage.'

Now her tone made sense. Ree jolted awake, her head coming away from the wall. 'What do you mean?'

'Improper care and attention. Bowstrings left in the open, metal against mud, unoiled, loose fletchings on arrows. Small things, but they could have been costly if I hadn't gone back to check.'

'Any chance it's just the way it was packed or unpacked?'

'Couldn't say,' the smith replied, but her eyes lacked their customary certainty. 'Like you said, it's been a busy day. Lots of coming and going.'

Now Ree raised an eyebrow. 'You think our friend the chained mercenary might have had something to do with it?'

She shook her head. 'My impression is that if that young man wanted something destroyed, it would not be up for interpretation. No . . .' She sucked at her lip, clicked her tongue. 'This is more . . . subtle. If I hadn't double-checked, the first time we'd have known there was anything wrong with the gear was the moment we needed it.'

'Then let's stay vigilant. The last thing we need is another unpleasant surprise. Right now, though, we've got more pressing matters.'

'The deadline.' Vida nodded. 'We need to get everyone inside the village. If you'll excuse me, I promised Mari I'd grab the last of our things before we close off the pasture.' She cocked a half-smile. 'You'll have plenty of company in the stables tonight.'

'Just bring that samovar, or at least some *kipir*. But before you go, there's the other thing I mentioned.' Ree pushed her aching, creaking body up from the wall and collected her walking stick. Her rest had been all too brief. 'We're going to need the others.'

FORTY-THREE

Javani sat down heavily on the cold earth beside Anri and nodded to the lower terrace, where Mani was conducting a small ceremony in the dying red of sunset. 'Aren't you missing the funeral?'

He only grunted, barely lifting his chin from his knees.

'I mean,' she went on, 'I don't want to speak out of turn here—'

'Never spoken in turn in your life, you haven't.'

'—but, well, I'd hate you to regret missing something, I dunno, important.'

He grunted again. 'Must be a monster, me, missing something important.'

'Anri, I'm really sorr—'

'So you keep saying, pest. Yet here we are.'

'I'm sorry I told you to grow up, too.'

He gave a bleak chuckle. 'It's possible you had a point, mind. Maybe I should be thanking you for keeping me alive and all.' He sniffed. 'For another few hours at least.'

'If you want to go back, the bridge is still up, at least for now—'

'What do I have to go back for? House is ashes, wife's dead.' He took a sudden, sharp breath that hitched in his throat, and when he spoke again his voice was thick and as rough as shale. 'All this time, all this fucking *time*, and it's not even like we . . .'

She waited a moment. 'We what?'

'Liked each other!' He snapped his head around, fixing her with a tear-filled glare. 'Happy now, pest? Happy to revel in my shame, are you?'

Javani looked back, brows and cheeks pinched. 'What do you mean?'

'What I said.' He turned away from her again, staring off down the slope to the gathering at the lowest terrace, where scattered graves were marked with small and varied cairns of river stone. She thought that might be it, but after a moment, he went on, directing his words to the frigid evening air.

'We were never a good fit, but when we got on, all was tidy. Tanith had drive enough for both of us, and me . . . I was content to be driven. But travelling together, stressful, isn't it.' He gave another bleak chuckle. Javani was nodding along, thinking of her own travails with Ree.

'Gods, that was your bargain, wasn't it?' She tried to peer around his hunched shoulders to meet his eye. 'Your part was to get her safely up to Ar Ramas, and then in return, you were going to leave . . . that was your reward. But she got ill on the way, and you couldn't leave . . . because you're *not* a monster.'

He didn't laugh, didn't snipe or scorn. Just sat with his arms wrapped around his shins, his chin on his knees. 'Yet here I am, missing her funeral. Not over there singing about how pure her bloody heart was, am I. Funny how they can spare people from digging for this, eh?'

Javani nodded down to where Mani was burying not just Tanith, but also the men from the Council House that morning. There was talk of erecting a cairn for Gumis, who by now was presumed forever lost. 'That's for other people, though, isn't it? You cared for her for years, even though you wanted to leave her. All those years, caring for someone you disliked. That's sort of . . . noble.'

Anri snorted. 'Had help, though, didn't I?'

Her brows climbed. 'Did you now? First I've heard of it.'

He leaned back and sighed, his breath a silver column in the air. 'What do you want from me, pest?'

'You know all about snares and traps and things. There are some meetings I think you should join.'

Ree stood at the edge of the upper terrace, gazing out across the darkening valley. Mariam and Vida stood to one side of her, Sweeper the other. From the corner of her eye, she saw the kid approaching along the terrace's edge, the dour and sour Anri slinking behind her. She leaned on her stick. She was very, very tired.

'Where's Keretan? He should be here for this.'

Mariam looked downslope. 'Last I saw him, he was building barricades by the river path.'

'Kid! Go and get Keretan from down there, will you? Yes, now. Yes, you do. Go on. Thank you.' She glanced up at the sky again. Sunset's arrival, and near-departure, was no longer possible to ignore. 'We'd better start without him,' she muttered.

'What are we starting?' Vida kept nearly all intonation from her voice. 'Is this another council of defence?'

'In a way.' Ree rested both hands on the top of the stick and let her weight flow through it. Her leg still throbbed, and the cold weather seemed to be making it worse. Maybe the kid was right, and she did need to give it a proper rest. She could rest it once this situation was resolved.

Across the valley, lights glimmered through the darkening forest, fires and torches, perhaps even a lantern or two. The lines of the bandit camp were clear. She wondered if Manatas was out there somewhere, or if he was still stuck on that thrice-damned ridge, peering down on them. She resisted the urge to give it a wave, just in case, and instead lifted one hand and pointed.

'Whether it's now, or at dawn, or some time later, we know they're coming,' she said. 'They have to. They're running out of food, and have barely enough warm clothes and shelter for the conditions. They're cold, hungry, undrilled, dissolute . . . and a lot of them don't like each other very much.'

'Trying to get us all excited to go off and die, are you?' Anri had arrived. He stood to one side, arms folded, his unstrung bow clasped to his body.

'Thanks for joining us, Anri, especially after your loss.'

'Gave me no choice, did she? Pest.' He didn't look particularly angry when he said it.

'We need to do something,' Ree went on, 'something to delay them. They have a lot of one thing we don't, and that's weapons of range. They're sitting on a stock of bows, crossbows and other missile weapons, and it's all stacked up in that shed at the back of the camp.' She gestured again. 'If they come at us with those, we'll be shredded before anyone gets within sharp stick range. We need to destroy them, and we need to do it now.'

Vida was regarding her with narrowed eyes. 'How do you know this, exactly?'

'My scouting trips. Learned a lot.'

'Uh-huh.'

'What can we do, then?' Mariam was still fizzing with energy, despite their exhausting day. 'Anri, could you, I don't know, land a burning arrow on it? Send it up in flames like? Might be a little bit of, well, you know . . .' She didn't want to say revenge, but the thought was transparent.

For once, the hunter deigned to answer the question without a sarcastic retort. 'No. Need to be a lot closer, maybe upslope, and it'll take more than a burning arrow or two to get that going. In the meantime, they'd damp the flames, and then, well . . . Come looking, wouldn't they.'

'I'll go.' It was Sweeper, back to using his soft, deferential voice in company.

This time Anri scoffed. 'You?'

'No.' Ree was emphatic. 'We need you here, when the time comes.'

'Eh?' Anri said.

Sweeper stepped around in front of her, still hardly meeting her eye. 'You don't. My skills were never on the battlefield, and I can't hold a bow or wield a spear.' He swallowed, larynx bobbing in the fading light. 'But I can travel with a light step, and get into places I'm not expected.'

'Eh?' Anri repeated.

'Gods,' Mariam breathed, 'you really think you could sneak into that camp and murder the bunch of bastards?'

'Mariam!' Vida chided.

'Eh?!' Anri's voice was beginning to crack.

'No,' Sweeper said, matching Ree's emphasis. 'This is not like before – they will be armed and ready and watchful. But I can at least make sure they have nothing to kill us with.'

Ree met his wavering gaze. 'Can you make off with anything, bring it back here?'

'I can try.'

'What in the name of roaring fuck are you gibbering about?' Anri bellowed.

'Doesn't matter now,' Vida said. 'We'll explain later.'

'Come to some meetings, she said,' Anri muttered. 'Suffer incoherent bollocks, more like.'

'Sounds painful,' Mariam said with a chuckle.

'Don't you fucking start as well!'

Ree walked Sweeper to the still-up-for-now bridge. There was, as he insisted, no time like the present. The ring of pretty-much-sentries waved them through.

Ree came to rest on her stick before the bridge posts. 'You've already got one of my knives. Anything else I can offer you?'

He patted the satchel on his back. 'I have everything I need.'

'You realise this could be suicide?'

'Atonement was never meant to be easy, was it? Otherwise everyone would be at it.'

She puffed a tired laugh, her mirth fading with the evening chill, and looked at him sidelong. 'You could have killed those men beating you. You could have left them dead by the roadside any time you wanted.'

His gaze wandered past the waterfall to the road's end. 'I figured I deserved it. You know.'

'Even if they'd kept going?' She took a slow breath. 'All the way?'

'I don't know. Perhaps.' His breathing matched hers. He was astonishingly calm. 'I'm sorry I caused even more trouble.'

'Nothing that wasn't brewing already.' She scratched at her neck beneath her cloak. There was a significant chance that this was the last time they'd speak. 'Did you really get to Arestan and come back?'

'I did. Really not my kind of place. All that rain . . . good for rice, bad for people. I meant what I said: Ar Ramas . . . it's the most peaceful place I've ever known. The best place. We should try to keep it that way, shouldn't we?'

She couldn't hold his gaze. 'Perhaps we should.'

He hefted the satchel. 'I should be going.'

'Are you really sure about this?'

He turned to face the bridge. 'I learned one thing on my travels. Bravery begets bravery. People see what one soul can accomplish if they conquer their fear, makes them more likely to get over theirs.' He gave her a flash of a smile. 'Best contribution to this place I'll ever make. Short of keeping the steps clean and the pots shiny.'

'So long, Sweeper.'

'So long, Ree.'

Then he slipped across the bridge and into the darkening forest, completely lost from sight.

A vociferous huffing announced Keretan's imminent arrival. She turned to see the big man clearing the sentries, sweat gleaming from his dome despite the evening's biting chill.

'Ree, what is going on? Where's Sweeper?'

'Gone. We should probably get back to the upper terrace, just in case he succeeds. Sorry to make you run all this way for nothing.'

His block-like head shook with force. 'It's not that. There's a newcomer at the riverside path, at the new gate. She says she wants to help us.'

'What? Who? How?'

He nodded helplessly. 'She said . . .' He furrowed his brow in recollection. 'Her name is Kediras, and she wants to kill Lado of Cstethia.'

FORTY-FOUR

Javani leaned on the slick timber of the ram pen and watched the new arrival being herded towards the stable. Mariam had her at the tip of an impressively clean-looking spear, held in a relaxed grip that nonetheless suggested it could be driven forward and through without a moment's hesitation. Either side of her marched a cluster of villagers of varying ages and shapes, all carrying tools that had taken the sudden cast of weapons – mallets, chisels, scythes and the like – or even some of the precious stock of official implements of war. They ringed their captive at a distance that implied a slim amount of trust and a wide amount of wariness.

The woman herself was, for want of a better description, spectacularly dirty. Mud caked her, her clothes – or armour, it was hard to be certain – lost beneath a layer of grime. Her hair was matted and filthy, and clattered every time she moved her head with force, which was fairly frequently given her visible distaste for her treatment.

'Let me go, you imbeciles! Do you know what's coming for you?' She came to a sharp halt and rounded on her escort. 'Clearly you have some notion. I see you've taken up arms at last, however feebly. I can help you. Release me.'

Mariam cleared her throat and gave her gleaming spear a gentle nudge. 'We'd be much obliged if you'd resume your pace. Would be a terrible shame if anyone were to be accidentally nicked by a feeble arm, wouldn't it.'

Hissing with irritation, the woman swung around and resumed

her trudge around the stables, finally coming to rest at the gate of the ram pen.

'Captain Kediras!' Tauras was up on his feet, still wrapped in several sheep's worth of fleece, trotting over to the gate to meet her.

'I'm glad to see they've fed you, Tauras. And for the last time, you can still call me Keds.'

Javani smiled at that.

Kediras's gaze slipped to the chain that draped from his iron collar and snaked away into the stable building, and her eyes widened. 'You have him chained like a dog?' she growled at Mariam, who was standing a safe distance back. 'Do you intend the same for me? Is this how you treat your captives?'

Tauras coloured. 'It's not so bad, really, just a little cold around the neck.'

'The other end isn't even connected to anything,' Javani added from her perch along the fence. 'We had to rip it out earlier.'

Kediras appeared to notice Javani for the first time, her unwavering gaze landing on her like a falling boulder. Filthy as she was, Javani was shocked by the fearsome clarity of her pale eyes, burning from the mud-slathered mess of her face. She looked somewhat beyond sane.

Javani did her best to hold the gaze, which seemed to be forcing her slowly backwards. 'You two know each other, then?'

'This is my friend Captain Kediras,' Tauras said with a proud smile. 'She's a chapter captain too, like Captain Manatas.'

Kediras kept her voice low and spoke from the corner of her mouth. 'Tauras, are you and the small person acquainted?'

'This is my friend Javani.'

Her brows flickered. 'Javani? That'll age badly.'

'So my mother says,' Javani sighed. She'd almost forgotten that – according to Anashe at least – Ree had literally named her 'kid'. Almost, but not quite. 'I'm still thinking about changing it.'

'And do you keep all your friends chained up, Javani?'

'I meant what I said, the other end is loose. He took it back in there himself! We'd have taken it off him by now but everyone's been busy with . . .' She gestured to the terraces around them, where work continued into the evening despite the dying daylight. '. . . Everything.'

Kediras's eyes were little more than slits. 'Are you somehow in charge here, child? Are you blessed with wisdom beyond your years, or perhaps imbued with the spirits of your ancestors? Are you charged with the heavenly duty of command? Because unless you are empowered to compel these simpletons to release me and return my weapons before we are all slaughtered, you are a waste of my time!'

Javani didn't know how to react to that. 'Uh, Mariam . . . ?'

'Into the pen, please, visitor.' Mariam gave the spear another meaningful wave.

'As I thought,' Kediras grunted with a scowl. 'Begone, you stunted ape.'

Tauras was making a humming sound, hopping from foot to foot, eyes shut, his hands pressed to his ears, the loose tips of his braids flapping. Kediras's snarl disappeared in an instant, and she slipped over the pen's fence and to his side in a single smooth movement. 'Hush, Tauras,' she cooed in a voice so soft that surely only Tauras and Javani could hear it, one hand on his beefy arm, the other stroking his back beneath the fleeces. 'I'm sorry. I didn't mean that. I'm very tired, and my temper is shorter than you deserve.'

Javani edged closer, leaning right over the top timber. 'What's wrong?' she whispered. 'Is he all right?'

Kediras flicked a brief glance her way, the pitch of her voice unchanging in its softness. 'Tauras doesn't like it when his friends argue, do you, big man? Friends should be friendly, that's what we say.'

Tauras mumbled something about friends in return, his gnarled hands moved a little way from his ears, his hopping slowed.

'In the past we had a few disagreements, Inaï and I,' she went on, still in the soothing voice, 'but it was never grave, never for long. All mended swiftly.'

'Inaï? Is he that captain who came to the bridge with you? All drawly drawly vocabulary sub-clause?'

A tiny smile teased one corner of her mouth, cracking a flake of mud from her cheek. 'Oh, you met.' She gave the calming Tauras another pat, then looked down to find the shaggy bulk of Tarfellian at her feet, looking up in expectation at getting some scritches too. Her brows lowered in confusion for half a moment, then with a sigh she gave him a brisk rub behind the ears and, to Javani's consternation, received a contented huff.

'That dog is an absolute disgrace,' she muttered. 'So much for Vida's caution around strangers.'

'Clearly this fellow is an excellent judge of character,' Kediras replied, letting him lick the tips of her fingers with a giant pink tongue.

Tauras beamed. 'He's my friend too.'

The anger had left Kediras, and in its absence Javani saw the terrible fatigue that weighed on her, the fear and uncertainty and determination that burned in those striking eyes. It was also possible that she was extremely drunk; up close the air around her seemed to shimmer with booze. 'Daughter of chieftain, chosen one, whatever you may be,' she said with a tired voice, 'you cannot keep me caged and chained, for your own good as much as mine. If you have any sway, impel them. Time is getting short.'

Javani spread her hands. 'Listen, you need to think about how it looks, you just turning up here with, uh,' – she looked behind Mariam, where another of the villagers carried two narrow, curved swords and a long, bladed spear, along with their captive's pack – 'a fair amount of weaponry, saying you want to help, when everyone knows you're with the company who's threatening to sweep in and plunder the place. You're lucky Volkan isn't here, he'd be shrieking you're a spy sent to murder us in our beds . . . You're not, right?'

That got only a weary sigh by way of response, so she continued. 'Now, Camellia will likely say the same, so we need to balance it out a bit. Mani likes to give people the benefit of the doubt, I think, and Vida could go either way, but if Mariam there puts in a good word, especially if she gets to know you—'

'Child. Please. None of this matters. A demon leads my company, a demon I must kill, or die in the attempt. Nothing else matters.'

'Oh.' Javani could offer only a pained grimace. 'Not much I can do there, sorry.'

A villager appeared with a steaming basin of water, which was carefully laid down inside the pen. 'There you go, then,' Mariam said, maintaining her comfortable distance. 'Thought you might like a wash. Sorry it's not a proper bath, we've had to leave a few things behind at the forge, you know, because of the circumstances and all. I'll bring some food along in a moment, you must be very hungry.'

Kediras's gaze flicked from the basin to Mariam to Javani and back, landing finally on Tauras.

'Nice here, isn't it?' he said. 'Will there be enough food for Captain Kediras as well?'

She'd barely rinsed the first layer of muck from her hands when Ree and Keretan came thumping down the terrace; to Javani's concern, Ree looked haggard and sweaty, and Keretan was obviously checking his stride to allow her to keep up. Despite her evident exhaustion, she marched right up to the ram pen beside where Javani perched, paying her daughter no heed at all, and addressed the kneeling woman directly.

'You must be Keds. We have a mutual friend.'

Something flared across the valley, a great bloom of orange light in the twinkling gloom of the forest. A moment later, it resolved itself into a roaring pillar of yellow flame, sending thick black smoke into the gathering twilight. It was coming from somewhere around the mercenary camp. Javani thought she heard faint shouts and calls on the wind.

'Nine sweet hells,' Ree breathed, as a few scattered cheers went up from the terraces. 'He did it. He fucking did it. Everyone, get to the perimeter! They could retaliate immediately.' She looked back at the woman in the pen, still kneeling, her face half-washed, mesmerised by the dancing fire on the valley's far side.

'Kid,' Ree said, 'let her out.'

Manatas quickened his pace over the frigid ground, thick brush pulling at his boots, feeling in the grinding of his bones every aching instant of his night and day spent prone on a freezing ridge-top. Flames were roaring now, their fierce, quivering light bathing the forest around him in shifting hues of gold and amber, casting jumping black shadows in the gathering gloom. Antulu and Mantenu kept pace either side of him, their faces stony, the regular barks of their breathing now swallowed by the crackle of the flames ahead and the cries and bellows that followed them.

'What in the name of all the gods . . .' Manatas gasped as they reached the camp's outer edge, the pickets vanished, the scene before them in uproar. Several tents were aflame, oily smoke rising in the breeze, but the centre of the inferno seemed to be . . . the half-built hut at the camp's rear. The place he'd told Ree that the company were hoarding their weapons of range.

He came up short, breathing hard, swallowing back a growing terror. How had she done it? Was she still here? Had she been captured?

'Arkadas!' Relief flooded him as he caught sight of his lieutenant, organising scattered troops to beat out what flames they could and gather water from the stream. 'Arkadas, what news?'

'An attack, captain,' the man replied. 'Our sentries have failed us, and we are assailed.'

Mantenu had drifted away into the brush, but now returned, dragging something behind him. It was, of course, a corpse, a man in company colours.

'Two more back there,' the Pashani said with an expressionless jerk of his head. 'Throats cut.'

'Our sentries have failed us,' Manatas echoed, his throat dry, feeling a wash of guilty relief that the dead man was not one of his chapter. Could Ree have done such a thing? Could anyone in the village? Who was she, this woman, after all? How much did he really know? He was sweating again, and he wasn't even that close to the flames.

Arkadas appeared to mirror his thoughts, his eyes alive with unease. 'Could it be a response from the village, captain? Is it possible that they are striking in return?'

'The fire on the hillside this afternoon.' Manatas met his uncertainty with grave disappointment. 'That was Lado, then?' He had never doubted it, and Arkadas had no need to confirm.

'One of the Seventh claimed to have laid a blade on an interloper, but who can say—'

'Captains!' The roar came from the pavilion at the head of the camp, through the smoke, accompanied by a frenzied ringing of the dinner bell. 'Captains, to me!'

Botrys had awoken.

Manatas picked his way across the camp as fast as his battered limbs would allow, ducking through smoke and sprays of sparks thrown across his way by the snapping wind. The uproar in the camp was settling now as the scale of the attack was gauged and attended; coherent orders echoed in his wake, not least from Arkadas, leading the efforts to prevent the flames' spread.

Botrys paced before the grand pavilion, the fierce light of the burning structure at the camp's rear gleaming gold in the shell of his ostentatious armour. He was dark-faced and sweating, a scabbarded sword that Manatas did not recognise but guessed had belonged to their late captain-general gripped in one hand. Around him, the house guards had formed a grim square.

'The insolence!' he bellowed as Manatas approached, his voice scratchy from smoke and volume. 'The audacity!'

Jebel was there, flame-light flickering across his scarred dome, the rings of gold in his ear glinting and dancing as he shouldered his way past the guards. 'We have contained the flames, lord adjutant.'

'Why has it taken so long?'

'Our attackers used something, perhaps lamp oil, and let it soak in the wood before the first spark. The structure is lost, but the camp will not burn.'

'Treachery, infamy, gall! Gather the troops!' Botrys was screeching now, the pitch of his voice grating over the sounds of coordinated fire-fighting. 'We cannot stand for such outrage. The Company of the Wolf will have its due!'

Manatas did his best to squeeze through the guards alongside Jebel. 'Do you mean to attack the village, Bo— lord adjutant? We appear to have lost our weapons of range. The villagers have been digging in this very day, it is clear they expect an assault from this direction.'

Botrys rounded on him. 'Then they shall reap what they have sown,' he snarled, brandishing the sword. 'Assemble your chapters, we march immediately! To arms!'

A low, dark shape behind Botrys caught Manatas's eye, and he realised with a shudder that it was Lado, lurking only a little way behind the strutting adjutant, somehow couched in shadow from the flames. He shuffled forward, into the dimming light, his head pitched in obeisance, and cleared his throat.

Botrys paused. 'Yes, acting commander?'

'If I might approach, lord adjutant?' On Botrys's impatient nod, Lado slid closer, and bent his head close to the other man's. Whatever he imparted was lost to Manatas, but he saw the expression on Botrys's face change immediately, the ardent rage draining from his waxy features. The sword drooped in his hand.

Jebel shifted, his mail clinking, the leather straps creaking against his rigid form. 'Are we to attack, lord adjutant?'

'I am clarifying my order,' Botrys replied airily. 'While there is a chance that some within the domain of our aggressors may yet see sense, it is incumbent on us to seek resolution through negotiation.'

Jebel's brows knotted, his entire scalp furrowed. 'Lord adjutant?'

'We stay our hand while they may yet surrender. Easier that way, is it not?'

To Manatas's eye, the sag of Jebel's shoulders suggested only disappointment.

Botrys waved his free hand around. 'Replace the lost sentries, double the perimeter guards, increase the patrols. This will not happen again. Acting commander, dispatch one final herald.'

But Lado's gaze was lost in the flames.

Her mother's exhaustion was plain to Javani, but still she insisted on keeping vigil at the bridge, so Javani insisted on keeping an eye on her. For a while, they waited for a retaliatory attack, huddled with the village guards behind the new timber barricades, restless eyes searching the forest's twilight gloom. After word reached them of the herald's visit, down at the riverside path, they waited on, far from convinced that this supposed final warning was not trickery. And even once the moon was high behind thick sheets of cloud and the only thing moving on the hillside was the wind through the shorn trees, plucking at the last of their lingering foliage, Ree still refused to give in to sleep, even as Javani watched her lids drooping as if anchored with lead.

'Ma, you need sleep. You can't stay awake any more.'

She shook her head, erratic and groggy. 'No, no. He might come back any moment.'

Javani looked out over the barren hillside. The fire was out across the valley, a few twinkling lights marking its thoroughfares and perimeter, a heavy pall still lurking in the churned air above. The valley felt empty, almost desolate.

'I don't think Sweeper's coming back, Ma.' She put an arm around her mother, trying to force her to stand. 'And if he does, someone will be here, waiting for him.'

'Maybe he went back over the mountains,' Ree said dreamily, her words slurring, her eyes half-closed. She was too much for Javani to carry, but she could just about steer her if she kept most of her balance. 'Or maybe he went back east, to see his old friends.'

'Maybe, Ma. Maybe.'

In the end, Tauras helped carry her to bed.

FORTY-FIVE

Manatas couldn't understand it. The loss of nearly every item that could launch something sharp, heavy or both beyond the reach of a single arm should have been more than a setback; it should have left the company giving serious consideration to abandoning its assault on what was, despite its reputation, a stoutly fortified and defended location. Instead, at the morning briefing, Lado and his cadre appeared . . . relaxed?

He watched the lank-haired acting commander sharing a joke with one of the Pashani, before offering an ostentatious salute to the dozing Botrys and moving to address the officers waiting in the cold. It was early, the ground still crusted with thick frost, each of the waiting enforcers manoeuvring to keep as close to the braziers and fires as possible. The lord adjutant was still in his chair, swathed in blankets, helmet pulled low over his eyes. Manatas could smell the booze coming off him from the other side of the brazier; it was a wonder it wasn't burning with a blue flame.

Manatas shifted his boots, finding anything approaching comfort an impossibility. His thoughts remained likewise unsettled. He thought back to Ree's question of the day before – *why do you chain yourself to this madness still?* The company had brought structure and order to his life, certainly, but that was not why he had lingered so long. The truth was that he had failed everyone who had ever depended on him through the worst traits of his nature. He had abandoned his principles time and again in search of an easier path, and now, as the walls closed in, they were lost to him. He was here because had nowhere else to go, and no path out.

And yet. And *yet*. Perhaps there was a way. Redemption seemed an impossibility, but this woman, and those she spoke for . . . They did not as such rely on him, but nonetheless found their fates entwined. If he should give himself to their aid, unshackle himself from Lado's enterprise . . . Perhaps there might yet be a friend unfailed.

'Captains, acting captains, the lord adjutant thanks you for your diligence and flexibility,' Lado proclaimed. Startled, Manatas held his reaction in check. Acting captains? That explained the new faces at the briefing. Botrys had thrown the by-laws by the wayside, and was now shaping the camp and the company around his whims. The man addressing them was proof of that made flesh. 'Last night's conflagration has necessitated some changes in our planning for the coming operation. Should matters not reach a favourable conclusion beforehand, we will begin our collective action at noon tomorrow.'

Again, Manatas kept his features rigid, but his heart had begun to gallop in his chest, sweat damp on his back despite the freezing morning. They were to attack after all, and at the height of daylight. It was almost as if Lado were trying to kill as many on each side as he could. He blinked, swallowed. Of course, it was likely exactly that.

'Thanks to the expert reconnaissance of our comrades,' – here, Lado shot him a sidelong look of sly mirth – 'we have determined three primary points of entry to the aggressors' hold: the narrow gap at the waterfall, currently bridged; the path from the river up the escarpment; and the trail down from the grazing land, which can be reached by a substantial but attainable march downriver. We shall be dividing into three detachments, each under the command of a captain, as well as a reserve and a command post.'

Beside Manatas, Jebel grunted in approval. He was rubbing his hands together, and not in a way that suggested they were cold.

'Chapter Captain Jebel.' Lado pointed with a flash of a silver dagger that had appeared in his hand without ever seeming to pass from a scabbard. 'You will lead the assault from the river. Our scouting reports' – again, that sly smile – 'suggest that part to be the most heavily fortified, and possibly prepared with pitfalls. You will take the most heavily armoured troops we have.'

Jebel grunted again and saluted. He seemed to be vibrating with anticipation.

'Acting Captain Antulu, you will be taking the long way around to the grazing land, to be in position for the start of action. We will discuss your departure separately.'

Manatas felt the tension in his shoulders climbing, a dull, burning ache his reward. Would Lado trust him to lead one of the attacks? Of course not. But what would he do with him instead? Hold him in reserve? Make him babysit Botrys at the command post?

'Chapter Captain Manatas, you will lead the assault across the waterfall gap. If the bridge is downed, you will need to engineer a replacement.' Lado cut a half-smile that had a whole raft of sneer in its parentage. 'Some athleticism may be required in getting across, so your detachment will be the lightest armoured.'

Ah, there it was. Manatas felt the tension move from his shoulders to around his chest, taking the burning with it. He was to lead a lightly armoured, senseless attack across a ravine, into the teeth of whatever the defenders had mustered. Then it struck him. If the bridge were cut, they'd be forced to fashion a replacement and attempt to cross the gap ad-hoc. Such a task could take considerable time and resources, perhaps even the duration of the combat elsewhere. Valiant attempts, repulsed before serious casualties were sustained . . . He could see it. He could see a way out.

But first, he needed to warn Ree what was coming, and when.

'Acting commander,' he ventured, trying to hit a pitch between defeated and deferential. He needed to judge this one carefully. 'If I am to lead such a charge, I will need to know exactly what defences lie in store, and the likely changes today will bring. Permission to send one of my command on a final scouting mission?'

'Granted, chapter captain, although the greatest of us lead by example, I'm told, and your diligence never fails to impress. Mantenu will accompany you.'

Manatas did not like to see Lado smile, even when he knew he was winning.

* * *

'Why in nine hells didn't you wake me? It's nearly noon! We could have been attacked sixteen times over by now.'

'I'm sure we'd have woken you for an attack, Ma.' Javani considered. 'Someone would have got round to it eventually.'

Her mother clomped past her into the feeble day, huffing and wincing from the exertion. 'Don't you *dare* tell me I needed the rest.'

'Wouldn't waste the breath on it,' Javani murmured, her gaze to the sky. 'Or on reminding you that you're not giving your leg a chance to heal. What would be the point?'

Ree swung around and glared at her for a moment, then resumed her trudge towards the growing earthworks at the lower terrace. 'I'm glad we understand each other,' she muttered. 'How are preparations?'

'Continuing. Fine, I guess. As far as I can tell.' Javani set off after her, matching her progress with an ease that was, if anything, a little unsettling. Ree was not supposed to be slow. Ree was not supposed to be old. They passed freshly dug mounds of fine soil, open pits being filled with slim stakes, barriers and barricades formed from anything and everything to hand around the village.

'Is it fair?' Javani asked. 'What we're doing.'

Ree didn't slow. 'And what's that?'

'Making them fight.'

'We're not the ones making them fight, my dear.'

'You only call me that when you're being condescending.' She came to a halt, and was gratified when Ree did likewise, turning to face her with one heavy hand on the walking stick. Bent as she was, they were getting on for the same height. Javani didn't like that much, either. 'You know what I mean, right?'

'I do.'

Javani gazed across the terraces, transformed as they were in the last day and a half, from cosy farming community into fortified garrison. There was Vida, instructing her apprentices; over there Mariam, leading a group armed with what looked like ropes and pulleys. Keretan was down by the new gate, shoring it up with timber and stone. Above them, from the high ledge on the Grandfathers, the sheet of grey cliff that backed the village, she knew Camellia would be looking down at it all, Mani and Volkan at her side, deploring everything they saw and once again cursing the day that Ree, Javani and their ponies came riding in. 'Are you sure they weren't happy before, with how things were?'

'They might have been content, but they weren't happy.' Ree leaned forward, holding her gaze with her own, her eyes deep, dark wells of certainty. 'Don't you see it, kid? They're fighters. *Almost* to a man.' She glanced around again. 'I mean, look at this place! Look where it is. Are you telling me they didn't know what they were doing?'

'What are you talking about?'

'You asked me before if I'd wondered how they came to be here. Well, rest assured: I did.' She set off again down the terrace. 'Come on. You don't want to miss all the digging.'

Manatas was almost to the edge of the camp, Mantenu his dour shadow, when Arkadas caught up with him.

'Captain, you're going out again?'

Manatas drew to a halt, shifting the cloak on his aching shoulders. It was too thin, but the fleeces would be waiting up at the ridge. He wiped any trace of smile from his face at the thought of seeing Ree again. Mantenu might have all the facial activity of lichen, but there was no telling what he might report back to Lado. At least he only had the one minder this time – perhaps that was a sign he'd won some trust after all?

'I am, Arkadas. If we're to be launching our assault on the morrow, it's incumbent upon me to have mastery of what awaits us.'

Arkadas lowered his voice as he leaned in, no less mindful of the blank-eyed Pashani standing tree-still behind them. 'I thought you were lukewarm on the notion of assault, captain?'

Manatas matched his volume. 'And so I remain, Arkadas. This excursion is, in part, an attempt to prevent matters scaling beyond our means of control.'

The other man's brows were lowered, confusion and disquiet furrowing his sturdy forehead. 'What are you saying, captain?'

Manatas paused. He trusted Arkadas, trusted him with his life, trusted him with his most treasured possessions and personal well-being, but there remained a wall between them. If he were to confess that he was in active collaboration with their martial foes, working to undermine the activities of the company to which they were both contracted, he was not certain how his lieutenant would react.

But then again, Arkadas was far from stupid. He knew what they were up against, and wanted bloodshed no more than his captain did. And more than anything, Arkadas was loyal.

'Arkadas, I cannot tell you the how, but you will already know the why. There is much already in motion, but we can yet steer a course through these choppy waters.' He put one hand on his lieutenant's shoulder, leaning in close. 'We will winter at the lake, my friend, and soon, and no part will we have played in the slaughter of defenceless farmers for their winter grain.'

Behind them, Mantenu grunted. Aggressively. It was time to move on.

When Manatas looked back, just as they passed the last sentries, Arkadas was still watching after them, his arms folded across his mail, his features completely unreadable.

Ree smelled Kediras before she saw her. The woman sat cross-legged outside the ram pen, two narrow, curving swords across her knees – one long, one short – running a sharpenstone across each blade in turn, her braids swaying with the rhythm of the movement. She reeked of alcohol. The empty skin beside her on the frosted earth suggested why. Another was propped beside her pack, this one full. Ree was tempted to ask for a swig, but the day was yet young and, from the acrid sting in her nostrils, the woman was downing aquavit so strong they could use it as a weapon. Ree considered asking her for the second skin with such intentions, but caught the look in her eyes and swallowed the question. Instead, she stood for a moment in the cold, toes numb and breath steaming, and marvelled at Kediras's facility with the stone over what looked to be two very sharp blades indeed, despite being a little short of pickled.

'Are you going to stare all day, or bother your arse doing something useful? I hear there is still much to do.'

'I could ask you the same question. You're not finished sharpening yet?'

Kediras looked up at her, barely squinting despite the day's grey glare. Her pupils were very wide, and her gaze drifted like clouds. 'A blade must be sharp indeed to kill a demon.'

'You mean this Lado character, right?'

She returned her unsteady gaze to the swords, the metal ringing with each sweep of the stone. 'The demon has my flute,' she muttered.

'Uh-huh. And the booze helps with this?'

'Once I started drinking, I saw no reason to stop.'

Ree was about to enquire further when Kediras spoke again. 'Return my bow to me.'

'Hmm?'

She gestured up the slope with the stone. 'They have it still, as well as my spear.'

Ree followed the movement and saw Mariam addressing some of the younger villagers, bundles of arrows and a small number of bows at their feet. Ree recognised the weapons from their hiding places in the forge, and Kediras's was apparently among them.

'You're a walking armoury, aren't you? How many weapons can you use at once?'

Again, Kediras's watery gaze found hers, but there was no withering comeback, only a profound well of pain behind the wall of booze in her eyes. Ree took a small step back.

'I'll manage without,' Kediras muttered, holding one blade up to what little light there was. Her eyes flicked back up to Ree. 'And how is it you are so friendly with Inaï?'

Ree shrugged, her attention already drifting to the steps down to the river path, where Vida was signalling to her. 'We share some common interests. Please excuse me.'

Kediras only grunted as Ree took her leave, her focus returned to the rhythmic sweep of stone over steel. Ree clomped over to Vida, still feeling a compendium of aches on top of the sharp stab in her injured calf that accompanied every step.

'Was wondering when you'd be up,' Vida said by way of greeting. She was streaked with sweat and grime, breathing freely, the dark border of her short hair plastered black to the nape of her neck. 'There's something you need to see.'

FORTY-SIX

Javani leaned on the slick timber of the ram pen, watching Tauras lifting Tarfellian up and down. The big old dog appeared to love the attention, his thick tail beating against the mercenary's chunky arm every time he hoisted him clear of the ground, his head bent around to try to lick the man's face with each elevation. Tauras was giggling at the dog's attentions but not deterred. Javani could only shake her head at the pair of them.

'Tauras,' she called, 'they're going to cut the bridge soon. Really, this time. I think we need to, well, let you go.'

Tauras paused his exertions, then slowly lowered the disappointed mastiff to the cracked mud of the pen. He was steaming in the cold air, pale vapour rising from his arms. 'Let me go?'

'Release you. So you can go. Before you get stuck here.'

'Go? Go where?' His eyes were hollow with concern.

'Back to, you know, your people. Your, uh, company.'

One hand on Tarfellian's flank, he edged forward, his chain clattering along the frozen ground behind him. 'Back to the company?'

Javani was getting impatient. 'Yes, yes. To your company, your captain, all your favourite people. It's not like there's anyone left to exchange you for.'

'But Captain Kediras is here.'

'She is, but your other captain isn't, is he?'

That made him think.

'Is my company really going to attack the village?' he said at length. His gaze verged on pleading. Javani wasn't certain what he wanted to hear.

'Ree seems to be pretty convinced,' she replied.

'So if I went back to them, I'd have to attack too?'

Javani puffed air through her lips. 'I guess so.'

He folded his arms and sat down in the mud. Tarfellian came and leaned heavily against him, producing a contented huff. 'I think I'll stay here, then, please, Javani.'

She rubbed at her eyes. 'You're not worried about what will happen if you do?'

He shook his head, piercings jingling like silver bells. 'No.'

She took a breath. 'Well, I tried.' She looked around to see if Ree had finished with whatever it was she'd set off to inspect, and saw no sign of her. But she spotted someone else instead.

Vida pointed with earth-stained fingers. 'See that?'

'Around the base?'

'Yup.'

'It's not anchored, is it?' Ree squatted down with a grimace, tracing the lines of the timber, where it should have been buried in the earth but was instead resting in a mound of loose soil. 'It looks like it is, but a serious shove and it'll flip over.' She pushed herself back up, leaning so hard on the stick its tip drove a finger's width into the frosty path, and met Vida's eye. 'Who put this section of the barricade up?'

She shook her head. 'It's been done since, maybe overnight. Was stout when it went in.' She ran a hand through her grey mop, leaving muddy streaks. 'It's luck I happened to be checking.'

'A sort of luck,' Ree countered. She rested one hand at the base of her back and stretched with a wince. 'We're beyond happenstance, then.'

'We are.' Vida's face was grimmer than ever. 'This is sabotage.' She took a long breath. 'We should gather the Council.'

Ree sucked at her lower lip. 'I'm not sure that'll do much good. Given our most likely perpetrators, and all.'

Vida's eyes widened with a cocktail of outrage and incredulity. 'You can't mean— When there are mercenaries within our walls?'

'Tauras and Kediras? One's meek as a lamb in a ram pen, the other is intent on killing her demon before she pickles herself. Neither seems the indirect kind.'

Vida grunted acknowledgement, her gaze at her feet. 'Let's inform Keretan at least, and the rest of our council of self-defence.'

Ree looked around for the village's big man, spotting him labouring over the defences with a tired-looking bunch of carpenters a little way upslope. 'Not in his armour yet? I'd prioritise getting that old suit off the wall and onto my body corporal, were I in his clod-hoppers.'

'I'm sure he has his reasons,' was all Vida would say, but Ree was no longer listening. Her eyes, drawn by what might have been habit and might have been wishful thinking, had caught something in the distance, up on a distant ridge-line.

'Don't brief anyone just yet,' she murmured. 'I need to pop out for a moment.'

Anri didn't even look up at Javani's approach; her level of concern deepened. He was standing on the upper terrace, staring out at the wintry woods, his unstrung bow in his hands, his gaze vacant and his jaw slack.

'Anri?'

His eyes slid to her for a moment, then resumed their blank stare off across the valley.

'Are you all right?'

He took a long, ragged breath, and when he spoke his voice had a raw edge that even Javani could recognise as dangerous. 'Am. I all. Right.' He seemed to chew the air for a moment, bristly jaw working, then he turned on her, gappy teeth bared in a fixed, unconvincing grin. 'Well, we'll take stock, shall we?'

He began counting on his calloused fingers, the bow cradled to his body. 'Let's see: my wife, the person I swore to protect with my every waking breath, is dead, and I am not. The cabin that I spent four years building and contained all my worldly possessions bar those currently strung about my person has been incinerated. I cannot hunt, I cannot even walk the hills because they are *rife* with prowling mercenaries that you and your lot have incited to violence. The entire bloody life I have built and lived for *years* has been torn away from me in the span of a dog's fart and none of it had the slightest thing to do with me and mine, and now I'm stuck in this accursed village of warbling piss-drinkers while we await death. So no, you pestilent cockroach, I am not – fucking – all right.'

Javani nodded, one cold finger on her chin. Her nose was beginning to run, despite the day's weak sun. 'I get it,' she said.

'What? What the fuck can you possibly get, pest?'

'A few months ago, Ree and I had a happy little life, down on the plains. We lived on a horse farm, we were building a winter feed store and a covered stable – well, Ree was, I was more there for moral support. I had friends in the town, we were getting by, we had . . . we had a future.'

'And? How did you and your shithouse of a mam fuck it all up?'

Javani met his wavering, scornful gaze, and held it. 'We didn't. Someone else did it for us. Killed my best friend in front of me, tried to kill me, killed another dear friend. We ran, and we lost everything. Left it all behind.' She swallowed, trying to keep the memories at arm's length, trying not to let the thoughts come rushing to the forefront of her mind. Then she wouldn't be able to speak, wouldn't be able to do much more than sob and hug herself.

She cleared her throat. 'So I know a bit about grief, and loss, and . . . dislocation.'

'Dislocation?'

It was a word Ree had used. 'When you've woken up and done the same thing, day in, day out, week by week, month by month, and then suddenly, in a blink, it's gone. It's not just the loss, it's the . . . change. Like the ground's been ripped out from under you, and you're just . . . floating. Unmoored.'

He grunted. 'Know about boats, do you?'

'I know what mooring is.'

'The people you lost, close friends were they? Known them a long time?'

She carefully stepped around the one she'd known for only a few days. 'A good chunk of my life.' Short as it was.

'Then what's your wisdom, pest? Because the sympathy of a sun-addled infant isn't doing much to shift the mire of shite that drowns me.'

Javani took a deep breath, and tried to come up with something. 'Maybe you need to keep busy, take your mind off things.' She gestured at the activity swarming over the lower terraces. 'It's not like there isn't a lot going on.' Her gaze lingered on Mariam and her cadre of proto-archers, now passing out fistfuls of arrows. Another group was drilling with long poles on the terrace behind them. 'You could, for example, help out with a little archery instruction, perhaps . . . ?'

'*Fuck. Off.*' His words were a whipcrack, a mirthless snarl. He hadn't even called her a polyp or anything equally baffling. She peered sideways at him, hoping for a hint of a self-satisfied smile, a little gummy indicator that it wasn't meant the way it sounded.

It was.

'Look, Anri, I know you're sad, but—'

'Sad?' He whirled on her, the bow twisting in his pale-knuckled hands. 'I'm not sad, I'm *incan-fucking-descent*.'

'Come again?'

He began striding up the terrace towards the buildings that hugged the base of the cliff-face, and she trotted to keep up. 'Years of my life, for what? And now I have to mourn her? I should be glad that she's gone, that I'm free, and all I feel is regret and fury and' – his voice caught, the words choking as tears filled his eyes – 'and I miss her so much, I miss how she used to be, I miss knowing that she's there waiting for me, even when she wasn't talking, I knew she was there. It was all there.' He collapsed to his knees in the scrubby grass, the bow held before him in both hands, his body racked with sobs.

'I understand. It's easier to be angry than sad.' Javani put a tentative hand on his heaving shoulder. 'I'm sorry, Anri. She deserved better.' Then, as an afterthought: 'And so did you.'

'Keep fucking busy, eh?' he sniffled. 'What kind of suggestion is that to a grieving widower, you rectal parasite?'

She seized on the tiny flash of grin beneath his tears. 'You don't have to teach me anything, really. But there are a lot of people in the village who could benefit from . . .' Her gaze drifted, following movement below them on the terrace: a figure, moving quickly despite her walking stick, making for the still-uncut bridge. 'In the name of all the— She's going out again?'

Anri lifted his head, his eyes red and rheumy. 'Huh?'

'The hills are crawling with bandits! What's she thinking?' Javani slapped Anri on the shoulder. 'There's something you can busy yourself with. Go out and protect Ree. She's going to get herself in trouble again.'

He took a long, rattling sniff, then cleared his throat, the trembling bow still gripped tight in his hands.

'No,' he said.

FORTY-SEVEN

Manatas was a little shocked by the surge of elation he felt when he saw Ree's grimy face pop up above the ridge-top, kept low against the sharp foliage of the vicious shrub. She looked tired, and sweaty, and her expression communicated both a pressing demand for explanations and a clear degree of scepticism that he still commanded his faculties, but it was good to see her.

'You made it,' he said, shuffling on his elbows a little closer to the crest. It was pleasing to see her in daylight again. The scar on her temple was quite striking in the silvery light, forked like lightning, carving a line towards her cheek.

'You're taking one hell of a risk, Manatee,' came her curt response, her words still breathy from the climb. She seemed bothered by pain, perhaps from her leg. 'Your erstwhile colleagues are spread across the forest like lice.' Her frown deepened. 'Unless you merely wanted to lure me here for their amusement? Trying to win back their favour?'

His words tumbled out in a rush. 'No, no, it is quite the reverse, I assure you. The thought that I might commit such heinous treachery is wounding to both spirit and—'

Her hand was already up. 'Captain, please. Consider me reassured, while there are still daylight hours remaining.' The hand dropped. 'You have something to communicate?'

Manatas nodded, feeling his throat tighten as he tried to form the words. 'Our acting commander has the men in full array. Preparations are in train, and cannot easily be interrupted. We are to attack tomorrow at noon.'

One of her eyebrows arched, stretching the scar. 'Noon? You believe that.'

'I do not. I expect it will be dawn, or a little before.'

She nodded, lips pursed, her gaze drifting. 'I'd conclude the same.' She scratched at her cheek. 'What form will the attack take?'

He held his breath a moment, feeling the slow thump of his pulse, the twitch of his chest against the cold rock below. He'd expected betraying his company to at least trigger a palpitation or two. 'Three primary groups, plus reserves. The main group will try to force their way up from the river, but the dangerous ones will be those that skirt around and come through the pastures. They will move into position most likely overnight. You are expected to cut the bridge, and it is with some relief that I note you have not yet done so, but nonetheless a third group will try to force a crossing by the waterfall, some time later when your attention is elsewhere.'

'I see.' She sucked her lower lip against her top teeth. 'And where will you be in all this?'

'I am expected to lead the third group, the ravine-crossers.'

One corner of her mouth rose, creasing her cheek. 'And what impact do you feel your leadership will have on this group's pursuit of its goals?'

He felt his own smile rise in mirror of hers. 'Despite my many years of experience and solid record of service, I fear that on this occasion we may struggle to achieve our objectives in a timely fashion. A small but dedicated force with pole-arms or long staves would likely hold the bank indefinitely.'

'That's good to know. Thank you.'

'I do not know how matters will unfold, nor Lado's part in it. He and Botrys will be with the reserves, but I would expect them to commit unless your defences fold at the first.'

'We'll endeavour to do otherwise. Oh,' she lifted her chin, a sparkle in her eye, 'your friend Kediras arrived.'

Warmth flooded his body at the news, and his breath hitched. 'She is whole?' he gasped.

'In body, I'd say, but I wouldn't vouch for what controls it. She's ready, nay, desperate to fight.'

'That is Kediras. She is a dear friend.' He took a tight breath, felt the warmth in his chest constrict around his heart. 'In truth I find myself pained by this news, for while I am gladdened to hear of her health, I am troubled that she should be so clearly seeking to end it.'

'She said she needs to kill a demon.' Ree paused for a moment. 'Possibly because the demon has her flute?'

'That would be Lado of Cstethia.' He shuffled against the cold, rough rock. 'And the flute is not hers, it is her sister's.'

'She didn't mention a sister.'

'It is unlikely she would, for the poor girl is dead. She was the baby of the family, cherished by all, and a dazzling musician with it. The Pashani . . .' He trailed off, collecting his thoughts, uncertain how much of Keds's intimates to share. 'She is dead,' he finished.

'Understood,' was all Ree replied.

'You will understand her animosity for the acting commander.'

'And yours, captain.' She rubbed one finger across her lip. 'You said something before, about him. That he "raised the bear". I'm assuming that's not camp slang?'

Manatas gave a deep sigh. The memory was painful, even now, but having shared a slice of Keds's history it would be churlish to refuse his own. The meeting already had a feeling of a final confession, given what awaited them in the morning. 'There was a bear, a real one. I stumbled over it on patrol out east. The mother had been taken by trappers, stripped of pelt and meat, but they'd missed the cub. A tiny thing, and so hungry. I, uh, I took it into my care.'

He waited for her glib response, but none arrived. When he looked across, she was watching him with steady eyes. 'Go on.'

'Well, he became my companion, for a time. I always knew I'd have to let him run free before he became too tame, but I fed him and carried him until his strength was restored.' He gave a wry chuckle. 'The horses were not best pleased, although in time they grew accustomed to his presence. He even became popular around the camp – he was happy to eat what others would not, and always grateful. We named him Duroj.'

'That just means "bear".'

'We were not inspired namesmiths, it's true.' He sighed again.

'I can hardly talk, given what I called the kid, but still,' she said. A note of caution entered her voice. 'What happened?'

'One day – it was spring, a day before the second festival, and our rations had arrived at the fort. I was out inspecting the line, and when I returned . . .' He felt his lips curl around his teeth, his breath hot in his chest. 'Some of the new men, the relief, had begun their celebrations early. They deemed it only fair to involve Duroj.' He could feel his throat tighten. 'They gave him drink, as much as he would take, which was as much as he could get. "See, Manatas, the little bear is drunk, look at him stagger." He staggered for a time, then fell. And he did not rise.' Tears formed at the corners of his eyes, and his voice was little more than a croak. 'They poisoned my friend.'

He looked away, one fist clamped over his mouth, trying to hide the tremble of his lip, and awaited her mockery. Instead, he heard only a sniff. When he looked across, he saw a glimmer of tears in her eyes, and she wiped her nose on her sleeve. 'I'm sorry, Manatas. It was a cruel act.'

He wiped at his eyes as if rubbing away sleep and cleared his throat, trying to cover the extent of his upset. 'Had they intended cruelty, I could at least have held them in judgement. Their crime was thoughtlessness, and stupidity, and those are the crimes of us all at our worst.' He shook his head. 'Yet still I lost myself to rage.'

'You killed them?'

'It was only from the intervention of my lieutenant I did not. His reward was to accompany me, and my surviving crew, to fresh endeavours. For those men were not of my command, and the by-laws are clear.'

'They sent you here as punishment?'

'Eventually, they did. Seekers of peace, circled by men of violence,' he muttered.

'You have my sympathies for your friend,' she said quietly, then sighed. 'I once had a cub in my care, of a different sort, clueless fool that he was. I sometimes wonder what happened to him.'

'I wish him a happier fate than Duroj,' Manatas replied, his voice still taut.

They rested in silence for a moment, conscious of the whisper of the wind through the creaking trees, the high calls of the lingering birds. In the distance, thunder rumbled, echoing from distant slopes.

Manatas squinted up at the slate-grey sky. 'I fear the weather may be turning.'

'Before we call it a day,' Ree said, shuffling up against the ridge until their faces were only a foot or so apart, 'is there anything else you can tell me about what's coming? No matter how inconsequential.'

He gave a gentle shake of his head. It was strange to believe he'd already betrayed the company, blown through his oath and voided his contract as if it were the most natural thing in the world. But then again, hadn't the company betrayed him first? 'As I say, I do not know where Lado will appear, but it's the Pashani you must watch for. He will send the lower infantry up the river path, knowing it is the most heavily defended, but the Pashani on the pasture trail will be the killing blow. I will do my best to labour operations at the waterfall.'

'That's appreciated.' She gave him a wry smile, her eyes crinkling with the scar, and something lifted in his chest. 'Thank you, Chapter Captain Manatas. It's been nice chatting to you.' The smile dipped a little. 'I hope we don't have to kill each other tomorrow.'

He had to swallow. 'I hope so, too.' A final thought occurred as she began shuffling away. 'Wait, there is one item, and it may be inconsequential in definition.'

She paused her downward wriggle. 'What is it?'

'Are you certain of everyone within the village?'

'What do you mean?'

His mouth twisted. 'In the briefing this morning, there was, I would call it, a lack of concern about the nature of your defences, which struck me as discordant with what I have observed of their potential efficacy.'

She spun a finger. 'Get to the point, Mantelpiece.'

'Is it possible that someone within your settlement is working at odds?'

Her lack of reaction surprised him. 'Thanks.' She resumed her downward shimmy.

'You are, uh, welcome.'

'Oh,' came her voice as her head dropped from view, 'should you find yourself on the wrong side of the barricades, watch your step.'

'I will endeavour so to do.'

'Hm.' She stopped moving, the very crest of her gleaming white hair still visible above the ridge-top, in the waving shadow of the briar. He liked her hair.

'Is all well?'

'Do you hear something?'

'I hear plenty, I hear . . .' Frowning, he stopped to listen, and then caught it. The crunch of boots on frigid earth, swishing through the slick carpet of dead leaves. It was coming from downslope, and was clearly more than just Mantenu. Then he picked out the voices, low and urgent, calling to each other. He swallowed again. 'There are people approaching our position.'

'There are. One of your patrols?'

'I would hazard so.' He took a sharp breath. 'Make your escape, I will distract them, call them away.'

One of her eyebrows rose into view. 'Are you simple? They will mark you as a traitor and execute you as they did those others, when we need you hobbling the left flank tomorrow. Keep your head down. No, if anything, call attention to me the moment I'm distant enough to deflect suspicion.'

His own brows lowered in disbelief. 'Are you certain? That is to say, your movement is not, uh, you have the, uh . . .'

A flash of her eyes over the ridge-line silenced him. 'Do as you're told. And keep your head down!'

With that, she vanished down the slope, and he waited as long as he could before he began to shout.

FORTY-EIGHT

'Stupid, Ree, very stupid,' she snarled to herself as she crashed through freezing scrub, wet branches slapping and dragging at her thighs, her injured calf jolting with a flare of agony at every step. Narrow trees flashed past her as she ran, their lowest branches whipping and stinging as she left them swaying in her wake. Manatas had left it late before raising his alarm, far too late to be prudent, but they'd spotted her immediately, their barks and cries loud in her ears as they echoed across the mountainside. At least three different voices, likely at least a pair per voice. She was in trouble.

Should have let him take the fall, should have let him call them away. Her breath was coming in hot little gasps, her lungs burning, the aches in her body still distant subordinates to the pulsing stabs of pain that leaped up her leg every time she planted it. Not as young as you used to be, Ree, not as fit or nimble, and maybe should have listened to the kid, should have rested that leg for—

Her good toe clipped a buried root and she tumbled, flying forward and downward through a slime of mud and mulch. Her scream escaped without her even knowing it, conscious only of its echoes as she rolled in dirt, spitting mouldering leaves and clutching at her blazing leg.

It took several halting breaths for the fog of pain in her mind to clear, to remember herself, to force her groaning limbs back upright. Her walking stick was gone, lost somewhere in the fall, but she could see her target. The weak sun revealed the forest's waning edge and the packed-earth road beyond, just another few dozen strides and another few dozen sturdy trunks down the slope.

'Come on, old girl, not far now,' she murmured through gritted teeth. 'And all downhill.'

'And where do you think you're going, spy?'

The accent was Vistirlari, the voice's owner a thin man in dirty mail and mud-smeared colours, a dull round helm perched on his head. He was unshaven and his mouth twitched when he spoke, animating the narrow scars that marked his jaw. The long-handled axe in his hand looked ill-maintained, but a little rust would be no obstacle to cleaving her head from her shoulders. He was blocking her path to the road, the axe held easily over one shoulder, his eyes round with excitement.

'Well?'

Ree performed a mental inventory. She'd been in too much of a rush to collect her sword as she left the village, too blasé about the risk, which now seemed like spectacular false economy. After her gift to Sweeper, she had two knives left, assuming they hadn't gone the way of the stick in her fall. Neither was likely to pierce the mercenary's mail, which meant going for either the lower legs or the face and throat below his helmet. And in her exhausted, anguished shape, she didn't much fancy her chances. Ten years ago, hells, even five, she'd have—

Quit it, Ma.

The kid's voice, loud in her head. *You've got to get used to who you are, and start living as that person.*

Easy for her to say. Still bent double, her breath wheezing barks, she reached for her belt.

Something clanged, sharp and hard, a flat bell struck with a hammer. The man before her yelped and doubled over, clutching the back of his head through the helm and nearly dropping his axe.

Ree did not need a second invitation. Without a thought to check what had happened, she burst past him, teeth gritted against the pain of her leg, spittle flying from her hissing mouth. Twenty strides to the forest's edge, then ten, only the thunder of her pulse in her ears, the bark of her breathing, then the yells and cries of the mercenaries as the rest of her pursuers closed. She was close now, so close, the initial shriek of her injured calf now battered to an acute numbness that suggested if she lived to see tomorrow she might never use the leg again. Well, that was tomorrow's problem.

'I'm going to make it, I'm going to make it—'

A shape in her periphery, something grey and black against the wintry forest. A running figure, keeping pace with her, the jingle of mail and gear like the tinkle of festive bells. He was more than keeping pace, he was catching her, a wicked cavalry sabre bobbing in his hand.

Close sounds on the other side; she turned her head as much as she dared to see two more mail-clad men moving to intercept her. One carried a spear, the other carried a long knife in each pumping fist. They were moving a lot faster than she was.

'Not going to make it . . .'

They bellowed at her to halt, ordered her to abandon her escape, yelled 'spy' and 'snake'. She kept her eye fixed on the narrow slice of feeble daylight ahead, kept her arms moving, driving one foot after the other. The first man was ahead of her now, circling to cut her off from the path through the trees, his sabre held up in warning.

'Stop right there—'

This time she caught the flash of movement, the whip of the arrow between the trunks before it split the man's thigh and sent him crashing to the festering earth, his command converted effortlessly to a piercing screech without even a pause for breath.

To her left, the two other mercenaries checked their strides, sudden hesitation in their charge.

Hissing with effort, Ree lurched for the forest's edge. She stumbled down the bank and collapsed onto the road, scrambling up on hands and knees towards the thick posts that marked the bridge's end. Standing beside the posts was Anri, bow in hand, smoothly sighting along another arrow. She almost laughed to see him, but the pain in her leg was back and furious, and her attempt at mirth came out as a piteous mewl.

She crawled on, palms thick with cold mud, fingers caked, one knee of her trousers almost worn through, ignoring the whistle that went over her head and the thud and cry from somewhere behind. Then hands were on her, small hands, familiar hands.

'Come on, Ma, on your feet, let's go.'

'Kid? I—'

'Move! Across the bridge!'

The kid was supporting her, her small body jammed under Ree's armpit, heaving her upright and limping onto the slick and swaying bridge. To their left, the falls churned on, thick mist rising around them as another twang and squawk announced Anri hitting his mark once more. Ree gripped the side rope with numb fingers as the bridge shuddered and bounced beneath them, remembering their first trip across the bridge, only days before. She'd been cleaner then, if not much. She concentrated on planting her good foot as best she could, letting the rope and the kid keep her steady. *We've done this before*, she thought, as she heard Anri loose again and the screech of pain that issued from his target; *she carried me into a mine, dragged me to safety when I was ready to face death once more.*

Huh. She was shorter then.

'Kid?'

'Ma, you're all right, yeah? We're going to be all right.'

'Have you grown?'

'What?'

The bridge shook with sudden force, and Anri came barrelling up behind them. 'Come on, dairy cows, get a wiggle on! They've brought their mates.'

He fairly shoved them forward, sending the pair of them tumbling into a heap on the bridge's far side. He came to a gasping halt behind them, clearly caught out by the burst of movement, signalling angrily if incoherently to the cluster of villagers who were waiting at the barricades.

'Now?' said one of them.

'Yes, fucking now!' Anri spat back.

Ree was sitting up, the kid un-sprawled beside her, suddenly aware of the quantity of armed men at the bridge's far end. They were flooding out of the woods and onto the road, maybe a score of them, although at the rear of the company she spotted a number who seemed to be prone or limping, clutching wounds to their legs.

She smiled, despite the pain in her own. *Below the mail, every time.*

Her smile didn't last. The mercenaries were converging on the bridge, and the ones at the front had thick shields and long spears. If they made it across now, they could raze the village before those inside had time to do much more than blow a horn.

With a series of thwacks and twangs, the sentries severed the last of the supporting ropes. As the mercenaries reached the support posts, the neat timbers of the rope bridge shuddered and twitched, then dropped away, clattering into the seething mist of the falls and out of sight. The bridge was cut.

The armoured men milled for a short time, then on what Ree assumed was the arrival of an officer, quite possibly her friend Manatas, they began to fall back, retreating cautiously back into the woods until the road appeared empty. All bar one – the first man who'd challenged Ree, who stood at the forest's edge with his axe still gripped tight in his hand and a thin trickle of drying blood leaked from his helmet. He raised the axe and pointed it squarely at where Ree still sat in the freezing mud, the kid's arm around her shoulders, and began to bellow a challenge over the rush of the falls.

'What's he saying?' the kid murmured.

'No idea. Don't really . . . care.' Ree's teeth were beginning to chatter, and she wasn't sure it was entirely from the cold.

Anri stepped in front of them, blocking their view of the shouting mercenary. 'Ah, shut your head, you grubby little testicle,' he muttered, then nocked an arrow, sighted and loosed in a movement of shocking fluidity.

The man fell momentarily silent as he registered the movement at the bridge's far side, and hesitated, presumably trying to calculate if he was safe at their distance.

His gargling shriek confirmed he was not. It took far too long for two of his companions to emerge from the woods and drag him away, his axe abandoned, as he moaned and wept and grasped at the arrow that was driven squarely through his groin.

Anri chuckled as the man's agonised wails receded. 'Off you fuck, then, choirboy.' He turned to witness the kid's horrified reaction. 'Bodkin head. Call it a ring-splitter. What? Kept my promise, didn't I? Camellia can't complain.'

'There's a difference between "not killing anyone" and . . . what you just did,' the kid snapped.

He shrugged. 'If I'm not allowed to kill anyone, I'll settle for some light maiming.'

'You shot him in the unmentionables!'

'Hoy. Saved your mam, didn't I? If I choose to hit a man below stairs, that's my business and mine alone.'

The kid waved a huffy little finger beneath his nose. 'We'll discuss this later.'

'Of that I have no doubt,' he replied with a gappy grimace. As the kid returned to Ree, who was still no closer to getting up, he leaned over them, blotting out the watery daylight. In the distance thunder boomed again. 'Don't forget,' he said, jabbing a finger at the kid.

'What?'

'You owe me seven arrows, you do.'

'Thank you for helping, Anri.'

He marched away without another word.

'Sorry about him. He's, uh, grieving. I think.' The kid put her arm back around Ree and gave her a deep, stern look. 'What happened to everyone stays inside the village, Ma?'

'Had to go out. Important.' Her teeth were still chattering. 'We're really in it now. They attack at dawn.'

The kid nodded gravely. 'Then you need to rest until then.' She wrinkled her nose. 'And have a bath.'

'There,' Ree replied with a weary sigh through her trembling jaw, 'I'm no longer inclined to argue.'

FORTY-NINE

It was nearly full dark, the rising moon lost behind vast rolling banks of gravid cloud, when the traitor appeared. The figure slipped through the thickening drizzle, skirting the patrol of very-definitely sentries, their lanterns hissing in the spotty rain, and stepped cautiously down the terrace steps towards the river path. The focus of the guards at the lower barricades was on the winding trail that led down the steep slope to the darkened valley floor. None of them was watching for a stealthy, cloak-wrapped saboteur moving softly behind them, a long-handled pick gripped in one hand, making for the barricade's far end. Damage to the foundations would be harder to spot against the curve of the escarpment, and the defenders would likely have no idea that one side of their barrier had been fatally weakened until it collapsed under the first charge.

The figure stole to the barricade's edge and set the pick carefully against the first of the anchors. It was then that Ree lifted the hood from her lantern.

'Good evening, Keretan.'

The big man did not reply. Caught in the lantern's sudden light, his mouth hung open, eyes narrowed and darting, one giant hand raised.

'Nice night for a walk?' she continued. She was sitting beneath a waxed cape, her back to the rockface, previously hidden by the curve of the path. It was cold, and getting wetter, and part of her was extremely relieved he'd shown up when he had, as her stamina for keeping watch in such an uncomfortable place was substantially diminished. 'Want to tell me what you're up to?'

He swallowed, the drizzle misting his great beard. 'Ree. I thought you were resting.'

She sucked her lip against her teeth. 'Gave it my best try, but just couldn't stay asleep. All that thunder, all afternoon. More than you'd have thought possible. And now the rain's finally here.' She watched his squinting eyes trying to make her out, trying to work out how much trouble he was in. One hand still wrapped the shaft of the pick. 'And before the thought even crosses your mind, Keretan, I should probably mention that Anri is over there, and he's developed a recent and intense passion for maiming. If that doesn't quite steer your judgement, a swift toot on this charming horn will bring a lot of people very quickly, quite possibly including Kediras, who is unlikely to show quarter to anyone she suspects is in league with her demon. Perhaps it's time to put the tool down?'

He did so, the pick dropping from his grip as his shoulders slumped. His hands went to his face, and a moment later he was sobbing. 'By the gods, by the gods,' he moaned. 'I'm so sorry.'

'There, there, big man,' Ree replied without particular warmth. 'Let's go and have a chat with the rest of the Council, shall we?'

The fires were low and the lanterns dim, while the rain drummed on the roof. Keretan sat on the central stump seat, beneath his gleaming, twisted, useless armour, his elbows on his knees and his head in his hands. His sobs – genuine, despite Ree's initial doubts – had calmed, but he sniffled and groaned and shook his great head with depressing frequency.

The rest of the Council stood in a semicircle around him, in a curious reflection of their normal arrangement, with the exception of Ree, who sat on the floor. She was too tired, and her leg was too ruined, to spend any further effort maintaining verticality. Mariam and Vida were blank-faced, their hands clasped; Mani was bent over his walking stick, looking truly bereft. Camellia looked on the verge of tears. Even Volkan seemed shocked.

Anri lounged against the back wall, his bow brazen in his hand, clearly delighted at displaying it within the once-hallowed hall. 'Always took you for a coward, Keretan,' he called. 'The big ones always are.' Skulking at his elbow, the kid shushed him, but she didn't look too upset.

'You're our saboteur, then.' Vida spoke without inflection. She and Mariam looked muddy and exhausted, but neither appeared willing to admit weakness. Ree, from her roost on the floor, was past caring.

'Why?' Camellia whispered.

Keretan looked up through red-rimmed eyes, his face blotchy. 'I'm sorry. I just . . . I couldn't. I'm so, so *afraid*.'

Mani's tone was gentle, weighed with emotion. 'We're all frightened, Keretan. Why didn't you speak to us?'

'What did they promise you?' Mariam's voice had none of Mani's sympathy.

Keretan's hands were extended, thick fingers spread in pleading. 'That we'd be spared! That our lives, that our children . . .' He broke off into sobs again, his entire body shaking. No one moved to comfort him. 'You don't understand,' he whimpered. 'We can't fight them. They'll kill us all, they'll murder our babies!'

Ree sighed, ready to state the obvious for the umpteenth time, but Camellia, of all people, beat her to it. 'Keretan, did you truly believe that they would uphold their side?'

He gazed at the floor, calloused fingers running over his gleaming dome. 'I had to believe. I had to,' he whispered.

'You know better than that,' Camellia said, her voice not cold but certainly chilly. 'In the last few days, we've all had to face aspects of the world we would wish to be otherwise. It has become plain that merely wishing changes nothing.'

Ree shifted on the floor, propping herself on one hand and trying to stretch out her damaged leg. She was a little off-kilter from Camellia's sudden display of sense. 'Keretan, it's true there's a chance that tomorrow they crush us. They swarm this place and slaughter us all, enslave our most vulnerable, burn this place to the ground, what-have-you. There's a chance.'

'*Ma,*' came the kid's insistent gripe from behind her, 'how is this helping?'

'But if we lay down our arms and wave them in, that slaughter is a damned-by-gods certainty. You know that, don't you?' She peered forward, meeting his furtive gaze. 'Don't you?'

'Oh, right, yeah!' The kid was joining in, to Ree's mortification, gesturing at the golden armour that hung so proudly above Keretan's head. 'What have you got to be afraid of, anyway? Weren't you a fighting man, a lancer? Haven't you faced down worse a hundred times and come away victorious?'

An uneasy silence settled in the Council House.

'Haven't you . . . ?' the kid repeated, uncertainty creeping in. She was still pointing vaguely at the armour, her arm a little drooped.

Keretan didn't respond, his gaze back at the tear-splashed earth at his feet.

'But you haven't, have you, Keretan?' Ree was getting cold on the floor, despite the warmth of the fires, and she shifted again in a futile quest for comfort. No one moved to speak, so she pushed on. 'That armour on the wall isn't yours. It likely wouldn't fit you even if it weren't so twisted, because it's . . . two sets hammered together.'

Vida coughed. Mariam gripped her hand tighter. Ree swivelled towards them. 'Tell me if I have this right, "smiths". You were lancers, both of you, and for some reason you fabricated the remains of your armour into a great contorted mess so Keretan could pretend it had been his. Why? Why the subterfuge? Why let him carry on like Behrooz Big Bollocks when you were the ones who had served?'

'How did you know?' Vida mumbled, barely a question.

'Because I pay fucking attention. You've given yourselves away countless times. Not only was the armour a mess up close, something I realised when men came into this place and tried to kill me, let's not forget, but the workmanship had a lot in common with that magnificent samovar of yours. There's no way it was ever a single suit.' She sniffed. The pain in her leg had dulled, possibly with the warmth of her righteous indignation. 'Beyond that, Keretan seemed to know precious little about combat, while you two have been all too familiar with our preparations. And any time there was a confrontation with the mercenaries, for all your claims about staying out of Council business, you'd show up and look the part. You both know how to handle and maintain weapons and armour, and you're covered in scars that aren't just from smithing . . . do I need to go on?'

'No,' said Mariam, who had the decency to look shame-faced.

'I get it,' Ree continued, attempting to sound mollifying. 'I know you stepped away from decision-making because you felt responsible for bringing the mercenaries to Ar Ramas. But why did you hide to begin with? Why pretend Keretan was what you should have been?'

'Because we wanted to avoid questions. To be left alone,' Vida growled. Her knuckles were white around Mariam's hand. 'Together.'

'Our relationship, before,' Mariam clarified. 'It was frowned-on.'

Ree was half up off the floor in vicarious outrage, the pain in her leg be damned. 'Because you're women?'

Vida coughed. 'Because, uh, I was her commanding officer.'

Ree's advance stalled. 'Oh.' Her leg began to throb. 'That's actually quite unprofessional.'

'*Ma!*'

'Our stations of birth were different, see,' Mariam expounded, her free hand circling. 'In Arowan, at that time, only those born to the right families, like Vida, could command . . .'

'You know military doctrine, always behind the times,' Vida added, her cheeks flushed, her gaze somewhere in the corner of the chamber. 'Should be the best person for the job, irrespective of—'

Ree had sunk back to the floor. 'I think we're straying a little here. Why Keretan, though? Why not just bury the armour and leave it all behind?'

'It was valuable,' Mariam replied, 'and, well, he offered, didn't he.'

Vida looked over to where the big man sat, staring in misery at the floor. 'He was our carter on the journey to the foothills.'

'Gods,' Ree murmured. 'Of course, "Keretan" is the Parsa word for "Carter".' She turned to the man on the stump. 'Do you have anything to say for yourself?'

'I'm sorry,' he rumbled, his voice thick. 'I wanted to be a figurehead. I wanted to inspire. For my children, for those who'd never known me before. I wanted to be what people always assumed I was.' He looked up, wiping at his eyes. 'I was always big, and strong, and . . . imposing. But I never did anything with it, never anything to be proud of.'

'So you stole valour.' Ree's lip was curled halfway up her cheek. 'Truly pride-worthy.'

'I wanted to be! I thought the act would be the making . . . and it was! Until now. Until I . . . failed.' He pressed one great fist against his mouth, tears running silently into his beard. 'I wanted a better life for my children, for everyone's children . . . I didn't want any of this.'

Ree rolled her shoulders, which had clearly had enough of supporting her weight, and turned her attention to Mani, Camellia and Volkan. 'And the rest of you knew about all this?'

Mani shook his head, Camellia muttered that it hadn't been her business to pry, but Volkan drew himself up. 'I always suspected, although I never expected he would stoop to treachery! It's clear that—'

Ree dismissed him with a wave of her hand. 'That'll do, thank you, Volkan.' She turned back to Keretan. 'Now what are we to do with you?'

He was slumped down, deflated, seeming at once half the size he had been before. 'I'm so sorry. I've failed you all. I will leave the village, unless you wish my exemplary suicide. Just, please . . . look after my babies . . .' He broke down into sobs again, his barrel chest heaving, hands pressed to his face.

'Keretan, stop this nonsense.' Camellia's voice was sharp across the man's tears. 'For the sake of the gods, pull yourself together. Of course we don't wish your death or exile.' She accompanied her words with a fierce glare around the chamber, daring anyone to contradict her. No one did. She approached the seated man, breaking his ring of isolation, and placed a gentle hand on his shoulder. 'Mani was telling the truth. We are all scared. Even those of us who seem keen to give battle.' This time, she did not look round, but Ree suspected that was meant for her. 'We are here because of our mistakes, because we were blind to our own failings. But that does not mean we are lost. It means only that the path from here is hard, and we must fight to take it.' She squeezed his shoulder. 'You want a better life for your children, to make them proud? Fight for it. Show them what it means to live free. Show them what it costs. Help them learn the lessons that we did not.'

He raised his head, sniffing, his tears and misery so incongruous with his size, but this time there was something in his eyes besides despair. 'I don't know if I can . . . if I have it in me,' he rumbled, his gaze searching hers for a reason for hope.

'I think you'll surprise yourself,' she replied with a smile that struck Ree as a little grim, but nonetheless seemed to do the trick.

'You think so?'

'I do. Be the man you always hoped to be.' She extended her hand and helped him to his feet. At once, he towered over everyone in the chamber, the shock of his presence seeming to change the very atmosphere. He looked more upright with it, his posture restored, and when he spoke his voice once again set the walls trembling.

'I owe you all a debt I cannot easily repay. But in the sight of the gods, I swear I shall try.'

That got a general murmur of encouragement.

Vida was stroking her chin, scrutinising the armour. 'Keretan, fetch that suit down. With a few adjustments, we might get it on you after all.' She met Ree's sceptical gaze as the big man moved to obey. 'Beats it gathering dust on a wall looking shiny,' she rejoined with a shrug.

'I always said it was valuable, I did,' Mariam added, pride in her eyes as she gazed at her wife.

'Dress him in tin all you like,' Anri muttered from behind them, 'he'll still be a gutless fucker.'

'Gods, Anri,' Mariam snapped, 'weren't you listening? We're all terrified of what's coming! You'd have to be *deranged* not to be scared!'

He puffed a breath through his bristly beard. '*I'm* not scared.'

'I think that tells its own story,' she retorted as she and Vida turned for the doors. One of Vida's apprentices, Parvin, was already there, hand poised to knock.

'We've got the last of the equipment down,' he reported when prompted. 'From the caves. How should we—'

Camellia joined the conversation, Keretan a pace behind, his arms piled with burnished metal. 'The last of it? From the third store?' When Parvin nodded, she addressed Vida. 'I'll handle this. You attend to Keretan.' Vida did not protest.

As Camellia went to follow the apprentice out into the drizzling dark, Ree caught up with her, her leg sluggish and grumbling. 'Hey, before you go – I, uh, what you said back there—'

Camellia shook her off. 'Please. I cannot watch you revel in my mistakes.' Without another word, she disappeared into the night in the footsteps of the apprentice.

'That wasn't what I . . . sod it.'

A figure appeared in the open doorway, half-lit by the lamps on either side, and for a moment Ree thought Camellia had returned in apology. Instead, the light revealed the banished mercenary, Kediras, her walk steady despite the heavy reek of booze that heralded her arrival.

'Are your internal histrionics concluded?' she asked in her deadpan voice, her pale irises almost swallowed by her pupils. 'We should check the defences before the rain thickens.'

'We should come and all.' Mariam nudged Vida, who was steering Keretan and his load towards the door. 'That armour can wait a short while, can't it.'

'Might as well join you,' Anri muttered, pushing himself up from the wall. 'I suppose I should know where the big holes in the ground are, and there's no one interesting left in here anyway.'

'Hey!' the kid squeaked, and he chuckled.

'I assumed you were coming too, pest – it's not like I can shake you, is it? You're like a galloping case of knob-rot.'

'Hey!'

They left Mani and Volkan contemplating the empty patch of wall and stepped out into the night.

They stood together on the upper terrace, drizzle misting their faces, the wind along the valley stinging cold. Ree counted them off: Kediras, beneath her wide-brimmed hat, the two swords strapped to her now surely as sharp as any blade in history; Mariam, who had taken to carrying a bow much like Anri's, no doubt one she had made herself; Vida, thick-armed and powerful, the smithing tools at her belt lent new purpose by circumstance; Keretan, massive and half-armoured, his conviction renewed; Anri, surly and unhelpful, and probably the most dangerous of them all. And herself, of course, her sword back at her belt and freshly furnished with one of Mani's spare sticks.

Across the rest of Ar Ramas, many had claimed they were ready to fight to preserve their homes, but how many would? How many would throw their lives away in the teeth of an assault by trained, experienced and armoured mercenaries? They had three fronts to defend. Her scant confidence began to evaporate in the freezing rain.

'It's not enough,' she muttered. 'Six just isn't enough.'

'There's seven of us,' the kid replied from beneath her waxed cloak, draped over her head.

'You don't count.'

'Rude.'

'Even if you did, it wouldn't—'

'What are you all standing about for? Isn't there work to do?' It was Camellia, approaching from the foot of the rockface, where the last of the bundles of equipment were being unloaded in flickering lantern-light. She looked different.

'Camellia, you're . . . you're wearing mail. Is that a sword?'

She didn't respond. Not only was a suit of mail shimmering beneath her open robe, but it looked very cleanly fitted. The gently curved sword at her belt was matched by the bladed spear she carried like a walking staff.

'Camellia—'

'Don't talk to me.' She joined the line, looking out over the rest of the settlement. Small lights burned along the perimeter, haloed by the wind-whipped drizzle. Ree couldn't stop staring at Camellia. The arms and armour were not an affectation. She carried them with confidence, with familiarity. The mail was hers.

'You *were* a soldier, weren't you? Before you came here.' She thought further. 'You came here because you were a soldier.'

'I told you not to talk to me.'

'You can't expect me to—'

The woman snapped, her braids swishing as she turned on Ree. 'I swore I'd never kill again,' she hissed. 'I swore by all the gods of sky and stars that I would live a life of peace after Flywater. And you have rendered my oath as ashes.'

'Camellia,' Ree said slowly, keeping her voice steady, 'for the last time, I am not to blame for what has happened in this valley. Save your righteous anger for the bandits who hunger to plunder this place.'

The mother of Ar Ramas took a long, shuddering breath, the spear creaking in her grip, then nodded. 'So be it. Let them reap their harvest at dawn.'

'Now you're talking,' Anri chuckled. 'Those pig-dicks aren't going to maim themselves, eh?'

'Let's complete the inspections, then,' Vida muttered. 'Gods know there's no shortage of tasks to attend to.'

'Seven of us now,' Anri commented as the group broke up, 'that ought to do it, eh? Six, that would have been daft, but seven, well . . .'

Javani lingered with her mother on the terrace after the others drifted away to their various duties. Ree was clearly exhausted, and in a great deal of pain, but Javani knew better than to suggest she take herself to bed. She tried something else. 'We should probably check the stables, Ma. I tried to set Tauras free but he was having none of it. I don't know what happens to him tomorrow.'

Tomorrow. It was really happening. The village would become a battleground, and people who were hale and whole today might be considerably otherwise in only a few hours. The thought was destabilising, and she almost missed a step as they descended the steps to the next terrace.

'You all right, kid?'

She covered it. 'Rain's made it slippery. Take my arm?'

The fact Ree did so without protest was testament to her fatigue.

They walked on through the thickening rain, huddled beneath their cloaks and making slow progress past the barricades and half-covered pits. For a time all Javani heard beyond the slap and thrum of raindrops against her hood was the rasp of Ree's breathing, the sharp little hitch each time she put too much weight on her bad leg. Should have rested it like I said, Ma. We should have taken our time on our journey. But then, where might we have ended up at winter's edge? Instead, they were trapped in a village, surrounded by bandits, and in the morning a lot of people were going to die.

'What is it, kid?' Ree's voice was tight against the exertion of the mud-slick walk.

'What's what?'

'You made a noise. Like you were hurt.'

'Oh.' Javani took a long breath. It felt hot and raw in her chest. 'I think I'm scared.'

'I'm not surprised.' Ree took another painful step. 'I'm scared too. I'm sorry, kid.'

'What? What for?'

'For putting you through this again. You know, after Kazeraz.'

'Yeah.' Javani concentrated on supporting her mother down the last set of steps as the stables came into view, the lanterns at the lower doorway now half-obscured by diagonal rain. 'This time it's different, though.'

'Different?'

'In Kazeraz, things were just . . . happening. Happening to us, all we could do was react. This time, we're here by choice. We could have left them to face this alone, but we stayed. We agreed. And . . .' Her throat got tight, the words suddenly hard. 'I'm glad.'

'Me too.'

'Don't die tomorrow.'

'Nor you, kid.'

'Then it's a deal.'

They were holding each other tight as they ducked inside the stable.

Tauras was curled up inside a wall of fleeces just inside the arch to the ram pen, his eyelids drooping, Tarfellian slumbered at his feet, snoring happily. Tauras snapped to attention when Javani approached, Ree left propped under blankets at the back of the structure 'to rest her leg'.

'Yes, Javani?'

'Tauras, the mercenaries are going to attack the village tomorrow.'

'Oh.'

'I know you said you didn't want to leave, but your former comrades are going to try to come into this place at dawn, and they're going to hurt a lot of people if they can.'

'Oh.'

'So there won't be much of a village left to stay in, if you follow.'

'Oh.'

'Tauras, will you fight for the village? Will you defend it against the bad men who've taken over your company?'

His jaw set, his lips pressed tight. The stubble between his braids was quite noticeable now. 'I don't want to hurt anyone.'

'I understand that.' She met his timorous gaze. 'We don't want to hurt anyone either. But sometimes,' – she tried to remember how Ree had once phrased it – 'if you refuse to fight, then the people who get hurt are the ones who can't, and they could be the ones you care about. Do you see what I mean?'

'I don't want to fight,' he repeated, sounding a little wild. 'I don't want to hurt anyone!'

'Tauras, it's not about—'

'No! I won't do it!' His hands were pressed over his ears, his eyes screwed shut. Tarfellian had lifted his head in sluggish concern, ears pricked.

'All right, all right.' Javani began to back away, palms raised. She wasn't afraid of him, but she didn't want his protestations to wake her mother. 'It's all right, Tauras.' He subsided, his hands lifted from his ears, but kept his eyes shut.

'But I want you to think about things,' she added in a low voice as she turned to leave. 'I want you to think about who you care about. The secret army needs you, Tauras. The people of Ar Ramas need you. Your friends need you. It's up to you what you do from here. Good night.'

'Good night, Javani,' came his meek reply.

FIFTY

'Gods, Arkadas, what time is it?'

'Not yet dawn, captain.' The lieutenant shielded the lantern with his hand, relieving the glare in Manatas's eyes. 'It's time.'

'Not noon, then?'

'No, captain.'

Manatas took a heavy breath. 'So be it.'

The camp was pitch dark but for the bobbing of shaded lanterns, only the faintest glimmer of light in the maudlin sky above the towering peaks to the east. The rain had finally eased, but the ground was sodden and mud squelched up to his ankles with each step. It was bitterly cold beneath his thin cloak, and his only hope was that the ground froze before he sank into it.

'I've roused the men, captain. Cold rations this morning. Half-rations. You can brief them before we move out.'

'Thank you, Arkadas. I will do so.'

The lieutenant's manner was even stiffer than normal, his movements jerky and tense. The pressure was getting to them all. The camp was eerily quiet, none of the shouts and cries and clamour of a normal morning; just the whispering hush and creak of a lot of activity taking place as silently as possible. Even the Vistirlari were keeping their habitual moaning to a background murmur. It was so disconcerting it made the hairs on Manatas's arms stand on end.

Even in the feeble light, it was obvious that the camp was thick with mist. The valley was staying true to form at the last. As his detachment gathered for their final briefing, he could barely see the men-at-arms at the group's edges. They were in full array, the previous day's preparations – the interruption of Ree's pursuit and dragging the wounded back to camp notwithstanding – well made. Or as well as could be expected, given their strange new leadership and erratic command structure. Manatas was no longer clear who reported to him aside from Arkadas, and what chain existed above him beyond simply Lado and his puppet Botrys. He was relieved to see neither at the briefing. If he could move his detachment out of camp and into position before they appeared, he stood a better chance of steering the rest of the day's events to a satisfactory conclusion. He'd been lucky to escape suspicion the day before, his delayed shouts of alarm at Ree's presence going some way to allaying respective distrust, and for a terrible moment he'd thought her lost anyway. But she'd escaped after all, and another seven of the company's finest lay in states of varying injury in Bau's forlorn medical tent. Another seven out of the fight. Almost a tenth of the company's strength. Perhaps the people of Ar Ramas stood a chance after all.

He surveyed the score of troops before him, or those he could see clearly at least. He did not wish them injury or death. He did not hate them. But he felt no loyalty, no kinship to these dead-eyed professionals who had chosen the sacking of a village of innocent farmers over seeking honest work. There was a word for such things, and Ree had used it at their first meeting. How stung he had been, how outraged, yet now he saw it from her perspective. What other word can you use for such a thing?

Still, he was their commander, for all the good it would do them, and he owed them something for their trust. 'Soldiers!' he barked. 'We shall be making our assault from the woods by the waterfall. The bridge is down, so we will be bringing our own. Your carrying parties are assigned, shield bearers with them – cover each other, be mindful of missile assault. The moment we are across, seek shelter. Do not bunch up! Move slowly, check the ground as you advance.'

He paused. He didn't owe them *too* much. 'There is no shame in falling back if conditions are not in our favour. And remember, it is in the best interests of all parties of this dispute that those manning the barricades and defences beyond are minded to surrender. As a proposition, that will be far more readily achieved if they do not believe their battle to be existential.'

One of the men-at-arms in the front row raised a gauntlet. 'Come again, chapter captain?' she said.

'Try not to kill them,' Manatas replied, 'and they will not fight so hard.'

It was worth a try.

'Are there any more questions? No? Then—'

'Ah, Chapter Captain Manatas. So glad we caught you.'

Out of the mist, as if materialising from demonic vapour, came Lado of Cstethia.

Ree hadn't expected to sleep, yet Mariam woke her some time in the gloomy pre-dawn hours. She left the kid wrapped in fleeces, snoring gently, and made slow, painful progress after Mariam out into the world. The kid would be swept up to the caves with the other non-combatants soon enough; best to let her sleep while she could.

Despite the uncivilised hour, the village was awake and humming with gentle activity, cooking smells carried on the chill breeze and lanterns bobbing along the barricades. Mist cloaked the valley, swirling around the gentle lights, giving them an eerie glow. The very air seemed on edge.

Keretan was waiting for them on the upper terrace, and he shone in the lamplight. He was coated from head to foot in golden steel, and shimmered when he moved. He saw them coming and beamed, his tearful confessions of the previous night forgotten. 'Ree! What do you think?'

'I think Vida has done a miraculous job.' She hobbled closer. 'How do you feel?'

The big man's eyes softened as he looked down at her. 'Terrified,' he said in a low voice. 'But ready to face what comes.'

'In that shell, you'll stand a better chance than anyone. Just don't let them get you on the ground.'

People were gathering before the Council House, emerging from the mist, clad in their thickest wools and whatever they could find to wear as armour, carrying the weapons and implements retrieved from the caves and adapted from their farming purposes, stepping carefully around pits and barricades. Here were the defenders of Ar Ramas, excluding the night sentries who kept watch at the village's edges, their horns clutched tight, and waited for the attack they knew would come. Ree released a long, shaking breath, watching it plume in the lamplight and merge with the drifting mist. There were so few of them. Their chances were slim, and they knew it.

'You need to say something.'

Keretan blinked. 'What?'

'You need to say something to your people. They're looking for leadership, inspiration. And you're the big fucker in the golden armour.'

He swallowed. Behind him she noticed the rest of the Council milling, passing around hot cups of what could have been soup, each clearly hoping someone else would step up. 'What do I say?' he whispered.

'Seriously?' She leaned on her stick, feeling the pinch of the sword belt in her side. It was not designed for a lopsided stance. 'Well . . . What would you want to hear in their position?'

'That our opponents were giving up and running away,' he replied with a grim smile.

She matched it. 'Come on, you wanted to inspire. What would inspire you? What did you dream of, when you offered to take Vida and Mariam's armour for them?'

He ran a hand through his beard, his gaze distant, took a long breath, then he turned. 'People of Ar Ramas!' he boomed. The nervous defenders shuffled closer. Ree noticed Camellia, Anri and the smiths loitering in his shadow. Even Kediras, bleary-eyed and bloodshot, was paying attention.

'This village,' Keretan intoned, 'is our home. It is our nation. And nations are built on stories. Our actions today will become such a story, for good or ill. Make this day a legend that will echo down the ages, that the children of your children's children will tell boldly, and with pride. Let this be the beginning, not the end. You have it within you all. For Ar Ramas!'

'For Ar Ramas!' came the answering cheer.

Beaming and flushed, Keretan turned to Ree, who mouthed 'Good work.' 'Ree, you had some words of advice for our people?'

'I did? I did.' She cleared her throat and took a painful step beside him, conscious of their absurd height disparity. 'Remember, the mercenaries attacking us today are little more than bandits. They are ill-disciplined, ill-equipped, cold and hungry. But they are still very dangerous indeed. If you find yourself in a confrontation, fall back. Always fall back! Do not attempt to fight them – remember what happened to poor Gumis. Let the traps and the barriers do their work. Memorise the locations of our defences – once they are armed, they are a risk to everyone, irrespective of allegiance. In the heat of the moment you do not want to step on something you'll regret. And beyond that, after we win, we're going to want to come back and fill in the pits, so please – do your best to remember.'

Her line about winning got a cheer, and she felt the corners of her mouth lifting as she spoke. 'They are covetous bullies who will not expect resistance. You're defending your homes, your families, your way of life . . . I know who I'd put my wager on.'

That got another cheer. Her chest tingled. She wished for a moment the kid had been around to hear it, but was glad she was still safely tucked up in the stables. It was still so early that it did not yet count as morning.

'Ar Ramas: remember what you're fighting for. Remember *who* you're fighting for. Look out for one another. Nobody falls, nobody gets left behind. Keep together, and victory will be yours. To your posts!'

The defenders dispersed, energised, invigorated, and no doubt still gripped by mortal terror. They were only human, after all.

Vida was beside her. She was wearing mail, presumably taken from storage, It did not fit her well. 'What of your large friend, the man in the ram pen? Will he fight for us like the one who reeks of alcohol, or draw against us if the tide turns?'

'Honestly? I don't know. The kid sounded him out. He didn't seem to know himself. He's his own man now, I guess he'll make his own decision.'

The corner of Vida's mouth twitched. 'How nice for him.'

'Ma?' a yawning voice enquired.

'Gods be damned, kid, you were supposed to be asleep.'

'And miss all the –' she yawned again, '– the this?'

Keretan cleared his throat. 'We still haven't finalised where each of us will stand. I'd like to volunteer to go where the fighting will be thickest.'

Ree raised an eyebrow. 'You want to prove yourself?'

'Well, that and . . . I have the most comprehensive armour.'

'That would be the pasture trail, then. My information suggests that's where the Pashani will attack from, after the main body come at the river path.'

'Pashani?' The sting of booze on the air announced Kediras's proximity. Her unsteady gaze landed on Keretan. 'Then I will come with you, golden giant.'

Ree tapped at her top teeth with a freezing finger. 'That covers the pasture. The bridge is down across the falls, and I have reason to suspect that the attack there will be poorly coordinated—'

Anri stuck up his hand. 'I'll go over by there, then. What? Got my eye in popping off a few yesterday, might as well carry on where I left off.'

'Keep our people in formation, working the pikes, and they should hold. That leaves the river path, and it will be busy. It's the hardest approach for them, but it won't be a feint.'

Mariam and Vida spoke as one. 'We'll go.'

'You're sure you want to be together? It could be a hard thing, if . . . things do not go our way.'

'It's a quandary we've faced before,' Vida replied stoutly.

'I would rather die beside you than live without you, my love,' Mariam breathed to her wife, which took Ree slightly aback with its intensity.

'Then . . . we're covered on that side. Camellia?'

Camellia looked up from a private reverie. 'I'll hold with the reserve. Coordinate communication and move to wherever needs support.'

The reserve, perhaps counterintuitively, were the ten most capable spear-wielders in the village, those with the greatest mix of ability and determination. Whether this came from military history or recent enthusiasm for each of them was their own concern, but Ree had been impressed at how well they had come together in such a short time.

She nodded to Camellia, surprised at her lack of hostility. Perhaps it was too early, or too late, for such things. 'I'll join Anri at the bridge, just in case—'

Anri scoffed. 'Like fuck you will.'

'What do you mean?'

'Look at you. You can barely stand, can't move fast, can't carry messages, almost certainly can't fight, and I have it on good authority you're dogshit with a bow.'

Ree glared at the kid, who had found a fascinating patch of mud to contemplate. 'Now listen here, you—'

'He's right.' Ree wheeled in shock at Vida's words. 'Maybe not about the bow, I have no information there. But you're struggling for mobility.'

'Look at the bloody mess you got yourself in yesterday,' Anri added for good measure. 'Fucking disaster, it was. Lucky there was a dead-shot around to wipe your arse for you.'

'Thank you, Anri,' Vida said, without inflection. 'We've already discussed it. We need you with the non-combatants, up in the caves.'

Ree's voice was colder than the southern wind. 'You've discussed it.'

'It's the best place for you and the child. You can keep watch from up there, signal us with the horns if you see something.'

'Assuming the mist clears,' Anri muttered, 'which it won't.'

'Thank you, Anri. Mani and Volkan are up there.' Vida leaned forward, meeting Ree's surly glare. 'They could use the help keeping everyone calm.'

She felt the words rising to her lips, driven by fury and instinct: *five years ago, I'd have . . .* She stamped them down, one eye on the kid. It was just possible that they had a point.

'Very well, I'll go up to the caves,' she growled. 'But if I see anything I don't like, I'm coming right back down.'

'You can use the hoist,' chuckled Anri, 'I hear it's very fast if you kick the counterweight.'

'Thank you, Anri,' said Vida.

'Anri, wait up!'

'What is it, pest? I've got a ravine to defend.'

'I was thinking—'

'"How are you, Anri?" Oh, thanks for asking, pest. Actually I'm feeling free, but confused, angry, ready to move from maiming to murder, you might say.'

'You have a lot of pent-up frustration.'

'Oh, I wonder why.'

'Listen! This could be, you know, the last time we talk . . . if things go bad today.'

His face curdled. 'Are you about to confess your undying love for me, parasite? I've only just eaten my breakfast, and I'm in no hurry to see it again.'

'No— *No!* By the gods! This could be your last chance to, you know . . .' She waggled her eyebrows and gestured intently, willing him to catch up. '. . . Give me some archery pointers.'

'You have got to be fucking . . . With a mercenary company ready to tear out our throats—'

'That's why! What if you die, and your knowledge and training dies with you? What if there's a moment where I can save us all with a bow-shot—'

'Well, then we really will be fucked, won't we?'

'Come on! A moment of your time, just some pointers, then you can rush off to your maiming appointment. Come on, Anri. What's wrong with my feet?'

He blew out a long, exasperated breath. 'Oh, by the gods of salt and piss, *fine*. Hold this.' He pressed the bow into her hands. 'Draw.'

She did so, and he immediately kicked at her feet. 'Ow!'

'There, you fucking gruel-fed dunce. Get them in line with your body, draw to your cheek, keep both eyes open. Both eyes! Keep them fucking open, I swear to all the gods. Keep your chest up and breath controlled, relax all three fingers at once, bang, hand drops, shoulders pinch, whoosh, "Surprise, dickhead." Do all that, well . . . you're in with a chance of hitting something, I suppose.'

'Hold my breath?'

He snatched back the bow. 'No. Keep it controlled. Gods above and below, if today rests on you we might as well exsanguinate ourselves now.'

'Thank you, Anri.'

'Fuck off!' he called as he set off for the ruin of the bridge.

'Javani, a moment please.'

Javani was surprised to see Vida beckoning her over.

'Vida?'

'I want you to do something for me, young lady.'

'What?'

Vida put her fingers into her mouth and whistled, sharp and long. As the echoes from the cliffs above died away, she stood back, arms folded. Javani waited expectantly for something to happen, but nothing did. She began to wonder if the pressure of the upcoming battle had got to Vida and she'd started communicating in whistle-form, when she heard thudding footsteps and heavy panting approaching.

'Tarfellian!'

Vida offered her a tight smile. 'Take him up to the caves with you, please? Away from all this.'

She gave the dog a vigorous rub along his giant flank. Part of Javani was disappointed that Tauras had not appeared alongside him. 'You want me to look after him?'

Her smile cracked wide. 'Oh, no, girl, he'll look after you.'

Ree found herself left beside Camellia as she waited for the kid to gather herself for the trip up the cliff path to the caves. Their silence was far from companionable; the earlier absence of Camellia's hostility had apparently been an oversight, and readily corrected. As they waited, apparently for Vida to do something for or with the kid, the pressure grew, until at last Ree snapped.

'Your idea to send me up to the caves, was it? Is this some sort of twisted revenge for making you break whatever mystical bullshit vow you made?'

Camellia raised her gaze to the starless sky, letting the bite of the wind ruffle one loose braid that had escaped tying back, and said nothing.

'Maybe it wouldn't have come to this if you hadn't been afraid to show your strength earlier, did you ever think of that?' Ree went on. Her leg was really sore. 'There are always going to be wankers out there, looking to prey on weakness, and if you make yourself a target you'll start attracting them sooner or later.'

Camellia closed her eyes and took a slow breath, then opened them again. A faint look of disappointment clouded her face, as if let down that the world had remained unchanged in the interim.

Ree was still going. 'You can make all the vows you want to any and all gods of your choosing, but you can't choose your destiny. Our decisions matter, our actions matter, they have consequences, and what we face today is the cumulative result of yours and the rest of the Council's. I know you say I wanted this from the beginning, but I swear to you now that I never wanted this. I never wanted anything more than for you to live in peace and prosperity, without threat and exploitation . . .' She fell quiet for a moment. 'I wanted you to stand up for yourselves, that's all. To show that you weren't afraid of them . . .' Another pause. 'It was never my intention to inflame tensions or incite violence, only to push them away with a show of resolve . . .'

Camellia closed her eyes again. The faintest glimmer of dawn was rising in the east.

'I realise that not everything I did made things better,' Ree continued. 'I acknowledge that I made some missteps. But my intentions were always to free the people of Ar Ramas from effective enslavement, you have to see that.' She took another breath, and rested forward on her stick. 'I'm . . . I'm sorry, Camellia. For everything I did to make things worse. I never wanted this, and I'm sorry.'

'I know,' Camellia replied, slowly opening her eyes. 'I should have listened to you earlier. One-woman argument that you are.'

Ree looked up, uncertain. 'And I . . . should have respected your intentions.'

'We can both be sorry, then.'

They stood silently for a while, as a giant dog came loping past and bounced to a halt beside Vida and the kid.

'Oh, shit,' Ree muttered.

'What?'

'We've reached an understanding.'

'And that's bad?'

'Right before a battle? It's deadly. By the law of fate, one or both of us are now doomed.'

'Is that so?'

'In my experience, yes.'

'What do we do? Start another argument?'

Ree shook her head. 'Too late for that. We'll just have to follow the advice of an old colleague.'

'And what advice is that?'

Ree took another sharp breath and pushed herself upright. From the river path side came the plangent, urgent note of a horn, followed swiftly by another.

'Don't die.'

FIFTY-ONE

'Chapter Captain Manatas, are you healthy? Your pallor strikes my untrained eye as that of a man below his best, and on such a crucial day as this. I trust the advance of our schedule did not cause you undue . . . discomfort?' Lado advanced out of the mist, flanked by his lingering guard of those Pashani who had not left the day before to take the long route around to the pastures. He was wearing armour – not the mail and panels of their standard kit, but a great armoured shell that gleamed in the lantern-light and squeaked at the joints.

'You're wearing Ridderhof's harness . . .' Manatas blurted.

Lado inclined his head, lank hair drooping. The helmet was beneath one arm. 'The lord adjutant and I discussed matters, and we concluded that his own suit fits him far better.' He gestured behind him with his empty hand, where through the mist Manatas saw Botrys sitting serene on his horse, swathed in Ridderhof's old cloak. Lado had a wolf-pelt strung from his shoulders. 'I am humbled to receive such bounty from the company, and can only strive to give my all to prove a sliver of worth.'

Lado took another pace forward, the Pashani either side fanning out, moving without evident coordination to encircle him. Manatas felt very cold, yet sweat prickled the base of his back. They were too close now, to close to run from, to close to fight. And how would that look? One man against the acting commander? He could count on Arkadas at least, but the rest of his detachment were unlikely to throw in with insurrection, especially at the brink of their great pillaging. Lado had offered them an excuse to indulge their worst impulses and call it natural justice.

'I assure you, acting commander, that despite the hour I remain hale.' Manatas clapped his hands together in an attempt at dynamism. The sound was flat, muffled and weak against the stillness of the dark. Somewhere, an owl shrieked. Undeterred, Manatas pushed on. 'We have concluded our briefing and are ready to move into position. Should we advance?'

Lado offered an armoured palm. 'By all means, chapter captain, by all means, with just one last piece of housekeeping.' He took another step, almost close enough to reach out and grab Manatas. Manatas was suddenly conscious of the wicked skinning knife clipped to Lado's side. 'The lord adjutant has seen fit to refine his plans. Chapter Captain Jebel will be leading the assault across the ravine.'

Jebel loomed out of the gloom. He didn't even look at Manatas, moving straight past him to the head of the detachment. He was followed by some of the Eleventh Chapter, carrying two long timber constructions between them. Siege ladders, for the ravine, already prepared in secret.

'I'd be obliged to hear of these refinements,' Manatas stammered, trying to keep the panic from his voice. 'What are my new duties? Should my lieutenant remain in attendance?'

With a few gruff commands, Jebel had the detachment moving out of the camp in a shuffling jog, their gear clacking and jingling. Lado watched them for a moment, his tongue wetting his cracked lips, before he turned back to Manatas. 'You are to come with me, chapter captain. Your lieutenant too. Duty has placed her mark upon us today, and we must prove our worth.'

'You see, chapter captain,' Lado remarked as they crossed the camp towards where the other detachment had formed, 'I was struck by something, not that long ago, but I felt it was important to verify my assumptions from a trusted source.' The acting commander was walking just ahead of him, hands clasped at his back beneath the wolf-pelt. Pashani flanked Manatas and Arkadas as they walked, some carrying lanterns. One of them could have been Mantenu, it was hard to tell in the low light. 'A prudent approach, you would agree?'

The other detachment was arrayed and waiting. The dregs of the company, the Vistirlari, the drunk, the questionably sane, the obvious scoundrels – the group assigned to storm the winding river path up to the now-fortified escarpment. He recognised Zurab near the front, the late 'Fingers' Ioseb's confederate, the man he'd forced to the mud and threatened for his insolence. Zurab's gaze now was glassy with hostility. He'd been increasingly sullen since his chortling comrade Rostom had gone off on a scouting assignment some days ago and never returned. Manatas wouldn't have been surprised if the man had made a break for freedom. He swallowed. He had no wish to lead the worst of the company's troops into the teeth of the village's strongest defences. Falling repeatedly back and eventually giving up would be a lot harder without the excuse of a lack of suitable access.

'Prudent,' he echoed, his thoughts already devoted to engineering a way to achieve honourable failure in their assault. It had rained heavily overnight, perhaps if the path was too slippery, they'd be forced to construct an alternative—

Something cracked him across the backs of the legs and he stumbled, shocked and reeling, before another blow clipped the back of his head and he plunged face-first into sodden mulch. Pain bloomed, stinging across his legs, sharp and piercing at the back of his skull. He spat leaf-carcasses and raised his head.

'What in the name of all the—'

Taut fingers gripped his cheeks, stifling his words, dragging him up to his knees. He found himself staring into the fringe-framed and quite mad gaze of Lado of Cstethia. One of the Pashani was holding Lado's helmet. Manatas couldn't see his other hand. Behind him, his own hands were seized and bound before he could think to move them. 'Do you know, chapter captain, the penalty for treason against the company?'

He could feel the eyes of the detachment upon him. He'd wager Zurab was looking a sight more cheerful now. Someone had a heavy hand on his shoulder, keeping him on his knees, presumably the same person who'd beaten him with what might have been a spear butt. Where was Arkadas? Had they subdued him too?

Lado still had his face clenched in one hand, his fringe swaying in the flickering lamplight. 'Well, chapter captain? Speak up.'

He tried to speak, but his lips were crushed beneath Lado's frigid, foetid palm. The man had removed his gauntlet for this, which somehow made it worse. Manatas tried to shift, planting one boot in an attempt to push himself up, when he felt a line of something cold and prickly at his neck. Lado's other hand had made itself known, and it was holding a knife to his throat. Manatas froze.

'We're all waiting for an answer. Do you know the penalty for treason?'

Deprived of alternatives, he nodded. Carefully.

'Indeed, chapter captain, it's not a hard thing to guess, is it?' Lado released his face and turned away to face the waiting troops, but the knife remained where it was, as did the firm hand on his shoulder and its inexorable downward pressure. 'Betraying the company, your oath and contract, your sworn companions, well . . . there can be only one punishment for a crime so grave, so contrary to everything we hold dear and true. Betrayal!' The knife jumped at the word, and Manatas tried to edge back from it without success. 'From one of our own, a man trusted to lead, trusted to advise, trusted to stand side by side with his fellow men-at-arms, to carry their lives in his hands. Betrayal!' he spat again. The knife remained at Manatas' larynx, its keen edge beginning to warm. He could not stop himself trembling. He told himself it was only from the cold. Where was Arkadas?

'The loss of our weapons of range was a stroke of ill luck, was it not?' It wasn't clear who Lado was addressing now, facing the gathered mercenaries but with one hand still very much at Manatas's throat. 'Or was it? Such a precise, targeted fire, a line cut through our sentries, you would almost think our aggressor had known the precise layout of our camp, our very intentions. As if they had walked among us, hearing our words, studying our ways. Or perhaps the next best thing.' At last Lado stepped away from him, and the knife came too. Manatas almost sagged, but the pressure on his shoulder was undiminished. He wanted to look round, to see what they'd done to his lieutenant, but he didn't want to take his eyes off the acting commander while he paced with that blade in his hand.

'I had my suspicions,' Lado continued. The knife pirouetted between his fingers, flashing in the light. 'I'm sure we all did. But yesterday, a man approached the lord adjutant, and confessed to knowledge that fair made my heart stop.'

Manatas's mouth was half-open in shock, in denial, in dread. Now he turned. The hand on his shoulder belonged to—

'Arkadas . . . What did you do?'

The lieutenant could barely meet his eye. 'You were meeting her up on the hill, captain,' he whispered, his words choked and hoarse. 'You told her everything. You were selling us out, selling the company out to die.'

Manatas twisted in his grip. 'I wasn't— I was trying to prevent anyone dying!' he hissed, trying to keep his words for Arkadas alone. There might still be a way out of this, if he could get the lieutenant to recant his confession, claim he'd been mistaken, they could—

'I warned you about her, captain,' came the hushed and accusing response. 'How could you? We were brothers!'

'Arkadas, no!'

Lado was back, standing beside them, the knife twirling in his hand, and Manatas twisted to face him. Faint slivers of pale light had crept over the eastern peaks to their back. The first trills of impertinent birdsong had begun to tease the hills. His standing knee was thick with cold, the icy mud slick and cloying. His mouth was dry, and he had an overwhelming urge to urinate.

'Needless to say,' Lado barked, resting his empty hand on Manatas's other shoulder, 'this information has precipitated a number of actions, not least the refining of the lord adjutant's plans. Then there is the matter of the aforementioned punishment. Treason against the company, my friends, my sworn companions. Treason and treachery against us all. There can be only one penalty, and justice must be swift.'

The knife flashed in a silvery blur, whipped across Arkadas's throat before he could react, before he could even blink. Manatas felt a soft, hot spatter against his face, then the pressure from his shoulder lifted as the lieutenant clamped his hand to his open neck, wall-eyed and gasping.

'Arkadas!' Manatas roared as he struggled to his feet. Lado kicked his foot from under him and he went crashing straight back to the squelching earth. 'Arkadas!' he bellowed again, half-muffled by mud and decaying plant matter. Lado rested one foot on his back to keep him down. Through tear-shocked eyes he saw his lieutenant stagger and drop, thick ribbons of steaming blood, made black by the lantern-light, coursing through his grasping fingers. Arkadas came to rest facing him across the churned filth of the camp floor, his lifeblood pooling in swirling puddles, his face pale and eyes darting as strength left him. Finally they seized on Manatas, first shocked, then pleading, then as his movements slowed, fixed with pitiful apology. His lips moved, shaped to speak, but no sound followed them.

'Arkadas,' Manatas moaned through a mouthful of clinging debris, watching the light fading from his friend's gaze. 'Arkadas, you'll . . . We'll . . . We'll see the lake again, you hear? I'll . . . I'll meet you there.'

Arkadas rocked gently twice more then fell still. His fingers dropped from the ghastly wound at his neck, which continued to pump ever smaller jets of blood in defiance of its owner's passing. Manatas lay with eyes locked on the vacant stare of his lieutenant, his friend, unable to tear himself away, unable to force himself up from beneath Lado's boot.

'A terrible thing,' the acting commander pronounced, 'but there was nothing more to be done. To engage in such egregious treachery, then attempt to engineer suspicion against his commander for his own crimes?' Lado tutted, no doubt shaking his head along with it. 'I cannot abide disloyalty. We must respect the chain of command. We must have *discipline*, or are we not animals?'

Manatas didn't see the signal, but he was hauled back to his knees by two of the Pashani. He knelt, one side of his face caked with stinking mud, flakes of decaying leaf mashed in with it, the bitter taste of death in his mouth. The urge to urinate was gone, replaced by a stifling numbness, a vague and growing distance from the world.

Lado had retrieved his helmet and was holding it up to the light. 'Now of course, Chapter Captain Manatas, while you cannot be blamed for the crimes of those under your command, we are a professional company, and we expect . . . accountability. The man was yours, and his actions . . . mark you.'

Lado stepped closer, running his other hand through his hair and this time holding it in place, revealing in the lantern-light the full extent of the grooved scars across his cheeks. Manatas started when he realised that beneath Lado's hand, the ear normally hidden by the fall of his hair was little more than a hacked stub. Perhaps this accounted for the tilt of his head, always favouring his good ear.

Manatas did not like where this was going.

Lado cast an eye up to the lightening sky, the heavy, sombre clouds now veined with tiny splashes of creeping copper through the mist above their heads. 'Time is against us, but these things are important, don't you think? We must have discipline.'

'Lado, acting commander, listen—'

Strong hands gripped his arms, keeping him immobile, his wrists lashed behind him, while another grasped a fistful of his hair and yanked his head back and to one side. He felt horribly vulnerable, his throat naked and exposed, just as Arkadas's had been, the side of his face open to Lado's caprice. He became suddenly conscious of the thud of blood in his ears, the whisper of wind across their surface, the burn of cold along their edges. In all his years of life, he'd never given much thought to his ears, but now he could think of nothing else.

'Now, what should it be?' Lado mused, swaying from foot to foot in Manatas's periphery. The knife was back in his hand, a small, sharp, silver thing that seemed to slither between his fingers as he contemplated. 'What will carry the message to our company that we are accountable for our actions?'

'Cut off his ears!' It was Zurab the Vistirlari, exuberant and rambunctious. With grit-toothed regret Manatas remembered his own threats to the man. *I have known captains who would carve the skin from your face at this time, cut the ears from your skull or sever your digits, and should I choose to mirror them, not a man in this camp would stop me.* Of course he hadn't meant it, it had been for show. For . . . discipline. How the world turns.

'Acting Captain Zurab is full of ideas,' Lado grinned. 'Such a good friend to my dear cousin, so . . . loyal.'

Acting captain? That stung as much as—

The knife slid into the flesh of his auricle, carving straight through the upper rim and almost to his ear canal. He felt the blade's tip score a line along his scalp beneath. Manatas shrieked. Manatas writhed. The knife remained lodged in his ear, its hilt still in Lado's hand, and the acting commander's head swayed as he watched its travels with what would otherwise have been comical intensity.

Clamped in the Pashani's grip, Manatas's struggles achieved nothing. Hot pain radiated from the mangled organ, as hot as the blood he felt coursing over his face and neck. His ear was gummed and sticky with pooling fluid, his hearing distorted, a ghastly feeling of air moving over the exposed edges of the cut, and *there was still a knife stuck in his ear*.

'Yes!' screamed Zurab. 'More!'

His voice was not alone. Manatas took an idle instant to reflect on his leadership of the chapter, and that he felt he'd done better than his current situation would otherwise suggest. It was hard not to feel a little hard done by when *there was still a knife stuck in his ear*.

'Do you feel it, chapter captain?' Lado's voice was low and close, muffled by the rivulets of blood that streamed into his ear hole. 'Do you feel accountable for your actions?' He leaned in close, his scarred cheek filling Manatas's limited vision. 'Do you feel the binding of law, or are we animals?'

There had to be a correct answer. What did Lado want to hear? Was there anything that would get the knife removed before it did more damage?

Manatas hissed through his teeth. 'Yes?'

'I wish I could believe,' Lado replied sadly. He turned away, and whipped out the knife as he went. Manatas screamed again. Not from the pain, but from the sight of a small triangle of flesh spinning through the lamplit air, trailing a gory arc as it fell. He fought to press a hand to the damage, to probe the extent of the wound, to staunch the reinvigorated cascade of blood down the side of his head. His arms were pinned fast, his hands still bound.

Lado regarded him, head tilted, his face slick and shiny beneath the shadow of his hair, as he slowly wiped the knife on a fistful of fallen leaves. 'You will feel it soon, chapter captain. You see, I was there when Ozuri fell. Do you remember? I was but a boy, and I saw what happened when the walls came down. To my family. To my neighbours.

To the people I'd known. It was then I learned, chapter captain, that there are no rules. There is no law but what we make for ourselves, what we take for ourselves. There is nothing but our will.'

Manatas tried to pull away when Lado leaned in again, but he was held fast. His ear throbbed like at least four hells. 'We make the world, Chapter Captain Manatas. We need only believe. And we are animals.' Lado's breath was hot and sour against his cheek. 'Do you feel it now?'

This time, when he nodded, feeling the pull of his scalp against the fist that gripped his hair, Lado smiled. 'Then we must proceed, for time is against us. Boys!'

The Pashani pulled Manatas upright. His knee ached and was coated with muck, and there was a weird and unpleasant whistling sound in his damaged ear. Then his hands were free, his bonds cut, and he almost collapsed when they released their hold on him. Rubbing his hands against each other, massaging the life back into them, he tried to summon the strength to test the extent of his maiming. Was that all it was to be? Was Lado truly a forgiving sort? Manatas did not entertain for a moment the notion that he had believed Arkadas responsible for the loss of their bows. His murder had been an act of vicious spite, and when the opportunity presented itself, Manatas would—

'Chapter captain, you are in no state to lead the detachment. Be reassured – the company provides.'

The Pashani were back around him, too many, on all sides, crowding him as he pushed up his arms to ward his ruined ear. His belt was snapped away, his sword and knives with it, then a spear was pressed into his hands. No, not a spear – the company standard, its sodden pennant drooping. One of the Pashani clamped his hands together around it, while another stepped around him, narrow cord in his hands. An instant later, Manatas stood unarmed but for a pole knotted to his hands. At least they were no longer bound behind him.

'What in the name of—'

'Perhaps a moment of quiet reflection would suit you, chapter captain?'

Something rank was forced into his mouth, old cloth that tasted of stagnant water, then lashed taut around the base of his skull. He gagged, or tried to, the foul mass in his mouth blocking anything more than an involuntary bob.

'About time he learned to shut up!' came Zurab's crowing.

'And now, something appropriate for your place as our standard carrier at the head of the column.'

Something heavy across his back, hairy and stinking. He thought for a moment they'd thrown a sheep's corpse over his shoulders, but then he saw the colour of the fur as they dragged the covering over his arms, tying it in place. Ridderhof's great bearskin. A terrible weight pressed on his head and neck, the pressure severe, then with a crunch they forced the animal's head over his own, his ravaged ear shrieking along with him as it scraped over his flesh. His view of the world was now blocked but for a slot of lantern-lit forest floor, framed by the poor dead animal's giant fangs.

Lado was not, after all, the forgiving sort.

'Fitting, don't you think, chapter captain?' Lado leaned in again to whisper. 'I like to think it's what he would have wanted, don't you?'

Manatas could not reply, his mouth gagged, his ear aflame, his vision obscured and his hands lashed to a useless length of sodden wood. He could only sob silently in the musty, stinking darkness of the bear's head. His wrists and waist were now roped to something else, a trailing cord he couldn't see through the bear's mouth. The line jerked, and he stumbled forward after it, trying not to trip over the pole lashed to his hands.

'Company of the Wolf! Acting Captain Zurab will be taking command of your assault, but Chapter Captain Manatas will be at the vanguard. The lord adjutant and I wish you good fortune, and remember . . . we'll be right behind you.'

FIFTY-TWO

'Are you sure you don't want me to carry some of that?' Javani glanced at her mother sidelong as they climbed the narrow, winding path hacked into the cliff-face up towards the caves. They hadn't yet travelled far from the upper terrace but already the drop to her right was precipitous. 'I mean, you've got your stick, and your sword, and the bow, and the arrows, and—'

'I can manage,' Ree snapped in a pained and breathless voice that very much suggested she couldn't. 'Their mistake . . . not to let me hold the line with them,' she groused between heavy breaths, 'I'm perfectly capable of . . . climbing . . . a hill.'

'Ma, we're scaling a mountain,' Javani replied, a little ashamed of how easy her breath was in comparison. 'Just one they cut steps into. Sure you don't want me to take something?'

'Carry your sacks . . . and keep quiet.'

Ahead of them, the trail kinked, and a gentle squeaking announced the passing of the hoist. The thick ropes ran through a series of pulleys overhead at the lip of the caves, running bundles of supplies from the stores to the terraces and back as required. A taut bundle of nets bigger than Javani rose past them bulging with river stone, while somewhere in the mist above the very last of the stored equipment would be making its gentle, swaying passage downward. It had never occurred to Javani to wonder how a village of peace-seeking farmers had so much ordnance hidden in caves. Now she was kicking herself that she hadn't seen it when Ree had: who wants peace more than those sick of fighting wars?

Javani watched the rocks squeak past, keeping one eye on the mist-slick steps ahead. 'We could have asked for a lift on the hoist. If we nip back down, we might catch it going back up.'

'I said . . . keep quiet.'

'Come on, Ma, you can understand why they sent you back from the line, can't you? Most of people in this place are young, fit, healthy – and they all work outside with their hands. How many more of them used to be soldiers, do you think? 'Cos it seems like more of them were than weren't. At this rate, I wouldn't be surprised if we got to the top and found Mani in war armour and toting a scimitar.'

'Will you . . . hush.'

'Can I have the bow? I've been practising, and Anri gave me some pointers. Finally.'

Ree came to a stop, leaning one shoulder against the pitted rock. Sweat stood clear on her brow in the growing dawnlight. 'No.'

'You still don't trust me!'

'. . . But you can have this.' She proffered something from her cargo, then hoicked it back as Javani reached for it. '*If* you keep your mouth shut for the rest of the climb.'

It was the hand-bow. She'd not seen it since they'd arrived at the village, not held it since she'd loosed the ill-fated bolt that had buried itself in a doomed mercenary's leg. Delicate, unreliable, inaccurate, weak . . . It was better than nothing.

'I'll take it.' She looked out into what should have been a magnificent vista of the valley at dawn, but was instead a drifting mass of paling haze, growing in light and colour as the distant sun finally crested the jagged eastern horizon. 'Do you think we'll climb above the mist? It would be nice to have a view.'

From the village's far side, another horn blared. Ree's tired scowl became a grimace. 'You might not like what you see, kid.' She pushed herself off from the wall, planting her stick on the damp rock despite her unwieldy goods. 'Come on, less yap, more, uh, soar.'

'Yes, Ma,' Javani sighed, and resumed her climb. Below them, the valley echoed with the squall of horns.

* * *

Mist cloaked the pasture, its rolling slopes buried under dense swathes of crawling cloud. From the crest of the thick timber barricade at the neck of the trail, Keretan peered down the widening path towards where he knew the forest resumed around the curve of the forge and the schoolhouse, but they and the smiths' hut were completely lost, even in the burgeoning gloam of dawn. In the feeble, greyish light, he could see little of the maze of pits and traps that marred the slope to their position, barely more than occasional patches of churned earth and drifts of swept leaves. Somewhere a woodpecker was calling. Aside from that, the scene was silent and still.

'Well?'

The mercenary, Kediras. She was right behind him at the barricade's foot, her acrid stink preceding her by a clear stride. Over her shoulder, the path wound down towards the shrouded village, the way blocked with a series of further barricades, and – although harder to spot – further traps. Their defence in depth. Another horn blared from somewhere on the village's far side, echoing from the cliffs, sending another flight of late-season birds into the bleak winter sky.

Keretan shook his head. In spite of Vida's efforts, the armour did not fit him well; it chafed at the joints, and the helmet was cold and heavy against his head. And despite the biting cold of the morning, sweat still crawled down his back and his fingers trembled. He had to keep his legs widely spaced for fear their quivering would make the armour rattle. His guts roiled, an urgent, phantom need to void his bowels vying with a queasy giddiness that surged up into his chest every few heartbeats. When he spoke, he could hear the shake in his voice. 'Nothing yet.'

Another distant horn, and the faint echoes of shouts from down-valley. Could that have been a clash of steel? From the pasture, only the solitary woodpecker. Kediras cleared her throat, the sound bristling with impatience. She was decked in mail and panels, two swords strapped at her belt, and held her long and wicked spear brushing the brim of her broad hat. Her meaning was clear: *I was told this was where the thick of the fighting would be, yet it seems to be everywhere else but here.*

Keretan already regretted his earlier bravado. He felt hollow and fragile, little more than a gold-shelled egg. And while he was glad not to yet be battling for his life and the lives of his friends and family, the thought that others might be for his only made the sweats and nausea worse. The long-handled hammer he carried, salvaged from the forge, seemed an imposter in his hand. Could he hit anyone with it, if the time came? He gazed across the barricade, at the other villagers alongside him and crouched behind, improvised weapons clenched in their equally pale-knuckled hands. Some of them had fought in the past, he knew that. But all had come to Ar Ramas because they wished never to fight again. And he and Camellia had failed them.

The mercenary cleared her throat again, then belched. She looked like she hadn't slept more than an hour for several days, and from the stinging waves of second-hand aquavit coming off her, he was amazed the woman could stand, yet alone purport to fight. That she bristled with weapons was no reassurance; she was as likely to take an arm off one of the defenders as any unseen attacker if she started swinging those swords around.

'The thick of the fighting,' she growled with prolonged enunciation.

'Ree seemed to believe that—'

'How much do you trust her? This woman who came out of the forest and made havoc for you?'

Keretan stiffened. 'I trust that she believed what she told us.'

The mercenary sniffed and adjusted her hat, swaying slightly. The cold didn't seem to touch her, possibly because she was cloaked in a finger's width aura of pure alcohol. The horns had stopped blaring, but now the cries and shrieks that drifted towards them from the edges of the village were unmistakable. He had to hope it was their attackers stumbling into the traps they had laid. Perhaps they would stumble and withdraw. Perhaps. He risked another sweaty look over his shoulder, the rim of the armour rubbing the skin of his neck through his undershirt. At least there was no mercenary company charging up the path behind them.

'She said the Pashani would come.' The mercenary's teeth were bared. 'Where are they? Did she lie?'

Keretan stepped down from the barricade to face her, suppressing the grimace from the creak of his knees as he dismounted. 'I think she deserves some credit, don't you? Or did you forget it was at her insistence that we released you to fight?'

The woman's stare was a thousand miles away. 'And does that strike you as a wise choice?' she murmured. She shook her head, only the faintest wobble of her hat. 'I must seek the Pashani.' She turned in the direction of the trail to the village.

'Wait, you're leaving? You can't leave!' Behind him, the other defenders stirred, unnerved by the mercenary's presence but aghast at the thought she might abandon them.

'Call for me if the Pashani appear,' she barked over her shoulder, her swords bouncing at her belt as she made her unsteady way back down the path, weaving between the first of the traps.

'That's—' Keretan paused, cocked an ear. Was that . . . He glanced around. The villagers had been distracted by the mercenary's departure, had anyone been—

A shriek rent the air, a howl of shock and pain. It came from the far side of the barricade. Keretan fair leaped back up it, peering into the mist. There, one of the leaf-piles had collapsed. Movement, a figure in a drab cloak trying to rise, then tumbling back into the pit and screaming again. His eyes adjusted to the drifting glow of the mist banks . . . other figures, crawling, hunched against the soft earth, moving silently towards the barricades. At least, silently until one of them had dropped into a shallow pit of sharpened stakes. His eyes scanned down. They were closer than he realised, closer than he'd thought possible. One of them . . . One of them was at the foot of the barricade, one arm poised to climb.

Keretan froze, his eyes locked on the man. He was staring back, and slowly he began to smile.

The smile vanished as Kediras's spear punched past Keretan's elbow and through the man's throat. He dropped, screaming, as a pungent waft of alcohol announced her presence. She craned forward over the barricade, squinting at the gurgling, thrashing man, one hand keeping the butt of the spear steady, and sniffed again. 'Not Pashani,' she muttered. 'Call me if they come.' She pushed the spear haft against him and slid away. 'Keep the spear,' was her parting shot.

One hand on his hammer, one hand on the spear, Keretan stared at the dying man at the base of the barricade, the torrents of his blood already turning the seething earth to oily mulch, and vomited.

Gasping, his convulsions passed in an instant, he found his height again. The urge to void his bowels had receded, his trembling stilled, replaced by a strange, delicate calm. He thought of his children, pictured their gappy, uneven smiles, felt the crush of their enthusiastic affections.

'Ar Ramas!' he bellowed, raising the hammer as the wave of mercenaries closed in. Behind him, their horn blew clear and true. 'To arms!'

Mariam stood rigid, gazing through mist. It drifted across the river path, rolling lazily over the network of blockades and barriers the villagers had erected along it, between the pits and wires and ropes they'd strung through every narrow gap along its winding route. She kept the bowstring taut against her fingers, just enough pressure to dimple their calloused skin. It had been a while, but her fingertips hadn't forgotten, and neither had she.

'Asherah, hold that arrow nocked,' she barked, keeping her voice low in the mist-dampened hush. 'Yasha, back straight, eyes front.'

Beside her was Vida's comforting presence. She drew strength from knowing her wife was there, silent and poised, watchful and ready; enough strength to suppress the gnawing anxiety that had edged out her natural dread of the coming confrontation. They'd sighted the enemy early, their horns in a chorus of alarm, but the mercenaries they'd spotted through cloud at the river bank on the valley floor had yet to cross. They were waiting for something, and whatever it was, she did not like it. In the meantime, horns blew from the waterfall side, urgent, insistent.

Vida grunted.

Mariam kept her eyes on the path. 'My love?'

'Anri's hitting that horn pretty hard.'

'Do you think he needs help?'

Vida grunted again. 'That was supposed to be their weak flank. They need to cross the ravine unsupported and into the pikes of our defenders. I'd guess Anri just wants someone to witness his brilliance.'

From behind them, running footsteps, thudding on cold earth, then a splatter, a slip, and a squelch. 'Great thumping sheep-shit!'

Now, she turned. 'Anri? What in the name of . . . why aren't you at the bridge?'

He looked up from the slick, muddy ground of the terrace, glowering through a caked layer of muck. His entire front was black with it. He'd managed to keep his bowstring clean, at least. 'Getting fucking overrun, aren't we?' he spat. 'We've been blowing on that horn like a lamb's cock, where's our support, then?'

Vida swivelled, her eyes intent. 'Overrun? On the weak flank?'

Anri picked himself up, brushing what sludge he could from his filthy clothing. 'Weak flank my pimpled arse. They brought stuff with them! Stuff!'

'Stuff?'

He waved a muck-caked hand. 'Their own fucking bridges! With sides! We kicked the first one off and sent them packing, but we can see they've got more.' He snarled. 'Busy little fuckers, they are.'

'We can't leave our post, Anri,' Mariam chided. She already felt guilty for diverting her attention from the river path. 'Camellia has command of the reserve – go and find her on the upper terrace.'

He raised his mud-slathered face to the sky. 'Going to make me run up the fucking steps now, are you?'

'You could have sent someone else,' Vida observed.

'Needed some more arrows, anyway, and everyone else has their hands full with poles,' he snapped, grabbing a fistful from Mariam's stock and tucking them into his earth-slick quiver. 'Go and run my little legs up to Camellia now, shall I?'

'Yes,' Vida replied, turning back to the valley.

'Though gods know if she didn't come for the signal, she'll no doubt have pressing business elsewhere,' he muttered as he shouldered his bow and turned for the path to the terrace stairs. 'Oh.'

A figure was marching down the path towards them. A figure in mail, two swords at its belt. Mariam's heart stopped. The mercenaries were already inside the village, they had—

Wait. It was Kediras. Ree had assured them she was friendly. Well, not hostile. Well, unlikely to murder them. Today.

'The Pashani?' the woman demanded as she approached. Close to, her steps seemed a little unsteady, although she did not slip in Anri's mud-patch. 'Are they here?'

'We don't know,' Vida said, not turning. 'Ours haven't crossed the river yet.'

The woman sniffed.

Anri sidled back a step. 'If it's conflict you're after, things are getting pretty tasty on the falls side, I have to say.'

'Are the Pashani there?'

He didn't even hesitate. 'Almost certain, I am.'

She didn't reply, just set off on her weaving march in the direction of the waterfall. Anri watched her go for a moment, then remembered himself. 'Right. Camellia.'

'You don't think Kediras will help?' Mariam asked as he made to depart.

'Between us,' Anri said as he moved away with careful steps, 'I wouldn't recognise a Pashani if one sat on my face and farted the song of its people, but I'm willing to bet that she would, and I'd like some backup present if it turns out I just chatted through my arse.'

He vanished into the mist.

Mariam chewed her lip. 'Should one of us—'

'No,' Vida replied.

'But what if—'

Vida put her hand on Mariam's arm. Her touch was still thrilling, even after all the years. 'If we go,' she said, meeting her wife's gaze, 'we go together. For now, we hold fast, we watch, we listen, and we wait.'

They'd been waiting for him, the advance line, waiting for the main body to join, waiting for their 'standard bear-er'. Zurab had come close to soiling himself with mirth at that one. He yanked on the rope lashed around Manatas's wrists, dragging him one way, then another, while the erstwhile chapter captain struggled to maintain his balance in the roiling mud left by the passage of dozens of pairs of boots before his, planting the pole where he could, trying not to slip and be trampled. He was half-deaf, half-blind beneath the bear, his ear burning and gummed with blood, his vision limited to a tiny, fang-framed slot of drab ground before him. He couldn't even tilt his head backwards, and if he tried to lean, Zurab merely jerked the rope again. At least, wrapped as he was, he wasn't too cold.

At a signal they forded the river. Acting Captain Zurab took particular delight in forcing Manatas into the icy, knee-deep water, while he walked over the low bridge himself, apparently indifferent to the risk of traps or snares upon it, leading Manatas like a recalcitrant hound. There were, disappointingly, no snares upon the bridge, but the moment they reached the far bank, and the scale of the great granite escarpment that came looming out of the mist became apparent to the mercenaries around him, the horns began again. An instant later, the first arrow hit, thumping into the smooth stones at the river's edge a little to his right, skittering and crackling. More arrows followed, their locations and targets lost to him in his great bear head, but the grunts and yowls around him suggested they'd hit more than stone.

The rope dragged him onward, boots scrabbling on soft earth as the bank rose steeply before him, the base of the weathered path along the cliffside a few impossible strides ahead. More arrows, hissing and whistling, a sound like cracking when they hit rock, a ringing thud when they hit flesh. More cries, some screams, and already a low keening, a wordless plea for salvation that would never arrive. And somewhere in the woods behind, floating through fog, the soft notes of Keds's flute, haunting, menacing.

The rope dragged him onward, into the mist and towards damnation.

FIFTY-THREE

'Ma, come away from the edge. Ma! You're too close.' Javani pushed herself up from the rock, folding away the hand-bow. 'Don't make me drag you back from there.'

Ree was at the very lip of the rock shelf that marked the junction of the caves, not far from the pulleys of the hoist, one hand on her stick, the other shading her eyes against the glare of what passed for dawn in the choked air of the valley. She was alone against the grey blur of sky; most of the villagers deemed 'non-combatants' for reason of age, infirmity or disposition were already ensconced in the tunnelled rock behind them, in the narrow areas until recently occupied by the shameful stockpile of tools of war.

Mani and Volkan remained in the open, however, although neither seemed inclined to resume the game of stones they'd seemingly begun at an earlier stage. Volkan paced, his gaunt face taut with unease, while Mani leaned heavily on his stick, head bowed, lips moving. Javani paused as she passed them.

'Mani, are you praying?' she asked. She'd not heard the old man mention gods once, despite the spiritual position he seemed to hold for the community.

Volkan snorted, the disquiet vanishing from his expression. 'Prayers in times of crisis are no true measure of faith, but a coward's gambit,' he crowed, derision dripping from his words. 'Were there such a thing as gods, how might they delight in the eternal torture of the deathbed convert, who thinks them too stupid to remark upon a lifetime of impiety!'

Javani regarded him levelly. 'You're not a believer, then, Volkan?'

He only snorted again, and turned away.

'Well, happens I know a little about gambits myself,' she muttered. 'Mani, are you all right?'

He blinked, and his filmy eyes drifted to her. 'All is well, my child. It is in times of stress and worry that we must remember what we love, and what loves us in return.' He offered a muted smile, his moustache bristling sideways. 'No matter the rest, it is our love that makes us, and it is our love that endures. Can you remember that?'

She nodded vaguely, mirroring his smile without really knowing why. She felt guilty for having the hand-bow on her. 'I'll try, Mani.'

'Good girl.' He looked past her. 'You may need to drag your mother back after all . . .'

'Oh, gods damn it all . . . Ma!'

Ree waved her away, free hand swiping in irritation, the movement taking her perilously close to the plateau's edge. Beyond it, Javani knew without needing to look, was only clear, cold air, and a drop of longer than she fancied towards the terraces below. She reached out a steadying hand and took a cautious grip on her mother's arm.

'You're too close, Ma. A strong gust and you're crow-food.' She paused. 'And they'd make me clear you up, I just know it. You wouldn't do that to me, would you?'

Ree didn't even smile. 'It's wrong, kid,' she murmured. 'Something's wrong down there. I can feel it. Gods damn this mist!'

Javani tightened her grip. 'Ma. Come away from the edge. The mist will clear soon,' – maybe – 'and when it does, we'll have a decent view from up here. It'll only be worse at ground level,' she added meaningfully.

Ree grunted in acknowledgement, but she did not move.

'We must fall back,' Keretan whispered, his voice hoarse and hollow. 'We must fall back to the third line.'

The outer ring was already lost, abandoned as the enemy pressed, and enough of them had now massed at the second row of bulwarks that it was only a matter of time before Keretan and his defenders were swarmed. So many of his people hurt, so many cut and fractured. Ree's words played over and over in his head. *Always fall back! Do not attempt to fight them.* She'd made it sound so easy. The reality was that turning their back on the enemy was tantamount to suicide, but engaging them in direct combat was little better. The traps had slowed them, thinned them, funnelled them, but not enough. There had to be the better part of thirty mercenaries in fighting shape forming up at the barricade, and if they left it too long to pull back they'd be caught in place and cut off. That would mean failure. That would mean death. Keretan would not fail.

But after the third line, there was only the village. The village of his family, of his friends, the village he had spent so much of himself to build. The village he'd claimed he'd lay down his life to protect. He hesitated. Perhaps if he sent the rest of the defenders back, he could slow the mercenaries' advance long enough for . . . long enough for . . .

He swallowed. There was no help coming. He could not fight the men and women clambering over the barricades towards him, he could only swing hammer and spear and try to beat them away. They would overpower him, bring him low, and through the gaps in his armour they would pierce him. He was no soldier, no captain. He was no leader. He would fail. Tears blurred his vision, and his throat tightened as he inhaled to give the order to retreat.

A shape in his vision, little more than a fuzzy silhouette, arrived with a cry and a call to arms. 'Hold! Ar Ramas, hold this line! Pikes to the fore! Archers, clear them!'

Keretan could barely speak. 'Camellia?'

Her braids were drawn and bundled, and her mail rippled in the silver light. 'Don't waste energy on conversation,' she muttered, her spear tight in her hands. 'Let's just get this done.'

It was scant comfort that Manatas could not see the carnage. Hearing it was somehow worse. He trudged slowly uphill, the weight of the sodden bearskin pressing upon him, the mud that alternated between slick rivers and frozen crusts taking both his concentration and the strength in his legs. He could see only downward, but for once he wasn't too displeased, happy to let Zurab steer him with yanks of the rope: unique among the mercenaries struggling up the cliff path, Manatas was watching his step.

They'd left the river bank behind and below, along with some of their less fortunate comrades, pierced by arrows or downed by whistling chunks of hard grey stone hurled from higher up the path. Those struck were unfortunate indeed; it was clear from the parabolas of the scattered volleys that the archers above them were well short of practised, assuming they could even see clearly through the mist. That said, his good ear was still ringing from a whistling stone that had glanced off the bear's head and splattered into the mud behind him.

And now, as they wound their way up the switchbacks of the narrow path, they met the traps and the obstacles that had been laid for them with such guile that he was, on one level, impressed, and on another, far more primal level, terrified. It was already clear that no matter how fierce the resistance they met, there would be no falling back, no retreat. The mercenaries around him were caught between a furious drive to take what had been promised to them and a dread of what might happen if they fell short in their attempts. Lado was behind them, that much was clear, although his exact whereabouts were a nebulous mystery, just vague enough to have them looking over their shoulders at the merest thought of withdrawal. The mocking trill of the flute was never far away, and never in the same place twice.

Manatas concentrated on getting one foot in front of the other, digging in with the base of the standard pole, keeping himself upright against the treacherous slope. Still it rained rocks, small ones that pinged and crackled, larger ones that clonked and thumped on their descent. Every attempt to take cover from the barrage turned up another surprise in waiting – a scree-banked pit, lined with stakes, had taken a man two strides ahead of him who'd leaped for what had looked like safety, and the stack of leaf-mould concealing an upturned scythe beside it had claimed the comrade who'd rushed to help him. Now progress was more cautious, every suspicious lump and divot probed from safety, but the cascade of falling stone had not eased, and the air around him was suffused with the agonised curses of injured or frantic professional soldiery. Their mail was stout, their helmets solid, and most would be little more than bruised, but the thud and clang of rock on mercenary and the echoing crump of rock on shields were distressing even if they didn't prove fatal. He didn't need to look up to know that carrion birds were gathering in anticipation of worse to come; he could hear the hunger in their caws.

A thwack and cry signalled another of his supposed comrades had encountered an unpleasant surprise at the next corner: the judder of a bent trunk, now straightened, and the gravelly tumble of the keening man from the path's edge, crunching down the cliff-side as he fell. Manatas realised the rope had gone slack; Zurab was no longer dragging him on. Had the fallen man been Zurab? Did that mean—

'Keep moving, standard bear,' came a snarling voice directly behind his good ear. It had a Vistirlari accent. 'You're the vanguard now.'

'For the sake of the gods, Ma, come away from the edge!'

Her mother was pacing again, her stick clomping, the sword slapping against her leg. This time, Javani took hold of her arm with emphatic force.

'What do you expect me to do, kid? The fucking mist is loitering like an unwelcome dinner guest, but even the Watcher of the fucking Rau Rel could see it's shaping up to be a disaster down there, and he was blind!'

'The what?'

'Never mind.' Ree twisted, pulling Javani with her, and pointed with her stick. 'Camellia's gone from the centre, and the bulk of the reserve with her. It's barely first phase! See over there, on the pasture trail? Keretan has troops at the second line already, and from the way his people are moving back they may not hold it long. If that's where Camellia and the reserve are . . . Gods! And listen – hear that? There's combat on the bridge side. Combat!'

'They're not supposed to be fighting?'

She nodded, her mouth a grim line. 'They should be easily pushed back on the crossing, not able to engage. Either my man lied, which I doubt, or he's no longer in a position to influence events.'

Javani read her mother's expression, the set of her jaw, the lines below her eyes. 'You like him.'

Ree blinked, and the only emotion left in her gaze was fury. 'We've got nothing in the centre, kid, and the flanks are about to collapse. You know what happens to the front line when it does?'

Javani raised her shoulders helplessly. The sooner they were both away from the edge, the better. 'It falls back?'

'It gets pulverised. Probably not far from the stables.' Ree stepped back from the edge, at last, and Javani unclenched herself. Her mother swivelled on her good heel, marking the progress of the narrow path back down to the distant terraces below. 'It's too far,' she murmured. 'Too far.'

'Ma – what are you thinking?' Javani's tone had a warning note that she was more accustomed to hearing than using.

'I've got to get down there.'

'Uh, what? You most certainly do not.'

'We're falling back too much on the pasture side – they should have been able to hold for hours, especially with the reserve. Something is terribly wrong. We have no idea how bad things are on the bridge side, but Anri has been dashing around like a post-decapitation bantam, which bodes very ill. We have no reserve left to commit, and our whole plan is based around falling back in the face of the enemy, which only works *if you have somewhere to fall back to*.'

'Meaning?'

'If one or, gods help us, both flanks fall in, the bandits are going to be *behind* our people at the front. When they try to fall back, they'll find heavily armed mercenaries waiting for them. They'll be ground like mill-flour.'

'What can we do? Send a signal? Use the horns?'

'How the fuck do you signal something like that, kid?'

'I don't know, I'm not a signals expert, am I? And it's not like you involved me in the planning, is it?'

Ree gave a short, amused snort. 'You sound like Anri.'

'Oh, piss off.'

'Yup, just like him.' Ree looked past her to where Mani and Volkan now held court with some of the younger adolescents who'd been dispatched to the caves, spared from the fighting for either their own good or the peace of mind of their families. Javani was glad to see Lali among them. 'Hoy,' Ree called, 'which of you knows how to operate this?'

She was pointing at the hoist.

'Ma? Ma!' Javani grabbed Ree's arm, pulling her back, and did her best to fix her mother with her fiercest stare. 'This is not a good idea. I need you to consider, just for a moment, the possibility that you might be wrong, that this time Camellia and the others know better. That this really isn't your business! Can you do that?'

Ree's frown was undercut by the panic in her eyes. 'I . . . can't. I can't leave it.'

'Ma! If you go down there, you may not get back up. And, and . . . someone else might, someone we don't want to see. Are you going to be comfortable with that outcome, with me and the others left up here, without you?'

Ree held her glare for a moment, her frown relaxing. 'I trust you, kid.'

And that was it. In short order, Ree had bound herself like a bundle of timbers, good foot through the bottom loop, and stepped off the cliff edge to swing in space. Javani quailed at the sight of it, her knees buckling beneath her; Mani had to hold her up.

'Listen up,' Ree bellowed to the young man who was operating the complex and, to Javani's eyes at least, terrifying mechanism of the hoist. His name was Arman, and Javani guessed he was no more than two years older than her, but his confidence in working the various brakes and pulleys reassured her that he at least knew a little of what he was doing. 'Once I'm at the bottom, haul this assembly right back up and lock the mechanism – we do not want anyone unexpected coming up the way I went down. Then watch the path, and if you see anyone climbing it you don't recognise, don't hesitate. Understand? Good. Now let's go.' She shifted the bow hooked over her shoulder. 'And don't fucking drop me!'

Javani swallowed hard as she watched the wheel begin to turn, Arman's hands steady on the draw handles, and her mother's feet slid out of sight. She was already rotating slowly. How many times had she watched Ree head for death and danger, with no certainty of return? And yet, she'd always come back. So far, at least.

Their eyes met just before she twisted out of sight below the lip of the shelf.

'I trust you, kid,' Ree repeated quietly.

'Sure,' Javani said, her voice tight. 'Don't be wrong.'

Then she was gone. Javani became aware of Lali, hovering uncertain at her elbow. She hadn't noticed the other girl's approach.

'Will she be all right?' Lali asked. She looked like she'd been chewing her nails again, and her lips were stained with ink.

'Yeah,' Javani replied, affecting a confidence she didn't feel. 'Definitely.'

In the distance, thunder rumbled.

'Fall back, Keretan,' Camellia hissed. Something bright had spattered her cheek, something that glistened in the gathering daylight. She twisted the spear in her hands and made another lurching thrust over the top of the barricade. No cry or clang followed. She was tiring, he could see it. 'Everyone else has made it to the third line.' Her words were breathy, her chest heaving, and sweat had darkened the base of her hair. 'It's time.'

'You fall back,' Keretan growled back. He knew he looked no better. His legs were lead, the muscles of his back and arms burning, and it was still barely full dawn. If he survived the day, they'd never get him out of the armour, he was stuck to it forever. 'I've got the plate.'

'We'll both go, together,' she panted, but he saw the lie in her eyes. An orderly retreat was beyond them; one had to stay, to block and delay. If they both turned their backs, they'd be cut down before they made it halfway to the next line. Keretan's great golden shell would count for nothing with a dagger through his visor.

'I won't leave you to face them alone,' he rumbled. The spear the mercenary had left him was gone, snatched from his hand as he'd jammed it into an assailant. Both man and spear had dropped from the side of the cliff, lost somewhere in the valley below. The hammer that remained had never felt heavier. He peered over the barricade again. The mercenaries had withdrawn a little, recovering their own breath, consolidating. Up to a score remained in view, upright and dangerous. They must suspect that the defenders were depleted, their volleys of arrows and stone fallen to nothing. They must suspect a breakthrough was at hand.

'Keretan, it's time,' Camellia insisted.

'It's still too early.'

'Think of your children!'

'I think of nothing else!' he roared, spittle flying from the gap of his visor. 'I will not have them remember me as a traitorous coward. I must not burden them with shame.'

'Then have them know you as a living father,' she snapped back, 'and make your retreat now while—'

Something shifted beneath them, the braced timbers of their improvised rampart wobbling.

'What's—' Keretan began, then one side of the structure collapsed, thick spars slithering over the side of the cliff as the earth crumbled away beneath them. Keretan and Camellia hovered for an instant in space, then their rampart slid sideways and they crashed to earth, curled into balls, arms raised against the tumble of falling wood. Heavy beams crashed onto them, one glancing Keretan's helmet, the next denting his vambrace as he tried to shield Camellia. He howled in pain, certain he felt the arm snap, then another thick log came to rest across his ribs, pinning him, crushing him.

'Ow,' Keretan groaned.

Camellia was prone beside him, struggling beneath a weight of sodden wood, a fresh gash on her forehead. 'I told you,' she gasped, 'it was time . . . to go . . . Now we'll both . . . die.' She smiled, and there was blood on her teeth. 'We tried . . . didn't we? For . . . peace.'

Keretan fought to take in a full breath against the weight of the timber. He'd been prepared to die in battle. He'd been prepared to give his life, heroically.

A creak and clatter joined the groan of shifting wood as the mercenaries took their first tentative steps over the collapsed barricade. It wouldn't take a moment to find them.

Keretan took another juddering breath, and felt tears running hot down his temples, wetting his ears, snot bubbling in his nose. This didn't feel heroic. This didn't feel heroic at all. He didn't even recall weakening this one.

'Pashani!'

The cry came from somewhere behind, down the path, clear and utterly, utterly furious.

'Pashani!' A string of syllables followed, nothing Keretan recognised, muffled as it was by the helmet. The slow creaks and clunks of the mercenaries' advance stilled, then resumed as a gallop. Shapes rushed past them, over them, as the enemy forces charged over the ruined barricade, and the two figures buried in its wreckage, to reach whoever was making the noise. Timbers jumped and rocked, thumping against him, crushing the air from his lungs, jolting his agonised arm, then falling blissfully still.

Then the sounds of combat began.

Beside him, Camellia's struggles had faded, and her face was slick and bloodless. 'Kediras,' she breathed. 'We should have . . . called her.'

Keretan thought of the woman's stern instruction. He'd lost the horn somewhere in the first retreat. He hadn't even realised the people attacking them had been Pashani. 'You know,' he replied, his own words little more than a croak, 'I plain forgot. Camellia. Camellia?' She was no longer moving, her eyes closed. 'Camellia! No. No! No one falls. No one gets left behind.'

Keretan strained. Keretan heaved. One-armed and exhausted as he may be, it would not end like this, not for her, not for him. Keretan roared.

And, little by little, something started to move.

FIFTY-FOUR

'What's happening now?'

'You could come and look yourself, Lali.'

'I know, I just can't bear to. But what *is* happening?'

Lying prone against the freezing rock, Javani stretched her head a little further over the edge to bring more of the terraces into hazy view. Her vision swam, her modest breakfast making a spirited run for her oesophagus. Cold sweat tickled her back. This was a lot to go through to impress a load of kids.

She squinted. Somewhere overhead, the sun was finally up, for all the good it was doing; the day was thick with gloomy cloud, and mist still roiled in the valley, thickest over the river and drifting in increasingly disparate swathes through the brittle black trees on the hillsides. The valley rang with shouts, cries, and clangs, and in the background a growing anticipation of corvids. Thunder rumbled periodically, but she saw no sign of a storm.

'There's movement at the base of the trail to the pastures, I think Keretan's lot are digging in at the edge of the huts. I can't see him, though.' You'd think a giant in golden armour would stand out. 'Lots going on at the top of the river path, although not sure exactly what, but they're holding for now. And . . .' she tried to crane her head around the cliff to take in the far end of the village, '. . . no idea what's going on by the waterfall.'

Arman had finished winding the hoist, and jammed the locking wedge into the master pulley. 'You really haven't told us much.' He'd spent Ree's descent explaining the mechanism's workings to a less-than-enthusiastic audience, but it had kept Javani's mind off other things for a while at least. Now he scooped up spools of rope and flung them past her, towards the cave's edge. 'Lali, tie that off, would you? Don't want it slipping loose, remember?'

'There's not much to see,' Javani retorted, trying to wiggle a little further forward to bring the winding path beneath them into view. Something snagged her trouser ankle, arresting her progress. She tugged, then harder, but her leg was pulled back, and then she heard the growl.

She turned to find Tarfellian with his jaws delicately clamped around the leg of her trousers, his feet braced. On making eye contact, he began to back away, dragging her trousers against her hips.

'Oho,' Arman laughed. He'd picked up a woodsman's axe from somewhere, and was hefting it like he'd know what to do in an emergency. As long as it was a tree-felling emergency, presumably. 'Looks like the old boy doesn't want you too near the edge either.'

Javani's choice was clear: retreat with the dog, or risk her trousers being yanked clean off her legs on what was still a bitingly cold morning. She scuttled backwards on elbows and knees, glowering at the dog, who simply glowered back. He'd evidently had more practice at it.

'Don't worry,' Arman called, resting the axe against his shoulder. 'I'll cover the path.'

Released at last, Javani sat on the slick, tiered granite with her arms resting on her raised knees, and gave the dog a withering look. 'Look after me, Vida said,' she muttered. 'Call this looking after?'

The big dog made two small circles, then flopped down beside her and sighed with satisfaction.

Ree had to take several good, long breaths on alighting from the hoist to regain her composure. She was even more wobbly on her feet than usual after her trip down the cliffside, and her stomach had done backflips for most of the journey as she'd swayed and twisted and jerked her way towards the ground. She'd closed her eyes in the end; the kid had been right, there was little enough to see once enveloped in the mist. She was cold to the bone, her arms tired and leg sore, yet still found herself wiping sweat from her palms on a day that promised to be sunless and bitter.

Feeling capable of movement at last, she made to set off and very nearly stepped straight into a pit. This one wasn't even covered, dug in a rush and left wide open at the foot of the cliff, the stakes within a mixture of sharpened and raw. She took another long breath, made a point of registering her surroundings, and set off.

The pasture trail was closest, the last line, the so-called third ring, just the other side of the terrace from where she'd descended. She found the barricades there milling with defenders, wandering in and out of cover. They were oddly hushed and anxious, despite no sign of imminent attack on them. She recognised a few of them from Keretan's crew – Farrad, Solheil, Parvin, a couple more whose names she'd never bothered to learn, mixed in with the ends of Camellia's reserve. They were battered and bloodied, several clutching at damaged limbs, two simply lying on the crusted earth, the rise of their chests the only sign they were alive.

'What are you all doing? Where is the enemy?'

They jumped at her voice, and eventually it was Solheil who replied. He looked very, very unhappy, and seemed to have lost a tooth. 'Master Keretan ordered us to fall back to here and hold it.'

Ree glanced around. 'Where is he?'

'Still up at the second ring. With Mother Camellia.'

She squinted up the trail into the mist. A hint of movement, of activity, whirling within the drifting sheets of cloud? The fact that the bandits weren't already racing down the hill was encouraging, at least. 'That's it? Just those two?'

Parvin shifted from foot to foot, then gestured up the trail with his improvised spear. Ree noted the dried blood that had streamed from a wound on his arm, black and sticky. 'The mercenary woman went past us. The one with all the swords.' His tone suggested he'd appreciate even one sword.

'Kediras? You just let her past?'

'Should we have stopped her?' Parvin replied.

'Could we have stopped her?' Solheil added.

'No. No, I guess not.' She snapped her gaze around. The defenders were all over the place, some creeping out of the line of defences, looking to edge up the trail towards whatever was happening at its crest. Others had collapsed against the blockades, exhausted despite the early hour. They're not soldiers, she reminded herself. Not all of them. 'Right, get shipshape you lot. No, you are not at sea, Parvin, but you need to be in position. A torrent of bastards could come tearing down that hill baying for your blood without an instant's warning. Be ready for them! Come on, get where you should be! Form up on the barricades, in ranks like you practised, and keep those spears facing forward.'

'What then?' Solheil said in a small voice.

'Do what Keretan told you: hold this line. Do not let anyone past unless you've known them since childhood. Got it?'

'What if we can't?' That was Farrad. He looked exhausted, blood down one side of his face, and was favouring one side of his body, arm cradled against his ribs. 'What if . . .'

Ree held his pleading gaze with all the strength she could muster and a fabricated quantity besides. If I get this wrong, she thought, all these people, all these lads and lasses whose names I've learned and those I haven't, they're going to die. And then so is everyone else. 'There is nothing behind you now. Understand? You. Will. Hold.' She took a breath. If they collapsed here, the village would be lost. But that was true of elsewhere, too. She had to keep moving. 'You lot, the reserve – with me. Now.'

As she left the terrace, her leg burning, she offered a silent prayer to any and all gods. You never knew your luck.

'What in hells are you doing here?'

They said it simultaneously. Ree stared and Anri, and Anri stared at Ree. 'Where are Mariam and Vida?' she demanded as he blurted, 'Why aren't you up at the caves?'

They held each other's glares for a moment, then Anri folded. 'Swapped, didn't we? Coming over right thick they were, more than we could peg back with arrows. That loony mercenary helped for a bit, then she just fucked off. Situation called for someone with a bit more, uh,' he mimed pushing something heavy, '. . . drive.'

'And? Have they had more luck?'

'Haven't got a clue, have I? Been stuck at the top of the path, chucking stuff at tin bastards.'

'And?'

'Well, it was working, but then the pig-willies all bunched up together, went slow. Wise to the traps now, they are. We've thinned out their numbers, like, slowed the advance and all, but, well . . .'

'They're still advancing.'

'In-bloody-deed. Turns out armour's rather effective at preventing injury, who knew.' He patted his quiver. 'I've still got a few bodkins left for when they crest the path, but after that . . .'

She nodded. 'Things are precarious – if we collapse at the waterfall flank, they'll flood round the stables way and cut you off. We can't risk it. Get everyone pulled back to the edge of the village. We can use the huts to thin and separate them, and there are plenty more surprises along the way they won't have the measure of. We know the layout. They don't.'

'Pull back now? I've not used my bodkins yet.'

'Save them. Get things moving while there's still time, before they're too close to drop back from.'

'And this is all part of the agreed strategy, is it? Got the rest of our council of defence singing in harmony, have you? Where are you going with the rump of our reserve?'

'For fuck's sake, Anri, do as you're told. Fall back. Now.'

'Oh, fine.' He turned away from her, then turned back. 'Hoy, forgot to mention, one thing struck me as rather odd.'

She was already making her jarring, painful way in the direction of the bridge, her uncertain detachment at her heel. 'What?' she snapped back over her shoulder.

'They seem to have a bear with them. Carrying their pennant. I stuck an arrow in the fucker's head but he just kept on plodding along. Do you need special arrows for bears?'

He didn't wait for an answer, and Ree did not have one to give.

They were moving faster up the path now, Zurab pressed to his back, forcing him on. Close to the top, he'd said. Close to the top. Manatas felt only dread and misery. If the myriad injuries and injustices weren't enough – the pulsing burn of his mutilated ear, the press of the wadded cloth in his mouth, the boots still sloshing with icy water – someone from the village had landed an arrow square on his head. He could feel it poking through the bear's thick hide, its point itching at his already distressed scalp, and, thanks to his bindings and the gag, he was entirely unable to remove it, or even ask for assistance. Zurab had giggled with glee hard enough to risk incontinence at the arrow's arrival, and found its continued presence an endless source of mirth, occasionally reaching up to give it a twang. Manatas knew he'd get no help there.

'They're falling back!' someone shouted. Not Zurab, but one of the men-at-arms who was keeping close to the acting captain and his standard bear. Manatas couldn't see what lay ahead but the hardy vegetation at his feet made him think of the shrub up on the ridge, which made him think of Ree, which gave him a strange pang in his chest that had nothing to do with the sodden ropes that bound him. Was she hunkering behind the defences at the top of the path? Was she already embroiled in the fighting elsewhere? Had she fled into the hills the moment he'd confirmed the attack? He couldn't decide which option he desired most, which compounded his guilt. *Let her not be hurt, let her not be in danger. And while we're at it, let me not be in danger, too.*

Manatas was not a praying man, his relationship with the gods somewhat arm's length but nonetheless respectful. Circumstances, however, were conspiring towards a reappraisal.

'Nearly there, boys, they're turning tail!' The man-at-arms again, whose voice he recognised – a caustic Vistirlari by the name of Zaal who'd done little to recommend himself in the duration of his service under Manatas. 'One push up this steep bit and— fuck!'

A rumble from ahead, not the distant murmur of the thunder that had started at the coming of dawn, but something close, and heavy, crunching down the path towards them. Unable to do much else, Manatas ducked. The standard jolted in his hands as something hit it, then the arrow was gone from his scalp, ripped clear as something whistled overhead. A great crash erupted from behind, a clanging impact that was nevertheless too wet for his liking. Shrieks and cries came after it, along with yelps and shouts of warning from further down the winding path, then another thudding crash, a smaller one, a prolonged quiet, then a final, distant crunch.

What in the name of all the gods . . . Manatas whimpered into his gag as he pushed himself blindly back to his feet. The standard pole felt a little easier to manoeuvre all of a sudden, and it dawned on him that its topmost section, complete with pennant, had been smashed clear.

'Fuckers chucked a tree trunk at us!' Zurab was somehow still at his back, growling into his good ear. 'Good thing you ducked when you did, standard bear, or that would have cleaned the pair of us out.'

And what a shame that would have been, Manatas sighed to himself.

'Come on, bear-boy, get climbing! Almost at the top!'

Unlike what Ree had found at the pasture trail and the cliff path, the scene at the mist-drenched ravine was open combat. As Anri had said, the mercenaries had strung a pair of pre-built temporary bridges across the gap to the escarpment's edge, long constructions of hacked tree limbs and thick rope, and were clambering across them in a steady stream. The defenders had bunched at the second row of barricades, villagers thrusting spears and pole-arms at the armoured troops who had already made it across, but with little cohesion. The situation was perilous – unless the replacement bridges were downed quickly, a critical mass of soldiers would be across, too many to fight back; they would lose the flank, and retreat in disorder. But a stand-up fight was everything she'd cautioned against – these were professional fighters, decked in mail and helmets, and carrying weapons that had neither spent a decade wrapped in wool in a cave nor been converted from farming equipment.

Ree was not surprised to see Vida and Mariam at the heart of the line, closest to the arriving mercenaries, Vida driving forward with a spear and toting a home-made shield while Mariam jabbed past her with a pike. Despite their efforts, they were able to do little more than slow the advance of the mercenaries making landfall from the bridges and cramp their area of disembarkation.

It was too soon to lose this flank. Anri had yet to pull everyone back from the river path. They needed to hold. Which meant dealing with . . . she counted . . . six mercenaries on this side of the ravine, with another seven or eight currently crossing. Ree needed to get involved.

She didn't hesitate, her hand flashing to the sword at her hip. It had been a while, but—

A spear of pain ran up her leg as she tried to adopt a fighting stance, and she yelped. 'Nine piss-blistered hells!' She let go a heavy sigh. 'Reserves, to the line! Fill the gaps, don't give them space to advance. Keep them away from you and your friends! I'll . . . I'll hold here.'

The sword stayed in its scabbard, and she shrugged the bow off her shoulder. It would have to do. She still had a handful of arrows, none of Anri's bodkin heads, but enough to give them something to think about.

Bracing carefully on an unoccupied barricade, Ree drew back the bow and took aim.

FIFTY-FIVE

They were at the top of the path now, somewhere on the lowest terrace. Manatas tried to remember the layout of the village, from his visits, from his observations. The river path had wound up the side of the escarpment and emerged close to . . . what was it, the stables? The little graveyard area? He could barely see, and what he could make out was unrecognisable. The ground had been transformed into hummocks and pits, every pile of banked earth a potential maiming lying in wait. The huts were sparse at the village's fringes, but the gaps between them had been filled with loose timber and woven boughs, some of them carefully laced with thorny briar, making it hard for the body of troops to maintain their cohesion as they advanced.

That was, of course, assuming they even wanted to. Already he heard their cries of triumph and jubilation, their excitement at having reached the village with all its hidden treasures. Lado had filled their heads with any number of poisonous notions, but high among them was the idea that every dwelling in the otherwise modest village was bursting with some level of riches that was there for the taking. Already the surviving members of the detachment were breaking apart as soldiers split off in ones and twos, eager to burst their way into huts and reap the rewards awaiting them.

By the gods, Manatas lamented mutely to none but himself, do not succumb to the urge to loot the moment you encounter habitation! Where is your discipline? Not only is the wealth of this village in its food stores, which are on both the uppermost terraces and in its store caves in the cliffs above, but the likelihood that your actions might be anticipated by those seeking your incapacitation is strong enough to suggest—

A scream erupted from his right, a dark blur at the edge of his vision suggesting a hut in the location. He swivelled in time to witness a mercenary tumble backwards into the mud through what he assumed was an open doorway. Something was buried in her chest, something, presumably, sharp enough to punch through her mail. He became aware of a sort of quivering noise. Ah. Another pole-tension trap. Perhaps that would be instructive for her comrades.

A shriek of pain from ahead suggested the lesson was slow in being learned.

'Keep moving, standard bear.' Somehow Zurab had maintained his own discipline. 'We've got a rendezvous to make.'

'Gods, woman, the pest wasn't chatting farts after all.'

'Anri? Why in hells aren't you getting everyone back inside the village like I said?'

'What? Gave the nod, didn't I? It's not like they need me to show them the way.'

'You are such a spectacular coward.'

'No I'm bloody not! Just enlightened. Came over here to help out, given my unique skills and sensibilities, thought I could tip matters in our favour, no matter the potential danger to life and limb, which if you think on it is actually quite heroic, like.'

'Shut up and shoot, will you? And what did you mean about the kid chatting farts?'

'Blamed her shocking bow-skills on her teacher, didn't she. Meaning you.'

'And? You'll get any excuse from her for her failings bar lack of diligence on her part. There. Are you telling me there was anything wrong with that shot?'

'Yes.'

'Oh, fuck off.'

'Just give me your arrows, will you? Mine have all disappeared into the fleshy parts of those who mean us mischief, and I left my bodkins up at the terrace, as you demanded.'

'I will not.'

'You can keep your pride if you want, that's no bother to me. Just be honest to yourself on its price, eh?'

'Oh . . . Nine fucking hells, here.'

'You've made a sound choice there, for once.'

'You *are* a dick, there's something else the kid was right about. No, aim low, legs and feet. Less armour, bugger their mobility, block up their manoeuvres.'

'You're telling me you were actually aiming—'

'Just fucking shoot, will you?'

'Hit their feet, eh? You have any idea how hard that is?'

'You're saying you can't do it?'

'Course I can do it, just wanted to check you knew how hard it was.'

'Shoot!'

'Step it up, standard bear, we're awaited.'

Manatas could not have replied, even had he wanted to. The gag was soaking and rancid in his mouth, and the stink of the ex-bear had not faded with prolonged exposure; if anything it was worse, intensified by his sweat, blood and tears, now a stinging hum in his nostrils as he trudged. The going was absurd – the mud was thick and churned, cloying and sucking at his boots, and he knew full well that anywhere likely to be used as a direct path by an interloper was almost guaranteed to feature an unpleasant surprise. He moved slowly, cautiously, despite Zurab's infuriated exhortations, his gaze fixed barely a step ahead. Already he'd checked his stride once and let one of Zurab's contingent stride past him and kick clean through a taut line of twisted wool running between two huts. The woman had been lost under a thunderous rush of rolling timber from a rooftop.

Zurab had been a mite less impatient after that, if only for a breath or two.

A new smell was on the wind, a pungent reek of animals in close proximity. They had to be close to the stables now. Manatas fixed his image of the village in his mind. Once they had taken the stables, there was a single stairway up to the terrace beyond, around the curve of the cliff to the spit of land that bordered the ravine, which had until the day before sported an impressive rope bridge. Zurab was in a hurry to reach it. Jebel was there, on the far side of the ravine, and he was clearly expecting to cross. Manatas had missed something crucial, and it pained him.

Ree watched the struggling mercenary hop backwards, swinging his sword in a wild arc with one hand while clutching his perforated foot with the other. He teetered at the sudden slick edge of the cliff, windmilling the sword and swaying like a spring-wood scarecrow, then the man plunged backwards with a wail, disappearing into the ravine, with any luck never to return. Ree leaned heavily on her stick. Only three fighters in mail remained on their side of the ravine, forming what defensive line they could before the temporary bridges, hemmed by a growing rank of reinvigorated defenders, their spears and poles levelled. Panic had struck the mercenaries who were midway through crossing – those closest scrambled to get all the way over before their bridge was toppled, those further back were caught in the uncertainty of whether to commit or withdraw, and, needless to say, they were not all of the same mind. Arguments were breaking out among those currently partway across.

It warmed Ree's heart.

'You know what,' she said to Anri, surveying the scene. 'We can tip this. Put a couple of shots in those stragglers and we'll be clear on this side, could rush the bridges.'

'I'm out of arrows again.'

'For fuck's— Already?'

'Quick on the string, aren't I? I did say we should have made more.'

She shook her head in exasperation. 'At the cost of what else? Too much to do, not enough time, not enough people . . . And it's not like you were fletching shafts all night, is it?'

'My contribution has been primarily tactical.'

'Get in there and fight! Drive them back before more of them cross!'

'After you, Mistress Ree. Not much of a, you know, metal-swinger, me. You're the one with the sword.'

Ree gritted her teeth and put one hand on the hilt. She could fight through the pain. She'd done it before. And if it got this flank secure, it would be worth it.

Vida and Mariam beat her to it. Vida sounded the charge, and the defenders advanced as one, pikes, staves and spears a bristling line driving the mercenaries back towards the bridge. Vida and Mariam were at the centre, bellowing orders and encouragement as they closed. The mercenaries battled furiously with their own spears, their shields locked, trying to keep the line at bay, while behind them those on the crossing redoubled their scrabble to make landfall, but Manatas had been right – the defenders had longer weapons, and now had the strength of numbers and a sense of a turning tide. The first mercenary took a heavy blow to the midriff, bending him double, then a spear clanged against his helmet and sent him reeling backwards. In a blink, he was gone, vanished into the ravine.

Vida was making for the first bridge-point, her shield high and a heavy hammer in her hand, meaning to smash it clear before any more soldiers made it across. The second mercenary moved to block her, but was caught between the line of poles that bore down on him as the outer flank closed. Jabbed and poked, he was forced back onto the structure of the bridge, into the face of his desperate colleagues, when Vida delivered a mighty blow to one of its anchoring hooks. The wood split and sheared, and the bridge twisted in mid-air, throwing the first mercenary into the ravine and leaving the others grasping desperately at the creaking wood. With a splintering sound, the second hook went, and the bridge fell away in a cacophony of clattering shrieks.

The final mercenary stabbed Vida. His own shield high, he lunged across and punched the blade of his spear through her standing thigh. Her scream was eclipsed by Mariam's howl of rage. She fell upon the man, who had barely enough time to yank back his weapon before a dozen jabs rained upon him – his shield clanged and boomed, then she found a gap to his foot and he faltered. Her final blow lanced through his open mouth as he bellowed; the jaunty ring of his helmet circling daintily on the projecting point of Mariam's pike as gore flooded from the hole at the back of the man's shaven, scarred head would stay with Ree for a considerable time afterwards.

Vida was down, one hand pressed to the pulsing wound at her thigh, but had still strength enough to wield her hammer and smash the hooks from the second bridge's end. It creaked and groaned as its construction splintered, and the few mercenaries who had persevered with crossing in the face of the villagers' assault rapidly reassessed their decisions. A few of them even managed to scramble off before the lashed timbers finally gave and the siege bridge tumbled, disintegrating, into the ravine.

Ree was at Vida's side with all the speed she could muster as Mariam and Anri dragged her back behind the barricades. The mercenaries might not have much in the way of weapons of range, but they'd demonstrated they weren't beyond throwing things when provoked, and the loss of their siege bridges would be provocation indeed.

The smith was pale and clearly in a lot of pain. She wasn't speaking, which proved nothing.

'How bad?' Ree said. 'Artery?'

Mariam shook her head. She was already binding the wound tightly, with bandages that she must have been carrying on her. 'By the mercy of the gods, no. But it's deep. And my darling girl is heavy. You're going to need carrying, my dear.'

Vida grimaced but said nothing.

'You can borrow my stick if you want,' Ree said with a forced grin. 'I'll lean on my sword.'

'At least you'll be getting some use from it,' Anri muttered, and was cuffed for his trouble.

'What are the mercenaries doing now, then? What's going on elsewhere?' Mariam said, her concentration on her stricken wife. 'We weren't expecting to see you down by here, Ree.'

'I wasn't expecting to see you here either,' Ree muttered, 'life is full of surprises.' She cleared her throat. 'They're regrouping, it won't be long before they come at us again – most likely from the valley floor.' She took a juddering breath. 'The pasture trail is bad, looks like the Pashani came in heavy. Everyone's fallen back to third ring, bar a couple still on the second.'

'Keretan?'

'And Camellia. And Kediras. Don't know how they are.'

Mariam tied off the bandage and fished out a waterskin. 'And if Anri's here with us, the river path must be under control, is it?'

'They flooded up the path. Everyone's back inside the village. We're letting the traps work but we need to pull everyone back from here before they cut us off. And they will.' Ree swallowed. 'We need to move right away, get back to the third ring.'

'Last ditch?'

'Last ditch.'

'Right, my love, my light, drink. Good girl. Now we're going to move. Ready? Anri is going to help. Ree would but she's only got one good leg to begin with. No disrespect intended, mind.'

'None taken,' murmured Ree, looking past her. The defenders were in a terrible state, had given everything they had to drive the mercenaries back. Vida was not their only casualty. She was feeling panic rising, fought to contain it. 'This isn't over. Even with Vida's injury, if we can form up around the village like we planned, keep a hard perimeter, we should have . . .'

Something had caught her eye, through the drifting mist that boiled up from the waterfall. Something at the fall itself, above and across from them, at the very pitch of the opposite cliff. Leading behind the waterfall, and out the other side, anchored to the empty scaffolding of the future water mill.

'Is that . . .' She swallowed. 'Are those ropes?'

'You know what, standard bear?' Zurab growled into Manatas's good ear. The man was pressed right against him, using him as an ursine shield against traps and projectiles as they crept around the side of the village. They'd not lost anyone since an unruly Vistirlari woman who'd gone by the name Ksenia had kicked open a hut door and triggered some kind of clay pot to swing back through the doorway and crack her on the skull. It had smelled a lot like honey, which had prompted Manatas to want to investigate further, but the man who dragged his rope had disagreed. It would probably have attracted bees anyway.

What, Manatas tried to reply, but even the thought was pointless. He didn't care what Zurab had to say. He didn't care about anything beyond finding a way for the attack to fail. The honey smell was a memory now, entirely supplanted by the stench of goat musk, complemented by a thick layer of sheep dung. He almost missed the bear stink; this close to the stables, the very air brought tears to his eyes.

'When this is finished,' Zurab went on, his voice a hoarse whisper in the sudden quiet of their slow approach. 'When this place is ours, and the skins of these fuckers are tanning in the winter sun. When we're gorging ourselves on flesh and sweetmeats, when we're warm and fat and comfortable . . . I'll let you go. You can go on your way, if you want, or stay with the company. No harm done. You've done a brave thing today, standard bear. You've survived. You've atoned.'

Really? Manatas couldn't help himself, although of course it came out as a muffled squawk.

Zurab's laughter was a patter of gravel and broken glass. 'Fuck no! I'm going to cut off your balls and make you eat them. That's after we finish your ear—'

Something was in front of them, casting Manatas's view in shadow. Something that had made Zurab go quiet.

'You go no further, bandits,' came a voice he knew, a voice that made his heart rise in his chest and brought fresh tears to his eyes. 'You won't hurt my friends.'

Manatas tried to shout, tried to wave, tried to communicate his predicament, but the gag was immovable and his hands remained lashed to the standard pole and the rope in Zurab's ruthless grip.

'I am ready to fight,' Tauras said in his biggest voice. 'And I'll fight your bear if I have to.'

'It's fucking . . . fucking ropes,' Ree spluttered, trying to beat the mist away with her scabbard. 'It's fucking . . . Oh, by the gods! They've crossed behind us!'

Javani heard a sound like squeaking in the background. It had been building for a while, but it was only when Tarfellian started to growl that she really paid it any attention. It was not the hoist swinging in the wind – the wheel was locked with its wedge, and Lali had slung the trailing ropes around the loose timber at the shelf's edge. The sound had a metallic edge to it, though, a resonance, a rhythmic clatter. A sort of music, too – an odd, gentle accompaniment of breathy notes, faint on the wind.

Then the great metal head appeared at the top of the cliff path, and she screamed.

Lado of Cstethia flicked up the visor on his magnificent armour as he crested the path and came to a halt. 'Well, well, well,' he said, head tilted, a thin tendril of hair sliding across his face within the helmet. 'What precious treasures do we have up here?'

FIFTY-SIX

Arman reacted first. Already standing not far from the hoist, he snatched up the axe he'd brandished earlier and charged with a roar.
'Arman, no!' Javani cried.

Lado didn't move. He stood where he was as Arman rained axe-blows upon him, the blade striking his armoured shell with great hollow booms. Arman swung again and again, smashing the axe against carapace, arms and legs, leaving little more than the occasional smudge on the gleaming metal. His swipes slowed as he tired, his breath coming hard, sweat on his brow, then as he launched one final attack Lado threw up a gauntlet and caught the haft.

Lado looked up at the nicked and scuffed axe blade, then down to Arman, who was straining with his remaining strength against the mercenary's grip. Somehow, he affected to look hurt. 'Why would you strike at someone you'd never before met?' he said in his soft voice. 'Someone who has raised no hand against you, who wishes only to see justice done?' Without releasing the weapon, Lado turned his head and spoke over his shoulder. 'You were correct, lord adjutant, the armour was a necessity in the face of such unprovoked aggression.'

Clanking up the path behind Lado was another figure in full plate, no less ostentatious than the first. Both men were wet, the armour beaded and gleaming, as if they'd walked through rain on their climb. The suits were the very opposite of that worn by the White Spear, the vast mercenary Javani had encountered in Kazeraz, and until that week about her only experience of professional soldiery – hers had been oppressive in its function, black and featureless, a contrivance of purpose and nothing more. These suits were gaudy, flared and ornate, embellished with useless affectations that made them no less fearsomely effective.

Arman grunted and struggled to free the axe. 'Leave it,' Javani shouted. She had barely made it up from the rock, one hand on Tarfellian's raised hackles. 'You can't hurt them.'

He seemed unconvinced, flexing his arms twice more before abandoning the weapon to Lado's possession with an exasperated growl. *Hells*, Javani thought, *even a mountain falling on the White Spear couldn't do much more than slow her down, what chance does a boy waving an old wood-axe have?*

The second armoured figure was alongside Lado now, and flipped up his visor to reveal a well-proportioned, if terminally self-satisfied, face. 'Such unprovoked aggression, acting commander,' the new man said. He looked inordinately pleased with himself, if breathless from the climb, and repeatedly shook out his great fur-lined cloak.

'It fair wounds the soul, lord adjutant,' Lado replied, the axe still held in front of him. 'Still, the Company of the Wolf seek only what is owed, no more. Justice must be served.' With that, he tossed the axe to reverse his grip, then whipped it around to smash the flat of the blade against the side of Arman's head.

Arman dropped without a sound, but the rock shelf erupted in screams. Tarfellian was up and barking, great throaty growls and snarls, Javani no less loud in her upset.

'Fair is fair, lord adjutant,' Lado said, inspecting the battered axe-head. A thin line of blood marked one edge. 'We are here for what we are owed.'

For once, Ree was ahead of everyone else, stomping at breakneck pace back along the terrace, dodging between hazards, her stick tearing up clumps of wet earth with every stride.

'Come on!' she barked. 'Come the fuck on, they have passed us!'

Anri and Mariam were labouring with the injured Vida and, despite Ree's urgent exhortations, the other retreating defenders were slow and hobbling in their wake. As Ree had feared, the villagers had given all they had, and now there was nothing left when they needed it most.

'Want to push on, do you?' Anri called back, his words strained by his efforts to keep Vida as comfortable as their progress would allow. 'Don't let us keep you.'

'And what the fuck do you think I'll achieve on my own?' she turned and snapped. She'd been ignoring the burning pain in her leg, the countless other hurts and scrapes, but there would be a reckoning. 'For all we know they've already got behind Keretan's line, or— Wait, do you hear that? From the stables!'

She made it to the top of the terrace steps in record time, skidding around the pits and channels, one hand on her walking stick and the other gripping the hilt of her sword. She was completely unprepared for what awaited her.

The ram pen was a crumpled mess, its timbers torn apart and crushed beneath a scattered mass of armoured forms. Five . . . six unmoving figures, strewn about like hayseed, some with limbs bent at angles that were a long way from standard operating procedure. At the centre of the carnage stood Tauras, massive and bloodied, his braids flowing loose and clotted.

He was trying to pull the head off a bear.

The pain was indescribable, and there came an interminable moment when Manatas became convinced that he had made a terrible mistake, that he should have been content to be glued inside a stinking bear's head by his congealed ear-blood for the rest of his days, that attempts to remove him would result, like a curse from myth, only in the tearing of his head from his shoulders, and his ear from even that.

And then came blinding grey daylight, and stinging cold air, and a sickening ripped feeling at the side of his head. He dropped to his knees with a muffled groan, still fumbling with bound hands at the hated gag, his eyes flooded with tears of pain and gratitude and pure, effulgent relief.

Tauras wrenched the cords from the gag and over his head, and Manatas did not begrudge his clumsiness a jot. He spat the revolting wad clear and sucked in a great lungful of clean, cold mountain air.

The big man was looking at him intently. 'It's really you, cap?'

His eyes were streaming and he could barely speak, but Manatas wanted to whoop, wanted to throw his arms around his comrade and declare his undying devotion for the man who'd freed him from within the bear. Instead, he tried to crack a smile and croaked, 'You ever doubted me, Tauras?'

'Yes, cap, I did. I thought maybe a bear had eaten you.'

He was starting to shiver. It was a lot colder outside the bear than in it. He pushed himself up and proffered his bound hands, the ridiculous standard pole still jammed between them. 'Would you mind?'

'Of course, cap, let me find something sharp.'

Tauras turned, and for the first time Manatas became aware of their audience.

'My lady Ree, is that you?'

'Manatas? Nine hells, you look like shit. What the fuck happened to your ear?'

'Would you believe a disagreement with a barber?' This time the smile came without effort. 'While I'd be delighted to claim that I have, in the past, suffered worse and survived, this may, in fact, be somewhat uncharted territory.'

'Hm. I like a man with a distinctive look.'

'Hoy!' A man was at the top of the steps leading to the next terrace, a shaggy-looking, mud-stained wretch with a bow slung over one shoulder. 'Thought we were in a fucking hurry!'

Ree blinked, and immediately her brow creased with worry.

Concern lurched in Manatas's gut. 'What is it?'

'Someone got past us. At the waterfall. They roped up the fucking mill fixings, and we were so focused on the bridges we didn't even notice. They're in the village already.'

'Who?'

'Don't know.'

'Lado?'

'Probably. He could be anywhere, he could get the drop—'

Manatas's head was shaking, almost like a tremor he couldn't stop. 'Where are the children?' he whispered, his throat dry.

All the blood left her face. Her mouth opened slowly, but no sound came out.

The man called again from the steps. 'Hoy! Are we going or what?'

Ree had turned to look past him, up at the great grey sheet of rock that rose behind the village into the mist. At the winding stepped pathways that led up its face to the ledges and shelves that marked its caves. Her eyes filled with tears. 'I can't get . . . I can't climb fast enough . . .'

Tauras reappeared, empty-handed. 'Sorry, cap, I couldn't find anything sharp.'

Manatas felt the thrum of his pulse, the terrible throb of his mangled ear. 'Tauras, we're climbing that rock over there, and we're doing it now.'

'Right you are, cap.'

Manatas nodded to the sword still held pale-knuckled in Ree's grip, then indicated his hands. 'Would you mind?'

She nodded, vaguely, and sliced through the rope that wrapped the standard pole. He let it fall with delight, whereupon Tauras caught it. Rope and cord still bound his wrists and his waist, but his arms were free, and he could deal with the rest later.

'Let's go, my lady Ree.'

She finally met his gaze, distracted from whatever miserable visions had seized her. 'You're with us, Captain Manatas?'

He nodded. 'I've heard it said that fighting for peace is akin to fornicating for chastity, but, well . . .'

'It's horseshit?'

'That it is. Today I choose peace, by the necessary means. Tauras! Let's go. Did you, by chance, see who had my sword?'

Ree's head whirled as they raced back up the terrace steps, one elbow hooked around a massive arm from the compliant Tauras. That evil, sadistic *fuck*. Of course Lado would head straight for the non-combatants, Manatas had hit the mark that she'd been too blind to see. And now they were far behind, and far below, and moving far too slowly, and her leg was burning like infernal spirits themselves had risen from the earth and were raking her calf with their flaming claws. The thought made her miss Aki.

'It's a long way up the cliff path,' she gasped as they neared the top. 'Lot more steps than this.'

'We'll get there, Ree,' Manatas replied automatically, sounding confident but still looking inescapably like utter shit. 'Lado is in full plate. Tauras and I will— *yerk*.'

He disappeared backwards, his legs vanishing from beneath him. Hands flailing, he hit the slick timbers of the steps and lurched downward, bouncing back to the terrace they'd just left. Ree blinked away her shock and focused her eyes. The rope – the rope that had still been wrapped around his torso. It had caught on something, snagged, and that was—

A figure stepped out from behind the terrace wall, a mail-clad, mud-streaked and well-bloodied man with a southern cast and a look of absolute murderous delight on his face. In one hand, he held a naked sword, its blade as dull and grey as the day. In the other was the end of the rope. Over their heads, a roll of thunder echoed from the hills.

Bruised and bleeding afresh, Manatas tried to rise, and the man whipped the cord again and sent him crashing to the mud. Ree turned, caught in two minds – she needed this man, she'd never get up the cliff without him, but every moment lost could prove fatal – but Manatas made the choice for her.

'Tauras, get her up there!' he called, waving them onward from his prone position. The big man grunted in acknowledgement, then with one arm hoisted Ree near off the ground. She yelped and protested as he set off at a jog, still carrying the broken standard pole in his other hand, and after a moment she allowed her protestations to subside. Manatas was on his feet, still roped, hands empty, against an armoured man who had made his intentions clear.

With a sigh, Ree unbuckled the sword from her waist, and wound up to throw.

FIFTY-SEVEN

Javani stared at the two mercenaries in their great steel suits. They seemed enormous on the little shelf of rock, disproportionately huge. She was still crouching beside the growling Tarfellian by the cave entrance, Lali to one side, Mani and Volkan to the other, behind them a terrified mass of non-fighting villagers who were suddenly conscious that the caves had but one way out. All she could think was *how*?

How had these two simply walked up the cliff path unnoticed?

How had they skirted every line of defence?

How could they be so thrice-damned nonchalant about it?

She reached the hand that wasn't holding Tarfellian back down to the satchel at her side. The hand-bow was tucked within it. She'd seen them used against plate armour, seen the little bolts spiral harmlessly away, but maybe, if she could line up a shot through an open visor . . . Ree had always—

Ree.

Gods have mercy, what if the reason these men were up here was because everyone else was beaten back, beaten down, or worse? Were they all dead? Was her mother dead?

Without meaning to, without even being aware it was a possibility, Javani started to cry.

Anri and Mariam had lowered Vida to the earth by the time Ree and Tauras caught up on the upper terrace, around the curve of the rock from the base of the cliff path. 'Why have you stopped? We need to—'

Anri pointed. Coming the other way, from the third ring of defences where Ree had begun her interventions what seemed like an age ago, was the shattered figure of Keretan. His golden armour was rent and twisted. One arm hung limp by his side, his other was wrapped around a bundle slung over his shoulder. Ree blinked. The bundle was Camellia.

'Nine hells,' Ree breathed. Did this mean Lado hadn't made for the caves after all? 'Keretan,' she called, 'were you ambushed? Bandits in plate?'

The big man shook his bloodied head. His helmet was gone, and vicious wounds gleamed from his dome in the bitter, silvery light. 'We held as long as we could,' he rumbled, his voice cracked. 'Kediras holds, still.'

'She's still up there?' The dawn had eased some of the choking mist, but the crest of the pasture trail was still lost to those by the terrace defences. 'Pashani?'

'Pashani.'

'Then she got what she came for. Is Camellia, uh . . .'

'Still breathing. For now.' He looked ready to drop. He'd not even taken in Vida's stricken form and Mariam fussing around her, or commented on Tauras's bloody presence. Ree felt a surge of impatience, a panicked urgency – Lado had taken the cliff path after all, then. She could not delay. She needed to get up to the caves, and there was no one to go with her. In the distance, thunder came again.

'Anri, get something sharp, you're coming up with me.'

'With respect, no. And by "with respect", I mean fuck off.'

'Piss of the gods, Anri, this is no time for your enlightened cowardice!'

'This is exactly the time for cowardice, it wouldn't be much fucking use if it waved through the odd suicidal tendency for a laugh, now, would it?' He snorted a great breath out. 'But it's not about that. You spotted the figures on the path yet? Lurking, they are. Cunning bastards. Five I can see, not sure how many above. Not going to get a shot off if I'm on the path with them, am I? The angles are flat, they'll cut my fucking arms off. So, with respect, I will be staying down here, and – now I've retrieved my bodkins – taking the shots that I can, and generally keeping an eye on things, because I don't know if you've noticed but things are rather shitty at the moment and our people could do with a bit of looking after.'

'Huh. Fair enough,' Ree grunted, then cocked half a smile. 'You said "our people".'

'Don't you have somewhere to be?'

Mariam was up on her feet, blood-dappled, casting around for where she'd put down her spear. Ree raised a hand as she set off towards the base of the path. 'Mariam, no. Stay with Vida. Stay with everyone, hold the line, keep them alive. Get them well.' *And don't get yourself killed while your wife bleeds to death elsewhere,* she did not add out loud. 'Tauras, with me!'

She was only a few paces from the first steps of the cliff path, not far from the pit she'd almost walked into when she'd dismounted the hoist, when something pinged in her calf and she collapsed in agony.

'You're looking different, standard bear.' Zurab moved sideways with slow steps, keeping Manatas at the full extent of the rope. 'Did you cut your hair?'

Manatas ignored him. He had eyes only for Ree's short sword, lying where it fallen to the earth excruciatingly out of reach, its drab scabbard now splattered with oozing mud. He could make a grab for it, but Zurab would have plenty of time to yank him back on the rope, drop him to the sludge and close in for the kill. If he kept both hands on the rope, he could weather such behaviour, but how would he retrieve the sword before it was swallowed by the sodden ground? It was very, very wet.

'It's incumbent upon me to remark upon your disappearing act at the moment when Tauras made his challenge plain,' Manatas said, keeping his eyes on the sword and trying a tentative step towards it.

Zurab immediately dragged the rope taut, pulling him back. 'Never cared for that great fat fuck. Eats enough for a battalion.'

'He also speaks very highly of you.' He tried another move towards the sword. Zurab was closing, coiling the rope as he advanced, keeping Manatas pinned. He twirled his own weapon as he advanced. It caught Manatas's eye.

'That is my sword.'

'Is that so?'

'That weapon was a gift to me, on completion of my third tour. It is a product of the Shukla Smithy of Mahavrik, you will see its maker's mark at the base of the blade.' Zurab did not look at the blade. 'I would appreciate its prompt return.'

'As I understand it,' Zurab said, taking another looping step across the mire, 'this weapon was confiscated from a traitor, a man who had turned his back on his sworn brethren, befouled his oath.' A sly grin pricked the corners of his mouth. 'Still, one piece of good news. It's going to be returned to you very promptly.'

Zurab yanked on the rope and lunged.

Javani cursed herself for a coward, but she could not stand. She was rooted to the cold rock, both hands now wrapped around Tarfellian's broad shoulders, trying to stifle her sobs in his matted coat. She felt a gentle hand on her shoulder, and looked up through swimming vision to see Mani offering her an encouraging smile.

'Do not be afraid, little one,' he said in his scratchy, squeaky voice. His tone was so warm, his eyes wellsprings of compassion. 'No matter what happens here, know that you are loved, and have lived a life of love. Know that love will linger after we are gone, every one of us, for love is power and it is truth.' He made a small movement to where the armoured figures stood, basking in the terror of those in the caves, and, in the case of the second man, still recovering his breath from the climb. 'Even these men deserve love. No matter what they do.'

That's easy for you to say, Javani muttered in her head, but she was far from capable of speech. Mani squeezed her shoulder once more, then turned to face the mercenaries. Beyond him, Volkan was hunched, his hands clasped. Volkan was praying.

Mani took a slow step towards the mercenaries, leaning on his stick. 'What is it that you want from us?'

Lado rocked back a little, as if astonished by the old man's audacity.

'Lord Botrys, I believe the enemy is attempting to negotiate. Is it not a little late for such things?'

The second man, Botrys, his wind restored, now seemed to inflate with outrage. He advanced on Mani, towering over him in his extravagant armour, one hand on the hilt of what looked to be a very fine sword at his hip. 'How dare you address me with such impertinence, villain?' He drew the sword with a flourish. It looked very clean, and very new. 'I will make you bleed.'

Mani bowed his head, both hands resting on his stick. 'If that is your wish. I will not stop you.'

Botrys hesitated, his sword still half-raised. 'What?'

'If I am to die at your hand, it will be with my forgiveness.'

'What?' The sword was wavering, and Botrys let his hand drop to his waist. 'What are you saying, you old fool?'

'That I forgive you. That you are loved, and are free to love in return. I know you do not truly wish my death, for it will bring you nothing. I know that you are just a man making choices, and thinking he can live with the consequences.'

Botrys's mood had passed from indignation through confusion and was now entering new territory. His certainty was gone, and in its place came doubt. 'Wh— Why?'

'We are all just people, travelling life's journey, alone and afraid. But you are not alone, and you do not need to fear. I love you as my brother, no matter our histories. We all deserve love, and can give it freely.'

Botrys had backed away a step, his sword-point scraping the shale floor. 'I don't understand,' he whimpered. 'Lado, why doesn't he plead? Why does he not fear me?'

Mani took another step, infinite kindness in his eyes. 'There's nothing to understand. Your choices are your own, and the consequences with them, but you have nothing to fear. If you choose to embrace love, we will welcome you on our path as one of our own. What, truly, do you feel? What does your heart wish?'

Botrys's sword clattered to the stony ground. His eyes were darting and confused. Javani felt a surge of impossible hope. 'I . . . I . . . Lado, what do I do?'

The man behind Botrys gave a weary sigh, his loose strands of hair swaying as he shook his head. 'Lord adjutant, the old man has already given you your answer.'

He took a small step to the side, tilted his head, and buried the axe in Mani's chest.

FIFTY-EIGHT

Ree's calf was a white-hot ball of pain. Her teeth were gritted so hard that a small part of her mind was worrying she was going to do them irreparable damage, while the rest shouted it down for insensible priorities.

Tauras's extraordinary face filled what passed for her vision. From his expression, she did not look good at all. 'Are you all right, mistress?'

'My leg . . . Ran it too hard.'

'Can you stand, mistress?'

She knew she could not. Stupid, so stupid, all the times she should have rested it, let it heal properly . . . But there'd always been something that needed doing, thrice-damn it, and she'd convinced herself it would take care of itself eventually. Well, now it had. Stupid, Ree, so stupid. Should have heeded the kid's words.

The kid.

A scream from above, piercing, terrified, echoing from the grim, grey rock.

Javani.

The pain from her leg was suddenly distant, absurd, irrelevant. The pain in her heart was all she knew. 'Tauras,' she snarled, 'pick me up.'

'Are you sure—'

'Pick me the fuck up, soldier! Carry me like a pack.'

He followed orders, and she had a strange reminder of a few days before, clamped around his back with a knife to his throat, threatening his life for the return of Gumis. The knife was back in its sheath at his side. It was funny how much could turn, and how quickly.

He supported her with one burly arm, while the other still held the standard-less pole. He went to discard it, but she stopped him. Her eyes on the climb ahead, she'd begun to have an idea.

'Now run, big man,' she barked in his ear. 'Run like fuck.'

Manatas was ready. He braced against the jerk of the rope, both hands tight around it, then swayed and ducked as Zurab launched himself. Two quick, slick steps brought him back out of range of another slash, but further from Ree's discarded sword. He could not afford to go to ground, that much was clear. The earth around them was little more than a squelching bog, and anyone who lost their footing or overstretched would struggle to escape its embrace.

Zurab circled, one hand on the end of the rope, the other swishing Manatas's sword in little figures of eight. He now blocked the way to Ree's sword, and without obvious thought he scuffed one filthy boot backwards and showered the weapon with a lumpy spray of muck. 'Oops,' he said.

'Zurab,' Manatas said, one eye on each sword, 'let us be candid. It is no secret that my time with the company has reached an end, but it may not be for the reason you think.' He took another careful step back as Zurab menaced him with the blade.

'That so?' the Vistirlari sneered. He was pushing Manatas further from Ree's sword with every risky step.

'The company, as we understand it, is in breach of its own by-laws,' Manatas replied, one hand on the rope at his waist, one hand out to balance himself. The ground slid beneath his boots every time he shifted his weight. A sudden move seemed more likely to dump him on his posterior than achieve any significant translocation, and after that would come something far less pleasant. He needed to keep Zurab's attention divided. 'Since the captain-general's death, we have failed to follow our agreed procedures, and the acting leadership have rendered themselves rogue by our own definitions.'

'Rogue, eh?' Zurab was getting closer again, giving little testing pulls on the rope every time Manatas looked like moving his feet.

I will not die by my own sword, Manatas vowed to himself. How would that look?

'As such,' he went on, his gaze now fixed on the keen edge of the familiar steel dancing at the rope's other end, 'the terms of our contracts are suspended, pending an investigation and ruling by the Confederation of Free Companies. Neither you nor I are currently bound by the Company of the Wolf.'

The sword-point jumped and capered a foot from his face. 'Oh, my,' said Zurab. He was nowhere near distracted enough.

'Meaning,' Manatas gasped, taking two scrabbling steps backwards, one hand flailing, as Zurab made a lunging stab for his leg, 'that we face each other now as two private individuals, carrying neither association nor obligation to anything beyond the laws of this place.' He tried to slide to one side, but the rope was too tight, and Zurab came within a whisker of removing his hand. Manatas pressed his arm to his body in panicked recovery.

'I think I preferred it when you were gagged. Still, won't matter soon.' Zurab was grinning now. Manatas was almost against the wall of the terrace, stone-lined and perpendicular, and soon there would be nowhere else to go.

'Thus, and in summary,' Manatas panted, 'I am making you an offer: yield now, depart in peace, and I will seek no further remedy.'

Zurab's scarred eyebrows rose. 'Do what?'

'Surrender the weapon, depart this place, and I will absolve you of your actions. No repercussions. This will be my only offer.'

'Are you serious?' The sword dipped a fraction as Zurab swayed in mirth. 'Surrender? To you! Fuck no!' He began to laugh. Manatas tightened his grip on the rope. 'I'm going to cut you into fucking strips, you garrulous—'

Manatas made his move.

'Hush now, be silent, all of you.' Lado raised one stained gauntlet. 'I will not ask again, for your piteous, self-indulgent wailing assaults my very senses, and shall be considered injury. Stay! . . . where you are, do not approach. You have proved yourselves as treacherous as those below, whose every word is the venom of snakes.'

'You killed him!' Lali shrieked, still halfway to where Mani had fallen, the axe haft jutting skywards from his slumped form. 'You murdered a sweet old man who offered nothing but kindness!'

'A spy who drips poison into the ears of those who engage in honest dialogue is perfidious perversion. We of the Company of the Wolf have only ever sought restitution for the injustices we have suffered. We have only ever requested that which we were owed. Yet at *every – turn* we have been met with assault, with betrayal, with *lies*.'

Javani could only watch, frozen, her arms clamped around Tarfellian, the one warm, solid thing in the world. His growl was constant, almost obscuring the echoes of thunder that rolled periodically over the valley. Perhaps if it finally rained, it would wash these armoured monsters from the ledge and out to sea. Perhaps.

Lado took a slow step over Mani's crumpled body without apparent attention, advancing on Lali. His visor was still up, and spittle gleamed from the rim of his helmet. 'The lord adjutant and I came to this place in the spirit of open discourse, to put our differences aside and see justice done. And how were we met?' He swung a creaking arm towards where Arman lay, blood pooled on the rock around his head. 'Unprovoked savagery.' The arm swung to Mani. 'Trickery and deceit. From a village that reneges on its commitments and harbours *murderers*!'

Javani felt her throat close. Murderers. She was the murderer, the killer of the man on the roadside. But they held Ree responsible. This man was here because of what they had done, together. This was their fault. Mani was dead and it was all her—

'So do not plead to me, child,' Lado snarled in his sidelong, shuffling way, as he moved slowly towards where Lali crouched. 'Do not mewl and wail of mistreatment. The only rules, the only laws, are those that we make – and what good is a law that is never enforced? The Company of the Wolf have made clear their laws, and now they will be prosecuted. We will see justice done, the world returned to the order of our making.'

He loomed over Lali, then snatched a handful of her robe with frightening speed and hauled her to her feet before him. When she screamed, he clamped his other hand to her face, crushing her cheeks in his armoured gauntlet, then turned her head slowly from side to side, his own head moving in mirror.

'They are convincing facsimiles, Lord Botrys,' Lado whispered, 'but little more. Spirits of deceit made flesh. We must purge them from this place.'

A hand dropped to his belt, where a skull-handled knife stood proud. Lali shook and wept silent tears, her hands vainly wrapping his arm, her face clamped in his armoured grip.

'Leave her the fuck alone!'

Javani was on her feet, though she had no memory of standing. Her legs were shaking uncontrollably, her fingers trembling. Beside her, Tarfellian rose tall and shook himself, then resumed his growl.

Lado's head turned towards her with contemptuous languor. 'Oh?' he said. 'Or what?'

'Did you know, Tauras,' Ree bounced along on his back as he thumped up the slick stone steps, her words shaking along with her, 'there's a festival, down south, held every third spring outside a town called Astarvan, called the Beggar's Tourney?'

'No, mistress, I did not.' His words came easily even as he moved at full pelt up the rocky steps, the shock of each crashing footfall jumping her on her perch on his back and sending a jolt of pain along her ruined leg. The man was a marvel, but this was not a comfortable way to travel.

'It's a low-rent version of the fayres they hold in Arowan and in the Sink, feats of strength, melees, that kind of thing . . . jousting.'

'Sounds fun, mistress.'

'But— Shit!'

Around the curve of the rockface, a figure hove into view as Tauras raced along the path, a figure in a grey cloak and mail. He'd heard them coming, and was ready, braced with spear jutting. She wasn't ready, she hadn't prepared for him to climb this quickly.

Something whistled from her right, a flash of movement like a speeding bird, and the greycloak ahead of her grunted. His spear dipped as he reached a hand down to the long, fletched shaft that now protruded, improbably, from the side of his thigh. He turned, eyes wide, and a second arrow punched directly into his mailed chest. He staggered backwards, bounced from the cliff wall, lost his footing through his injured leg and stumbled over the path's edge, spear and all, dropping from sight as Tauras powered past.

'Thank you, Anri,' Ree murmured. 'Maybe you're not so useless after all.'

'Sorry, mistress, you were saying?'

'I was, wasn't I? The thing about this festival, Tauras, or at least in the tale of its beginnings, is that nobody can afford horses . . .'

FIFTY-NINE

Zurab was not expecting Manatas to pull on the rope. He took a lurching step forward, off-balance, the sword thrown out to one side, then his foot slipped sideways in the slime and he fell.

Manatas was on him in an instant. One knee pressed down on his arm, pinning the sword to the ground, the other on his chest. Manatas reached for a knife that wasn't there, and instead settled for punching the Vistirlari square across the face. Zurab flailed with the sword, trying to wrestle Manatas off him, trying to free his limb from the oozing sludge, and Manatas punched him again, then wrapped the loose coil of rope around Zurab's free arm and looped it over the man's helmet, yanking his arm tight against his own head.

'Get off me, you—'

Manatas punched him again, then with one hand hammered at Zurab's exposed wrist until he let the sword fall. Manatas snatched it up and pressed the blade to Zurab's exposed throat, drawing a thin, bright line in the dark and muddy smears.

'Well,' he said, 'here we are again, Zurab.'

'Leave her alone or I'll release Tarfellian. He'll go for you.' Javani couldn't stop her legs shaking, but hoped the mastiff's bulk would obscure how terrified she was. 'He'll rip out your throat.'

Lado's head was still inclined, and he made no move to release Lali. 'Is that so?' His hand came up, the wicked, gleaming knife held in the silvery gauntlet. 'You fancy your hound to dig through cold steel?'

Now he did release Lali, discarding her to the shabby rock at Volkan's feet – Volkan, who was still, to Javani's distant but intense irritation, praying. Lado shuffled sideways to face her and Tarfellian, stepping over the loose rope that Lali had looped over the stacked timber by the cave entrance. He peered forward at the dog. 'This fellow would have been quite the concern in his younger days. But now?'

He tossed the knife from hand to hand, twirled it over his clanking fingers, his eyes never leaving Javani. Beside her, Tarfellian's snarl was a low, constant thing. 'Would you make me do it?' He took another step, rope scuffing beneath his armoured boots. 'The choice will be yours. The fault will be yours. I am merely fate's instrument.'

He grinned, grimaced, bared his teeth in a strange and unsettling flex of his mouth. 'What is it to be, child of lies? Are you so keen to see your hound's viscera?'

Javani swallowed. 'Tarfellian,' she said in her biggest, most commanding voice, which was not saying much. 'Sit.'

The dog ignored her, his snarl undimmed, but he did not move.

Lado's expression of twisted mirth fell away, and he simply turned away from her. 'Lord adjutant, we have been threatened and harangued enough. These creatures cannot be trusted.' He walked slowly, back along the path of the loose ropes, towards where Mani lay. 'Only one path lies open to us.'

'Uh, acting commander . . .' Botrys appeared no less assailed by doubt since Mani's felling. He was sweating beneath his helmet, beads clear on his cheeks. 'Might we not, uh . . .'

Lado put one foot on Mani's body and wrenched the axe clear. 'It is them or us, lord adjutant. They have wanted war from the beginning, and war they shall have. If we must cleave every head on this mountain from the shoulders below, so be it!'

Revulsion pushed Javani to act, hearing Mani's agonised gasp as Lado pulled the axe clear, the shock of realising he still lived matched to the horror of his continuing suffering, the thought of Lado taking that axe to the terrified, harmless villagers who cowered behind her in the caves, her sheer physical *disgust* of the man. Her hands moved without express thought, and as Lado turned back, the axe slung over an ornate pauldron, he came face to face with the pointy end of the hand-bow.

'Oho,' said Lado of Cstethia with a wide, mad, grin. 'We have our first volunteer.'

Anri had already downed the next guard before they reached her – Tauras vaulted over the woman's prone form and the wide, dark puddle around her, an arrow jutting proud of the side of her neck. Then they were around another switchback and climbing again, Tauras's breathing coming in regular barks, his heavy hands now clamped to her shins. Ree felt a little perilous in her new position, but it had freed her hands, and as they clattered up the weathered steps towards the next greycloak's emplacement, the astonishment and confusion on the man's face made the extreme discomfort entirely worthwhile.

'Tauras, charge!'

Tauras barrelled up the steps, Ree riding high on his shoulders, the standard-less pole couched beneath her arm like a lance. The mercenary ahead had no idea how to respond, how to set himself as they bore down on him, the sword in his hand suddenly too small, too puny. He turned one way as if to retreat, thought better of it, turned back and caught the tip of the pole square on his shield.

The shock of it rocked Ree's arm and shoulder as if she'd hit a wall, and even Tauras slowed a stride, but the impact on the mercenary was enough to drive him pinwheeling backwards, twisting in space, then over the path's edge and out of sight.

'You all right, mistress?'

Ree shook the life back into her grumbling shoulder. The pole had survived intact, at least. 'All right if you are, Tauras.'

'I'm all right, mistress.'

'Then onwards and upwards, soldier. As fast as you can.'

'I gave you fair warning, Zurab.' Manatas held the sword firm across the struggling man's throat, mindful that he would have at least one more knife on him and it was only a matter of time before he went for it. 'I told you that improper conduct would lead to punishment. I told you that failing our standards would make you their victim. Did you forget, Zurab?' He was breathing through his teeth now, hours' worth of suppressed fury, suppressed outrage surging up through him. Days', perhaps – he'd been so angry, for so long, and it had built within him with no outlet. Zurab had become his outlet.

He pressed the sword tighter, watching a bead of bright blood bloom beneath the blade. Zurab's kicking and hissing only intensified.

'Did you forget I was *good* at this, Zurab, you dung-brained buffoon? Did you forget that I, like you, am a man of violence? How do you think I became a captain?'

Zurab tried to spit, tried to wrestle himself clear. The trickle of blood at his neck thickened. 'You said . . . you'd let me go,' he gasped.

'I made you an offer, which you *refused*,' Manatas snarled. 'And I will not repeat myself. It is the eternal failing of the bully to mistake compassion for weakness.' Abruptly the fury left him, burned out, the incredible pointlessness of their conflict draining the energy required to sustain it. 'I'm so tired, Zurab,' he murmured, 'so thrice-damned tired. And you have delayed me too long.'

Now Zurab went for his blade, jack-knifing his body in an attempt to get his arms free. Manatas rode his spasms and whipped the sword across his throat, then pushed himself to his feet as Zurab rocked and gurgled, both hands clasped to his pulsing neck. Their eyes met, the Vistirlari's wide with panic and reproach as he sank slowly into the blood-sodden mud.

'You had your chance,' said Chapter Captain Inaï Manatas, before turning and walking unsteadily away.

They knocked another mercenary clean off the path before the pole snapped. At least one more remained between them and the top, and Tauras was finally tiring, his breath coming harder now, his pace beginning to flag. Still, the man had run up a cliffside carrying another human the whole way, and Ree was inclined to let him off the last part. Until she heard the screams from overhead.

'Tauras, fuck, keep going, please!'

'I am . . . going, mistress.'

Ahead of them, ready and waiting, not one but two of the mercenaries, blocking the final turn of the path. The rock shelf that marked the entrances to the caves was directly above them; if Ree craned, she could see the machinery of the hoist projecting over its edge, the great net sacks of river stones swaying gently in the chill breeze. If she stood on Tauras's shoulders, could she reach it? Could she climb it from here, and bypass the greycloaks and their bristling armoury?

Not a chance.

'Tauras, apart from your knife, what other weapons do you have?'

'One other knife, mistress.'

'Right. Can I borrow it, please?'

'Of course, mistress.'

'Thank you. Now for this bit, I'm going to need one last favour.'

'Yes, mistress.'

She shifted her position on his shoulders, sizing up the approaching mercenaries, their shields, their gleaming swords, their excellent formation.

'When I say, you're going to need to throw me.'

'Righto, mistress.'

SIXTY

Javani swallowed hard, trying to still the trembling of her hands, the judder of the little bow. Her mind swam with urgent, unanswerable questions: would the bow even shoot? Would it go where she pointed it? Could she hit a part of him that wasn't draped in glossy steel? What would happen when she failed?

Lado regarded her along the length of the slim bolt, head inclined, the axe unmoved from his armoured shoulder. 'You disappoint me, child of lies, but I am not surprised. Even when I thought we had arrived at congruence, you have one more betrayal in store.'

'Shut up! Stop *whining* about everything!'

'Am I to fall silent to spare you the truth of your actions?'

'By the gods! Have you ever taken responsibility for anything in your life?'

'I do not care for your tone.' He took a slow step towards her, crossing the centre of the shelf. 'Just what is it you think you'll be doing with that curious little device?'

'Back down. Back away, go back down the path and don't come back.'

His brows lowered, quizzical, challenging. 'Or?'

'Or I kill you with this.'

Another swaggering step, his boots kicking rope. 'Put that weapon down, child of lies, before you hurt yourself. We both know you don't have it in you.'

'Last chance.'

'Likewise, creature.'

One more step. This was it. Anri's words buzzed in her brain: *Feet in line with your body, keep both eyes open. Control your breath!* It wasn't a proper bow, but it couldn't be far off, could it? Don't second-guess yourself, Javani – Ree trusts you, you can trust yourself.

Javani set herself, sighted, controlled her breath, and squeezed the trigger.

'Now!'

Tauras heaved. Ree sprang from his upturned palms, one leg ablaze with pain, and sailed through space. The cliffside rushed towards her, a wall of pitted and mottled rock, and she angled her body to push back from it with her free hand and good leg. Then she was over the astonished mercenaries, landing in a tumbling ball on the path behind them, tucked and rolling and hissing from the jolt to her leg. At least she'd given it a rest on the way up the cliff. Sort of.

'Long time since I've done anything like that,' she breathed to herself.

She pushed herself to her good foot, Tauras's knife already clear in her hands. The mercenaries were milling, both turning to her, both turning back to Tauras, finally reaching some kind of equilibrium with one facing each way. They took too long. Tauras was on them, grasping the wrists of the closer man, delivering a mighty head-butt that dropped him to his knees. The second wheeled, exposing his back to Ree, then spun back in panic.

'You go, mistress.'

'Thank you, Tauras.'

She set off at a rapid limp, broken pole in one hand, the knife in the other, leaving Tauras facing the fully armed and armoured mercenary. She knew who her money was on.

'I'm coming, kid,' she breathed as she scudded up the last turn of the cliff path. 'Ma's coming.'

Manatas reached the top of the path with a sword in each hand, his lungs burning, to come face to face with a wall of spears. He let his arms drop.

'Where is she? Did she go up?'

'Who are you, then?' Lurking behind the wild-eyed spear-wielders was the filthy archer who'd shouted at him earlier. Beyond him, injured villagers were clustered around the foot of the cliff, albeit at something of a distance from it. A ring of broken bodies across the torn earth of the terrace suggested why. On closer inspection, some of them looked familiar, which pained him. 'That odd friend of Ree's, is it? On our side now, are you?'

'Did she go up?'

The archer rubbed a hand over his bristly chin. 'Did at that, her and the big bugger with the hair. Keeps dropping little presents for us.'

As if on cue, a tumbling figure in a grey cloak came bouncing down the cliff, thumping twice against the rock before crunching into a circle of splattered earth.

'Don't mind me, like,' the archer said, setting off for the fallen figure with a knife in his hand. 'Just need to make sure the fuckers are dead. Let him through, boys.'

He would not fail another friend. Manatas sucked in a hot breath and ran for the steps.

The rock shelf lay in silence, the terrible hush of an audience who had seen something horrifying and had no idea how to react. Javani stared past the shaking hand-bow at where the bolt had passed clean over Lado's shoulder and thumped into something on the other side of the ledge.

The acting commander of the Company of the Wolf regarded her contemptuously. 'Well. That was a needless waste of time, wasn't it?'

Javani wasn't looking at him. She was looking at where the bolt had struck home, within the mechanism of the hoist. She was looking at the locking wedge, which had, fractionally, started to shift.

Lado brought the axe off his shoulder. 'Do you pray, child of lies?' He nodded at Volkan. 'He does. Shall we see if it makes any difference?'

With a slow groan, then a jolt, the wedge moved. The counterweight sack of rocks dangling from the hoist dropped a hand's span, then stopped, jerking and swinging.

The noise drew Lado's attention. 'Now just what—'

The wedge pinged clear, and the sack of rocks plunged from view. The pulleys began to spin, and a hissing noise came from the spooled rope beside it.

Lado looked at the rope, then traced its path across the shelf, all the way to the loose loops coiled below his feet.

He stepped to one side. 'Oh, very clever, child of lies. Did you intend that?'

The rope whipped taut as the hoist exhausted its slack, a sudden line at chest-height erupting from the shelf's floor. Lado watched it tremble with amusement dancing in his eyes. He reached over and tapped it with a gauntleted finger, delighting in its hum.

'That was quite the shot, child of lies. How sad for you that—'

The pile of timber where Lali had lashed the rope produced the most terrible groaning sound. Lado's eyes widened, the path of the rope suddenly no longer a source of entertainment. He tried to bring the axe around, fumbled it, grabbed for the skull-handled knife at his belt.

The groan from the timber became a splitting sound.

'Surprise, dickhead,' Javani whispered.

A spar of timber as wide as Javani's torso and three times as long burst from the pile and rocketed across the shelf. It caught Lado square in the armoured chest and his eyes met Javani's as the force of it carried him up in the air and clean off the ledge. The pain had not hit him, but the terror had. As Lado of Cstethia went over the edge, he was wailing with fear.

SIXTY-ONE

Ree was three burning paces from the top when a sound like the thunderous ringing of a bell near-deafened her. She looked up to see a pillar of shining steel arc into the air beyond the cliffside, glittering in the feeble light, as wooden chunks and splinters rained down around it. Then it dropped, falling like a stone through the last of the drifting mist to the distant terrace below. It seemed to be keening. She barely heard the noise it made when it hit.

A man in similar armour was retreating down the path, his fur-cloaked back to her as he edged off the shelf. Ree flicked up the knife and stepped in close, wrapping her arm around and pressing the edge to the astonished man's exposed cheek.

'Boo,' she said.

'I surrender!' squeaked the man, as his sword clattered to the rock.

Manatas had been only a few steps from the bottom when the man had fallen, close enough to hear the archer's exasperated sigh. But this one had not fallen like the others, no bounces or scuffs from the cliffside. His drop had been straight down, a vertical plummet, and the noise of impact had been gruesome. Say what you like about full plate, Manatas cautioned himself, it does not cushion a fall.

He walked slowly over to where the body had landed, by sheer ill luck, half-in and half-out of an unfinished pit at the foot of the cliff. Armoured legs stuck out at impossible angles, and within the pit wooden stakes lay splintered and snapped, but some had been driven into the gaps between the plates. The visor was still open, jammed up against the helmet by the force of the landing, but Manatas paid it and its contents no attention. Instead, he knelt carefully beside the pit and rummaged in the armour's belting and pouches until he found what he was after.

'There are rules,' he said softly.

Then, without another word, Manatas turned his back on the ruin of Lado of Cstethia and walked back to the path.

Javani and Lali cradled Mani between them. The old man's blood saturated their clothes, the stone beneath them sticky and vile. Lali wept uncontrollably, and Javani wasn't far off herself, but he reached out to them, placing a cooling hand on each of theirs. His moustache was mottled with dark spots, but he still managed to smile.

'Love . . . everyone,' he mouthed.

'But it didn't work!' Javani cried. 'They killed you!'

'It doesn't mean . . .' came his whispered response, 'you shouldn't try.'

His chest moved for a short while longer, but Mani spoke no more. Javani was conscious of little more than hugging Lali as they wept, of Tarfellian's wet nose on her cheek, his attempts to soothe her with great rasping sweeps of his tongue. Then Ree was there, levering her up from the freezing ground, cradling her in her arms. Even Volkan was bereft, hot streaks of tears travelling his gaunt cheeks as with only the slightest hesitation he let Lali embrace him.

'Are you whole, kid?' Ree's voice was little more than a murmur through her hair.

Javani nodded, sniffling and wiping at her nose. The mist was finally lifting, the cloud breaking, and the occasional shaft of low, golden sun shone through the gloomy mass overhead. Thunder rolled on over the peaks, but there was no storm in the valley. Not any longer.

'You?'

Ree nodded in return, then caught herself. 'Leg isn't good,' she admitted.

'That why it took you so long . . . to get back up here?'

'Maybe. I'm sorry I wasn't there for you, kid.'

They embraced again, Javani's breath still coming in shivering gasps.

'I am sick to death . . . of seeing people I care about . . . murdered in front of me! He killed Mani, Ma. The sweetest, kindest old man . . . and he killed him. So I . . .' She swallowed. 'I killed him back.'

'I heard.'

'Not much doubt on whether this one was my fault.'

'How do you feel?'

'Horrible.'

Ree cupped her chin in her hand. 'Let me reassure you of one thing, kid. The sad truth is that the world is better off without some people in it, and that prick was one of them. You've done the rest of us a favour today.'

'It doesn't feel like it.'

'Maybe one day it will.' Ree squeezed her shoulders again. 'And you showed I was right to trust you.'

'Trusted me not to die? I guess I'll take it, but it feels a pretty low bar.'

'Sometimes it's all you need.'

'What about partners now, Ree?'

Ree ruffled her hair and pulled her close. 'Next decision's on you, kid, no matter the scale. And what's this I'm hearing about you threading the needle with that hand-bow? Knocked the wedge from the hoist from fifteen strides?'

Javani's cheeks coloured, proud while not-proud. 'Maybe eighteen. I didn't shut my eyes!'

'That's my girl. All my training finally paid off.'

'Uh, sure, Ma. Something like that.'

'Hey, kid, he could have had it worse. You could have hit him in the unmentionables.'

It took a long time to clear the shelf and start moving everyone down. Arman was breathing but still unconscious, which did not bode well. Mani was draped in woollen cloth from the stores and carried down in Tauras's arms. Javani walked arm-in-arm with her mother ahead of Volkan and Lali, their progress slow and expressly painful. Tarfellian followed behind, stiff but regal. Nobody suggested using the hoist. It would likely require substantial repairs.

When Ree's leg became too painful to continue, they stopped to rest on the path, and Javani looked out over the spread of the terraces beneath them, the escarpment and the river below, still dogged by trailing fronds of mist at its heart, then the rising spread of the valley's opposite side. The trees were thick and leafless, the snow of days before washed away by the previous night's downpour. The opposite slope was devoid of smoke, of movement, of anything suggesting life beyond whatever creatures dwelt within the forest. The mercenary camp was empty. In the distance, thunder boomed again.

'Where in the name of the gods is that storm?' Javani muttered. 'It's been all talk and no substance.'

'Reminds me of countless men I've known.' Ree chuckled, then winced and massaged her calf.

'Tauras could carry you down, if you want,' Javani suggested, scratching the patient Tarfellian behind the ears. 'If you wait for him to come back up.'

'No. I'm finished with being carried. Until I'm in a shroud, at least.'

'I'll let you walk, then.' She looked out over the valley again. 'Oh, the hawk's back. Ma, he's back!'

'It's probably not the same one, kid.'

'It is. It's definitely him.'

She waved. It was definitely him.

Javani found herself beside Volkan as they resumed, allowing her mother enough space to swing her improvised walking stick and curse every step on the journey down. The councillor was still visibly upset, his cheeks more hollow than normal, the lines beneath his eyes pronounced.

'I'm sorry about Mani,' Javani said, because walking in silence seemed more awkward than stating the obvious. 'I wish I could have saved him.'

'We are all the poorer for his loss,' Volkan replied. 'None more so than me.' He took a long, sad sniff. 'Who else can hope to test me at the stones now?'

They descended another half-dozen steps, careful on the damp rock. 'Volkan,' Javani said, 'do you remember telling me that the godless turning to prayer in times of crisis was, uh, a coward's gambit?'

'Hm,' the old man replied. 'I may have said something similar.'

'But weren't you praying up there?'

'Perhaps I was, perhaps I wasn't. But either way, it worked, didn't it?'

Ree found Manatas waiting at the bottom of the path, given a wide, wary berth by the rest of the villagers, which might have been for any number of reasons. He looked, if anything, even worse than before. One side of his head was a black matted mess of dried blood, and he was covered in a tarry mixture of mud, blood and gods knew what else. He could still offer a pleasant smile on seeing her descend, hobbling and agonised as she was.

'I, uh, have something of yours, my lady Ree.' He held out her sword, took it back and tried to wipe away some of the coating of filth on the scabbard, then offered it again. 'I had no need for it in the end, but I appreciate your kindness and generosity of spirit in a time of great peril.'

'What? What in—' The kid was a pace behind her, little face puffed in outrage. 'You *gave* him your *sword*? The sword you never lend anyone, the sword you—'

'I did,' she replied, taking the weapon, their fingers grazing, then doing her best to clean off the remaining mud. 'But you heard him, he didn't use it.'

'But that's *worse*!' the kid shrieked.

'How are you, Captain Mandlebras?' Ree said, a hint of mischief in her smile, despite the pain and exhaustion. Around them, people were spontaneously bursting into tears, many from relief, from elation at still being alive at the end of it all; some, on the other hand, for far less celebratory reasons. Ree felt like joining them, but there was too much to do yet.

'I am . . . uncertain, my lady Ree,' he replied.

'I feel like we have a lot to discuss.'

'I would concur without question, but if you'll forgive me, I have someone I must see first.' He patted a pouch at his belt, which meant nothing to her, but she nodded him on.

'See you presently.'

His gaze lingered a moment longer before he departed, and she met it.

She made slow progress to where Vida still rested, now sitting up, her leg tightly bound, and barking orders at her fleet of apprentices who had emerged from their various hiding places and were being dispatched on a raft of tasks with barely a breather. Ree caught Mariam's eye.

'How is she?'

'Irrepressible,' came the response, matched to a tight smile that spoke of joy, and relief, and sadness, but most of all of love.

'Are we, I don't know, safe? Is the village clear? Just because Lado the dipshit is a smear in a pit doesn't mean—'

'The perimeter is secure,' Vida barked from the ground. 'We're just corralling prisoners now.' She puffed out a frustrated breath. 'Damned shame about the ram pen, we'll need to use something a little more substantial.'

'Keretan? Camellia?'

Mariam jerked her thumb across the terrace to the Council House. 'Both alive, both injured, both desperate to get out and start doing things. Honestly, the bloody lot of you!' She reached down and ruffled her wife's hair. 'You're all as bad as each other when it comes to letting yourselves rest.'

'Resting doesn't get things done,' Vida and Ree said in unison, then exchanged wary looks.

Ree took a breath and asked the question she'd been dreading. 'Casualties?' was all she could manage.

Vida and Mariam looked at each other to see who would reply. At length, Mariam released a sad breath. 'Mani is dead, and Arman may never wake. If that weren't enough, we have multiple broken bones, some worrying head injuries, at least three lost fingers, several very nasty cuts and gashes, and my darling here.' Vida inclined her head in acknowledgement. 'The damage is significant.'

Ree blinked, shook her head, played Mariam's words back in her head to make sure she'd heard correctly. 'Are you saying that . . . one person died? One?'

Mariam inclined her head. 'It's a tragedy.'

'It's a fucking miracle!'

'Some of those injured may have mobility problems for the rest of their lives! And blood poisoning is no laughing matter—'

'Nine skull-dancing, piss-gargling hells, Mariam, only one person died! Every soul in this village could have been slaughtered today!'

'You don't have to sound so cock-a-hoop about it.'

'It was a good plan,' Vida averred from the ground.

'It was, wasn't it?' Ree could hardly keep the laughter in now, a hot feeling in her chest that seemed to clog her throat as it rose. 'It was.'

Ree burst into tears.

Javani found Anri milling around the bottom of the terrace, ostensibly supervising the rounding up of their prisoners. The bulk of said prisoners were injured mercenaries, victims of traps and volleys, left stricken and abandoned by their more mobile comrades. It wasn't clear when it had happened, but at some stage a critical mass of them had reached the conclusion that taking the village was no longer worth the trouble – possibly around the fifth or sixth encounter with something sharp and unexpected – and begun a staged withdrawal. The withdrawal had become an expedient retreat, and from there it was only a short hop to full-on rout. Many had abandoned their weapons and equipment in their haste to flee the village, and collecting up their leavings before an infant found them was becoming a full-time task.

The one exception was Botrys, the man Lado had called lord adjutant. He was stripped of his armour, standing in his undershirt in the ruin of the ram pen and looking very cold indeed. A suspicious dark patch marked the front of his hose.

Javani sidled up to Anri. 'Did you hear about my bow-shot?'

He didn't seem to hear her, so she nudged him. 'I said—'

'Oh. Hello.'

'Hello?'

'Yes, hello.'

'What happened to "Gods save me from your vapid pestering"?' She looked closely at him. Beneath his thick coating of mud, he seemed unharmed, but his eyes had a vacant quality that she didn't like at all. 'Are you all right?'

'Am I all right,' he replied, but without the customary rancour that should have accompanied it; it sounded a genuine pause for consideration.

'Anri?' She put a tentative hand on his arm. 'What is it?'

He was looking off over the terrace, over the valley and into the milky distance, but he likely saw none of it. 'Do you know what I thought, the moment that fucker crashed to earth, the moment I knew it was all done?'

'What?'

'I can't wait to tell Tanith.'

'Oh.'

'Couldn't stop myself. Was looking forward to getting home, kicking off the boots, getting the fire raging, then telling her all about it, all about the insanity of it all. That we faced them down. That we won.'

'Oh, Anri.'

'But I can't fucking do that, can I? Because they killed her. And they burned my fucking house down.'

'I'm so sorry, Anri.'

'That's the point, though, isn't it? She's been dead for years, dead to me, I mean. I just carried on talking at her, even though she couldn't talk back. I've been fucking kidding myself for years, pretending I had a life. Just fucking pretending. It's not like I even built that whole house myself, I had loads of help.'

'I, uh . . .'

'Ah, I don't know what I'm complaining about. My life was shit before, when you think about it, which I never did. I've not been a happy man, pest.'

'Really.'

'I reckon it's time for some new horizons, don't you? This lot have sorted themselves out at last. When are you and your mam moving off, then?'

'Oh, I . . . uh . . . Can I let you know on that?'

Manatas sat slowly down beside Kediras, easing himself to the sodden earth, then reached across and placed the flute into her open palm. A little down the slope lay a swathe of grey-cloaked corpses, the ground around them saturated with their blood. The sightless eyes of Antulu gazed unblinking at the silvery sky, the slack-jawed head some distance from the rest of the acting captain. Manatas did his best to ignore it.

'There you go, my friend,' he said. 'I am sorry that it took me this long to secure.'

He gazed back over the corpses. Carrion birds were already gathered overhead, turning slow circles of ravenous expectation, despite the lateness of the year. 'I counted them, you know,' he went on, 'as I passed. Eighteen. Eighteen Pashani no longer walk the earth. This may be the last of them. I hope this pleases you.'

They sat in silence for a little while, staring out, past the savaged bodies and the uproar of the village downslope, watching the last of the mist fade at the valley's foot. Birds called, trees creaked in the wind. It was not a warm day, but it was an improvement on those that had come before.

'I still intend to go to the lake,' Manatas said, 'but there are matters to attend here that must take precedence. I must find where they left Arkadas. Too many good souls deserve better than they received.' He sniffed against the cold. 'Tauras will come. He has no love for the mountain climate, especially in winter. We will spend the season by the lake, and recuperate, and consider. The world has changed too much since we last made our plans.'

He put one arm around her and rested his head against hers. When he next spoke, his voice was cracked and hoarse. 'It will be a harder journey in your absence, Kediras, and a poorer world.' He reached up with gentle fingers and closed her eyes. 'Sleep well, my friend.'

Manatas put his face to his knees and sobbed.

SIXTY-TWO

'Are you sure you're up to this?' Ree asked as they made their painstaking way across the valley floor, her stick leaving divots in the soft earth.

'I feel I should be asking you a question of similar intent,' Manatas replied. 'Your state may be worse than mine.'

'Nobody cut my ear off this morning.'

'Perhaps we can merely align on the notion that neither of us has experienced an optimal start to our day? Nonetheless, I have obligations on the far side of the valley that I will not delay.'

'Well, there's still some daylight left, so as long as we don't move at the pace of a wounded animal there and back, we'll be golden, eh? Oh.'

'You are a droll person, my lady Ree.'

'Cheer up, captain, you're still alive, which is more than can be said for a good number of those who thought killing us was a good idea. And that accursed thunder has finally stopped. Things are looking up, I'd say.'

The camp was almost unrecognisable. It shouldn't have been, Manatas had left it only hours before in that strange, indigo wash of pre-dawn, but in the intervening time it had been stripped of any semblance of an operating military encampment. Survivors and scavengers had torn through it, making off with whatever they could carry, and a few things that, from the way they had been dumped in the mud, they apparently could not.

He found Arkadas with little effort. He'd simply been left where he'd fallen, the mulch around him stained and curdled. He spent some time apologising to his late lieutenant, regretting that he hadn't placed greater trust in him from the start of the affair, commending him for his duty and diligence and his belief in the ideals of the company, before stumbling to a tear-choked halt.

He had no strength to do more. His idea of securing a proper send-off had been foolish; he would have to wait until Tauras made his way to the camp, as was his later intention, and between them they would either transport Arkadas back across the valley to rest with Kediras, or secure his final resting place on the hill. At this stage, Manatas was too tired to think any further ahead than that.

A whistle from up the slope drew him away from his melancholy. Ree was standing outside the grand pavilion, admiring its construction.

'Hey, chapter captain. This one yours?'

'I regret it is not, it is the official residence of the captain-general. Mine is the—'

'I don't care, come with me.'

The pavilion was oddly undisturbed, as though the looters had expressed some curious reverence to its contents and left it alone. The inside was cold, its braziers unlit, but the furniture was untouched: the folding tables, Ridderhof's cursed bathtub, the comfortable chair that Botrys had had carried in and out to suit his whims, the great fur-laden bed at the pavilion's rear.

Ree was leading him by the hand through the pavilion. Manatas followed meekly, half-awake, no longer attempting to fight his confusion, to reason his way through an unreasonable world. Once he had recuperated, he would approach matters afresh. Once he had been permitted a chance to rest.

Ree tossed her stick to one side and commanded him to undress, and Manatas obeyed without question.

It was some time after, in the glow beneath the furs, that Ree became aware of the noise. No longer the incessant, sourceless thunder, nor even the knocking and squeaking of the great bed. This was coming from somewhere outside the pavilion, if not by much, and sounded like an animal in distress. Eventually, it proved annoying enough to force them up and back into their clothes, and they went, swords in hand, to investigate.

The noise was coming from a stack of wood-framed boxes, piled up in a rotting stack on the slope behind the pavilion. One of them was rocking and producing a sort of honking noise.

Ree gestured with her sword. 'What is this?'

Manatas squinted past it. 'Had some chickens here, long ago. This was their coop.'

'And what is it now?'

'At this time, I cannot rightly say.'

'Open it.'

'Are you sure? Gods only know what manner of—'

Ree was firm. 'I'll cover you.'

He went, muttering, 'And how are you going to do that from there?' but in a good-humoured way, at least.

The wood was rotten, and took very little levering. A moment later, a bundle of reeking filth bounced free.

They stared at the bundle.

The bundle stared back.

'Nine piss-drenched hells,' Ree whispered. 'Constable Gumis?'

It took some convincing before they could even get the gag off him, let alone cut his bonds; Gumis seemed almost feral, and not without justification. But he was alive; despite torture, injury, hunger and depredation, he was extraordinarily alive.

'I guess they just forgot about him,' Manatas murmured.

'By all the gods,' Ree muttered, 'if this keeps up the village is going to end up with more people than it started with.'

Finally, the gag was off, and the former constable glared at them with open hostility. 'You,' he hissed at Manatas through broken teeth. 'You,' he swivelled and hissed at Ree. 'You're in league with them? Of course.'

'Oh, my boy,' Ree sighed. 'You have a lot to catch up on.'

The day that followed was strange, and sad. More rain fell in the evening, slowing the clean-up efforts, and driving the survivors back to the homes that were still safe to enter without triggering something unwelcome. Overnight the temperature dropped, and Ar Ramas awoke the next morning to find itself once again blanketed in a layer of fresh powder. It was still snowing, albeit gently, when Javani braved the cold in Mariam's footsteps and went to help serve breakfast from the Council House, which had been converted into a temporary kitchen and resting place. Tarfellian kept pace alongside her, his giant paws leaving great holes in the fresh crust.

Gumis was recuperating in the Council House, along with many others who'd suffered injury in the attack. He seemed stunned by events, and his own personal tribulations, but by the time Javani and Mariam were ready to leave, he had begun to regale some of his fellow patients with tales of his heroism in the face of mortal danger, and Javani guessed he couldn't be all that damaged. She was puzzled to see that Sweeper's prized pots were missing, though.

They fed the prisoners next, a motley, piteous lot, watched over by Tauras and a rotating cast of Vida's apprentices.

'What are you going to do with them?' Javani asked Mariam sidelong as they spooned out hot porridge. 'There's no one left in the mercenary camp to hand them back to . . . and even if you did, they have no supplies or equipment left. Ree said the others had stripped the place bare.'

'Well, it's not up to me,' Mariam replied, her eyes on bowl and ladle. 'But I imagine, if the Council agrees, that we'll keep an eye on them while they recover from their injuries, and then over winter if they're in no hurry to strike out into the mountains, then let them make their own choices from there, isn't it.'

'How do you mean?'

'If they want to go, or stay.'

'You'd . . .' Javani blinked. 'You'd let them join the village? After they attacked it?'

Mariam shrugged, poured out another steaming dollop of rich oats. 'Few of us here led perfect lives before we found this place. Seems only fair to extend the same opportunity to them, doesn't it? I like to think it's what Mani would have wanted. Perhaps your captain friend will keep them in line.' She passed the bowl over.

'Speaking of which, have you and that mam of yours come to your own decision yet?'

Javani bit her lip, which was getting numb with cold. 'No. Not yet.'

They performed the burials later that day, as sombre as would be expected, but doubly so for Mani's loss – his absence in conducting the service was keenly felt. Volkan took over, and delivered what Javani would have termed a Mani impression for the duration, which wasn't to her taste but seemed to satisfy the rest of the village. Kediras had been added to the rolls of the dead, as had poor Arman, who had not recovered from his terrible injury. Javani watched his family weeping at his graveside with a bitter knot in her stomach and a stinging like vinegar in her eyes.

The dead mercenaries were rolled into the valley and burned. Javani watched the black plumes rising high into the air, billowing into the day's thick cloud, and was glad that the wind was carrying the stink down-valley. She had no idea what had happened to Lado's remains, but she hoped he was sizzling away inside that horrendous armour somewhere at the base of a pyre.

'You all right, kid?'

'Huh? Yeah.' She sniffed and wiped her nose on her sleeve. 'I'm all right.'

'Don't do that, kid. By the gods, we only just got your clothes clean.'

Javani ignored it. 'Ma, did we . . . did we do the right thing? Knowing what we do now, if we'd just left things as they were, if we'd never got involved . . . would Mani still be alive? Would Arman? Would everything have worked out?'

She expected Ree to slap her down, dismiss the notion out of hand, but instead her mother put one hand on her hip and blew out her cheeks. 'Well, kid, we can't know anything for certain. Maybe Captain Manatas would have got things under control for a season or two . . . but who would have come after him? Running a settlement on the goodwill of heavily armed and hungry soldiers just isn't a viable long-term strategy.'

'It's a shame. I really like the idea of living in peace.'

'So do I, kid. And who's to say there isn't some way of making it work out there, just waiting to be tried?'

Javani sniffed again.

'Ma, what are we going to do? It's so late now . . . I'm not sure I can go out again.'

Ree sucked her lips together. She was looking better than she had in a long while, Javani had to admit. Maybe she was finally resting her leg. She'd heard something about her using a tent in the mercenary camp, presumably she was grabbing some relaxation time where she could. 'We're a few days behind where we might have been, sure, but if we want to go, we can go.'

Javani swallowed. 'And if we want to stay?'

Her mother let the question hang for a moment, watching her with steady eyes. 'What happened to finding our new life in the west?'

'Well . . .' Javani rubbed the heel of one boot against the other. 'I guess what I really wanted was to live somewhere, you know, nice. Comfortable. Somewhere I could . . .' Across the terrace, she saw Lali, helping to deconstruct a barricade. Lali waved. '. . . Make some friends.' She cleared her throat. 'What do you think?'

Ree turned slowly, scanning the devastated, uprooted terraces, the huts still buttressed between fortifications, the Council House, where many wounded resided, and finally to the graves before them. 'It may not be up to us, kid.'

Javani bowed her head. 'I understand.'

'Sorry, kid.'

'Yeah.'

SIXTY-THREE

'Mistress Ree, may I trouble you for a moment?'

'Camellia! Should you be up and about?'

The councillor was moving stiffly over the snow, a thick bandage around her head and one arm pressed to her body. 'I think we both know the answer to that.' She flashed a quick, nervous smile, and Ree wondered if that might be the first attempt at humour she'd seen from Camellia. 'How . . . How are you?'

The question caught Ree off-guard. 'I'm . . . all right. Mostly. Leg still isn't great.'

Camellia nodded thoughtfully, giving Ree's words more consideration than was due. Ree was disconcerted to realise that Camellia was nervous.

'And you—' Ree began, while Camellia said, 'Are you busy now?'

'I'm waiting for Captain Manatas to return from the camp. We have some matters to discuss.' Camellia didn't even blink. 'And Mariam said Vida had a message for me, although she's confined to the forge. It seems her injury isn't stopping her ordering those poor apprentices around.'

Camellia nodded again, her smile bright and brittle.

Ree gave up waiting. 'Was there something you wanted to discuss?'

'Mm, mm, yes.' Camellia wiped her free hand down the front of her robe. 'You'll be aware that we have a lot of clearing up to do. A monstrous amount, to quantify it correctly.'

'Yeah. Sorry about that.'

'And we have, of course, Sun's Night. If we can get things squared away in time, we might yet be celebrating as planned.'

'You're going ahead with that?'

'It feels the least that the people of Ar Ramas deserve, don't you think?'

The thought of busting a gut clearing the village only to bust several more putting a festival together in a few short days gave Ree a psychological hernia, but thank the gods it wasn't her problem. 'Sure. Why not.'

Camellia took a slightly unsteady breath. 'We've not always seen eye-to-eye, Ree, but . . . well, I've talked with the other councillors, and quite a few other people besides, and . . . we'd like you to stay.'

'Excuse me?'

'You and Javani. If you wish. We'd like you to stay in the village.' She cleared her throat, straightened her shoulders. 'I'd like you to stay.'

'You're sure? After, you know . . . everything?'

'I think,' Camellia said, not quite meeting her eye, 'that in the grandest scheme, it's possible you were right about more than you weren't. I think . . . I think we can learn from each other. And we need new candidates for the Council, of course . . .'

Ree put up a chilly hand. 'One thing at a time, please!'

Mariam approached, beaming. 'Did you tell her, then?'

Camellia nodded, and Mariam's smile became worryingly broad. 'I'm so glad. Think your captain friend will want to stay, and all?'

Ree felt her cheeks glow, and cursed their treachery. 'Who can say?' she managed.

'Oh, and Vida's message: she said she hasn't forgotten about your pony's shoe, she'll get round to it as soon as she's up and about again. Ha, which won't be any time soon if I have any say in it.' Mariam paused, then slapped one hand to her forehead. 'Plains ponies, that was it!'

'That was what?'

'Don't need shoes, do they? That's what they're famous for. That and running their little legs for days.'

Ree stared at her with wide, twitching eyes. 'Are you telling me,' she growled, 'that we've been waiting all this time to fit a shoe that we don't need?'

Mariam shrugged. 'Who can say?'

Ree turned to Camellia for some kind of acknowledgement, but the councillor's attention was fixed on the far side of the terrace. 'There's . . . something, on the road. Coming this way.'

They made what haste they could.

The procession that came to a halt on the far side of the ravine stole Ree's breath from her lungs. Riders, half a dozen of them in a loose column, dressed in exemplary cold-weather gear – fur-trimmed long leather coats, thick boots and down-lined, wide-brimmed helmets, their fine burnished breastplates gleaming through the gaps in their outerwear. Long sabres hung from their belts, but stowed at each saddle-point was a weapon Ree had no trouble recognising: a mechanical hand-bow. The lead rider bore a lance with a pennant she didn't bother inspecting; it was no mystery who was on their threshold.

'It's . . . it's the fucking Guild,' she breathed, feeling her heart turning somersaults.

'What are they doing here? How are they here?' The kid was beside her, her breath great white streams. Ree turned to see Anri already arrived, his bow in his hands, and even Keretan was making his lumbering way up the path towards them, one arm in a sling beneath his thick cloak. 'There's no road, right? Not all the way.'

Words tumbled through Ree's mind: *there's a way down, but you'd have to move a mountain or two out of the way to make it quick . . .*

'Godshit!' she gasped. 'That thrice-damned thunder we kept hearing – I knew it sounded wrong.'

The kid met her eye. 'You mean – they've been blasting? They cleared the way?'

A sound of running footsteps over frozen turf drew her attention to her left. Pelting over the churned, packed earth was Manatas, his cloak streaming behind him. He arrived in a crash and jingle of mail, hands on his knees, barking between pants, 'Armed column . . . coming up from the old road . . . think it's Guild . . .'

'Thanks, Inaï.' Ree nodded to the other side of the ravine. 'We spotted them.'

He lifted his sweating head, breath coming in hard gasps, and groaned. 'Gods be damned . . . I am getting old.'

She put a hand on his shoulder. 'You and me both.'

'Ma.'

She was instantly defensive, but withdrew her hand as if caught with it in a jar of candied fruit. 'What, kid?'

'One of them's coming.'

The lead rider nudged his horse up to the lip of the ravine, a few paces from the posts that marked the start of the now-fallen bridge, and gazed down in visible disdain, then across at the assembling villagers.

'We saw smoke,' he called in a lowland accent, nodding in the direction of the black plumes still rising from the mercenary pyre at the valley floor, staining the crisp wintry sky. He was unshaven and hard-eyed, his voice carrying easily in the leaden air. 'Thought it was late in the year for a wildfire.'

He scanned the terraces, taking in the sweep of the cliffs, the huts, the barricades, the snow-dusted debris and detritus, then leaned forward on his saddle-point. 'Seems you've been through a lot, so consider this some friendly advice. This land has been granted to the Chartered Miners' Guild of Serica. You are on Guild territory, and this is an unsanctioned settlement.' He leaned back, regarding them from beneath the brim of his helmet. 'The Guild are generous people, but you'll be taxed from the date of the grant; first collection, given the lateness of the year, after the thaw. A joyous Sun's Night to you all.'

'Ma, you're grinding your teeth, I can hear it from here.'

The rider was already turning, signalling to the rest, and a moment later they were off down the road in a jingling clatter and thud. Soon there was nothing left of them but echoes and hoof-prints in the snow.

The villagers stood in stunned silence on the terrace. Ree turned to face Camellia, seeing her shock written in the lines of her face, the pallor of her complexion. 'Camellia, listen,' she began, 'if after everything—'

Camellia wasn't listening, or didn't hear. 'To go through all that,' she whispered, 'to fight and kill and suffer and die . . . to face extortion from someone else?' A bitter smile pulled at the corners of her mouth. 'This was what the mercenaries should have protected us from.'

Ree shook her head. 'They'd have cut and run, or taken a percentage from the Guild to carry on as they were.'

This time Camellia heard. 'Yes. Yes, that's probably true.'

'I was going to say, if you want to accept their terms, then . . . I understand.'

Camellia's gaze focused on her, her shock now pure affront. 'What are you talking about? Of course we won't accept. Things are not the same as before.'

'They're not?'

'No. Now we know what we're capable of.' She looked out over the assembled victors of Ar Ramas, bruised, bloodied and proud. 'And come the thaw, they'll find out too.'

'Camellia, are you sure? This is the Guild. They don't stop. They don't back down. This won't be settled by another skirmish, this could mean a *war*—'

'Then so be it.'

'You're going to become a village of warriors, after all?'

'No. Do not misunderstand, Ree. We'll take up arms again as circumstances dictate, but we will put them down at the earliest time. And so on, for as long as necessary. We will always return to peace. We will always return to our family.'

'May Ar Ramas stay ever peaceful,' Ree replied with a wry smile. 'Perhaps we really did learn something from each other. You think you can be ready for when they come back?'

Camellia's gaze was steely. 'You can count on it.' She flicked to the kid and back to Ree. 'And you? Will you be with us? To war, for peace?'

Their eyes met, but it was the kid who answered.

'You can count on it.'

REE AND JAVANI WILL RETURN

ACKNOWLEDGEMENTS

Profound thanks and gratitude are due to the following people and nonhuman aggregate entities, without whom this book would have made it no further than a vague idea I had once:

To my hardworking agent, Harry "Air Miles" Illingworth, Kirsten Lang, and all at DHH;

To my sublime editor, Laura McCallen, and the editorial team at HarperVoyager: Natasha Bardon, Rachel Winterbottom, Elizabeth Vaziri, and tireless champion Chloe Gough; to superlative copy-editor (I'm going with the hyphen this time) Rhian McKay, and proofreader Anna Bowles; to the cover art dream team of Emily Langford and Gavin Reece for yet another phenomenal cover;

To fabulous subject matter expert Bethan Hindmarch, voice coach and corrective influence to Mariam and Anri;

To the denizens of the Illers' Killers/Team Henry/Whatever Stupid Name Ryan Has Given It This Week Discord server, my buddies, my pals, my distributed nervous system; to my convention stalwarts, too numerous and splendid to name in toto, but with special mention to Anna Stephens, Tom Lee, Sunyi Dean, Jen Williams, Pete Newman, Steve Aryan, Justin Lee Anderson, RJ (Ronnie James) Barker and Ryan Cahill; to Francesca Haig;

To the bloggers, podcasters and YouTubers (you tubers?) who have done so much to support me and the series, not limited to: Nils and Beth of the Fantasy Hive, Holly Hearts Books, Andrew Mattocks, The Brothers Gwynne, Stefan of Civilian Reader, David "LordTBR"

Walters and Adrian Gibson of FanFiAddict and SFF Addicts, Night at SoManyBooks6, and so many others;

To Matt and the team at The Broken Binding, for everything, and more; to Phil, Magnus, Caro & everyone at SRFC; to Adam Iley, James G Smith and Laz Roberts;

To my spectacular wife Sarah, who keeps threatening to write a book of her own ("it can't be that hard if you can do it"), and my ever larger daughters, who keep threatening to read a book of mine; to my family and friends, who continue to buy my books, despite everything I've put them through; to you the reader, for getting this far – I know I don't make it easy, and you should at least get a little badge or something for reading all the acknowledgements. Maybe in book 3.

Love and thanks to you all.

Hitchin, February 2024

CREDITS

Agent
Harry Illingworth

Editor
Laura McCallen

Voyager Editorial Team
Natasha Bardon
Rachel Winterbottom
Elizabeth Vaziri
Chloe Gough

Audio
Fionnuala Barrett
Ciara Briggs

Design
Emily Langford
Gavin Reece

Production
Robyn Watts
Emily Chan

Marketing
Emily Merrill
Indigo Griffiths

Publicity
Susanna Peden